street fighter

Also by Bill Kent

Street Hungry
Street Money

Under the Boardwalk
Down by the Sea
On a Blanket with My Baby

BILL KENT

street fighter

Thomas Dunne Books / St. Martin's Minotaur ✺ New York

THOMAS DUNNE BOOKS.
An imprint of St. Martin's Press.

www.minotaurbooks.com

ISBN 0-312-32883-4
EAN 978-0312-32883-2

First Edition: May 2005

10 9 8 7 6 5 4 3 2 1

For my wife, Elaine,
who liked the way this started,
and my son, Stephen,
whose love of Sherlock Holmes
rekindled my own

acknowledgments

This book would not exist without the enthusiasm of family, friends, librarians and readers who liked the previous books and supported these efforts in many ways. This series would not exist without my editor, Ruth Cavin, and my agent, Jake Elwell.

Fighting techniques illustrated here represent many martial art styles. Instructors Judson Sumbler and Jonathan Maberry made sure the punches landed where they should. Investigator Joseph Shannon provided Sherlockian insights. Dr. Mark Gilbert and Dr. David Cohen contributed medical detail. Avery Dub, CPA, only had nice things to say about the accounting profession.

Events in this novel pertaining to the Vietnam War never happened. They were inspired by conversations with veterans, as well as reporting in *The Secret War Against Hanoi: Kennedy's and Johnson's Use of Spies, Saboteurs and Covert Warriors in Vietnam* by Richard Schultz, Jr. Details about Matthew Plank's Corsican adventure were found in Dorothy Carrington's *The Dream Hunters of Corsica*.

Philadelphia does not have a neighborhood called Westyard. The characters, locations and events occurring there are imaginary and are not meant to reflect on existing persons, places, things, restaurants or artworks. I remain grateful to the war veterans, poker players, police officers, restauranteurs, self-defense students, developers, lawyers and so many others in and around Philadelphia who shared some of their lives with me.

Μεμνησο απιστειν
"Remember to be distrustful."

—motto of Prosper Merimee (1803–1870),
French civil servant, journalist, archaeologist, translator,
politician and author of *Carmen* and *Colomba*

street fighter

1
putting on the finger

If you didn't know him better, you'd say Paulie Small was a condemned man eating his last meal.

And what a meal: antipasto for two, clams casino, oysters Rockefeller, mussels marinara, shrimp scampi, osso buco with broccoli rabe, spaghetti with sweet Italian sausage. Garlic bread like you wouldn't believe. A full carafe of the house chianti. Double espresso, amaretto cake, the cannoli plate, consisting of plain, vanilla, chocolate and, because this was the Villa Verdi, a green peppermint.

Paulie Small was a big man, tall and wide in a brown suede sport coat and a black turtleneck shirt rolling out over a gut you could ski down. He just about ate this meal himself, because the short, scrawny woman he was with, the one in a clinging pink sweater and the shiny black disco pants, spent more time moving the food around on her plate than putting it in her mouth. She'd lift up every one of the shrimp in the shrimp scampi, turn them over, put some of them on one side of the plate, some of them on the other. You could say she ate like a bird, except for the spaghetti and sausage. When that arrived she poked the sausage with her fork, and ate it slowly, giving Paulie Small these looks that would make him break out in a sweat and drink his wine a lot faster.

A man and a woman in their late fifties, spending serious money at the Villa Verdi, giving themselves little looks, you just know it's going to lead to a hot night. You had to hand it to Paulie Small: he only had eyes for Teal Cavaletta. You should've seen how she ate those cannoli in front of him.

She was wearing her wedding ring, but it was turned around, as if, with the diamonds not showing, nobody would be able to recognize her. Teal Cavaletta let her husband and daughter go off to the suburbs while she stayed in the city because her husband was one thing, but Paulie Small was the grand passion of her life and, if you're Italian in South Philadelphia, or just pretending, you don't argue with passion.

You might not even blame her, if you had seen Paulie Small back when he was younger and thinner, before he got in big with the politicians and became the man through which all this government development money ebbed, flowed, dripped and dropped into so many different pockets. When Paulie Small came back from Vietnam, and started getting his CPA on the GI bill, he had the charm, he had the smile, he had the ways to loosen up the local widows and get them to put their money into insurance policies, annuities, reverse mortgages, mutual funds that nobody ever heard of that sometimes went belly-up. When that happened, you would never hear those widows say a thing about him, other than they had to rush home because he was coming over for tea and they didn't want to be late.

And you never wanted to play against Paulie Small in the poker games he'd run at the firehouse, at the truck stop down by Essington, and at the veterans' social club that his war buddy, the cop Jack Ferko, set up. You'd play against Paulie, and it would seem that everybody else at the table was winning more than Paulie. And then, one by one, everybody would fold until, at the very end, it was just you and Paulie and you knew that, no matter what he was holding in his hand, Paulie Small was going to win the pot because Paulie liked his card games to resemble his life: you start small, you take a little, you let the other guys win some, but you make sure you go home with more than you came in with because that's the way it's got to be.

There was something terrific about a guy who lived that way. Maybe ten individuals in the city could do Paulie's kind of work, but Paulie got more business because he was a lone gun and unconnected to any of the big law firms. More than any accountant in the city, Paulie offered "deniability." If he had to, he could claim that he was "above it," "out of the loop" when it came to pay-to-play politics. Officials with reputations to protect could tell those who were expecting a major feed and didn't get a crumb: my hands are tied! You got a problem, talk to Paulie.

And Paulie would turn on the kind of charm that would make a sucker think he was anything but a sucker.

Teal Cavaletta was never a sucker for Paulie's charm. He never had to talk her into believing she was anything but what she was: his partner, his right hand, his "insurance policy," his best girl. They had known each other as children and she was always too smart for the little street-corner scams he used to work. When Paulie Small got kids that were even older than he was to bet on the outcome of a game of stickball, Teal would have none of it. She had a better head for numbers and details than he did. She could do things with computers that left him running his fingers through the thin strands of hair on his head that he dyed and brushed straight back. That's why Paulie trusted her, took her to the meetings that happened after the meetings, where she would take notes on her laptop computer and go back to her little row house and create the paperwork so the right people got what was coming to them, just as if it was the natural order of things.

Money is sexy, and so is power, but, for Paulie Small and Teal Cavaletta, the sexiest thing of all was to be the only two people in the city who knew "where the money was buried." They didn't consider themselves partners in crime. They weren't making kickbacks—even the ones that were legal, proper, aboveboard—for the money, at least Teal wasn't. To make Paulie's deals legal, or appear to be so, was, for her, a labor of love.

Still, Paulie paid her well enough, on a piece-by-piece basis, so that, with what she got from the tax returns, bookkeeping and putting her notary seal on documents, Teal could put her crazy daughter Lucia through four years at Ohio State. This, despite the fact that Lucia decided to move out with her father—Teal's ex-husband, Frank—who thought it was okay for their baby to learn all that karate stuff. And what was Lucia doing with a BA in Physical Education? Teaching women in Columbus health clubs how to beat up men! What kind of man is going to want to marry a girl that can beat him up, unless he's in for that sort of thing?

Let them both stay away. The three-story row house that she and her husband had moved into just after they got married was now set up the way she liked it: she had a television in the parlor and a television in the bedroom, a nice kitchen with a gas stove, an office next to the parlor where she would meet with clients and another office upstairs where she would do her accounting work for the neighborhood.

For Paulie, it had to do with keeping score. He paid himself rather grandly. Looking decent was part of the job, so he spent his money on clothes, but never on fashion. He ate food, preferably Italian, but nothing fancy. He bought big American cars that he could trade in after they were a year old. He had a top-floor apartment in the Pickle Factory, a Westyard luxury rehab whose government financing and bountiful city tax breaks he helped arrange. The Pickle Factory had set off a gentrification boom along Westyard's northern edge that Paulie was especially proud of. He'd drive through the gentrified sections and see his handiwork in the prim and pointed row houses, with their planter boxes out front and the fancy iron grates on the windows and the doors, the coffee bars, the cozy Italian BYOBs where it was arugula with this and polenta with that, and the empty-nesters come back from the suburbs, wearing their dark clothes and looking for their high-end, street-parked automobiles whose car alarms were always going off.

No question, Paulie Small was proud of how some of the government money coming into the city ended up in Westyard in particular, a fiercely insular, two-and-a-half-mile, cucumber-shaped swath of one-way streets, row houses and old factories just waiting to be turned into luxury lofts.

Whenever an especially large gush of funds came Paulie's way, he would pick up Teal Cavaletta in front of her row house in his newest black Lincoln and they would drive two blocks—that's right, two whole blocks—to the Villa Verdi, where, if it was a Friday and Saturday night, they'd listen to the owner, another Vietnam war vet named Angelo Delise, come out and sing his thing—tenor arias from Italian opera, mostly. They'd put on a huge feed and then Paulie would drive Teal back to her row house on Brixton Street and spend the night.

On weekday nights at the Villa Verdi, the music was a prerecorded South Philly mix of Sinatra, Dean Martin, Pavarotti and Mario Lanza, the South Philadelphia kid who will be canonized on the day that the cardinals in Rome convince themselves that having a voice can be a bona fide miracle.

On this Tuesday night in October, Paulie had things on his mind and Teal knew better than to ask him what they were, because Paulie told her everything, sooner or later, and you had to save some things for the night. She listened and put things together: ever since the mayor made his ridiculously arrogant "you gotta pay to play" speech, the Feds were dropping hints that people were talking to them, and, even though nobody important was talking to them at the moment, you couldn't be sure, anymore, who wasn't going to talk, if the Feds put on the pressure.

Paulie dabbed his mouth with a green cloth napkin that had seen hazardous duty. He said to Teal, "Some people in this city, you put your finger on them, and they just pop."

Teal said he could put his finger on her anytime, and he smiled at that, a little. One of the things he was doing this week was putting the finger on people. He wasn't actually touching anybody—putting the finger on was what Paulie called telling what wasn't a secret, to people who couldn't keep secrets, so that it seemed that those who had to know things a little bit ahead of everybody else would feel that they were on top of it, in the loop, connected, close to what was happening.

The finger of the week was huge: government funding was almost in place for a $350 million, mixed-use, three-phased development that was going to do for the south edge of Westyard what the Pickle Factory had done for the north edge, on the site of the Eisley Bros. Meatpacking Plant, right behind the Sisters of Zion Hospital. The development would be a public/private partnership, the same one that built the Pickle Factory.

The project would also "stop those Asians from taking over," Paulie said. "Stop 'em right in their tracks."

Paulie didn't like the Thais, Cambodians, Koreans and Vietnamese who had filled out the southern edge of Westyard since the end of the Vietnam war. He saw them as obstacles to the total gentrification of the neighborhood. "You got empty-nesters coming into the city, they're not going to drop a couple a' million on a condo, with Little Saigon going nutso on the street," Paulie told Teal as he finished the wine in his glass. "They're going to want trees on the street, good restaurants, places to park. They're going to want it decent."

"You really think so, Paulie?" she said. "You really think that they're that different from us?"

For all her life, Teal never said a word when Paulie went off about the Asians. This time, she saw the strain in his face. He was having problems with his health, his blood pressure was up, he needed to get more tests about his diabetes. She couldn't tell him to cut back on his eating: for Paulie, what he put in his mouth was his to put in his mouth. It was his right.

For once, she didn't want him to get mad, about anything. She wanted to see the tension go out of his face and see the gentleness return, as it did when he would fall asleep after making love.

She reminded him that the Asians could be decent, in their own way. When Frank Cavaletta, Teal's ex-husband, needed a loan to buy a new moving truck, he borrowed from one of the Asian community banks. And there was that time when Paulie had to come up with $2 million to save the Pickle Factory project. The Asians had been more than decent then.

But Paulie didn't see it that way. "Politics is all about what side you're on. Anybody that wants to keep a lid on things needs somebody he can point a finger at and say, 'We're not that. That's not us.' Only decent thing about those Asians is they don't complain. They learned right: the ones that complained got deported."

"And how decent was that, Paulie?" Teal said. "What they're going through is what our parents and grandparents went through when they came to this country."

"Nobody gave them any breaks," Paulie said.

"You know that's not right, Paulie. Sure, there were lots of people that didn't like us, that put us down, said we were dirty and ugly and had no morals and didn't eat right. But we didn't get where we are on our own. We worked hard, but we got breaks. We found good people and they found us."

"Good people," Paulie said. He looked around the dining room. Twenty years ago, it had been staffed by Italian boys and girls. Now it was staffed entirely by Asians, and they weren't doing such a bad job.

He made more cell-phone calls: to the real estate columnist at the *Philadelphia Standard,* the gossip guy at the *Philadelphia Press,* a couple of the talk-show hosts. "You didn't get this from me," he would tell them, "but Veterans Plaza is going to be the biggest thing to happen to South Philadelphia. Bigger than big."

He put the phone down and looked at the Asians in the room again. "I had to work for those breaks. The stuff I did . . . There's a lot I'm not proud of."

"So why not do something you'd be proud of," Teal said. "Do something that's totally decent this time."

The concept shocked him. "I've done stuff I thought was decent," Paulie said. "But not totally. Somebody's always got to get screwed. You need losers if you're going to win. That's the way you play the game."

"So play it differently this time," Teal said. "We've won enough fights. We've taken our share. Now let's have it come out so it feels good."

He gave her a little wink. "Totally?"

"Totally."

He put food in his mouth and Teal could almost hear his brain working as he chewed. "I'd have to get some changes made. There'd be risks involved."

"There's no risk now?"

He chewed some more. And more. And more after that.

Then it happened: the tension, the concern just melted from his face. He gave Teal a little wink, which gave Teal the shivers. Paulie was the most charming man with everybody else. With her, he could be the big, crude, lovable oaf, and she would still love him. Her ex-husband, Frank, was a nicer guy, a friend to everyone and, without question, the absolute best-looking lifeguard on the Wildwood beach. The difference between them, as far as Teal could figure it, was that, while Frank Cavaletta looked good on the beach, Paulie Small looked like he owned it.

Paulie excused himself and said he had to "go into the back." This meant a call he couldn't make on his cell phone because he wouldn't want the call monitored or traced back to his number. She watched him put his big hands on his cane and push it down on the threadbare green carpet. He was using a cane these days because of gout and a knee that was never good and wasn't getting any better. The Villa Verdi had pay phones by the restroom but Paulie wouldn't use those, either, because it was a point of privilege for him to be able to go up to Angelo Delise, who stood in his custom-made green suit with gold piping at the cash register, and ask to go into the kitchen and use the office phone. Angelo Delise would give him a look, and Paulie would give back a different look, but he would always let Paulie use the phone.

This time Teal watched them say a few words. She couldn't hear the words, but Angelo Delise was surprised, then suspicious, as he went with Paulie into the kitchen.

When they came out, Paulie had a folded piece of paper in his hand—was that Teal's raised notary seal on the edge?—and Angelo seemed happy. Now it was Teal's turn to be shocked. She had never seen Angelo Delise happy. Not in the seven years since his daughter was killed and his wife left him.

Now she did and it was amazing.

By the time Paulie returned to the table, Teal had added up the bill, calculated the tip to the penny, entered the numbers on Paulie's credit card receipt and signed Paulie's signature. The waiter, an Asian fellow, brought their hats and coats.

"You're good people," Paulie said to the waiter. The waiter was shocked, because Paulie had been a pain to wait on, but now . . . he said that like he meant it.

The bracing October wind blew garbage and a few leaves this way and that. When you grow up in Philadelphia, you get used to garbage because garbage comes from people, and if you leave it where it is it'll blow somewhere else. But leaves come from trees and leaves get wet and they turn into this sticky, disgusting brown mess that doesn't go away until the city cleans the streets, and the city only cleaned Westyard streets once a year, right before Election Day, which was three weeks away.

Teal remembered that Westyard didn't have a single tree until the Pickle Factory opened seven years ago. Somebody had the idea to put trees on the sidewalk in front of the place, these gingkos which, every fall, would drop these walnut-sized berries that smelled like vomit. What could be more disgusting than walking around and stepping on those things?

Now, with all the gentrification going around on the north edge, trees had been planted in all these holes in the sidewalks, and leaves and the vomit-berries were making a mess out of the neighborhood.

But now, there was an energy in Paulie's step. She walked with him, arm in arm, and the leaves and garbage whirling around them seemed okay. Paulie stuck the hand that wasn't holding the cane into his pants pocket and pressed the button on his keychain so that the headlights on his big, black Lincoln blinked and the alarm whooped, like a dog grateful for its master's return. Paulie held the door for her, as he always did. Soon they were inside the car's soft, gray leather womb, the bright headlights making the familiar streets seem darker, more menacing.

Paulie parked a block away from Teal's house, and the walk back to her house seemed longer than it should have been. Once inside she kissed him, but he was distracted. She went upstairs to the second bedroom, now one large closet, where she changed, while he went to the third floor, where she had her office and the room with her files. There he put copies of documents from things he had been involved in, computer discs, and other items that he did not want to leave in his office or his apartment.

He sat on the edge of the bed, holding the phone in one hand and some folded papers in the other.

Teal came in and saw her notary stamp on those papers. She wanted to show him her new robe. He hung up when he saw her.

"Damn," he said. "That's *in*decent."

She rubbed the back of his neck and his shoulders but the tension did not go away. Finally he said, "I left the lights on."

"What lights?"

"In the car. There's a gadget in the car that turns them off automatically but I think I pressed the button that leaves them on."

"You'll turn them off later."

"It bugs me. I can't get it out of my mind."

She had read somewhere—it was in the *Philadelphia Press,* the "Mr. Action" column. Someone had written Mr. Action about people who leave on a trip and then come back an hour later because they're *sure* they forgot to lock a door, turn off an oven, water the plants, and they find out they did lock the doors, turn off the oven and water the plants. Mr. Action said that this was actually a neurological problem, a sign of aging, and that the best thing to do was let people go back and make sure that their memory was correct so that they learn to tell the feeling of forgetfulness from the real thing.

So Teal watched him bear down on his cane and slowly rise, this big, lumbering man made her feel like a schoolgirl when the lights were out. She stretched out on the bed and heard his steps recede on the stairs. She closed her eyes when she heard the front door close.

When she opened her eyes she realized she had fallen asleep and that someone was hitting the front door knocker, hard.

She pulled her robe around her. As she came down the stairs she heard a voice she knew too well. "Mrs. Cavaletta? It's Sergeant Ferko, Philadelphia Police. I need to speak to you right away."

She opened the door and felt the cold wind rake her skin. She saw the lights from the police cruisers and the ambulance flashing across his face, a face that told her that he needed to cry. He needed to run in and cry, the way he did when Vinnie's brother Errol would beat him up and Vinnie had no place to go, or when Vinnie's mother had finally died from the cancer.

Cops are supposed to get thick skins from all the terrible things they see on the job. Vinnie's father Jack Ferko had a thick skin before he retired and got in big with the war veterans. Vinnie's brother Errol had a thick skin—Paulie always admired Errol as the kid who had what it took, too much of what it took—"that punk wants to take over," Paulie told her. "He wants to move in on my turf, like it's his due. What a punk."

But Vinnie was still Vinnie, so she stepped back and began to think about putting the coffee on and looking for the most recent batch of pizzelles she had made.

She noticed that Vinnie was holding Paulie's hat in his hand, but it couldn't be Paulie's hat because it had one of those disgusting rotten leaves clinging to it, and Paulie was particular about dirt on his clothes. A few nights back, when they had been out on the street together and the wind had blown Paulie's hat off his head, Paulie had watched calmly where the hat went and pursued it slowly, not rushing, not moving fast, his cane making the steady beat on the sidewalk until the wind jammed the hat up against a car wheel in a gutter. Then Paulie had reached down with the grace of a big man who never has to be in a hurry, picked up that hat and smacked it against himself until there was not the slightest trace of dirt and grime.

So here was Vinnie with Paulie's hat, with a leaf on it. She wanted to snatch that hat out of Vinnie's hand and smack that leaf off, until she noticed the red feather along the side.

Paulie didn't put feathers in his hat. She took a closer look and was surprised. What looked like a feather was actually a dark red paint, shiny in places, crusting and dark in others where the wind had blown and dried it out.

Paint that looked exactly like blood.

2 emotional lift

Dear Mr. Action,

Why are airlines so messed up? I need to fly to Philadelphia because of a family emergency. Not only does it cost twice as much money to buy a ticket on less than two weeks' notice, but I have to change planes twice, so it will end up taking me about three hours less than if I rented a car and drove. What's the deal?

Fighting mad, L. C., Columbus, Ohio.

Andrea "Andy" Cosicki stuck her thumb in the air, signifying approval. Lucia's question had survived the final edit and appeared, intact, in the Friday morning edition.

She hoped Lucia would be surprised, and pleased, at seeing part of their Wednesday night phone conversation recast as the lead item in the *Philadelphia Press*'s "Mr. Action" question-and-answer consumer column—one more way of welcoming Lucia Cavaletta home.

She took her fingers off her word processor's keyboard and felt a glow of satisfaction that you get when your work comes out more or less as you intended—she found some cuts had been made in Mr. Action's rather long explanation of how the airlines route flights and price tickets—but, on the whole, the column looked good.

She looked around the drab newsroom that, despite this being a Friday morning, had the warmth, conviviality and friendliness of the city bus terminal at 3A.M. She sat in a corner far from the windows, the autumnal colors in her baggy sweater bleached out by the pale, buzzing fluorescent lights. She saw the reporters and columnists straggling in, grimly taking position at the cluttered desks, grimly facing the task of finding something, anything horrible, scandalous, or awful to write about in this second no-news week.

Whose fault was it that there were too few calamities in the world? Why, of all times, were there no major economic crises in the nation, no scandals in the government, no ghastly violence to put on the tabloid's cover? Neither the president, the governor or the mayor was up for re-election in November. The judges, city councilmen and state representatives on the campaign trail had failed to create controversies. Reports of a councilman who had been driving for years without a license, and a judge who owed more than $26,000 in back taxes failed to excite the electorate, and *Press* editor Howard Lange, in his weekly "Off My Chest" column, scolded the city for assuming such venalities were "business as usual."

Not even an excessively ballyhooed multipart series on the effect of video game violence on teenage IQs sold papers. Circulation figures had fallen dangerously low. Advertising revenues had also dropped, as retailers saved their pennies for the November-to-December Christmas season, which, according to the advertising department, now began the morning after Halloween.

Hey, Andy wanted to say, I have a friend coming home. That's news to me!

But not news to them, even if the births, deaths, fires, drug busts, car jackings, domestic disputes and robberies continued. There had been a small item in the paper two days ago, in the citywide "Police Story" column, about a Paul Small, who was in a coma at the Sisters of Zion

Hospital from injuries received during a street mugging—the robber had evidently beat Small with his own cane.

When Andy had come in this morning, she had found Neville Shepherd Ladderback, the old, dusty obituary writer in the rumpled dark suit, faded white shirt and black necktie, at the desk to her right, frowning at his word processor screen.

She saw he had a printout of a coroner's report labeled SMALL, PAUL on his desk.

"Is that the same guy who was mugged on Tuesday night?" Andy asked.

"It is a report about the death of an individual who was assaulted on Tuesday night, yes," Ladderback replied testily.

Would it be news to Ladderback that Andy's friend Lucia not only knew "Uncle Paul" Small, but was returning to the city after spending seven years away—two living with her father in Ardmore and four attending college in Ohio—to stay with her mother, who had done accounting work for Small and was—Lucia had told Andy when calling from Ohio—in such a state of shock over what happened that she had refused to leave her house?

It would be different if Ladderback weren't so grumpy. He could be that way, in the mornings, at lunchtime, in the afternoons and the evenings when he worked through the dinner hour. When Andy had been coeditor of the University of Pennsylvania's student newspaper, she had known that reporters got grumpy, usually when sources proved difficult or a story didn't quite turn out as expected. The grumpiness usually gave way to manic elation when a reporter finally got the "nut"—the essential element that defined the story—or an important phone call was returned.

In the five months since Andy had graduated and had got her first journalism job, not at the *Philadelphia Standard,* the city's staid, provincial, suburban-oriented broadsheet, but at the scrappy, tabloid *Press,* she had never known Ladderback to express elation, gratification or even satisfaction. Concern, yes, and sympathy—Ladderback would spend hours on the phone coaxing quotes out of friends and relatives of the dead people he wrote up—but anything approaching happiness was foreign to his nature. It was as if the loss and sorrow in which he worked had rendered him permanently wary of shoes about to drop, disaster about to strike, latent sickness and disease waiting to turn contentment into despair.

"You know what your problem is?" Andy told him.

He blinked.

"You need an emotional lift," Andy said. "You need to be happy about something. I have my best friend coming back to town. You need something like that."

He took a long breath. "I am attempting to determine if this subject is appropriate," he said.

"And you can't be happy until you do, right?"

Ladderback had told her previously that he couldn't write up just anyone who died. He had to find a balance among people of different religions, different ethnic and racial categories, different economic backgrounds, different residences within the *Press*'s circulation area.

Andy could understand how you could get so obsessed over the little things you wrote about. She had to find a similar balance with Mr. Action. She couldn't have too many items about credit cards, or banks, or computers that wouldn't work properly, or tradesmen who failed to finish jobs, but she could still find things to do that she enjoyed.

"Mr. Small's parents and siblings are dead," Ladderback went on. "His secretary was a part-time employee and said that, in the event any accident or fatality he might suffer, she was to say nothing to the media."

He went to the enormous file cabinet that took up the wall beside his desk. The cabinet contained just about every obituary, with notes and background material, that Ladderback had written in more than forty years at the *Press,* as well as newspaper and magazine clippings that Ladderback had found interesting enough to save.

"In an early article about the development of the Pickle Factory, it is mentioned that rehabilitation was done as a public/private partnership venture with the nonprofit veterans assistance organization, Not Fade

Away. Mr. Small founded Not Fade Away with Jack Ferko, a retired police captain and fellow Vietnam veteran. Captain Ferko told me earlier this morning that there would be no funeral—Mr. Small wanted to be cremated. He had already informed Mr. Small's half-sister in Canada of his death, who agreed that there should be no funeral. Captain Ferko said that it would be best to have an obituary about him, though he would not elaborate as to why or for whom this might be best."

Ladderback opened his Small file and withdrew a printout from a fax. "Here is the preliminary report, signed by Captain Ferko's son, Sergeant Vincent Ferko. Though Mr. Small's death occurred on a residential street, Sergeant Ferko could not locate any witnesses who provide meaningful information about the robbery. One witness mentioned hearing shouts through the walls of her row house. Another thought that the assailant might have chased something up the street. Police were summoned when Mr. Small, with whatever life was left in him, pressed the 911 emergency call on his cell phone. He was discovered unconscious, having suffered severe trauma about his face and skull. His wallet was missing."

"Sounds like a robbery," Andy said.

Ladderback frowned. He opened another file. "Mr. Small appears to have made a very good living for himself in what is variously called project positioning, fee disbursement or commission scheduling. This has put him in close proximity with several local and regional political figures, some of whom have said, through spokespersons, that though they are saddened by Mr. Small's untimely departure, they had very little contact with him on a personal or professional level. I also have calls in to a few developers, suppliers and contractors who worked on projects whose fee payment system Mr. Small scheduled. These calls have, so far, not been returned."

Andy looked at the newsroom clock. It was around 10:30. Ladderback had been busy.

"So," Andy said, leaning back in her swivel chair, "you need somebody to talk straight about him."

"Captain Ferko offered to do that informally this evening. He and his staff eat a late dinner at Jimmy D's."

"Your favorite place," Andy said.

Ladderback ignored that. "He said that his eldest son Errol was quite close to Mr. Small, and that, after Mrs. Ferko died, Mr. Small helped look after Errol and was responsible for his choosing a career in consumer and small business financial services. Errol Ferko has a financial services business in the city. I called Errol and Errol was profoundly emotional about Mr. Small. He told me that Mr. Small had been killed by an Asian gang that is preying on older Caucasian residents of Westyard. He said that Mr. Small hated Asians and was not beyond making his feelings known."

"And you believed him?"

"In the composition of obituaries, the cause of death is never as important as the fact of death," Ladderback said. He closed a folder. "What troubles me is that Errol Ferko was not aggrieved. His emotions, in speaking with me, were of profound pleasure. Rapid mood swings are a symptom of the shock that a death can bring. Mr. Ferko's did not seem that way. He supplied me with several meaningful anecdotes about Mr. Small that he felt would be worthy of inclusion in his obituary."

"So you got what you were looking for."

"I did not," Ladderback said. "I found Mr. Ferko's responses disturbing."

"This person you can believe." Andy went to her desk and wrote down a telephone number. She told him the number belonged to the mother of her friend Lucia, who was flying into town tonight.

"She calls him Uncle Paul, because he hung out with her mother enough to be like family, even if he wasn't. Teal did a lot of number crunching for him and Lucia figures they'd been having an affair, probably during the time Teal was married. Teal's really messed up about him dying, but she could probably tell you some things about him if you catch her when she's calm."

His eyes stopped moving behind his glasses. He was surprised. "How did you come to know this person?"

"We met in high school, in gym class, at the beginning of our junior year. She decided she was going to live in Ardmore with her father. We had to line up in alphabetical order. She was in front of me and she made it clear that she hated gym. I was standing behind her and I also hated gym."

"But you're athletic," Ladderback said. "The shortness of your finger-nails and the calluses on your hands indicate that. You play basketball."

"I do *not* play basketball," Andy said. "I do layups by myself, for myself. It's a personal kind of workout. It has nothing to do with team sports. I do not *do* team sports."

"Neither do I," Ladderback said.

"Have you *ever* held a ball in your hands?" Andy said.

"What I meant," he scowled, "is that, I, too, have difficulty coping with social dynamics."

"Lucia's into all these different kinds of martial arts," Andy said. "She was always signing up and quitting them because the instructors were assholes. But she was really into it because she had a friend that got killed right before she left the city and it messed her up pretty bad. I think she's got three or four different black belts and she wants to open up a women's self-defense school when she gets settled."

Andy handed him the telephone number. Ladderback accepted it and appeared to study her handwriting. He said, "If Mrs. Cavaletta was emotionally involved with Mr. Small, and has not left her house since his assault, my speaking to her may increase her discomfort."

"Or it may help," Andy said. "You told me once that you think writing obituaries is the most important journalism there is, because it helps the living cope with loss."

"That isn't precisely what I said," Ladderback replied.

"Close enough," Andy said. She started opening her mail when she caught, through the corner of her eye, Ladderback grinning.

She stopped. "Are you okay?"

He pointed to his Small, Paul file. He pointed to her. He pointed to the piece of paper she'd handed him. "Small world," he said.

She tore open her mail and ignored him for the rest of the day.

Andy had to admit Lucia looked better than it was possible for anyone to look in a baggy, dark Ohio State sweat suit. Her chestnut-colored hair was cut in a close, layered sweep. Her eyes were deeper, her cheekbones had an athletic hollow and, even when she yanked her duffle bag off the baggage carousel, she didn't walk as much as she glided through the airport's parking garage to Andy's red Ford Focus hatchback.

On the way, Lucia told Andy that last night, when Lucia's mother had hung up on her again, Lucia had phoned in a reservation to the Villa Verdi restaurant because she wanted to go someplace that she really, really loved, that reminded her of home, of her childhood, of the fun she had playing with Mr. Delise's daughter, CeCe, and the nights that, when Cavalettas went there as a family, her mother and father would stop their snippy little fights.

"I want to give myself some time before I see her," Lucia had said. "I want to feel good to be home for a while. Is that okay with you?"

It wasn't. What Andy wanted was a place that was loud and greasy and filled with people their age, or close to it, where they could just fit in and not care, like they had done in the Main Line bars when Andy looked old enough not to get carded.

She was not in the mood for big heavy plates of pasta in tomato gravy—not at all—but she thought she'd just be pleasant about it. Lucia sensed it though, right away. "It's my turn to be grumpy, okay?" Andy said.

As she merged on the airport exit ramp onto I-95 north, she explained. The question Mr. Action had spent most of the day trying to answer was the naive gripe about developers getting tax breaks and government funds to tear down buildings to put up new ones when the old ones were perfectly good. Andy had called the reader—a cranky guy who used to live in the Bala Busta neighborhood but had to move to a senior adult complex when his assessments went up and a developer came in, with tax breaks and government money, to level the whole block and put up new row houses with parking in the back.

Andy tried to call the developer, Nashua Eagleman, and was referred to his sales and marketing department, which then referred her to a public relations woman who said that it costs so much to build in Philadelphia because of union labor, zoning compliances, security and permitting and insurance bonding and infrastructure improvements, that no developer could recoup his costs without government incentives, and even then, there was risk involved: not every development sold through fast enough to make a profit.

Andy expected this kind of response. What she wanted to get at was, if government money was needed for any new or rehab construction beyond a single dwelling, to what extent did politics determine who would build, what would be built, and where it would be built?

It was a complicated question and the spokesperson mentioned several names in city government she could call to get "some kind of handle on it," including the mayor, but the one who had the greatest influence, in terms of where the major funding went, was State Senator Henry Tybold.

She called Tybold's office in Philadelphia and got an aide who said he was "qualifying" her question, so it could be "prioritized in a timely manner." What was Andy's position at the *Press*? How long had she been working for the newspaper? Did she normally write about political matters? Was she a resident of Philadelphia? What was her political affiliation?

You don't ask a reporter these questions, Andy said. You either answer the questions, or you refer the reporter to the person who can, and, if that person isn't available, who is?

Andy was put on hold. Then she was disconnected. She called back again and got someone else who went through the list of questions again. Andy called the senator's Harrisburg office and was given a different list of questions to answer, and cut off when she objected.

She tried people in city government. She even left a message with the mayor's press secretary. Everybody promised to get back to her and nobody did.

All the while, people were returning Ladderback's calls. She couldn't help but hear him, thanking people for getting back to him, being so sincere and concerned and sympathetic. You'd expect nobodies, friends, relatives and enemies of nobodies that Ladderback wrote about to call back. To them, the media was like this big spotlight that was always shining on the rich, famous and spectacularly vile. When the spotlight wandered into their neighborhood, even if it was for an obituary, they would scramble over the top of each other to be in the reflected glow.

Andy was aware that State Senator Tybold was in the spotlight all the time. He gave weekly scheduled press conferences. To get in, you had to apply in advance to get a press pass and then you had to show up half an hour early to go through the metal detectors.

Or you had to know somebody who knew somebody.

She looked around the newsroom and, there, in the columnists' ghetto, was the cluttered desk of Chilly Bains, the *Press*'s "kleptosexual" ("I'll take anything, from anyone, anytime!") gossip columnist, who was supposed to know *everybody*. He hunched in his chair with the phone jammed in his ear, playing with his mustache, snickering as if he was listening to the dirtiest joke ever told.

She went over to his desk and figured she'd ask him when he got off the phone. He never looked at her—not even when she tapped him on the arm and showed him a piece of paper on which she had written "Can you help me with something?" He just waved her away. This would have normally enraged Andy, but the quest for the quote had worn her down.

She went back to her desk, dropped heavily into her plastic, static-proof chair and followed the developer's spokesperson with "city officials, as well as State Senator Henry Tybold, did not respond to several requests for comment."

She wrote her column, hoping that editors would just skim the lead but it was bounced back from the copy desk, with a note: NEEDS MORE ATTRIBUTION.

The lead item became the Internet Web site and Andy was furious at having wasted her entire day as she rushed to get her car out of the garage so she could get Lucia to the airport in time.

She was still grumpy as Lucia gave her directions to the restaurant.

She parked easily, which, Lucia said, wasn't a good sign. "You couldn't park anywhere near this place on a Friday night when I lived here."

The green stucco on the outside of the restaurant had cracked in places. The inside was dark, but inviting. They were shown to a table across from the kitchen and Andy pulled her bomber jacket around her sweater and shifted uncomfortably in her chair. She didn't like the green wallpaper, the empty wine bottles and plastic green grapes hanging from the ceiling, the dimly lit paintings of Italian scenery on the walls. Where was the waiter? Did she feel a draft in this place? Were they skimping on the heat?

"You'll love it when he comes out and sings," Lucia said. "He's an old guy, and he doesn't have much of a voice left but, spirit is content, you know? He just has it."

Andy wasn't sure what Angelo Delise and the Villa Verdi were supposed to have. Andy could imagine, maybe ten years ago, an old pasta mill like this would get a crowd on a Friday night, but now? The restaurant was nearly empty. The green carpet had weird blotches on it. The sesame seed twist bread was pretty good, warm and chewy, but Andy had finished her water glass and she didn't see anyone in the restaurant who might fill it.

"This bread," Lucia said. "I missed this bread like you wouldn't believe."

"They didn't have Italian bread in Ohio?"

"Not like this," Lucia said.

Andy took a breath. "You look great," she said finally to Lucia.

"We'll see how I look after I see my mother." She looked at her watch. "He comes out and sings at eight on the dot."

"He's late," Andy said.

"He's never been late. Even when he's sick, he sings. He sang when his daughter . . ."

Lucia didn't finish the sentence and Andy hoped she wouldn't bring up CeCe Delise's death, because Lucia had brought it up too often when Andy had first gotten to know her. Sure, it was horrible to have a best friend turn up raped and murdered in some ruined place, but you get over these things. Andy had had to get over the death of her father. It takes time, but you move on.

Andy saw Lucia look at her watch again. "The kitchen's right there," Andy said. "You can go in and ask him what's up."

"You don't go into Mr. Delise's kitchen without asking first," Lucia said. "Only CeCe and very special people could do that."

Andy looked around again. Nobody was at the bar, not even the bartender. She saw, against the wall beside the kitchen doors, an electric organ, and next to it, a big silver microphone resting on the empty music stand. Was that one of those pop-in-a-cassette-and-it-plays organs, or did this guy have his own accompanist?

She was not looking forward to this. She wanted a waiter to bring them menus, at least. "Lucia," Andy began. "You know I don't hear music."

"Oh, I'm sorry," Lucia said. "I forgot you were born with that thing. You're super tone-deaf."

"It's called *amusa*. I can hear words. I can hear sounds. But music is just noise to me." Here it was sixteen minutes after eight. Lucia was getting nervous.

And Andy couldn't find a waiter. She wanted to find a waiter, which was why she got up and told Lucia, "I just have to find somebody to take our order."

"Andy, don't go in there!" Lucia called but Andy stood up and, with the same easy, unquestioning audacity that makes a reporter pick up a phone and try to get the U.S. Attorney on the phone to issue a statement, took two steps forward, put her hands on the door marked *in,* pushed it open and walked into the kitchen staff, waiters in green uniforms, lined up against the side of the kitchen. All eyes were on her, but Andy was six feet one inch tall, so she was used to all eyes being on her. She was about to ask for somebody to take her order when she heard someone hiss behind her, "What the fuck?!"

She turned around and saw a short guy in a ski mask holding a pistol, aimed right at her.

3 i know you!

At around the same time on Friday, about three miles north of the Villa Verdi, Shepherd Ladderback came into Jimmy D's basement kitchen through doors that, according to the legend, were connected to the Center City's underground concourses so that Prohibition-era patrons in the ground-floor dining room could run down the stairs to the kitchen and escape a police raid.

No one in the kitchen had ever asked Ladderback why he never came in through the restaurant's front door, because, back in the days when Jimmy D's was the top power restaurant in the city, where you would find all the city's "movers and shakers, and even a few Quakers," the really big celebrities who didn't want to be seen on the street came in through those doors, and left by them, too.

Ladderback ate at Jimmy D's several nights a week. When he came in through the basement doors, he made a point of saying hello to the staff, some of whom recognized him as the "guy who wrote up the dead people" for the *Philadelphia Press*.

On this Friday night, he arrived later than usual, having knocked off an incredible, start-to-finish, three obituaries in one day. He glowed with the righteous weariness of a job well done. So why was the kitchen staff on edge?

A glance or two at the clouds of steam near the pot sink told him why.

A short man with jowls that hung down to the brilliant, cream-colored scarf wrapped around his neck had perched himself on the backless barstool reserved for users of the unlisted "pot-watcher's" telephone.

Named for the proverb, a watched pot never boils, the pot-watcher's phone had been installed by the restaurant's previous owner so that, in the days before cell phones, those who had eavesdropped on the conversations of the city's rich and powerful, or just had to make a telephone call and could not be seen doing anything as déclassé as stuffing coins into the pay phones near the lavatories, could excuse themselves, go down the stairs and use an unlisted telephone in a relatively private area.

Hatless, reading glasses hanging on the end of a pointed nose, the man on the pot-watcher's phone wore a broad-shouldered midnight blue chesterfield coat from which stuck out short legs of precisely pressed ash gray woolen trousers and gleaming brown brogans. Beside him stood two young, handsome, smartly dressed acolytes: an imperious male with a jutting chin and dark skin in a similar but not quite as dark chesterfield coat and a lighter-skinned female with the eyelids and cheekbones that indicated the possibility of Hispanic origin. Both acolytes looked warily about the kitchen, aware that this was yet another of those peculiar places where State Senator Henry Tybold did his business, so they would put up with the steam, the noise and edgy stares from those who worked with their hands.

As a state senator, Henry Tybold was supposed to be seen and heard in Harrisburg, but he was almost never in Harrisburg. Harrisburg was Pennsylvania's middle-of-nowhere capital city, invented because it was far enough away from the scheming, magnificently corrupt industrial cities of Philadelphia and Pittsburgh to pretend it had escaped the taint.

One reason that State Senator Henry Tybold was the most powerful politician in Philadelphia was that most people in Philadelphia couldn't figure out what Harrisburg was for. It was a little more than a two-hour drive east "up the turnpike." It had the governor's mansion but it didn't have the Eagles, the Flyers, the Phillies or the 76ers. If it had an orchestra, ballet or an art museum nobody cared. It certainly didn't have an Ivy League university, or actors dressing up like Ben Franklin and Betsy Ross walking around on the street and posing in pictures with tourists in front of Independence Hall. Harrisburg probably had cheese steaks, hoagies, Tastycakes, roast pork sandwiches, turtle soup and thick, doughy soft pretzels that you ate with yellow mustard squirted all over, but who the hell goes to Harrisburg for a quick bite?

Unlike Philadelphia's mayor, an infamously "aloof" presence whose "pay to play" politics confined his attentions to his largest campaign contributors, or the bickering, sputtering city council members, whose districts were a mismatched, crazy quilt of insular neighborhoods and irregular border zones designed to keep residents in a perpetual state of rage and confusion—especially on election day—State Senator Henry Tybold's district included "anybody in this great city who needs somebody to stick up for them."

And God help you if you didn't want the senator to stick up for you.

Ladderback had seen plenty of pictures of the senator and, as is the case when you finally glimpse people who have been photographed too many times, the senator seemed smaller, older and less senatorial in person. He could have been just another well-dressed geezer, except he had the phone jammed between his ear and the coat's immense padded shoulder and was making small notes with an expensive fountain pen in a worn, leatherbound notebook on which had been hand-tooled in gold: "In gratitude for all you done."

Ladderback said his hellos, moving inevitably toward the stairs beside the dumbwaiter (that took the food up, and dirty dishes down) that led to the dining room, while keeping Tybold in view. Would the senator want Ladderback to recognize him and say hello?

Then he saw the female acolyte whisper to the senator and the senator get off the phone, and Ladderback acknowledged why so many politicians who have no skills, no education, no ethics or morals get more votes than the intelligent, the competent and the idealistically righteous: they know how to make a person they've never met feel as if he is the one person they've been waiting for all their lives.

Tybold slipped off the stool came up to Ladderback, cocked back the black fisherman's cap and put his hand in Ladderback's. He said, "I know *you*," with such warm, convincing bombast that Ladderback did not try to deny, refute or amend it.

The senator added, "I heard you come in here."

That was true. "I am Neville Shepherd Ladderback, of the *Philadelphia Press*."

"You do such a great job," the Senator said. "You make nobodies sound like somebodies."

Ladderback wasn't sure if he had been flattered or insulted. "I have never met anyone I failed to find interesting in some way."

The senator cracked a respectful grin, as if Ladderback had said something profound. "Upstairs there's a fellow named Captain Jack Ferko who said you'd be meeting him here."

"We were to speak informally," Ladderback said.

"About Paulie Small, Jack told me," the senator continued. "Jack, Paulie Small and I go way back. Jack said you were considering writing Paulie up."

"I am considering it," Ladderback said.

"You know it's funny how this great city can bring people together," the senator resumed. "Jack and Paulie came back from Vietnam and had problems getting their veterans' benefits. Jack's father—he'd served in Korea—came to me and I wrote letters on the boys' behalf that got them their benefits. Later I helped Jack get state funds to build up Not Fade Away and Jack, God bless him, delivered the veterans' vote to me. I've helped him build a new headquarters, put up housing projects. We did the Pickle Factory together."

"I mentioned that in my obituary of Noah Zyman," Ladderback said.

"And it was in today's paper, wasn't it?" Senator Tybold asked the woman beside him, who nodded in agreement. "She does my reading for me," he told Ladderback. "Anybody ever tell you how that deal went down?"

"I confined my research to Mr. Zyman's life," Ladderback said.

"I was the one that got Sunset Zyman to deed it over to Not Fade Away as a tax write-off. He never could see a place that stank of vinegar as a luxury residential rehab. But look at what it did for Westyard. You been down by that neighborhood recently?"

"No," Ladderback said.

"Well, you'll have a reason to, soon. This I tell you for your ears only: Matt Plank's next restaurant is opening there. You been to his places? That boy's a genius. Raises the food bar wherever he goes."

Ladderback found the senator's phony confidentiality insufferable. He was sure that other ears had heard about this, and any other secrets the senator might reveal to him.

"Anyway, Jack's up in the dining room, down in the dumps—understandably—over Paulie, a friend of his, friend of mine, an old soldier, a solid neighborhood guy, a private kind of person who, when you really look at what he did, wasn't all that interesting, I don't think, from a media standpoint. I know for a fact that, beyond mentioning that he died of injuries, the *Standard* isn't going to have anything more to say about him. He was involved in payment schedules, contract allocations, permit acquisitions, stuff that probably won't translate well. You're not the only one from your paper who's been asking questions about him, but I think it's safe to say that your editor and I are of like minds: there really isn't much of a story in this."

Ladderback blinked. "Which editor was this?"

"The top one. Lange. He didn't mention it to you? I'm sure he'll get around to it." He snapped his fingers and the man at his side produced a business card. He handed the card to Ladderback. "You come across anything that you want to ask me about, don't be a stranger."

As Ladderback took the card, Tybold asked him if he had been in the military.

"I did not serve," Ladderback said.

"Jack was in Army Intelligence. Spend a few minutes with him, and you'll wish you'd been there. I can't tell you how happy I am to have met you." He picked up the phone, signaling that the conversation was over.

The male acolyte stepped aside so Ladderback had a straight path to the stairs.

Ladderback put the card in his jacket pocket and took the path up. Had the most powerful politician in the city spoken with Howard Lange, the most powerful editor of the *Philadelphia Press*, to kill an obituary that Ladderback wasn't even sure he wanted to write? Though journalists and politicians behaved like hereditary enemies, they were actually much closer, in type and demeanor. Both exploited public attention in order to further agendas that, on occasion, were more similar than conflicting.

The senator had also said that Ladderback was not the only person "from your paper" asking questions about Paulie Small. Who might that other person be?

Ladderback recalled that Andy had a friend whose mother had been close to Mr. Small. Was Andy making inquiries on her behalf?

If so, Ladderback hoped she would remember to be distrustful, of everyone.

The square glass window in the Out door provided the best view of the Villa Verdi's kitchen, though you had to be careful when looking in, because waiters came through that door carrying trays heavy with plates, and Mr. Delise would throw a fit if a waiter crashed into someone standing by the Out door and dropped a tray.

Anyone but CeCe. Mr. Delise let his daughter and her best friend Lucia play in the restaurant because he thought she could do no wrong. CeCe would sometimes crouch by the Out door and, if a waiter came through that she didn't like (usually the best-looking boy), she'd stick out her foot and down would come dishes, waiter and all, with Mr. Delise right behind him, saying how could he be so foolish as to almost step on his baby girl.

Of course, CeCe had to know who was coming through so she could drop down beside the door and stick out her foot at just the right moment. CeCe would get a soup spoon from the cutlery rack beside the gleaming espresso machine that filled the wall space between the Out and In doors. She would then hold the spoon up to the window so that it showed her a curved, upside-down reflection of what was going on.

So now, with Mr. Delise's performance still unaccountably delayed, and Lucia's current best friend in the whole world having gone into the kitchen and not emerged, Lucia put her hand around a spoon on the table. She stood and moved near the Out door.

She held the spoon up to the window. The reflection she saw was of an inverted, dark mass. What could that be? Mr. Delise's waiters wore pale green long sleeved shirts over black pants. His maître d' always wore a dark green jacket, as did Mr. Delise when he performed. So what was this dark black blur?

She had to see it with her own eyes, so she decided she'd move by, as if she were on her way to the restrooms, and just happen to glance in.

She saw a few waiters grouped together, their faces nervous and fearful, and Andy, looking mad. Andy was always mad, but there was no reason to be mad in the kitchen of the Villa Verdi unless Mr. Delise was yelling at her, and if Mr. Delise was yelling at her, Lucia would have heard him.

Then, at the very edge of the window, Lucia saw a dark shape with a knitted blue stripe across it.

It was the back of a ski mask, pulled down tight over someone's head. In a kitchen, men with beards might wear a mesh face mask to keep stray hairs out of the soup, but nobody wears a ski mask in October this far south of the Poconos, unless he's robbing the place.

Lucia could call the cops on her cell phone if this was a robbery in progress. She always told her self-defense students to call the cops if they ever felt threatened, but that you could never depend on cops because cops had their own way of doing things. In most Philadelphia neighborhoods, those in South Philadelphia especially, you call the cops as a very last resort, because even if the cops that answer the call were born and raised on the next block over, by the time they become cops, they are no longer people from the neighborhood. They have become city employees. They might mean well, they might do a million good deeds daily, but they don't want to solve problems as much as they want to stomp to pulp anyone who might even think of breaking the law. Cops will utterly destroy the peace in order to preserve it.

Besides, if a robbery wasn't taking place and Lucia called the cops, Mr. Delise would scream at her for bringing them into his place so that now he had to give them free food or they wouldn't go away.

Lucia glanced toward the front of the kitchen, where the cash register sat. If anybody was going to rob the restaurant, he'd hit the cash register, which sat in a corner of the dining room with a fake TV camera over it (Mr. Delise never wanted to spend the money for a real surveillance system). But, with nine out of every ten checks paid for with credit cards, the most the thief could get would be a few tens and twenties.

What could possibly be worth robbing in Mr. Delise's kitchen? A meatball recipe?

Lucia moved toward the In door. She moved it gently with her fingers and saw that it wasn't blocked. Waiters could go in but they couldn't go out. One human being in a ski mask couldn't keep Mr. Delise's criminally underpaid waiters away from their tables long enough for them to annoy the customers and lose their tips, unless this human being was large enough to be physically intimidating, or he had a weapon. This one was somewhat thin and as short as she was.

So he must have a weapon. And he had stationed himself so he could catch anyone coming through the In door.

Lucia became suddenly, rapidly, utterly afraid. Her throat choked up. Her back got stiff. She felt a crackling energy around her shoulders and she started to ask herself if she knew what the hell she was doing.

Then she reminded herself that, if you spend almost half your life learning the fighting arts, you're going to get moments when you're scared and you can't let the fear stop you. You have to get beyond it. You have to *do* something.

The Villa Verdi's kitchen had an entrance off an alley, a door wide enough for deliveries that opened into an alcove where Mr. Delise's tiny office was. Go to the right, and you'd enter the kitchen, coming up rather fast on the ovens. Go past the office, and you'd hit the stairs going into the basement where Mr. Delise kept his wine, bundles of clean linens, extra plates and dishes, cases of canned food, restroom and cleaning supplies.

Lucia guessed that anybody who was going to wear a ski mask, flash a weapon and keep people in the kitchen would probably have another guy on that door. The only window in the kitchen looked out onto that alley and had been covered with a steel grate after someone had broken in one night and made off with a few cases of Mr. Delise's wine.

Lucia ran past the In door and turned left down the hall leading to the restrooms. She prayed that the ladies' room would be empty.

Once, when they were playing hide-and-seek, Lucia had chased CeCe into the women's restroom. CeCe had asked her to wait until she flushed the toilet. Lucia heard the toilet gurgle and rushed in to find the room empty.

It had taken Lucia only a few seconds to notice the green wallpaper didn't quite line up under the sink. CeCe had slipped through, and then replaced, a panel under the sink. Lucia had removed the panel and found CeCe grinning at her beyond a dingy snarl of pipes. CeCe took off and Lucia pursued her, crawling into a cramped, dank tangle of plumbing that fed the kitchen's dishwasher, which filled the space on the opposite side of the ladies' room wall.

The ladies' room door was locked. Lucia wiggled the door handle.

Behind the door, a woman's voice said, "In a minute."

What's a minute? Lucia was charged up, locked and loaded. She grabbed the door handle again.

"I *said* in a minute."

Was the handle loose enough, the door thin enough and the lock weak enough for Lucia to rock back and kick the door open?

The lavatory hall was too narrow for Lucia to extend her leg fully and get full power from the kick. Why not try a palm heel strike? She had used one to break three boards once, but it had hurt her hand because she had tried to push the flat of her palm through the wood, instead of pulling the power up from her feet, through her legs and into her hips, twisting back and firing it forward like a cannon ball.

She planted her feet and put her right hand flat on the door, just beside the knob. She took a breath, pulled her hand back, twisted her hip and paused.

She told herself she shouldn't be so . . . charged up. She wasn't afraid, she wanted to do something and she wasn't sure what she should do so she was . . . charged up.

But one of the aims of self-defense training is developing a heightened awareness of your surroundings. You can't be aware of much of anything when you're charged up, except, perhaps, the feeling of being charged up. Instead, you must stay calm so that when your charged-up, locked-and-loaded opponent comes at you, you can see the situation clearly and act accordingly.

Lucia let her hand go loose. Less than a second later, she heard the lock slide back, saw the knob turn. The moment the woman left, Lucia was in, on her knees under the sink. She popped the panel off and a hot, humid gust of steam from the dishwasher rolled over her face.

In the dim reflected glare from the kitchen, the pipes appeared darker, dirtier and more formidable. The dishwasher roared and gurgled, its fittings leaking drops of steaming water. What had seemed a wide, inviting crawl space when she was six years old was tight, filthy, cramped and reeked of boiling detergent and decaying garbage that had missed the jaws of the Disposal.

She stuck her head in. She followed that with her left arm and shoulder. She wrapped that arm around a pipe, brought in a leg, squeezed in further.

And found herself wedged in. One pipe was hard against the back of her head, another trapped her knee, a third pipe pinned her shoulder. She pulled her left hand back and a pipe that had been cool was so hot it scalded her wrist. She lost her calm in a rush of panic. She wanted to get the hell out and, like a cricket in a spider's web, every twist and turn seemed to tighten the trap. She couldn't remember the moves she'd made on the way in. The rough, corroded edges of the pipes scraped painfully through her clothes and the water dripping from the fittings had begun to touch her skin.

She felt the scalding water and she suddenly wanted to scream or cry but her throat was so tight she couldn't even do that.

She took a breath and felt her throat loosen, and wished, for a moment, she could be back in a practice room, doing one of the flowing, beautifully graceful kung fu eagle forms. She imagined herself flying, swooping, fluttering away from this awful trap.

Not flying, she realized: flowing. She had been loose when she got in. The only way out was to become even more relaxed.

She took another breath and pretended she was in a tediously complicated yoga posture in which every muscle wants, begs, pleads to tense itself into a knot, and the point of the posture is to relax, to look inward and tease, coax and tickle your muscles to loosen up, let go, liquify and accept that, yes, the position is annoying and crazy and unlike anything you've ever been in before, but you're not going to fall, you're not going to get hurt, you're not going to suffer if you can find a way to relax.

She took more breaths and her wrist fell against the hot pipe. She pulled it back and noticed that the pipe wasn't as hot as the last time. The water that had passed through the pipe had taken some of its heat. She could just twist her arm around it and lean forward instead of back and stretch her leg out here and . . .

She told herself that the two pipes she had to pull herself through were not so close together, that this was *not* the time to kick herself for being fifteen pounds overweight, that she could not be jealous of one yoga student she'd had who had never taken yoga but could still bend and stretch herself in ways that Lucia had never even thought possible. She had to stay loose and reach through the pipes, turn her arms out and down while letting the pipes roll down her side.

They snagged on her hips.

She took another breath. She imagined she had the body of one of those emaciated British fashion models and that she *had no hips.* None at all. It was a straight drop from the waist on down.

She let her legs go limp. Then she squirmed against the slick tile floor. One pipe pressed hard into, and then over, her right hip. The left did the same and then, she was through. She crawled under the conveyor belt that moved the racks of clean dishes out of the spray and stood up.

To her right was the wet gray wall of the dishwasher, and the big metal pot sink, the mop and wheeled bucket and a narrow, open stairway leading to the basement. Just past the stairs was the glass box of Mr. Delise's office.

Directly in front of her was the butcher-block surface of the prep table, strewn with colorful chopped, sliced vegetables in varying stages of disassembly beside a big, long-handled saucepan. Next to that were some knives and several large containers of spices. Above the table was a rack of spoons, ladles, strainers, wire whips and saucepans.

On the other side of the table was the chef's station, where plates were garnished and examined on their way out of the kitchen. Beyond that were the burners and the ovens, and a man in a short, crumpled toque who glared with contempt at a crowd of mostly Asian waiters with Andy Cosicki towering above them. They stood bunched together beside the dessert station in front of the walk-in freezer.

They had mixed expressions—anger, fear, a would-you-get-this-thing-over-with annoyance—as they gazed at the man in the filthy black jeans, faded T-shirt, ski mask and pistol, blocking the Out door to the dining room.

Andy saw Lucia first. Why did Andy have to notice her? Why couldn't Andy have seen her, maybe, out of the corner of her eye, and just ignored her? Or pretended to ignore her? The guy with the gun started to turn her way.

Lucia didn't see anyone else with a weapon, which meant that, if this was a robbery, there was another person involved and, if he wasn't out in the dining room hitting the cash register, he was most likely trying to get into Mr. Delise's office safe.

Lucia couldn't quite make out what was going on in Mr. Delise's office—the glare on the glass was too bright.

The guy in the ski mask pointed at her with a big, shiny, nickel-plated automatic pistol that he held with his arm straight, as if the gun was a magic wand and he only had to wave it to get things to fly through the air.

So Lucia picked up one of a half dozen bruised, cracked, angry red tomatoes on the prep table. Just as his brain was thinking: *Hey, I have the gun, I have all the power, no way she's going to hit me with that,* she let it fly and it missed, and the second one bounced off his shoulder, but the third tomato got him on his shirt and the fourth hit just above that and the fifth got him right in the crotch. He yelled something that sounded like "What the fuck?" and started to come around the table, passing a busboy cowering in a corner past the In door.

Lucia ran out of tomatoes, ignored the knives (never use a weapon that your opponent can use against you) and hit him hard in the face with a peeled onion. The small dish of dried rosemary missed, scattering the tiny curled leaves across the floor. She threw a second spice dish at him. This one bounced off his gun arm, kicking up a dark cloud into his face.

He yelled and Lucia caught a whiff of powdered black pepper. He covered his eyes with his free hand. Lucia pulled the saucepan off the table and hesitated just long enough to see what he would do with the gun. He seemed to be more intent on screwing his hand into his eyes, so Lucia kicked the gun out of his hand (her spinning crescent kick was somewhat wobbly, she noted, but the gun went flying). She used the momentum from the spin to bring up the saucepan and hit him hard enough against the side of his head to lift him off his feet and knock him down against the side of the prep table.

She hit him one more time on the top of his head, stepped back and, when he didn't appear to be moving, looked up and saw the waiters had turned toward Mr. Delise's office, where a thicker and stronger man had emerged with Mr. Delise's chopping knife. He stood just outside the office, waving the knife as if he just might know what to do with it.

He was too far away for her to throw the pot at him. She dropped the pot and was moving toward him when she stumbled on the rosemary leaves and would have fallen had she not managed to grab on to the edge of the pot sink, banging her knee against the metal. She didn't have time to see if she was hurt. She grabbed the flexible spray nozzle used to blast grime off the pots (how long ago was it when Mr. Delise punished her, and not CeCe, for playing hide-and-seek in his restaurant kitchen by making her scrape and clean the hardened, burnt remains from the soup pot), pushed the hot water lever all the way to full, and sent a beam of water toward where she hoped the guy would be.

He wasn't exactly where she expected, but it was much easier for her to adjust the direction of the water spray than for him to get close enough to her to do anything fancy with the knife. She got him full in the face, filling the ski mask with steaming hot water.

He bellowed, put his empty hand over his face, hunkered down and charged toward her with the knife extended. She kept the spray on him and tried to back away but the knee that had banged into the sink suddenly gave out. She stumbled forward again, grabbed the mop handle for support and planted a kick that knocked him away.

But not out. He fell on the floor, pulled the ski mask off his reddened face, pulled himself back up and fixed Lucia with a glare of pure hatred as he raised the knife to throw at her.

With one hand holding on to the pot sink, Lucia grabbed the handle of the mop's water extractor and tilted the bucket toward him. The rush of filthy, ammonia-tainted water on the floor drew his eyes to his gleaming silver mesh athletic shoes, so he didn't see Lucia lift the water extractor and smash it into his chin. He fell back and banged the back of his head against the edge of the prep table.

Lucia waited a second to see if he would get up. When he didn't, she used the mop as a crutch, hobbled over and kicked the knife out of his hands and down the stairs leading into the basement.

She limped into Delise's tiny office. Mr. Delise, so frail, cadaverously thin, was in his dark green "singing suit" hiding under his office table beside his unopened safe. His mouth was covered with duct tape. Three of the fingers of his left hand had been broken and bent back horribly.

"It's okay," Lucia said. Holding the mop, she knelt down and put her fingers on the duct tape.

Delise shook his head and squirmed.

"It's just pain, Mr. Delise. You can take it, after what you've been through."

He raised a hand but she yanked the tape hard and he said, "I'm going to kill that bastard!"

Lucia turned and saw the terrified face of the busboy who had been in a corner of the kitchen away from the group of waiters while the first guy in the ski mask had covered them with the gun. Now he was standing in the office doorway, holding the gun with both hands.

"How come you had to . . . ," he said to her, the gun shaking in his grip.

"She's going to kill you, Tommy!" Delise yelled at him.

Lucia wanted to tell Mr. Delise to shut up. You don't tell someone who has a gun pointed at you that he is going to die, especially when he's close enough to you for you to see that the gun's safety is off and that he is so scared he just might squeeze off a round.

"Tommy, don't you recognize me?" Lucia asked, hoping to calm him down. "It's Lucia, CeCe's friend." Just before she got killed, CeCe had dated Tommy Nguyen. What was the American-born son of Nguyen Li-Loh, the "giant" of South Philadelphia's Asian community, doing working as a busboy?

And, more important, what was he doing with a gun in his hands pointed at her?

Lucia smacked the mop handle down on Tommy's wrists, hoping that the pain from the blow would deflect the gun and maybe loosen his grip.

It didn't. But the blow startled him, giving her a split second to plant her feet, knock the gun away with her right hand and drive her left fist into his side under his ribs. He staggered back out of the office, but he did not drop the gun.

Lucia grabbed the mop in her right hand and followed him. He backed away, the gun aimed directly at her.

Lucia told herself: Don't look at the weapon. Look at the person who is holding the weapon.

That person was frightened. "Don't hurt me," Tommy said. "I didn't mean it."

Lucia limped slowly forward. He moved slowly back until he was almost, but not quite in front of the stairs going down to the basement.

"Lucia!" Andy screamed. "That's a gun!"

Then Tommy stopped in his tracks. He began to tremble. "I have to. I have to do this."

The first rule of self-defense is, whenever there is even the possibility of danger, get out of the way.

Lucia couldn't wait to see if he would fire the thing. He was too close. She was in the path of the bullet and she had to get out of the path, even if the slightest movement might make him fire.

Lucia wiggled the mop handle, hoping Tommy would look at it and not see her left foot, which she was shoving forward, about to execute a sweep that, she hoped, would knock Tommy backward, giving her enough time to put her hands on his arms and aim the gun away.

It might have worked if Andy Cosicki hadn't chosen that moment to jump on him, knocking him down. Tommy collapsed and the gun went off. The bullet went past where she had been standing. It shattered the glass office window and buried itself in the leather spine of the reservation books on the shelves surrounding a massive combination-dial safe.

And Tommy's face landed hard on the edge of the stairs leading to the basement. He took his weight, and Andy's, on his jaw, which made a crunching sound as his body slid forward, bringing Andy down the stairs with him.

Lucia fell in a heap. The loud crack of the gun had numbed her ears. She couldn't quite hear him tumbling into the basement, stopping with a loud smack.

Her eyes found the gun on the floor. It wasn't near anyone. She was going to get it, but her knee was screaming at her, so she let the gun stay where it was.

She heard a few sharp groans coming up from the basement. She remembered that Andy had this way of *trying* to kick the crap out of guys she really, really didn't like. She rarely hit these guys because she would haul her long legs back, so just about anybody could see the kick coming and get out of the way.

This time, Lucia guessed, Tommy couldn't get out of the way. "Think you're going to hurt my friend!" Andy yelled in the basement. Lucia heard her kicking Tommy once, twice, a third time and "one more, just so you remember!"

Then Andy bounded up the stairs. She crouched down beside her and asked Lucia if she was okay.

It took a while for Lucia to recognize her. She didn't remember Andy's eyebrows being that dark. Then she saw the nose. Only her best friend in the whole world could have a nose like that.

Before she could say anything, Lucia heard someone say, "Wow." Someone else said, "Way to do it."

Then there was a cheer, followed by another cheer and something that might have been the beginning of applause until Mr. Delise came out with his damaged hand behind his back, and said, "Back to work. Back to work, all of you."

He stopped in front of Andy. Lucia could see he was about to yell, but he stopped. Andy gave him a look and he just said, "You shouldn't come in the kitchen."

"I *am* in here," Andy said. She put her arm around Lucia. "Are you all right?"

Mr. Delise told his maître d' to get some other waiters and "throw them out on the street." He glared at the gun. "The bastard had to go fire a gun. Now the cops are going to come." He told the maître d' that whatever the cops ate was on the house.

Andy saw the gun and stared at it for a few seconds as if it were a snake that could bite her. Then she helped Lucia to her feet.

Lucia was trembling. It was just adrenaline, she told herself. Later, she would replay the events in her mind and get angry about all the things she could have done. She would remind herself that it was only because of years of tedious, frustrating practice sessions when she would lose her balance, wobble on her ankle, fall down flat on her face and then repeat those jumping, spinning back kicks until she could do them without thinking, was past boredom—that she had survived.

Because the truth is that you never know how a fight is going to come out. You can never be sure that you can walk away. With the throbbing pain in her knee, she could at least walk.

"You," Mr. Delise said as he pointed to Lucia. "There's an angel up in heaven telling me I should let you eat on the house."

Lucia forced herself to breathe calmly. "It's okay, Mr. Delise."

He looked at his broken fingers. Then he went past Lucia and Andy, stood on the landing and spat into the basement. "It's not okay. Not for a minute."

4 stay away from the media

"I found Senator Tybold on the kitchen phone, Whitey," Ladderback told the owner of Jimmy D's Bar & Grille as he took a seat at the bar.

"And what would be so unusual about that?" Goohan said. "He still comes around."

"He looked like he could pay for a call," Ladderback said.

"Ahh, but not paying is the whole point with a fellow like him," Goohan replied. "The day he has to reach into his own pocket for anything is the day we put him in the ground."

Ladderback ordered the house drink, a Jimmy D'Tini, also known as a Jimmy Deet, or just a Deet. It was a basic dry martini made with bottom-shelf gin and vermouth, adulterated with two shakes of black pepper.

Goohan adjusted his electric wheelchair so he had a view of the dark, wood-paneled dining room with lobster pots hanging from the ceiling. When Ladderback and Goohan were young and Philadelphia had yet to take its place on the map of restaurant cities, the city's "power dining room" would have been filled with boisterous, happy, thickset, male gluttons with their wives or girlfriends making slow progress through a gut-bursting binge of shrimp cocktail, steamed mussels in wine, clams casino, snails in garlic, iceberg lettuce salad with Roquefort cheese dressing, turtle soup, oyster stew, Salisbury steak, coquilles St. Jacques, lobster Newburg, filet mignon crowned with béarnaise sauce, cracked lobster tail drowned in butter and an inch-and-a-half thick aged T-bone, baked potato and sour cream and chives, lubricated by stiff bar drinks and finished with cheesecake, chocolate mousse, bananas foster or the ultimate, baked Alaska.

But tastes had changed, and what was "continental" then was boring to a younger generation that ate "eclectic cuisine" in extravagantly designed dining "salons" lit like movie sets. Jimmy D's was less than half full.

"That phone used to get a workout on a Friday night," Goohan said. "Back in the days when I could stand on my own feet, I'd get decent money to put the eavesdroppers at a table next to the mayor, or the bank president, or the senator, or the union president, or a newspaper man like yourself, Mr. Ladderback."

Ladderback flinched. According to correct usage, "like" denoted an exact similarity and, as far as Ladderback knew, there were plenty of newspaper men, but none was "like" him.

But you don't correct the grammar of the few friends you have left.

Goohan sensed Ladderback's discomfort. "Well, not quite like you, Mr. Ladderback. But, before everyone and their baby was carrying a cell phone, there are fellows that had to be near them. Like the fellow they had writing the gossip for the *Press,* before that Chilly Bains took over."

"Lincoln Fretz," Ladderback said. "He called his column L. Fretz Alley."

"His name is in my reservation books. I've kept them all, you know, so I can remind myself who passed through this place. Fretz would sit beside the big-name stars playing the theaters on Walnut Street, and they'd say all kinds of things that he would write down like it was the gospel, and then he would run down stairs into the kitchen, and I swear, there were times when he had a line forming at that telephone, all the pot-watchers waiting to get their turn, and, it always struck me, Mr. Ladderback, that the pot-watchers all ate, drank and came from different places, but they had one thing in common."

He paused to permit Ladderback to guess. Ladderback touched the condensation dripping down the stem of his martini glass. "They did not want to be seen reporting what they heard?" he offered.

"They was all cheap bastards," Goohan said.

Voices in the dining room toasted a "dead soldier," and Ladderback turned on his bar stool to see five men in sweaters and sport coats sitting at a round table close to where he customarily ate his dinner. They drank and one of them waved a glass, demanding a refill.

Goohan set off toward the table.

Ladderback pulled from his pocket the piece of paper Andy had given him. He found enough coins in his pocket for the pay phone.

He moved slowly past the table with the men who had toasted the dead soldier. Which one was Captain Ferko? They weren't in uniform. They wore no insignia indicating rank. What remained of the hair on their heads wasn't groomed in the severely short trims associated with armed services' conformity. The one with the mustache was just as round and out of shape as Ladderback.

He picked one of the five pay phones near the cloakroom, added coins and dialed.

The woman's hello was short, sharp and suspicious.

Ladderback introduced himself. "Please forgive me for calling late, Mrs. Cavaletta. I was hoping you might help me regarding an obituary that I haven't quite made up my mind to write."

"About who?"

"Paul Small." He heard a quick intake of breath. "If this is not a good time . . . ," he offered.

"I won't be having good times anymore," Mrs. Cavaletta said. "Paul was a great man."

"I am told he worked in financial matters."

"Ac*counting* matters. There is a difference. Money doesn't mean anything if nobody knows where it is, where it came from and where it's going."

"I understand that, Mrs. Cavaletta. You are an accountant, also, is that correct?"

"It is my profession," she said proudly. "And it was Paul's, though, the thing about Paul, he could look a person over, and he'd be right on the money, if you know what I mean. That was his gift. But he couldn't add a column of figures. I had to do that for him."

"Mrs. Cavaletta, I am getting conflicting advice about Mr. Small. While I have found that there is no such thing as an uninteresting subject, some have suggested that I should not write about Mr. Small."

Her tone became sharp. "You think what an accountant does is boring? You think all we do is sit around and count beans all day? Or help people cheat on their taxes?"

"I didn't say that, Mrs. Cavaletta."

"An accountant is the conscience of the business world. An accountant is the moral center. An accountant can make a rich man feel poor, a poor man feel rich. An accountant is the estimator of hope."

"I'm sorry, Mrs. Cavaletta. I don't understand how the maintenance of records has anything to do with hope."

She hesitated. "With Paulie gone, they're going to come after me."

"Who would come after you?"

"The ones that didn't get what they think they deserved and think it was Paulie's fault."

"Who are these individuals?" Ladderback asked. "Do you have any evidence that Mr. Small was being threatened?"

"Don't come at me about evidence. I can show you a row of figures and add 'em up backwards and forwards and what will they mean to you? Nothing. You gotta be told."

Against his will, Ladderback found himself drawn into an argument. "I've been led to believe that accountancy is an objective profession that bases its conclusions on facts, Mrs. Cavaletta."

"Facts don't win a fight. Facts don't make people fall in love, or get a divorce. Facts don't get you through an audit. Facts don't get you off the hook in court. What gets you what you deserve is what you are willing to believe. Paulie made people believe. He was like the priest who could tell you why bad things happen, even if you've been good, and you'd believe him, except Paulie didn't do it for God, he did it for money. Paulie could explain things to people, all kinds of people, so they'd accept what they were getting, what they weren't getting, or—most important—what they were losing, like it was the natural order of things."

"This doesn't sound like accountancy, Mrs. Cavaletta."

"What it sounds like is the truth, even if you don't want to hear it."

"I won't dispute what you've told me, Mrs. Cavaletta. What concerns me is your belief that you are in danger. Have you informed the police?"

She hung up on him.

Ladderback replaced the handset. He turned around and saw Whitey Goohan in his wheelchair. "Which of the gentlemen at the round table is Captain Ferko?"

Goohan introduced him to the guy with the mustache which reminded Ladderback of the wide, flat brush on the end of a vacuum cleaner hose. The man had the skin of a man who drinks in quantity.

Ferko's hand was wet when he took Ladderback's and shook it. He introduced his cronies. He told Ladderback he had read his obituaries of veterans and that those obituaries were framed and mounted on a wall in Not Fade Away's headquarters in Westyard.

"I like the things you say about us," Ferko said. "We're raising our glasses to the memory of Paul Small."

Ladderback thanked him. Captain Ferko made a place for Ladderback at the table. Goohan had Ladderback's soup brought to him.

"You don't need nothing in the paper about Paulie because if there was ever a monument to Paulie, it was the Pickle Factory," Captain Jack Ferko told Ladderback as he buttered his bread. "That building wouldn't've happened without him."

State Senator Tybold had claimed credit for the Pickle Factory deal downstairs, but Ladderback sipped his turtle soup and said nothing.

Ferko leaned forward. "We got something coming down the pipeline that's going to transform the south edge of Westyard. Veterans Plaza: mixed-income residential, retail and offices, on the site of an old meat-packing plant back of the Sisters of Zion Hospital. Paulie was working it but I've asked my son Errol to take over. Errol's a capable boy. He'll do Paulie's memory proud."

"I have heard some speculation about Mr. Small's death," Ladderback said.

"There's no end to it." Ferko sighed. "You ask me, Paulie was in the wrong place at the wrong time. He was no spring chicken. He moved slow, with a cane. There's always a bad element that's going to prey on the elderly, even if Paulie wasn't that old."

"You were in charge of the district that included Westyard. Did you have any knowledge of Asian gangs?"

"They were a fact. Still are. They prey mostly on their own. Westyard had a huge population of illegals, some of whom were undesirables who were, in my opinion, responsible for a lot of the crime we had there, and at least one murder, that, I'm sorry to say, we could not close. That was Angelo Delise's daughter. He's the fellow who owns the Villa Verdi. A terrible case. Absolutely terrible."

Ladderback made a mental note to find out more about Angelo Delise.

"We tried to round up and deport as many of the Asian undesirables as we could find," Ferko added, "but it was always a cat-and-mouse game."

Ladderback risked a neutral question. "How long did you know Mr. Small?"

"Paul and me were born in Westyard. We've known each other for as long as you can know anyone."

He went on to tell Ladderback how it was Small's idea to create a neighborhood organization for war veterans. "Paul and me didn't know what we were doing with ourselves when we got back from Vietnam. We started hanging out with other vets and we figured that VA wasn't doing enough. Hell, we had to fight just to get our benefits. Paul went out, trying to get people to donate to help them. While I was at the police academy, and Paul was getting his CPA, we still hung with the troops. I'd bring them into my home, give them meals, introduce them to my sons. We got them involved politically, as a group. The reason we started up with Hank Tybold was that the senator had an open-door policy about helping veterans."

"As long as they voted for him," one of the guys quipped.

"And why shouldn't they?" Ferko said. "Not Fade Away wasn't more than a telephone number and a desk in the back of the senator's office when the senator started steering state and federal grants our way. I dealt with the vets. Paul was the money man."

"And ladies' man," another guy put in.

"Old ladies," a third agreed. "Always inviting him over for coffee and cake."

"Let's not speak ill of the dead," Ferko said. "Paul liked his gals unattached, and you never heard one of them complain."

Ladderback's prime rib arrived, with brussels sprouts and a baked potato. He had that first bit of beef in his mouth when Captain Ferko asked him if he had enlisted.

Ladderback put down his fork. "I considered applying for conscientious objector status. My draft lottery number was never high enough to warrant that."

"You must've thought that those of us who fought were fools."

"I did not," Ladderback said. "I knew of many who volunteered. At the time, I believed my decision to object was the right choice."

"Ah, but what about those that can't choose?" Ferko asked rhetorically. "Paul thought we should see the world. I told you he had a half-sister up in Canada."

"She did not return my calls," Ladderback said. He resumed eating.

"Not surprising," Ferko replied. "That side of his family were a bunch of outlaws. They had an indoor pot farm just outside of Quebec City. But for working class boys like us, there was never a question that we would serve. There was another reason, of course. In peacetime, about the best we could hope for was to follow in our fathers' footsteps."

One of Ferko's buddies said, "You became a cop anyway."

"As did my son—the screwy one, the one that moved out. But Errol's gone places, hasn't he? Errol always looked up to his Uncle Paul. If Paul could do something, Errol would want to do it, too. You spoke with him?"

Ladderback nodded. "He offered me an anecdote about Mr. Small coming up with $2 million to save the Pickle Factory."

"It was a little more than seven years ago, before the election," Captain Ferko went on, "and a lot was riding on that project breaking ground, and suddenly it came up short about . . . what was it . . . somewhere around two mil. Now, you say, what's $2 million when you're talking $130 million in total costs, public/private, with the unions agreeing to supply the contractor with veterans for the principal construction, and the contractor agreeing to hire veterans for all positions not covered by union representation. Now, what Paulie does is, when the money comes in, from wherever it comes in, from the federal, state and local government, from the private sources, from a dedicated funding going to Not Fade Away, from negative enhancements like tax abatements, Paulie comes up with a timetable that basically says who gets what, and when. It's an incredible thing, really, because, in a complicated situation like the Pickle Factory, with money coming from so many different sources in so many different amounts, with allowances for overruns, delays, liability issues and, this being Philadelphia, political situations, the timetable is not as important as the ability of a guy like Paulie to step in there and massage it, to stretch it here or tuck it in there and make it work when things start screwing up. So, before we could even get it going, we come up $2 million short, and we needed it fast and there wasn't a lender in the city that would give it to us without asking the proverbial arm and leg."

He wiped a tear from his eye. "And then Paulie, God bless him, he just comes up with it. I didn't get all the details—I hadn't retired right then. I was still putting in my forty hours on the job. Paulie just found the money. Pulled a rabbit out of his hat. The project broke ground and the rest is . . ."

"History," one of Ferko's cronies said.

"A remarkable accomplishment," Ladderback said. "It would be worth mentioning in an obituary about Mr. Small."

"I don't know about that." Captain Ferko rubbed his chin. "The problem is, you tell a story about Paulie pulling two million out of a hat, and there might be somebody, I'm not saying who, that'll ask where did it come from? I'm not saying Paulie did anything underhanded, but in police work, we talk about the gray area, and I'm not saying Paulie worked that gray area, but this isn't the time to bring it up, because Not Fade Away has other development deals pending."

"You mentioned Veterans Plaza," Ladderback said.

"We're waiting on the federal money before we can announce it."

One of the cronies asked Ferko why the wait had been so long.

"The Pickle Factory was mostly Pennsylvania grants that the senator got for us. This time it's a lot more millions, and the Feds have different ways of doing things. We have to meet some kind of good-character standards that the Bible-belters in Congress wrote into the grant release process."

"You'll meet 'em, Commander," the acolyte said.

"I was telling the senator that it all depends on how deep they want to go," Ferko said. He turned to Ladderback. "In 'Nam, Paul and I were involved in what were called deniable activities. To this day, the military will not admit to the things we did. I'd tell you what we did, but then I'd have to kill you."

Ladderback didn't react.

"Just a joke," Ferko continued, "and one that you've heard before, judging from how I didn't see you show any fear. You'd've been a good soldier after all. Not afraid to make the ultimate sacrifice."

Ladderback let that pass.

"The problem we had," Ferko continued, "was that these snot-nose reporters were listening to Cong sympathizers, who were telling them all kinds of horseshit about the deniable operations. If you ever come across anything pertaining to the Beach of Good Choice, I'm asking you to go over it with me. Just to make sure it's accurate."

"I'm sure I can find military historians who will confirm what actually occurred," Ladderback said.

"That's where you're going to run into difficulty," Ferko said. "Shortly before the war ended, a fire broke out—some will say it was allowed to break out—in a military records facility in St. Louis. Made it almost impossible for Paul and me to get our benefits when we were discharged. We had to get a signed affidavit, and then get Senator Tybold to back us up, before we got our benefits. But we got 'em."

Ladderback's second Jimmy D'Tini arrived.

"What we did was secret stuff. Covert ops. Counterintelligence," Ferko said, eyeing his buddies. "There've been books written about it, but you won't find Paul and me in those books. We were part of a team that would fake the enemy out."

Again, Ferko's tone of voice, his twitchy, forced casualness, told Ladderback that the man was hiding something. "How so?" Ladderback asked.

"We'd invent things that we wanted the enemy to believe. It got to be quite an elaborate operation. Ever hear of the Beach of Good Choice?"

Ladderback shook his head. He had heard of the Good Choice Market, a supermarket that served the diverse and thriving Asian community in South Philadelphia.

"Someday, you should write a book about it." Ferko eyed his buddies, as if asking for permission for what he was about to say. "You should know the media doesn't rank highly with me, because it was the media that decided that war was wrong, not us, not the men living and dying for freedom."

Ferko's statement wasn't true: many of the most significant protestors were members of the Vietnam Veterans Against the War. But the American news media had been notoriously selective in its war coverage. Ladderback recalled that a distorted account of a "surprise attack" on two American Navy vessels in the Gulf of Tonkin led to a congressional resolution that permitted President Johnson to escalate the war when, in truth, the vessels had intended to provoke a response from the North Vietnamese. And, having discovered an attempt to suppress news of a massacre by American troops at My Lai, American journalists considered it their duty to emphasize wartime mistakes, deaths and atrocities, whether these were caused by American military operations or someone else.

Ladderback could have said all that, and more, but he stayed quiet.

"I want to tell you that I consider you an ally," Ferko said. "Your newspaper has consistently promoted our activities and put us in the best possible light. Veterans Plaza will have a financial counseling center that we'll dedicate to Paulie. You might want to write up something about him then. But not now."

He rose. "Now we go to salute the troops at half a dozen VFW halls." He put his hand on Ladderback's shoulder and squeezed it. "I'm grateful that you were thinking of writing Paul up. If it was part of the mission, I wouldn't't've hesitated to aide you in its execution. But we have different missions awaiting us," he said solemnly. "I'm sure you will fulfill yours to the best of your ability."

Ladderback tried to finish his meal but couldn't manage it. Listening to too many lies made him lose his appetite.

The police sergeant was just *too* serious, and too good-looking, to be true. Sure, he acted like he was in charge. He didn't appear bossy or patronizing. He didn't even try to be cool, or to calm anyone down. He and his men stepped lightly through the Villa Verdi's kitchen, with the sergeant radiating such sincere concern that Andy was sure it was an act until Lucia saw Andy scowling at him and said, "he's like that. He has to feel the pain."

Andy had walked Lucia back to the table where she had been sitting. Lucia was still for a while. Then she found Andy's hand and squeezed it.

Andy held Lucia's arm up in the air, as if she were a boxer and had won the fight. "Fearless Lucia," Andy said.

Lucia shook her head. "Andy, I hate to tell you. I was scared. I still am."

"So let's go someplace and talk about it."

"We have to stay here." Lucia glanced at the sergeant. "Vinnie has to talk to us."

The police had jammed chairs in the doors so they would stay open as they carried out Lucia's victims on stretchers. From their table, Lucia and Andy could watch the sergeant handle the situation and, with Lucia refusing any care or attention, Andy was forced to admit that she liked watching the sergeant.

He was a head shorter than Andy, dark haired, in his mid-twenties, with a smooth, wide-jawed face that, if it weren't so annoyingly sincere, Andy might look at for hours. She kept waiting for him to give up his act, to get just a little bit flustered when one of the waitresses interrupted him while he was interviewing someone on the kitchen staff. The waitress had been among those trapped in the kitchen. She started yelling that she didn't have all night to wait around. As long as the dining room had cleared out, she couldn't see why she had to stand around waiting for him to talk to her, so if he didn't mind, she was going home right now.

Any other cop would say he *did* mind and that she wasn't going anywhere until he said so. The sergeant said he understood that she might be upset after what she had been through, and that if she wanted, she could leave her phone number with him and he could call her on the following day. The waitress said she didn't want to give her phone number out to anyone, even a cop, and he turned his beautiful brown eyes on her and said, "Please."

And she gave him the number.

He asked—he did not order—his men to assist the medical technicians as they moved the injured onto stretchers and carried them out. He seemed aware of Lucia, but he made a point of avoiding her.

When it seemed that Vinnie wouldn't be talking to them soon, Andy reached into her shoulder bag, withdrew a copy of the *Philadelphia Press* and showed Lucia the "Mr. Action" column with Lucia's question at the top.

Lucia said, "This is so cool!" She smiled weakly at Andy. "You have that look. Like you're in charge. I remember when we'd shoot baskets after school, after the guys had gone home, you'd have that look."

"You are the only person I ever shot baskets with," Andy said, "and if I had any kind of look, it was only because you were easy to beat."

"You were, what, an even six?"

"I'm six-one now, maybe a little more."

Lucia looked back at the newspaper. "When you told me you got that job with the *Press,* it was like, wow—I actually know somebody who is following her dream." She picked up a rounded seeded loaf of Italian bread that was still warm from the oven and tore it in half. She found herself looking at Vinnie again.

Andy had to ask, "What is it with you and him?"

Lucia curled her lip. "History," she said.

"So how come he hasn't said hello?"

"He's saving me for last. He knows I'm going to want him to not report this and he's going to want to report it, but, without me or Mr. Delise pressing charges, he's going to have nothing much to report."

Andy checked Vinnie out, was it the third or the fourth time? His proportions were near perfect: black leather police jacket open to show a dark blue police blouse pulled tight over a compactly muscled chest. His arms and legs just long enough to fill out his uniform, broad shoulders and chest, belted waist from which his mace canister, handcuffs and holstered pistol hung like kitchen utensils from a rack.

Mr. Delise avoided him. He clutched his wrist and wouldn't let anyone give him first aid.

Lucia had put the newspaper in her duffle bag by the time Vinnie finally approached the dining room table where she and Andy sat, Andy could feel his eyes on her, rather than Lucia. Then he asked Lucia if he could speak with her and waited a few awkward seconds until Lucia said, "Vinnie, you never had to ask to speak to me."

"I'm asking now," he said. He picked up a chair and gently put it down near the table. He sat in it backward and rested his notepad on the top of the chair back. He rolled his pen in his hand and said, "It's good to see you again, Lucia."

Lucia looked away.

He introduced himself to Andy as Sergeant Vincent Ferko. He put his card on the table. He offered Andy his hand and got a little jolt when she felt his calloused fingers wrap around hers. She liked it when he asked her, "How you doing?" How was she doing? She was liking that hand, liking the solid warmth seeping into her skin and running up her arm. Should she tell him that she knew people who were cops, that her grandfather was a cop who died before she was born, that she liked holding Ferko's hand?

She forced herself to let go. Ferko asked Andy what she saw when she came into the kitchen. She told him. He asked her for a number at which she could be reached. She recited the newsroom's number and her extension.

"Something about that number. I must've called it some time ago but I don't remember. Is that a residence or a place of business?"

"Call it and see," Andy said.

Ferko pondered her response, as if he had to wring every nuance from what was . . . what? Did Andy really want him to call her?

He caught her eye. She wanted him to call.

"I'm very sorry this had to happen to your evening, Miss Cosicki," Ferko said, pronouncing her name slowly, as if the sound was jogging his memory.

Andy said, "Can I ask you something?"

"Anything that's on your mind," Ferko said.

"How did you ever become a cop?"

Lucia rolled her eyes.

Ferko put down his pen, folded his hands and thought about it as if this was the first time he had ever been asked. "I thought it was a decent thing to do."

"He became a cop because he can't stand his brother," Lucia said, exasperated.

"Errol has nothing to do with it," Ferko continued, flustered because he didn't like Lucia getting personal. "I got accepted to the police academy, I studied as hard as I could and I graduated. I'm currently the youngest sergeant on the force and I'm studying for detective."

He rolled his pen again and asked Lucia if she was going to stay with her mother and, before she could give him her mother's address, Ferko said he hadn't forgotten where it was. "You see your mother yet?"

Lucia said, "I just got off the plane."

"How long you staying?"

"Forever."

He asked Lucia if she had a cell phone.

"You know the number," she said.

Then he put down his pen and told Lucia that she was lucky she wasn't dead. "You don't mess around when somebody has a knife or a gun. You don't start a fight, you don't try to finish a fight. You call us. You dial 911 and we send three squads in, and we solve the problem, or we call in more squads. With what happened here, somebody could've got slashed and bled to death, or the gun could've gone off and the shot could've gone wild and who knows how many people would've gotten hurt. This is not the way it's done."

Andy became angry. "What she did was incredible."

Ferko again turned his eyes on Andy and she gave him a look of withering contempt, her infamous Cosicki Intimidation Beam.

But he wasn't intimidated. He almost grinned. Then he turned to Lucia and said, "You messed those guys up pretty good. I'm expecting you to give me a statement and press charges."

"Talk to Mr. Delise," Lucia said.

Ferko folded his hands again. "Mr. Delise wants us to forget this happened. I told him I came into this on a shots-fired call, and now I have three unidentified Asian males on the way to the emergency room and a roomful of people who saw you put on a show."

"She wasn't putting on a show," Andy said.

Ferko consulted his notepad. "What I have ascertained so far is that a pistol was fired. I also have witnesses that say you beat up three guys pretty bad. We can file an unlawful weapons possession charge against the shooter, but, given who the shooter was . . . If Mr. Delise won't press charges and you won't press charges, those guys can turn around and press charges against you. And then you have to pray nobody in the media hears about it and blows it up until it's out of control."

Andy ignored the slight about the media. "Police reports don't always get filed." She enjoyed every second that Ferko stared at her.

"Do you have any idea," he began, "what kind of trouble can happen when reports that should get filed, don't get filed?"

Andy didn't blink. "My grandfather was a police sergeant and my father used to work with the police," she said. "His name was Benjamin Cosicki. Around City Hall, they used to call him Benny Lunch. He'd take people out to lunch and he'd work things out."

He looked at Andy even longer. "I heard about him. He was supposed to be shorter than me. I can't see you as Benny Lunch's girl."

"Daughter," Andy said. "I'm his daughter. I got my height from my mother."

He cracked a grin and Andy felt herself loosen up far too much because he had a truly great smile. He said, "If you got your height from your mother, what'd you get from your father?"

"An education into how you do things, if you want to do something decent." Andy smiled back.

He stopped smiling. "Police work is the hardest job there is to do right, especially when you get people who should know better telling you how they think you should do your job."

Andy was about to stand *up* so she could look *down* on him when Ferko turned to Lucia. "If you know what's good, stay away from the media."

Lucia looked at Andy. Andy grinned, folded her arms and said, "Sure."

Ferko said, "Have a nice evening," rounded up the other officers and left.

Lucia watched him go. The restaurant was empty; the staff had gone home.

Lucia found Mr. Delise and told him that he had three broken fingers on his hand that a doctor had better see.

"The ovens are still warm," he said, trembling with pain. "You don't leave a kitchen when the ovens are warm." He had difficulty locking the doors and wouldn't let Lucia turn the keys.

In Andy's car he talked of the food wasted and the money he would lose. As Lucia gave Andy directions to the Sisters of Zion Hospital, Mr.

Delise grumbled about the police rushing in, frightening the customers and making so much noise that it was no wonder the dining room cleared out. When Mr. Delise's father had the place, he said, it didn't matter what the problem was, the cops always asked permission and came in through the back door.

Andy hit a pothole and the jolt must have been painful enough to make Mr. Delise stop grumbling. That's when Lucia asked him about the safe.

"You don't talk about that," he threatened her.

Lucia wouldn't be threatened. "It had to be the safe. If they were going to rob you, they would have hit the cash register in the dining room. They wouldn't have gone near the kitchen because the only thing in the kitchen is your office with the safe in it, and they had you in your office with tape on your mouth, and they were breaking the fingers of one hand so you could open the safe with the other one."

"Forget about the safe," Mr. Delise snapped.

Andy wanted to tell him he should speak politely to the woman who saved his life, but she saw the hospital tower rising over the row houses about two blocks east. Lucia had given her directions that would take them two blocks south and then east, but she saw that the alley on the left would take them there faster. She turned the car into the alley and Mr. Delise groaned while Lucia said, "Oh—my—God!"

Andy slowed. "This looks like a shortcut."

As Lucia said, "It is, but—"

Mr. Delise sputtered, "No!"

Andy stopped the car. "I can see the sign for the Emergency right down at the end of the second block. Is there a big pothole or something in the way so I shouldn't go down here?"

Lucia whispered, "Yes."

Mr. Delise took a long breath and finally said, "No. You go down it."

"Back out, Andy," Lucia said.

"Don't listen to her," Mr. Delise grumbled. "You go where you are going."

Then Andy experienced one of those incredible intuitive leaps that, if

59

it had happened anywhere else, would have confirmed for her that journalism was her destiny. This time, it gave her the creeps. "This is where CeCe . . ."

"Keep going!" Mr. Delise yelled.

Andy waited for Lucia to contradict him. She heard a sob coming from the backseat, then, "Might as well."

Andy took her foot off the brake and let the car inch forward at idling speed. The rowhouse on the right gave way to another alley, and then a long row of chain-link fencing ending in a gate with a door off the hinge. Just beyond the fence rose the brick and concrete walls of an abandoned factory.

"It hasn't changed from the day they found CeCe," Lucia said, her voice quavering.

"Sure it has," Mr. Delise growled. "No more people are in it. It's sealed up now. You had families from Vietnam, Cambodia, Thailand, Laos, who were dying by the truckload and my girl had to get herself killed before anybody noticed. And now they want to turn this into another Pickle Factory."

When Andy passed by the gatehouse, Mr. Delise put his good hand over his face and said, "Mother of God!"

After Andy crossed a street they were silent. She continued down the alley toward the white, glowing EMERGENCY ENTRANCE sign. She turned right, on to Fifteenth Street and pulled the car into the narrow driveway leading to the emergency room. Mr. Delise opened the door and insisted on walking up to the entrance by himself. "Anybody ask anything," he told them, "it was an accident in the kitchen. You got that?"

Lucia told him that she did.

"Nice meeting you," he said to Andy as he threw his shoulders back. Andy waited until he was inside before driving back to Fifteenth Street.

"Nice guy," Andy said.

"He's been through a lot," Lucia said. "Oh, God, I can't believe you took us there."

"I would've backed out."

"He wouldn't let you. He's like that. If it's anything to do with pain, he has to show you that he can take it. I guess that's how he copes."

Andy paused at a stoplight. "Did it ever bother you, him being so mean?"

"Not really," Lucia said, some of the sadness leaving her voice. "In their own way, my parents were worse. Are you and your mother still not speaking to each other?"

"No. I mean, yes, we're not speaking," Andy said. "She calls me, though. She leaves voice-mail messages about parties she's going to be attending around here. She wants me to get all flirty with these rich guys so the Logo—Logan Brickle, the guy she thinks I should marry—will get jealous."

"He's rich?"

"He's a jerk. But she keeps after me to go to the parties. There's one tomorrow night at the Pickle Factory. One of my mother's artists is doing an installation, which is a fancy way of saying the painting or whatever will be on view for the first time. You want to go?"

"This guy she wants you to marry going to be there?"

"He's in Europe, being irresponsible. He's supposed to come back sometime soon. You met him once. I took you to a Halloween party at his house."

"It had all those rooms," Lucia remembered. "And there was this total asshole who couldn't stop telling me about riding his motorcycle into the pool."

"His mother owns the Hampton Bank, but she thinks he's incompetent so she torments him, hoping he'll straighten up and stop being a slacker, which only makes him try to annoy her even more," Andy said.

"And your mother wants you to spend the rest of your life with him?"

"She has reasons," Andy said.

"My mother hated me doing martial arts," Lucia said. "She told me it would never help me get married. Why is it that our mothers want us to get married? They act like they want it for us, but I think they want it for them."

Andy let the car move forward. "You sure you want to stay with your mother?"

"I want to try," Lucia said. "With Uncle Paul gone, she needs me."

Andy followed Lucia's directions to Brixton Street, put the car in front of a fire hydrant and carried Lucia's duffle bag to the row house's front step.

She watched Lucia swing her leg out of the car and give it a little weight.

"You going to see someone for your knee?" Andy asked.

"It's swelling up now but it'll be okay in a few days," Lucia said. She braced herself against a parked car, moved awkwardly toward the sidewalk and sat down on the step beside the bag.

Andy sat on the steps beside her, because row house steps aren't just a way to get into a house that had to be built so many feet above the street level, that, in another century, the guy who delivered the coal could dump it down a chute through a window into the basement. The steps were an in-between place where you could be close to the street without being completely in it, or at home without being in your home. You could sit on the steps and watch people and cars go by, or you could sit and notice how different things were, how they'd changed from what you remembered. This house had awnings hanging down over the windows while another one had a red door set in a shiny aluminum frame.

Lucia pulled her sweat jacket around her. "Vinnie was right. I should-n't've come down on those guys. What happened was, I got mad at them. I hurt them far more than I had to. You're not supposed to get mad in a violent situation. It only makes things worse."

"Vinnie was wrong," Andy said. "When you open up your self-defense class, I'm signing up for the full load."

"There's no load," Lucia said. "It's mostly about practicing simple movements, over and over and over, until they sink in. And a few tricks."

Andy became like a kid at a magic show. "Show me one!"

Lucia gently took Andy's right hand, flipped it over until the little finger was up, bent the wrist until Andy's arm was shaped like a Z, and then tilted Andy's hand toward her.

Andy yelped. The pain that shot through her arm was sudden and excruciating. Though she was sitting, Andy felt herself crumple forward. She snatched her arm back when Lucia let it go.

"It isn't broken," Lucia said. "That's a trick, a joint lock that the aikido people call *nikyu,* because *nikyu* means 'Number Two' and this is the second wrist lock technique usually taught. This technique isn't that practical because you have to get your hands on the arm and set up the lock. You have to be careful about teaching this, because a student can crank the wrist too far and cause damage. But if you get an asshole into it, and crank it a little, the pain usually stops everything."

Andy asked Lucia to show her the technique again. She practiced it a few times.

"Now I've turned you into a danger to society," Lucia said.

Andy imitated Vinnie Ferko's low voice. "You know better than to try that stuff."

Lucia pointed to a row house across the street, two doors west. "Vinnie grew up in that house. When his mother died, he and his brother would hang around here with me and CeCe after school while his father was working. My mother and I liked Vinnie more than Errol. Losing his mother made Vinnie appreciative and grateful for what he had. Errol went in the opposite direction—he was always angry, dissatisfied, looking to pick fights. He'd beat up Vinnie all the time. Jack Ferko thought we might all get along better if we enrolled in Mr. Ishimura's Heian-Do school, but that didn't work either. Uncle Paul eventually took Errol off our hands while Vinnie became like the brother I always wanted to have, and I couldn't help having a crush on him."

"So much for history," Andy said.

"He threw me over for CeCe, but he was always around. His brother and his father moved out, but Vinnie still lives in that house. He keeps his motorcycle in the living room. He was the first to call me when Uncle Paul got hurt."

"So how come he didn't seem happy to see you?"

"I think we both wanted to show each other that we're not the same people we were when we were kids," Lucia said. She rose slowly and picked up her duffle bag.

Andy made sure Lucia knew her cell phone number. "Call me if it doesn't work out," Andy said. "Anytime. Night, day, whatever."

Andy liked to turn her cell phone off when she drove but this time, she left it on because she had a feeling a call was going to come. She was in West Philadelphia, circling Clark Park in search of a parking place near her apartment, when the cell phone chirped.

It was Lucia. She was in tears. Her mother didn't want Lucia in the house. Lucia needed a place to stay.

Andy drove back and picked her up. They went to a greasy, noisy bar near the Penn campus. They were walking back to Andy's apartment when Lucia's cell phone went off.

It was Vinnie Ferko. Someone had broken into Teal Cavaletta's house. "They hurt her really bad," Lucia told Andy, as Andy gunned the car's engine. The shock wasn't yet hitting her. "She's breathing, but that's about all."

5 good for each other

Ladderback took off his shoes and tie. He opened the buttons of his fraying white oxford shirt far enough to show the top of his undershirt. He assumed his place on the throne-like brown recliner at the center of his studio apartment.

Would he finish the night with a book? Another try at the decadent ruminations about sex and love in *Justine*? Did he want to return to Lawrence Durrell's arid, horrid and treacherously beautiful Alexandria tonight? A hardcover of the Dutton edition he had ordered from the Internet, lay on the table beside the recliner with a flap of the terra cotta–colored dust jacket marking the page. Near the book was the remote control for his television, and the wireless keyboard that used the same wide screen as a computer monitor.

He let his recliner enfold him. He turned on his computer, accessed the Internet and did a search for the "Beach of Good Choice." This led him to the Research and Studies Annex, the innocuous name of a division in Army Intelligence that had operated an island camp where an insurgent guerrilla force had been trained during the Vietnam war.

He scrolled through pictures on several Web sites showing former

RASA personnel and found a young, thinner version of developer Nashua "Nash the Slash" Eagleman, a scar along his jaw gruesomely visible as he sat atop a camouflaged Army Corps of Engineers bulldozer, a private first class. Another photo showed a smiling American soldier with big ears playing what appeared to be stickball with Vietnamese children. The man was identified as Corporal Angelo Delise of Philadelphia, Pennsylvania.

But nothing about Jack Ferko or Paul Small. Ladderback did a search-within-results for their names and, again, found nothing.

Jack Ferko was mentioned on several Web pages as the founder of the non-profit Philadelphia-based war veterans assistance organization called Not Fade Away. Not Fade Away had "partnered" with Eagleman on several development deals, including the Pickle Factory, which had benefited from government funds secured by State Senator Henry Tybold. When Paul Small's name came up, it was usually among a list of "business professionals" assisting with the deals.

Ladderback picked up his telephone. She should not be at the number he was calling, but if she was . . .

She answered on the first ring. "Legal Help Line, Rachel Prentiss."

Ladderback identified himself. "I'm surprised to find you at the Help Line, Mrs. Prentiss."

Rachel Prentiss was a lawyer, the married daughter of Noah "Sunset" Zyman, whose obituary had appeared in today's *Press*.

"I'm surprised to find you calling. Are you in trouble?"

"I don't expect to be. I thought you would still be in mourning for your father."

"We're sitting *shiva* at my mother's but I've been on the Help Line every Friday night for my entire professional career and my father wouldn't have wanted it any other way. We buried him yesterday and . . . it was beautiful, what you wrote."

Ladderback thanked her. "I was touched by the way your father would permit his employees to leave their posts to go to the top of the factory and watch the sun set," Ladderback said.

"We were all happy you put that in. Why didn't you put in that he paid the same wage to citizens and illegal immigrants?"

"I could only include so much."

"The illegals were a big problem in South Philly when he had the factory. They were mostly Asian. They lived in terrible conditions in an old meatpacking plant. My father knew about it but there was nothing he could do for them, other than to pay them the same wage as the rest of his staff."

Would this be the same packing plant that Jack Ferko wants to turn into Victory Plaza? "Did you ever think of instituting legal action on their behalf?"

"The only rights they were permitted under the law was transportation to a deportation site. They were housed right behind the Sisters of Zion Hospital, but they couldn't go to the hospital for medical care because the hospital would just call Immigration and Naturalization and out they'd go. The hospital, which bought the plant ages ago for an expansion wing that it never built, finally sealed it off about seven years ago after a teenaged girl from the neighborhood was killed there."

"By 'a girl from the neighborhood,' you mean someone who was not one of the immigrants?"

"It's the old story: poor minorities suffer from every kind of crime, hardship and abuse, but the ones that get the attention, and the best treatment, are from the affluent majority. I didn't live near my father's factory—we moved out to Huntington Valley when I was a baby. But he'd talk to his employees and tell me what these people endured."

"What happened to the immigrants after the building was sealed?"

"Li-Loh Nguyen absorbed some of them in his businesses around Westyard."

Ladderback called up a Web page. "I was doing a search earlier this evening and I came upon a Nguyen Li-Loh—in Vietnam the family name comes first—as a leader of an American-backed insurgent movement during the war. Is that the same man?"

The RASA/Beach of Good Choice Web page showed a photograph

of a towering Nguyen Li-Loh in an imposing black robe standing beside a diminutive, imperious man in loose-fitting American combat fatigues. The smaller man was identified as Hideyoshi Ishimura, "weapons consultant."

"I don't know if he was involved in the war," Rachel Prentiss answered. "Most of the Asians in Westyard came over after the war ended. It could be him. He wanted Nash Eagleman to develop the meatpacking plant as low-income rental housing for Asian immigrants, but he didn't get the political approvals."

Ladderback again called up the photo of Nash Eagleman.

She said she didn't think Ladderback had called just to keep her company.

"I am calling regarding an accountant named Paul Small."

"The one who got robbed? My father had some dealings with him when he sold the factory to the veterans group," she said. "It won't harm my father's memory if I tell you he hated him. Among the things Paul Small did in Westyard was act as Senator Tybold's bag man. He would come into my father's office and tell him about a donation in cash or goods that the Senator wanted my father to make, or that the employees should vote the way the senator wants, or that he should hire a person the senator wants hired, or, finally, that he should sell the factory because the senator felt it was worth more as a luxury condo than it was as a livelihood for 266 employees who had to move out when the factory closed down."

"Did your father ever make his feelings known to the authorities?"

"The senator *is* the authority at that end of town. He isn't the only one—there are mobsters, city councilmen, union business agents who all come around with their hands out. But the senator gets the most. You don't complain about him and expect to stay in business."

"No one in this city has absolute power," Ladderback insisted. "Someone must have challenged the senator, or Mr. Small, at one time or another."

"Angelo Delise was supposed to be a holdout. He never liked the Senator, which is probably why his restaurant has suffered. He also had a lot of Asians working for him and was friendly with Li-Loh Nguyen. They both wanted the meatpacking plant turned into low-income housing but it didn't happen."

"I was told today that Mr. Small was working on a development deal involving this plant."

"If he was, it's not the one that the neighborhood needs. My father's factory was supposed to have been a low-to-middle-income housing and office complex for veterans and poor people. Have you seen it? It's a luxury apartment house. I think the only veterans living there are Nashua Eagleman and members of Jack Ferko's organization. My father would never have sold his factory if he knew what the result would be."

"Why did he sell, then?"

"Paul Small wore him down."

Teal Cavaletta was delirious as she was wheeled to the MRI room, then to X-ray. She was one of several people on gurneys: South Philadelphia victims of Friday night stabbings, gunshots, heart failure, falls, auto accidents.

They sent her to a corner of the emergency room, where a small, quiet, intensely serious Asian woman in a somber black dress and burgundy sweater introduced herself as Lieutenant Nancy Nanh from the Philadelphia Police Sex Crimes Unit.

Lucia remembered her. "You talked to me about CeCe. Caprice Delise," she said.

Lieutenant Nanh remembered. "A very sad situation. You were her best friend. I questioned you about it, yes, but I was just a sergeant then. I was not the lead investigator."

A deep, sincere voice joined in: "My father handled that case. That was the last case of his career." Leaning against the wall, his arms folded, was Sergeant Vincent Ferko.

Lucia glared at him as though she wanted to tell him what she thought of his father's career. Lieutenant Nanh crouched down and tried to ask Teal some questions. Teal's answers were indistinct.

Lieutenant Nanh's face was drawn and faintly lined, as if the horror of what she had seen had made cracks around her eyes and mouth. She addressed her remarks to Ferko. "You must be as patient with her as you would a newborn baby. It will be awhile before I can talk to her and, even then, she may have short-term memory loss."

"From getting hit?" Andy asked.

"Sometimes, from the concussion, from the physical trauma that can injure the brain," Lieutenant Nanh said. "But there is also the shock. The doctor told me that there is no sexual violation, but shock from her injuries can be so terrible that her conscious mind may not accept it. She might shut it out, or, sometimes, create an alternative memory."

Andy was aware of Ferko studying her. She turned to Lieutenant Nanh and tried to ignore him. "You mean she'll remember something that never happened?"

Ferko took out his pad. "She hit the 911 speed dial on her phone before blacking out. We can start with that. We could ask her what she thought they wanted. The neighbors said she opened the door to at least one male. The place is pretty well trashed. There's no way of knowing if anything's missing."

Lieutenant Nanh said, "We must see this from the victim's point of view. To a victim, this is the worst that can possibly happen. It might take her years to come to terms with this. She may never come to terms with it, because to do so requires a return to the suffering, and questions about guilt, responsibility, complicity."

Lucia said, "There is no way my mother could be responsible for this."

Ferko pushed himself away from the wall. "She's going to feel responsible. You see that happening in these cases."

Lucia went to him. "What are you doing here?"

"Sergeant Ferko is in training for my unit," Lieutenant Nanh said. "He asked to be here."

"He didn't ask me," Lucia said.

"This happened in my district," Ferko said. "She's as much family to me as she is to you."

"That won't be good," Lieutenant Nanh said to him. "To get involved personally, the emotions can make it difficult to see clearly."

She turned to Lucia. "You, as the daughter, you can help her. You can show her that it is possible to survive, that when we can put our lives back together and care for each other, then that can be the best possible thing."

Lucia tried to look at her mother. "If I'd have stayed just a half hour longer, I would've been there. I would have killed whoever did this . . ."

"You help her now." Lieutenant Nanh put her arm around Lucia. She left some forms and her card. She asked Lucia to write down anything that might be useful and promised to visit again on Sunday, sooner if Lucia called her.

Lucia asked Ferko to leave.

Ferko said, "Sure." He didn't move.

Lucia waited a few seconds. Then she told Andy that she had to wash her face. Would Andy just stay with her mother for a few minutes?

Andy told Lucia to take as much time as she needed. She watched Lucia go into the bathroom.

Ferko stayed near the wall. He said to Andy, "You could've told me you were in the media."

Andy went to the side of the bed. She noticed that Lucia had her mother's eyebrows, and that the mottled patch of yellow bruises on Teal's face was rapidly turning dark red. Her eyes were swollen shut. Her upper lip had been cut. Her dyed, blue-black hair was tied up in pink curlers. An emergency room nurse had tried to remove the curlers that had been smashed, but Teal had screamed when her head was touched.

"Your name stuck in my mind," Ferko said. "A couple months ago, you called the substation, about this old couple living over the grocery store at Sessick and Sixteenth saying that drug dealers were taking over the corner. You actually got to the captain. He put my patrol on it and you happened to be right. I been reading that column ever since. The captain told me Mr. Action was a woman. There aren't that many Andrea Cosickis around, so Mr. Action has to be you, right?"

Andy heard Lucia sobbing in the bathroom. She wanted to go to her, but Ferko was now standing close enough to her for her to smell some kind of cologne. She looked at him suddenly and almost backed off. Almost.

"The man who called me said he'd called the police a dozen times to do something about it," Andy said. "So how come I had to call before somebody checked those people out?"

"Because we didn't do our job right," Ferko said simply, his eyes open and guileless. "We don't do it right all the time. Somebody on the day shift thought they knew what was going on. He should've sent someone to check it out."

If Andy hadn't been so tired from lack of sleep, she would have been surprised. The only other Philadelphia cop she had met who ever admitted the possibility of police error was Lieutenant Jeffrey Everson, a homicide investigator who also let her know that much of what is blamed on police error was not an error at all, but a result of byzantine political complications that he was never willing to explain fully.

"So the media isn't so bad," Andy said.

"Sometimes we can be good for each other," Ferko said. He was standing just a little bit too close to her, but she didn't find him threatening. If she knew him longer, if she could believe that he really was as caring as he seemed to be, she might lean forward and maybe bend her knees a little bit so she could rest her head on his neck and close her eyes and forget, for a few moments, the awful things that had happened that night.

When the bathroom door opened Andy and Ferko almost jumped. Ferko took out his pad and flipped the pages.

"According to the attending physician," Ferko read, "Mrs. Cavaletta has had fractures in the skull and on her left arm and right hip. They hit her with something thin and hard, a metal rod or a cane. She could have held up her arm to try to stop it."

Lucia bent over her mother and tentatively touched the broken curlers. "It's me, Mama," Lucia said. "I just want to take these things off."

She waited but Teal didn't react. Lucia slowly began to remove them.

"Lucia, I got to ask you something difficult," Ferko said.

"I told you the first time," Lucia said. "I have no idea why anybody would do this to her."

"You stopped that robbery at the Villa Verdi," Ferko continued. "It's pretty well certain that at least one of the three suspects was trying to get Mr. Delise to open that safe of his. The one that broke Mr. Delise's fingers is a known member of an Asian street gang that runs protection rackets inside the Asian community. They drive around in vans."

Lucia said, "What's this have to do with Mama?"

"This gang likes to use sticks, canes, aluminum poles as weapons." When Lucia said nothing, he added, "You went to your mother's afterward. You think other members of this gang could have followed you?"

Andy waited for Lucia to get mad. "Vinnie, if they wanted to get to me, they could have gotten me while I was there."

"Lucia, I'm asking you to think about it," Vinnie said. "I live on that street. I see what's going on and, believe me, I am the last guy who wants to pin what happened to Teal on an Asian gang. But I want you to think about it."

"Because your father tried to hang CeCe's death on them?" Lucia snapped.

"Now that's not right," Vinnie said. "My father did his best with that."

"Your father alienated and terrorized the Asian community by dragging in their kids and browbeating them," Lucia said.

"The gangs are real, Lucia," Vinnie said. "Shi-Bin doesn't kill people, but he likes to beat them up really bad. I'm not saying he's involved in hurting Teal, but he was definitely involved in hitting Mr. Delise's place. You got any theories as to why they wanted to get into that safe, I want to know them. Same with why they would go after Teal."

"What about Uncle Paul? You want to hang that on them, too?"

"I'm not hanging anything, Lucia, because . . . what they're doing is what the Sicilians used to do when they were on the bottom of this town a hundred years ago and nobody was going to let them in. The Sicilians got blamed for a lot of criminal activities that they didn't do. But they did enough to earn their reputation."

"Go easy on that, Vinnie," Lucia said. "I got some Sicilian in me."

"You're not the only one, Lucia." She locked her eyes with his and Andy had one of those moments when the deepest secret between two people was as obvious, blatant and in-your-face as one of the one hundred-foot-tall animated signs on Interstate 95.

As much as they glared, hissed and annoyed each other, Lucia and Vinnie were naturals together. Andy could imagine them side by side, arms locked together, walking down those narrow Westyard streets without having to look where they were going because they knew the place, and each other, so perfectly.

That they never got together was no surprise. Sometimes the person you think is most perfect for you is the absolute last person you'd want in your life. The whole point of falling in love, Andy figured, was that it proved that being with this person was not a choice, not an option, not an exercise in free will. The two of you *had* to be with each other. There was no other way.

Andy could see that both Vinnie and Lucia had been waiting for something that would settle what was, or wasn't, going to happen between them. Before she could wonder how long they would have to wait, Ferko's cell phone went off and he went out of the room to answer it. When he came back in and he said he had things to do before he finished his shift.

Then he gave Andy his card.

"I already have one," Andy said.

He took her hand, opened it, put the card in it and held it closed. "You could've lost the first one."

"I didn't," Andy said. She knew Lucia was watching, but the warmth of his hand soothed her, calmed her, gave her strength that she didn't need, but didn't mind feeling.

"Good," he said. He glanced at Lucia, who was pretending to be involved in taking the curlers from her mother's hair. "I want you to know I'm sorry about all this, Lucia."

"You say you're sorry too much, Vinnie," Lucia said.

He asked her where she'd be staying.

Lucia said something about her mother's house. Her gaze was on Ferko's hand.

Ferko noticed he was still holding Andy's hand. He gently let go. "I'll check up on you soon," he promised as he left the room.

With his hands comfortably folded over his middle, Ladderback thought about deniable activities. It seemed that the Vietnam war had prepared Paul Small for such a life, if his career included that of being Senator Tybold's "bag man," as Mrs. Prentiss described it.

He did not remember picking up his remote control, but it was in his hand now, and he was scanning the evening's cable options. His thumb rested on a 1974 Sonny Chiba movie called *The Street Fighter.* The explanatory notes indicated that this was a classic martial arts movie, the first in a series, whose influence on filmed violence was even more important than Bruce Lee's *Enter the Dragon.*

Or he could choose Alfred Hitchcock's *Vertigo.* Ladderback found Hitchcock's films to be excessively mannered and heavy-handed, but *Vertigo* appealed to him, not merely because he suffered from an illness similar to that of Jimmy Stewart's detective.

Yet, he found no comfort in watching the likable Stewart, in a spotless, cream-colored Ford, slowly pursuing Kim Novak in a green metalflake Rolls-Royce through the sun-bleached, daylight maze of San Francisco. Stewart, of course, did not realize that he was being manipulated, that each turn and stop along the way drew him more deeply into a trap.

Ladderback fretted at the famous rescue scene at the foot of the Golden Gate Bridge (why didn't Stewart kick off his shoes before plunging into the glistening water?). The faked suicide from the bell tower disturbed him more deeply, because Ladderback's parents had been medical examiners. They imparted to him enough knowledge from what his father merrily called "the family business" to understand that a competent forensic pathologist would have examined the body's lividity—the areas about a corpse in which blood begins to clot at the moment of death—to determine that the corpse had been transported to the top of the bell tower before it was tossed off.

Then came the scene in which the perky Barbara Bel Geddes tries to cheer up the man she was meant to marry. She finds Stewart in a mental institution, deep in a catatonic funk from what he feels was his failure to prevent the death of Kim Novak, and encourages him to listen to Mozart.

Alas, Stewart, driven temporarily insane by the loss of Kim Novak, played dumb. He just didn't hear the music, but Ladderback did. The deliriously merry orchestral strings tickled his ears. He turned off the TV and found among his CDs the Clarinet Concerto in A major, the last concerto Mozart was believed to have written. The composition was proof, as far as Ladderback could tell, that Mozart was not suffering from any kind of delusional disorder at the end of his life. An addled brain could not compose the eager, grandly civilized anticipation of the first movement, the sublimely sentimental second movement, and the sudden, slippery dancing melodies of the third.

Ladderback listened to the performance with headphones clamped around his ears. The clarinet became a musical effervescence that, like good champagne, made what was so dark and troubling become light and frivolous, so that the only remaining necessity was sleep.

onward and upward

Morning sunlight streamed through the open window of the shared hospital room that was assigned to Teal Cavaletta after she was judged safe to move. The nurses who lifted her into the bed raised restraining arms on the bed's sides. Andy yawned and leaned against the wall as Lucia sat down in the room's only chair.

Lucia was in the chair for less than a minute when a man came in and paused beside the curtain that separated the beds. Frank Cavaletta said, "This is my fault."

Lucia stood. When Teal heard her ex-husband's voice, she said, "Get out of my house."

Frank Cavaletta looked to Andy for reassurance. "I turn my phones off at night. When I woke up I checked my messages and came over as fast as I could."

"I turn off my phones, too," Andy said.

His round face was unshaven. He wore a pajama top under a beige windbreaker that said ONWARD AND UPWARD.

"Dad," Lucia began, "you remember Andy Cosicki? From high school?"

Before he could answer, Teal snapped, "Out of my house!"

They didn't move.

"What's wrong with the TV?" Teal said, with her eyes shut. "Who turned off the TV?"

Lucia saw a wall-mounted TV set. She found the controller and turned it on. Cartoons flickered. Lucia dropped the volume, but Teal raised the arm that had the IV drip stuck in it and wiggled her thumb, as if she were holding a remote control. Lucia raised the volume until Teal said, "That's about right," and lowered her hand.

"We have to take turns sitting with her," Frank said.

Teal said, "Get *out,* Errol!"

He held up his hands. "Okay. We were just leaving."

He didn't move. Andy tried to watch the cartoons. She saw a pig hit a duck with a baseball bat and she looked out the window instead. The view showed a buff-colored brick wall. After a few minutes she heard a loud, gurgling snoring. "She always snored like that," Frank Cavaletta said, sitting down in the chair Lucia had vacated.

Someone wheeled a tray of food to the bed behind the curtain. The odor of toast made Andy's mouth water.

Lucia turned the television volume down, then turned it off. Her mother didn't stir. "The doctor said that, when she finally gets to sleep, the stuff they gave her will put her out for at least six hours."

Frank looked at Andy. "Maybe we could get some breakfast?"

Lucia took a long look at her mother and then said, "Okay."

They went down to the cafeteria. "I'm buying," Frank said.

"You don't have to," Andy said, reaching for the purse she kept in her shoulder bag.

"He's buying," Lucia said, picking up a tray.

Andy wolfed down the extra large tea, scrambled eggs and sausage so quickly that she wasn't sure if it was the sweet sausage or the hickory smoked sausage. The tea was some bland domestic orange pekoe—she gulped it anyway and felt the heat burn away the weariness from being up all night.

Beside her at the table, Frank Cavaletta excavated portions of his bowl of oatmeal but didn't eat. Lucia used a knife and spoon to examine each of the raisins in her bowl of Raisin Bran cereal. The raisins she found objectionable she put on a paper napkin.

Andy sensed that they had to talk, so she said she was going to check out the gift shop. She saw a magazine rack nestled beside the refrigerated flowers case, below the shelf of stuffed animals and foil-wrapped boxes of chocolate. She bought a copy of the Saturday morning edition of the *Press,* and came back to the cafeteria to see that father and daughter were exactly as she had left them. She chose a seat far away from them so that she wouldn't be in their space.

She turned through the paper to her "Mr. Action" column about developers and saw that it had been cut back so much that the only item that ran was a reader question that, in her opinion, she had answered badly.

She turned past Ladderback's obituary page to the section called "Police Story," a roundup of burglaries, robberies, car stops, domestic disputes and other reported police activity throughout the city. She turned to the listing for Westyard and saw a "shots fired" mentioned on the block where Mr. Delise's restaurant was. "Police quelled a fight among three Asian males, one of whom was in possession of an illegal firearm. All were treated for minor injuries."

Vinnie Ferko had filed a report in such a way that the police reporter was not inspired to pursue the story. She gazed at the cafeteria's beige dropped ceiling and wondered if any of those that Lucia had fought had also been given beds in the hospital.

Andy scanned the rest of the "Police Story" items. At the bottom was an account of an assault and attempted robbery of a Mrs. Teal Cavaletta at her Brixton Street row house. Police suspected Asian gangs.

Andy forced herself to remember how Brixton Street had seemed when she had been sitting on the steps with Lucia. The block had been quiet. A few cars had passed. Not many people walked by. She hadn't seen any Asian gangs, let alone Asian people.

Andy looked back at Frank Cavaletta picking at his oatmeal. He may have been, as Lucia had insisted, the best-looking lifeguard on the Wildwood Beach Patrol, a man who always had a lot of cash from moving people in and out of summer homes. He had grown bald and soft.

Frank looked up, the way some people will when another person is staring, and Andy quickly buried her gaze in the newspaper. She was thankful that, so far, no one from the *Press*, or the *Philadelphia Standard*, the *Press*'s broadsheet competition, had arrived to talk to Lucia. Andy had not called the newspaper to volunteer for the job. She couldn't see herself turning into a reporter and asking Lucia questions like "How did it feel when the police called . . . ?"

She reminded herself she would have to come into the newsroom later today to write more for Monday's column. But first, she had to sleep. The long night had caught up with her. If she put her head down on the table she'd be out cold. She kept her head up and, to stay alert, she listened to Lucia and her father.

Frank Cavaletta said, "I'm going up to see Teal one more time. Where you staying?"

"I'm going back to Mama's and clean the place up. With this coming on top of what happened to Uncle Paul, she'll feel a lot better to come back to a house she can live in."

"Uncle Paul . . . ," Frank said. "Did you know he introduced me to her?"

"You never told me that."

"There are things a father hopes to tell his daughter after she gets married, not before."

"So tell me now."

"Paul had an idea that I should help him move people into summer homes in Wildwood. I was happy enough just sitting in my chair and being lord of the beach—no way I wanted to do any heavy lifting. Then he shows up with your mother and she said the one thing she always wanted was for a guy to drive her around in a big truck."

"You fell for that line?"

"I not only fell for it, but after a couple of trips to Canada and back, I proposed to her in the truck."

"You must have been smoking something," Lucia said.

"We were very happy with each other." He came around to give her a kiss on her forehead. "A couple of days from now, when you get settled, we'll spend some time. Deal?"

"Deal," Lucia said.

Before he left, he told Andy that it was nice seeing her again.

Lucia and Andy went to her car in the garage behind the hospital.

"About you and Vinnie—" Andy began.

"There is *nothing* about me and Vinnie," Lucia said.

Before Andy could respond, Lucia squeezed Andy's hand. "You've been the greatest, Andy."

"No," Andy said, "*you've* been the greatest. I'm going into the paper later today. You need a hand with the house, or anything else, call my cell. Deal?"

Lucia nodded wearily. "Deal."

If he kept the hours in the night city editor's job description, Bardo Nackels should have been gone and sleeping sometime before dawn. But, as of 10 A.M. Saturday, he hadn't left the newsroom.

A sloppy, pugnacious, pear-shaped blob of a man, Nackels was addicted to the false but supremely seductive notion that, as long as he dwelled in a cheaply furnished, balefully lit, quarter acre of office space on the eleventh floor of the crumbling *Press* Tower on Market Street, he was close to everything important that was happening in the city. And, as long as editor-in-chief Howard Lange wasn't around, Nackels was in charge.

Newsroom intoxication can make you stay hours past the time when you've ceased to function sensibly, when your mouth is hoarse from yelling at people who don't need to be yelled at, your eyes focus only with effort and the synapses in your brain sputter and crackle like the last embers of a fire that's all but dead.

But you can't leave. You can't leave because something else could happen, and you can't give up the possibility that you could get even closer, not to what was happening, but to the feeling of being connected, wired, jammed into a flow that was sampled, siphoned, shaped, sliced, chopped, and, ultimately, edited into what became the day's news.

Nackels's great gut fell forward between his legs. His thick forearms pinned down a messy stack of page proofs. It took Nackels about a minute to see the man in the hat and lumpy gray raincoat carrying a battered satchel. "Shep-pah-dee-*doo*-dah," he said finally. "You should've stayed in bed."

Ladderback did not reply.

"Lange cut the news hole again. With what you filed yesterday, you've got enough obits in the can through to Tuesday."

Ladderback glanced about the listless newsroom. The only indication that the weekend had arrived was the abundance of faded trousers, jerseys, chamois shirts and athletic shoes of suburban leisure worn by all except for Chilly Bains, the *Press*'s stacked-haired gossip columnist, wrapped in the white dinner jacket and electric blue Hawaiian shirt that he wore when doing his Friday night Pub-'n'-Party Crawl column.

Ladderback noticed Bains writing with unnatural energy.

"Wait until Chilly finds out his Crawl's getting cut," Nackels confided. He called to the desks in the columnist's ghetto. "You might as well bag it."

Bains spun his swivel chair around. "You *will* run this. You have to." He touched one of the ends of his mustache. "Last night, I finally, finally, *finally* found out where Matt Plank's next restaurant is going to be."

Matthew Plank was the city's "genius chef" entrepreneur whose extravagantly decorated themed eateries had put Philadelphia on the national foodie circuit. At the mention of his name, the newsroom's background bustle quieted. No other publication had penetrated the black shrouds of secrecy surrounding the master restauranteur's projects.

"You wouldn't believe it," Bains said. "He's had a sign out in front of it for at least a week. It was a *plank*, get it? But nobody recognized it because it's right on the north edge of Westyard. The place is right on Broad Street, in the old 'K-O on the Corner' fight gym, and it's opening Halloween—'costumes mandatory!'"

"Me no think so, Chills," Nackels said. He raised his voice at the newsroom. "I am in need of a fat lead. Any contenders?"

A fat lead was a story about events that were so sensational, it took precedence over anything else in the paper.

"Let's run with Plank," Bains said. "His restaurant's name is still super secret, but, after finding out he spent five days in Corisca last week, I am ninety-nine and forty-four hundredths sure that it will be called Vendetta. The theme will be food as revenge, with a special menu that is 'best served cold.'"

For a second the newsroom was absolutely silent. Then Ladderback noticed a few *Press* staffers picking up their telephones.

"If I want cold food, I go to a refrigerator," Nackels said. "Our readers don't get excited about restaurants."

"They will because Westyard is heating up. With Plank coming in on the north edge, and another huge development going in on the south, the action is shifting there. Tonight, there is this *humongous* Fortini installation in the lobby of the Pickle Factory."

"You had an item about him collecting trash for it," Nackels said.

"It's going to be *so* Vegas, and because you refused to let me do a Page Three interview with the artist, we have been banned from the festivities. The art crowd thinks this newspaper doesn't care about art."

"It doesn't," Nackels said.

Ladderback saw Nackels look past Bains, at a newly hired reporter. The reporter whispered into his phone, a little too loudly, *"Best served cold."* He noticed Nackles glaring at him and hung up quickly.

Nackels turned to Bains. "All right. Plank stays. You get one paragraph."

Bains punched air and said, "Hoy, hoy!"

Nackels shuffled the page proofs beside his elbow. "Now we have enough obits through to Wednesday. Shep, you ever want to take a vacation?"

"No."

"You should take a vacation, Shep. See the world. You might not want to come back."

Ladderback merely turned toward his desk.

7 this thing of ours

After a few hours of fitful sleep, Andy awoke tired and cold with a cramp in her neck. She sat up slowly and pulled her blanket around her. A breeze rattled the windows that surrounded her futon mattress. She looked outside at the gray, tiled roof sloping down and saw a few more of the fading red and gold leaves blowing off the upper branches.

Her apartment consisted of two rooms. Her bedroom was the inside of the rooftop cupola of a large, subdivided West Philadelphia mansion. She had replaced the ratty curtains on the windows surrounding her bed with wooden oak venetian blinds and eggshell curtains that reflected back the warmth from her reading light at night.

The bed rested on a platform with a few drawers for clothes. Beyond the mattress, there was just enough room for a small end table, a book-shelf and a place to stand and walk to the ladder-like stairs leading down to a tiny sitting area, a small electric kitchen, half-sized refrigerator, half-sized sink and, just behind the kitchen, a windowless bathroom so narrow that she banged her hip against the sink every time she stepped into the shower.

But Andy loved it. When she found the apartment she thought it would be the most incredible place in the world to spend lazy Sunday mornings with the guy she was in love with.

So far, the only other living being to share this apartment had been a single cockroach she had surprised one night in the bathroom sink.

Not even Logo, the jerk her mother called her "intended," had visited the apartment. Logan Marius Brickle, heir to the Hampton Bank, was in Europe trying to find himself.

You wouldn't think that Andy's family, with its working-class roots, would have anything to do with one of the richest dynasties in the city, but in Philadelphia, what seems to be the very high, and what seems to be the very low—well, not that low but close enough—are never as far apart as you might think. Two people who should have no reason for being close could get close enough to feel like brother and sister, if only because their parents were so hard to understand.

Though he was in Europe, Logo would call Andy on the phone at night because he needed to talk to someone who didn't think he was as worthless as he aspired to be.

She went downstairs and found, in the apartment's only closet, a dress on a hanger way off to the side. She pulled it out and threw it on her bed. It was small enough to be mistaken for a napkin.

Back in June, shortly after Andy had graduated Penn, she had gone with her mother and Logan's mother, Belissaria Brickle, to a Bryn Mawr clothing boutique where Main Line mothers spent too much money on their daughters.

And there, Andrea Cosicki came into possession of a ridiculous, sleeveless black cocktail dress with swirling, frilly, art nouveau silver strands sewn into it. She also received a tiny purse and two sets of pumps, one with half-height heels, the other with pearl-inlay four-inch spiked heels that Charlotte had sneaked toward the cash register when Andy wasn't looking.

The dress was supposed to be one of many that Andy would wear when she accompanied her mother to numerous social functions among the Main Line "set," and then, if Andy "behaved"—at the Hamptons,

Bermuda, Palm Beach, Vail and anywhere else Charlotte's art buying clients might invite her.

Andy only had to give up her journalistic ambitions for the highly medicated, heavily therapied, disorderly deficit attentions of potential upper-class suitors, who, Mrs. Brickle was certain, would "swoon" for what Mrs. Brickle referred to as Andy's "spectacular bones and habitual contempt." With other suitors interested, Logo just might become jealous and propose marriage.

Mrs. Brickle wanted the match because she was certain Andy had every quality her son lacked. Andy was smart, proud, dedicated, furiously hardworking and capable of standing up, as Mrs. Brickle had, to those who believed that running the nation's oldest existing financial institution was something other than woman's work.

Unfortunately, Mrs. Brickle never stopped informing her son of what a miserable ruin she thought he was. That this might be the reason Logo rode a motorcycle into his swimming pool, took drugs not prescribed by his overpriced claque of therapists, got himself arrested for being loathsome in public and otherwise refused to develop qualities of any kind did not occur to Mrs. Brickle.

Andy had refused to wear the dress in public. She refused to give up a career in journalism—she had a restless need to "find things out," even if she preferred not to think about some of what she found out about her parents and the dysfunctional Brickle-Wadcalader banking dynasty.

Would Logo really like her in that dress? Would anyone?

Andy yawned. She was still tired and cold and the cramp in her neck hadn't gone away, but she suddenly felt very good to be here, alone, in her own place.

But she still couldn't remember whatever the hell it was she had heard about Lucia's mother that was so important.

She turned her cell phone on and checked her voice mail. One from Ladderback, one from her mother, one from a cell-phone number she hadn't seen previously and one that just left a telephone number.

"It is Saturday and I am about to leave for the newsroom and I am hoping to see you there," Ladderback said gruffly. "I have an assignment for you."

Then: "*This* is your mother. I am aware, Andrea, that we're not speaking, but there is a person who identifies himself as knowing you in some capacity, who is clearly attempting to use *my* relationship with *you* to gain entry to an exceptionally restricted gathering tonight at which I must represent the gallery, in Philadelphia, as it happens, and if he *is* who he says he is he might be someone who might advance your career, as much as you seem to want one. I will permit you to bring an escort, if you wish, but you will have to clear it with me in advance. As long as I have you on the phone, please tell Logan, the next time he calls you, that even if *he* isn't speaking to his mother, that Mrs. Brickle has asked me to inform him, through you, that the bank will no longer cover his debts and that if he wants to waste any more money, he will have to return to this country and take a position at the bank and pay his debts from his salary. There are plenty of entry-level positions in customer service, where, Mrs. Brickle believes, he can learn the value of a dollar, as you have. You should know that Mrs. Brickle still says nice things about you, Andrea. She has always considered you a positive influence on Logan. Do you understand what I'm telling you, Andrea? Have you any idea what that means? If you can persuade Logan to behave reasonably—something we both know he has never done but Mrs. Brickle never gives up hope—she will be very grateful. Mrs. Brickle's gratitude has always been significant in our family. You understand what I'm saying, Andrea?"

Andy understood. Anytime she wanted to be a bank teller at a Hampton Bank branch, all she had to do was ask.

Finally: "Andy, Andy, Andy, my colleague, compadre, fellow ink-stained wretch, it's soooooo amazing that we work at the same newspaper and that we haven't so much as air kissed! This . . . *thing* of ours is such a lonely business until disaster, fortune, scandal *hurl* us together and, well, because you read my column—doesn't everybody?—a simply magnificent work of art, a Fontini trash-er-oo, is being installed tonight, in the lobby of the Pickle Factory and . . . I happen to know—and please don't ask how—that Charlotte Cosicki, the marvelous executive with the Kaplan Gallery of New York, London, Paris, Bruges, Milan and Hackensack, New Jersey, for all I know, is also your mother and that Kaplan, of course, not only represents Claus Fortini but Charlotte is so squeezy-squeezy with Lyssie Eagleman, who has, quite understandably, banned representatives of ALL media from tonight's hanging, but your mother, with whom I have just finished speaking, said that I may accompany you as a kind of date? She's worried about you and, even though she assured me she wouldn't *speak* to you directly, she would love to see you in . . . proper company? She wants you to call her right away and, when you do, you're going to tell her that you will definitely, unquestionably let her see you tonight at the Fortini installation, and that you will be arriving with me, your favorite kleptosexual! Call her soon, because I can be *very* persistent when I wish to be taken! Seriously!!! Use my toll-free, ultra private line."

Andy extended the middle finger of her left hand. Then she dug into her shoulder bag and found Sergeant Ferko's card. The telephone number on the card matched a number, left as message, on her cell phone.

She took a long shower and banged her hip getting out of the bathroom. Then she sat down on the edge of her bed and asked herself, just by way of speculation, what Sergeant Vincent Ferko might look like naked. She couldn't quite keep his image in her mind, so she closed her eyes to concentrate and had one of those dreams where she knew she was in a dream.

And did not want to wake up.

Ladderback thanked the assistant director of the Mount of Olives, hung up his phone and made a small note for his SMALL, P. file: *cremated at request, and additional payment, from Mrs. Alise Perrigore, half-sister.* A Frank Cavaletta of the Upward and Onward (or was it Onward and Upward?) Moving Company was shipping the ashes to Canada at Mrs. Perrigore's request. Ladderback stood, went to the file cabinet along the wall, located the Small file and was about to slip the note in when he decided to make one more call to the phone number Small had supplied as his next of kin.

He heard the flatly nasal Quebecois French on Mrs. Perrigore's answering machine. He left a message in English. He identified himself, reminded her that he had called previously, mentioned that he had some questions about her half-brother and that he would appreciate if she would call him collect.

He replaced the file and, returning to his desk, Ladderback moved today's copy of the *Press* close enough so he could smell the acrid, unsettling odor of the ink. He tilted his head back so he could look through the lower part of his bifocals.

It was the Saturday late edition, the last of two editions published for Saturday newstand sale. The cover was a photo, taken at a football game, of a Philadelphia Eagle who had been arrested Friday night in New Jersey for drunk driving. A bottle was superimposed over the football he was carrying. Smeared across the man's face was the legend: CRUISIN' FOR A BOOZIN'?

Ladderback touched the newspaper carefully, savoring the rough texture of the paper on his fingers. He ran a finger along the dovetail-cut side edges. The pages, having been compressed into a tight stack, resisted his first attempt to separate them.

Ladderback turned the pages, skimming the mix of national and local news. He would return later and clip items he found interesting for his files. Ladderback opened a drawer in his desk and was about to get out a pair of scissors to cut out the obituaries he had written when he noticed the "Police Story" column. He found the "Police Story" items disturbing because they were derived from police reports that rarely presented a complete picture of what had happened.

The lead item was about a Mrs. Teal Cavaletta who had been violently assaulted in her Westyard row house during an attempted robbery by what police believe to have been an Asian gang. The report added that because police had previously responded to a "shots fired" incident at the nearby Villa Verdi, their prompt arrival may have saved Mrs. Cavaletta's life.

He read the story again. She had been assaulted less than an hour after he had called her.

Ladderback clipped the column. He saw Andy's empty chair. He had called her before he left his apartment to tell her he had an assignment for her. Where was his assistant? Was she covering this story? Did she find it odd that Asian gangs were said to be involved when there had been very little coverage, if any, of Westyard criminal activity attributed to Asians?

He got out a new file, put those items in it, as well as the piece of notepaper with Teal Cavaletta's telephone number on it, and wrote *Small, P* across the top.

He paused to look at his great wall of file cabinets. Everything he had ever written, all his notes, everything he had found interesting, everything he read that he thought was worth keeping, was in those cabinets.

And there wasn't an item in them about Asian gangs.

But he did have a file about an accountant, or, rather, an accountant who wanted to be Sherlock Holmes.

Ladderback inserted the SMALL, P file and removed a folder: MURPHY, O. J.

At the top was a handwritten note: *See Murphy, Michael M., obit.* This was followed by a clipping from the *Press*'s "Police Story" column about a brawl that broke out among three Drexel Business School students. The fight allegedly began during a high stakes poker game. O. J. Murphy, an undergraduate accounting major who escaped injury, was among those facing disciplinary action.

After this came the business section of the *Philadelphia Standard,* with the headline MURPHY'S LAW DOOMS HMO CHIEF. It was an interview with the assistant director of the Pennsylvania Special Investigations Unit, who said the skills of a recently hired Drexel graduate named O. Jonathan Murphy had been crucial in bringing down an embezzling health maintenance organization executive. The *Standard*'s reporter mentioned that Murphy had offered to play poker with the reporter, but declined a request for an interview.

After this came a press release from a Philadelphia accounting firm that had just hired an Osiris Jonathan Murphy as a consultant to its forensic division. "Mr. Murphy comes highly recommended by the United States Secret Service, the Federal Justice Department and the Pennsylvania Commonwealth Fraud Investigations Unit."

Then came an article by the *Philadelphia Standard* about Atlantic City casino poker players: POKER CHAMPS OR ARE THEY JUST BLUFFING?

ATLANTIC CITY—The man who calls himself "Murphy, just Murphy" has no phone number, no address and carries no identification or credit cards. He says he is a "risk management consultant" who fills his spare time playing solitaire at the Winged Victory Hotel's Patience Society.

You'll get a different story if you ask any of the Saturday night regulars inhabiting the Frontenac Casino's Carte Rouge Room and they'll tell you Murphy is "a street fighter you wouldn't believe."

In poker, a street is a round of betting. A street fighter is a player of such legendary betting skill that he can turn the game in his favor in a single round.

Ask the professional poker players who compete in regional and national poker contests and are easily recognized Atlantic City poker celebrities, there are "less than a dozen" pseudonymous street fighters like Murphy haunting the Boardwalk. They dress and talk as if they are anything but masters of the game, the better to fool their unwitting prey.

The only way to call the bluff of a street fighter is to play against one. That, says one recent loser who asked not to be identified, can be so expensive that, "if you want to get an education, college is cheaper."

The article showed a picture of a man's thick, scarred fingers holding a hand of cards that hid his face. One of those fingers wore a battered, chipped Chestnut Hill Friends Academy class ring.

Ladderback replaced that article in his file and paused before examining the last item. It was a fading photocopy of a page from the Chestnut Hill Friends Academy yearbook that showed, in one corner, a photograph of a fearsome, wide-faced, broken-nosed Osiris Jonathan "Card" Murphy. A short description below his photograph said Murphy's interests were math puzzles and games involving playing cards.

In another corner was a photo of a confused, unsmiling, bespectacled Neville Shepherd "Holmes" Ladderback. Interests: History, Jazz and Classical Music, Arthur Conan Doyle Society.

Ladderback closed the file. He looked at the chair to the right of his. Andy still hadn't shown up. Ladderback couldn't go to Atlantic City by himself.

Or could he?

a pattern of harassment

When she woke the second time, Andy did not want to go back to sleep. She crawled out of her bed, went down the steep stairs to the tiny kitchen, opened the cabinet above the two-burner stove and picked her favorite of the dozen cannisters of loose tea: a strong, dark *keemun*. She sprinkled tea leaves into a mug, filled it with water, zapped it in the microwave and, while waiting for it to steep, turned her cell phone and checked her messages again.

Yes, there it was: Vinnie Ferko's number. No message. What did he want from her?

It was followed by twenty-seven messages from Chilly Bains. She picked, at random, message seventeen.

It was his voice, pre-recorded: "Please, oh, please! Why haven't you called Chilly Bains, the famous *and* notorious *klepto*sexual chitchat columnist back on his super-private toll-free 800 number? You could be busy. You could be out of touch. You could be doing something *dangerous.* You could be thinking that you have more important things to do, or wondering how it is that Chilly Chilly Bang Bang gets all those people to call him back? Well, *one* of those ways is this *diabolical* device that will keep calling you, over and over and over again, until you do. All it takes is a return call, just one call, to the super private toll-free 800 number, leave a message for me that includes whatever it is I asked you about, and the machine turns itself off! And it'll turn itself off *even if I don't pick up.* And I might not, because, hey, I could be busy, out of touch, doing something *far* more important than waiting for you to get back to me. By the by—if you don't leave the message that I want to hear, I'll put the machine back on, and it will keep calling you, until you do. Hoy, hoy!"

He was harassing her. The jerk hadn't spoken to her, never even *looked* at her since she started at the *Press*, now he was harassing her!

She called Howard Lange, the paper's editor, who was in charge of everything that happened in the newsroom, and got his "I'm in the office today but I'm either not at my desk or on another line" voice-mail intro.

Andy was about to complain but she remembered how the numerous complaints sounded on her voice mail. No matter who was talking, people who left angry voice-mail messages sounded like . . . her mother.

Andy wasn't about to sound like her mother. She would tell Lange in person that she would not be harassed. She gulped her tea, put on some old black jeans, a warm, faded red flannel shirt and her nasty brown leather bomber jacket that looked better as it got worse, and was out the door with her shoulder-bag banging against her hip and the fallen, faded leaves of autumn swirling around her legs.

Andy remembered the column she had done on telephone harassment. Even with the current prohibitions against unsolicited telemarketing calls, it wasn't illegal in Pennsylvania as long as a "business relationship" existed between the callers. The victim also had to prove a "pattern" of harassment.

Twenty-seven recorded messages constituted a pattern. More than that, an employee of a newspaper should be not harassing anyone, for any reason. And on cell phones, where every second of use was billable, this was a law suit waiting to happen!

When Andy arrived at the newsroom, she found Chilly Bains's desk was piled high with press releases, invitations and odd boxes of promotional junk. She saw a beige plastic box plugged into his phone. She heard the modem in the box dial a number. She opened her cell phone, accessed the voice-mail list and saw message number thirty appear.

Howard Lange wasn't in his office, or anywhere in the newsroom that she could see. She would wait for Lange by going over whatever reader mail had come in, and, if Lange hadn't returned by then, she'd go back to Bains's desk and yank that damned black box out.

Then she saw Bains sitting at her desk, in her chair, talking on her phone, his fingers (with the single red painted nail) on her word processor's mouse, his red tasseled penny loafers propped on a mound of her mail.

"Hey, *Ms.* Action," Bardo Nackels called from the copy desk. "We're short on space. I cut your column in half. You can go home."

She ignored him. Ladderback sat at his desk, reading a long list of articles pulled up from the newspaper's database.

Ladderback noticed her and said, "Would you like an assignment?"

"Later," she said. She pointed to Bains. "How long has he been sitting in my chair?"

"Too long," Ladderback said.

Andy turned to Bains. "Excuse me," Andy said to him.

Bains didn't look at her. He waved a hand for her to go away.

She took two big strides. She told herself she was waiting exactly thirty seconds for Bains to get off her phone. Thirty seconds became sixty and she was about to yell at Bains when Ladderback's phone rang.

"Yes, I'll accept the charges," Ladderback said. "Mrs. Perrigore, thank you so much for returning my call. You were away this past week? I'm sure it was difficult to return to such unfortunate news. I want to tell you how sorry I am to be calling you regarding the loss of your brother. . . ." Andy watched Ladderback sit straight up in his chair. "I'm sorry, did you say his death was no loss?"

Andy began to get really angry. Not only was Chilly Bains talking on *her* phone, he had *her* word processor signed on and was working on his column on *her* keyboard. He had jotted down some notes for his column. "So he isn't calling it Vendetta?" Bains said. "What's it going to be, then?"

"I need to talk to you," she said.

He spun around, putting his back to her. "I definitely want the list of discarded names. You can reach me at the toll-freebie, no, call me at . . ." he looked at the extension on Andy's telephone and repeated the number.

"Get off the phone," Andy said.

He waved her off again. "I am *bored*," he went on. "I have to camp out here at the desk of this hissy little galley slave who's coming in to take me to the Fortini installation. My sources tell me she is—get this— the *shortest* female the newspaper has ever hired."

Short? Andy would have smiled at that but she was angry and she was aware that it would take only one small thing from this point to make her really mad and that, once becoming mad, she would do something that many people would later tell her she shouldn't have done, and that she would be asked to apologize for, which would only make her madder and she would *absolutely* not apologize.

"Her mother thinks she's God's gift to the art world," Bains said, "but she's just working-class trash and her father was the slimy little fixer that died in that old nightclub in Redmonton."

He was putting her parents down. Andy put her parents down all the time, but you can only do that when you're related. "I'm sorry," Andy said.

"The slave is supposed to be nearly illiterate so she comes in on the weekends because she's so slow. The only thing I like about her desk is that it is even messier than mine and I adore a mess because it hides so much and we *all* have something to hide."

"I said, I'm sorry," Andy repeated, standing behind him.

Bains put his hand over the phone's mouthpiece. "Stop apologizing and just leave me alone." Again, he didn't look at her.

"I'm apologizing because of what I'm about to do," Andy said. "Because, after I do it, nothing's going to make me apologize, and you'll just have to deal with that."

Bains waved her away a third time. She reached over, took the phone out of his hand and slammed it down. Bains took a second to notice that the phone wasn't against his ear. Then he grabbed the phone.

Andy clamped her hands on his wrist, put on the *nikyu* joint lock Lucia had shown her, and cranked the wrist, hard.

Bains said, "YAHHHKKK!" and dropped the phone. Andy let go of his hand and Andy *gently* replaced the phone.

Ladderback asked Mrs. Perrigore if he could call her back.

"What did you *do* to me?" Bains exclaimed, clutching his wrist.

"Get out of my chair," Andy said.

Ladderback hung up his phone.

"I am the most important columnist on this newspaper," Bains howled, gripping his wrist. "Did you break this? It feels broken. I am going to have to get this X-rayed and you, you little . . . little . . ." he was fumbling for a word because she was definitely *not* little, "are going to have a lawsuit on your hands."

Andy put both hands on her waist, fists balled tight. Then she looked down, *way* down on Bains and emitted a brutalizing blast of Cosicki Intimidation Waves. "Who are you calling *little*?"

"Chilly Dilly!" Howard Lange yelled.

Everyone turned to see the editor-in-chief of the *Philadelphia Press* tossing his fleece vest through the door of his glassed-in office. He approached them with a take-out latte in one hand. "Nice to see you and Andy getting acquainted," he said.

Bains froze. Then he unfroze. "Charmed," he said, extending his other hand, and then, thinking differently, pulling the hand back.

"This asshole has been harassing me," Andy said to Lange.

"You poor *girl*." Lange strutted up and popped the lid off his latte.

"She tried to break my arm!" Bains whined.

Andy waited for Ladderback to come to her aid. He said nothing.

She pointed to Bains's desk. "Did you know this asshole has that box that put thirty messages in my voice mail, he was sitting in my chair, using my phone, and trashing me and my parents!"

Lange replied, "So?"

Andy and Bains both looked at each other. "There is no way that I," Andy said, "or anyone—deserves to be treated that way by this . . ."

"Columnist," Bains offered.

"Shithead!" She glared at him. "Who told you I was short?"

"I did." Lange grinned.

Andy looked down on him. "You're the editor of a newspaper and you deliberately gave out false information about an employee?"

"Yup," Lange sipped his latte and licked foam off his lips. He thought it was all very funny.

"And you have no problem about him using that thing on his telephone to harass me?" Andy said.

"You didn't call him back," Lange replied.

"He wouldn't even speak to me when I wanted his help," Andy said. "Now he wants to use me to get into that party and I'm supposed to just . . . do what he wants?"

"Yes," Lange said. "You're supposed to do that."

"We'll see what the union says about this," Andy said, reaching beside Bains to open a small drawer in her desk where she kept the Newspaper Guild handbook.

"Your father worked with unions," Lange began. "I'm sure he told you that there is always a difference between what a union says and what a union does. Chilly is a columnist. You have a column, but you don't have a by-line. Nobody reads Mr. Action because Andrea Cosicki writes it."

That wasn't true, Andy wanted to say. Vinnie Ferko read her column because she wrote it. He told her so!

"I can hire anyone to do your job," Lange continued. "But, according to demographic surveys and reader questionnaires conducted in sixteen shopping malls within our circulation area, well over half a million readers pick up this newspaper just because Chilly is in it." He patted Bains on his stacked red hair. "Great job on being the first to find out about Plank's new restaurant, by the way."

"I could have told you that!" Andy said. "I was with him when he came up with the concept."

"Then why didn't you tell us?" Lange said.

"Because I consider him a friend and he didn't want me to!"

Ladderback opened his mouth, and then closed it.

Lange beamed at Chilly. "Chilly doesn't do favors for his sources. He doesn't have to sleep with them."

"Not *all* of them," Bains added.

"I didn't sleep with Matt Plank!" Andy said.

Lange shook his head with mock sorrow. "In terms of your job security, it might have been good if you had. Chilly has contacts and relationships with who-knows-how-many wealthy, powerful, influential, important people in and outside this city. You don't. If we have breaking news and we need to get to anyone that Chilly knows, I can call Chilly and he *will* return the call, and we will get to that person."

"I needed to get to Senator Tybold," Andy said. She pointed at Bains. "He didn't help me."

"Part of having relationships with important people," Lange continued, "is not bothering them over every little thing. Chilly has only so many cards he can play. If he plays the wrong card, or if he plays too many, the relationship suffers."

"He didn't even ask me what I wanted," Andy countered. "He *ignored* me."

"I don't think that will happen again," Lange said, inspecting Bains's wrist. "I told you that Andy was the shortest woman we've ever hired because I wanted to see if you would check out my story."

"Gossip is my beat," Bains said. "It doesn't matter if it's true."

Ladderback finally spoke. "The truth always matters."

"Thank you, Mr. Shep," Lange sighed. "Any more platitudes from the man on the dead beat?"

Ladderback went back to his word processor.

Lange told Bains that he had made a call and that Bains was "set" for the installation party tonight. "You're on the list. You don't need her to get you in there anymore."

"*Who* do we know?" Bains asked.

"Invitations were sold to this, as a fund-raiser for Not Fade Away," Lange said.

"We're the media," Bains said. "We don't *buy* tickets."

"We contribute free advertising space to Not Fade Away when it sponsors veterans events in the city. Captain Ferko is a personal friend. You just go there tonight and ask for him. He'll let you up."

"Hoy, hoy!" Bains said. He popped out of Andy's chair and touched her hand. "Charmed," he said. Then he scurried happily off to his desk.

"He was rude and abusive to me," Andy said to Lange.

"And you gave him the best scare he's had in years," Lange said. "He needs that every once in while. We all do, right, Shep?"

Ladderback didn't respond.

"I hope you're not doing any more obits than the one's you've filed," Lange told him.

"Just background," Ladderback said.

"Nothing *small*, is that understood?" Lange took a sip and wandered away.

Andy sat in her chair. "Thanks for sticking up for me," she said to Ladderback.

"Would you like an assignment?" Ladderback replied.

"Not now!" She confronted the messy chaos of her desk: the day's stack of unopened mail, copies of the today's *Press* and *Standard,* other forms and letters she had received pertaining to problems and column items. She checked her voice mail. Vinnie Ferko had called her again!

She called him, and he answered on the first ring. "Hey Andy. How you doing?"

He said it almost as her father said it, how you *doon.* His accent was flatter, deeper South Philly, his voice was low and earnest.

"I'm doing okay, Sergeant. How you doing?"

"I'm off duty right now, so it's Vin, okay?"

"Not Vinnie?"

"Well, it's like, there are people who call you what you want, and people who call you what they want. Everybody I grew up with calls me Vinnie. On the job, when I'm on the witness stand, anything official, it's Vincent. But, if it's you . . ."

"I'm going to call you Vinnie," she said. "So why'd you just leave your phone number the first time you called?"

"Because it wasn't anything major. I just wanted to know if you slept okay."

He sounded as if he really cared. Really! "I slept for two hours, I think," Andy said. "I just woke up and then I went back to sleep for another two or three."

"Me, too," he said. "Uh, I'm not taking away from your work, am I?" he asked.

"That depends," Andy said. "My job is supposed to be answering readers' questions and solving problems."

"I got a problem and I got a question. The question is, you hungry?"

She was famished. "I could be."

"I got a '98 Harley FXR2 with a Twin-Cam 88 engine and an extra helmet. Can you handle riding a Harley?"

Andy had never ridden on a motorcycle in her life. "I can handle it," she said.

"I'll be out front, in half an hour."

For a second, she thought about calling Lucia. Then she hoisted up her shoulder bag and blew out of the newsroom.

the roar of the open road

You get only a few times when something blasts into your brain and stamps itself into your memory so that, for the rest of your life, you will refer to this event, you will compare subsequent experiences to it and you will find, more often than not, that no matter how many goals you achieve and dreams become true, there is nothing like a first time.

For Andy, standing on the northwest corner of Thirteenth and Market Street, that first time began with a sound she would never forget: a low, flat, puttering, internally combusting growl that she didn't hear as much as she felt somewhere in her belly.

Then she turned in the direction of the sound and saw the traffic part and a man in a black helmet and a weather-beaten black leather jacket zoom toward her with his growling, gleaming, chrome and black enamel beast growling between his legs. She watched him aim for a handicapped ramp and glide onto the sidewalk.

He cut the engine when he was in front of her, as if the bike were a wild, snorting stallion that, by turning the key, it politely fell to sleep.

Vinnie put a booted foot down on the concrete and swung his tightly muscled, snugly blue-jeaned leg over the bike. Andy took a step back.

"Something tells me you've never been on a motorcycle before," he said.

"What makes you think that?" Andy said.

Vinnie had a wide grin under his sunglasses. "The way you're standing."

"This is the way I always stand." Then she tossed her shoulder-length, muddy blond hair in such a way that it would catch the breeze. The breeze caught her hair, and she had a magic moment where she imagined she resembled one of those models you see on the shampoo commercials.

But the wind switched back and she ended up with a mass of hair in her mouth. She hoped he wouldn't see her blushing as she pushed the hair off her face. She found a rubber band in her shoulder bag.

While she gathered her hair into a ponytail, Vinnie unfastened a white, scuffed helmet that had been tied to the back of the bike. He held the helmet briefly over Andy like a crown, fitted it gently on her head and flipped down the visor. Then he stood back and said, "It looks good on you."

How many other females he may have said that to. Had he ever said that to Lucia?

He grinned again at her and she suddenly wanted to pull open his leather jacket, crawl inside, and pull it and him around her and . . .

He turned to the bike. "You sure you want to ride with me?"

"Am I standing here or what?" Andy said.

He nodded at that. "This is where you're going to sit," he said, patting his gray suede gloved hand on what looked like a curling black lobster tail on the back wheel, "and this is where you're going to put your feet. You got any gloves? You might want to put them on because it gets cold when you're going fast. You can hold on to these grips here, or you can hold on to me. You do whatever's comfortable; it doesn't matter to me."

Sure it didn't matter, Andy thought. She sat on the bike, felt it yield under her weight. She put her hands around the grips. She didn't have any gloves. What did she need gloves for? The grips were awkward to hold on to, but she told herself she would get used to it.

"When I turn, you have to go with the turn," Vinnie said. "You have to lean into it as I lean into it. You can't fight it. You have to trust me and go with it. I'll go around the block a few times to see if you can handle it."

"I told you I can handle it," Andy said. She watched his butt lower onto the seat in front of her. He slid back until he was close enough for her to wrap herself around him, which she absolutely wasn't going to do, because, in that seminar she had taken on violence and the American hero, she had seen a sneering, surly Marlon Brando roar up in a movie about biker gangs, and she knew that the American preoccupation with motorcycles was an atavistic perpetuation of the frontier outlaw mystique, which originated in the dualistic, European colonial romantic fantasies of the noble savage and the highway robber.

He sat in front of her and she clamped her hands on the grips and leaned back so she wouldn't quite feel his back pushing against her. He looked back and said, "One other thing. You're allowed to scream."

Andy curled her lip. "I don't scream."

"When I'm riding and I get to this point where there is so much air and noise, that I really can't hear anything. I just let it all go."

"Is this like a warning? If I hear you scream, I'm not supposed to get scared?"

"I'm just saying you can scream if you want. With all that happens on the job, it feels good to let it out every once in a while."

He started the engine and Andy felt the sound in every part of her body as the bike slipped forward, slowed, went down a ramp and into the traffic and then stopped at a red light so quick that she slammed into his back and smacked her helmet against his.

When she was in a car, she was safe, insulated; the other vehicles floated about her with an aloof anonymity, the people in them dimly glimpsed and easily ignored, unless a driver cut her off or moved too fast or stupidly.

Now she felt exposed, vulnerable, surrounded by moving walls of dirty, rusting colored metal so close to her that she could smell the rubber of the tires and hear, over the bike's low growl, the angry grind of other engines.

"I told you not to fight it," he shouted.

"I'm not."

"Hold on," he said and the bike charged ahead and then swooped to the right so that every internal organ below her throat sank down, way down, and she dug her fingernails into her hands and leaned away and the wall of metal seemed to part around them and they zoomed ahead with a liquid grace that could have been flight, except she was sitting down with a man between her legs, looking over his shoulder at the street rushing into her face.

He stopped in front of City Hall and her helmet hit his again. "You're going to have to trust me," he said.

She was about to tell him that she didn't need him to tell her what to do, that she wasn't about to trust anyone, much less a man who should be her best friend's boyfriend, but he gunned the engine and the bike shot forward so fast that everything she was thinking spilled out of her ears and she clamped her legs around his, reached up under his arms, grabbed his chest and squeezed herself tight against his back as the bike dipped low to the right again and swerved into the traffic circle around City Hall.

He stopped at another traffic light and this time their helmets didn't bang together. He put his hands around hers and loosened their grip. "That's more like it," he said, "but let me breathe."

She loosened up and he went around City Hall and back on to the eastbound side of Market Street. She tried to anticipate the stops by watching the traffic and stoplights, but the bike went too fast. They were almost at the end of Market Street, in the tony restaurant district around Third Street, when he pulled over and asked her if she was "particular" about her eggs.

"About my *what?*"

"It's a little early for dinner but we could eat here. Or I could take you someplace in Westyard that you'd like for decent Italian or Vietnamese or something like that. But I've been working nights for a while and, when you work nights, you get to like having breakfast when you wake up, which is when everybody else is usually having dinner, and there aren't that many places that can do breakfast at four in the afternoon, and do it right. I know this place that's not fancy."

"A diner?"

"Better. They make other stuff, but they're very good with eggs and they're the absolute best with donuts."

Andy hadn't seen, or felt, any donut flab on him. "I didn't think you were the kind of cop that ate donuts."

"This is the best donut you will ever have. I'm saying this because, to get there, we'll have to go out south on I-95, which will mean a pretty fast drive, and you might get uncomfortable. If you do, you should think of a donut."

"While you scream?" she asked.

Vinnie said, "Sure," and slipped the bike into the flow of cars going into the downward spiral ramp to Columbus Boulevard, then roared south up a ramp onto I-95.

Andy felt a brutally cold wind pushing against her, bouncing her shoulder bag against her side like a boxer training on a punching bag. It crept into every crack and cranny of her body that wasn't covered by clothing. They flew past billboards, warehouses, the old brick shot tower and shopping centers while her hands became numb. She pulled her left hand off Ferko's jacket and tried to hold on to the grip, but her fingers wouldn't bend.

As they soared onto the bridge over the Philadelphia Navy Yard, Andy put her hand back over his chest, over the zipper. She tried thinking of a donut and it just didn't work. There was only one thing to do. She found the tab on the zipper pulled it down until she could put her hands inside, against the smooth, warm cotton of his shirt.

If he said anything there was too much wind and sound for her to understand him. She rocked her body forward. She dug her fingers into the fabric and felt the hard muscles of his chest rippling with the bike's vibration.

Then she heard him. He wasn't screaming—it didn't sound as if he were in pain. He wasn't expelling the tensions and frustrations of his job.

What she heard was more like exultation, a wordless cry of complete and overwhelming joy. She held him tighter and he took one hand off the handlebars and put it on top of hers. She heard the sound of his happiness again. It merged with the roar of engine and the wind and she had an urge to match him, to yell out loud that she could not for a moment imagine anything better than to be with him on this recklessly exhilarating speed machine, going, going . . .

Vinnie roared past the airport and the swampy wildlife refuge swamp, shot up the exit ramp, made a hard left and stopped, finally, at a red light.

She was about to take a breath. She was about to pull her hands off his chest when he started the bike again and they flew on to a wide, commercial street lined by motels, little houses that had been converted into offices and shops and then another left into a broad asphalt plateau where, at one end, tractor trailers were parked so close together they were like domino tiles about to be tumbled over. Vinnie zoomed between the parked rigs, slowed and stopped in front of a sprawling, two-story complex of garage bays that ended in a red-and-white striped aluminum shed with a tremendous illuminated clock over the front doors. The clock was surrounded by what could either be a truck tire or a donut. Written around that, in neon script, was WIDE LOAD CAFE.

He cut the engine and Andy just sat for a minute in the sudden silence. She took her hands off Vinnie's chest. Vinnie got off the bike and removed his helmet.

Andy let her legs fall away. Her shoes hit the asphalt. She rose slowly, backed away from the bike, yanked off her helmet, pulled the rubber band off and the wind came up, lifted her hair up and she knew, from the way Vinnie looked at her that he wasn't thinking about a donut.

He opened the Wide Load Cafe's glass door for her. The place smelled of grease, but good grease. Against the far kitchen wall, a tremendous triple-drum aluminum coffee urn rose like a pipe organ. Thrusting from that wall was a U-shaped white Formica-topped counter with small jukeboxes and telephones mounted within easy reach of anyone seated at the alternating red and blue barstools. Two men sat at the counter: one played with a handheld computer game, another surfed the Internet on a laptop. Other men, with family, inhabited the red-and-white-striped banquettes. He led her to a table near a window, where a passing tractor trailer briefly blocked the light of the sun completing its arc across the sky.

The waitress was an older woman in a pale blue uniform who did not call Vinnie "hon." They ordered their eggs. Andy had tea; Vinnie had decaf coffee. When Andy couldn't decide what kind of donuts she wanted Vinnie suggested a plate of "assorted glazed."

Vinnie was absolutely correct about the eggs, and the donuts. Andy could eat a third. And a fourth after that, no problem. She gulped her tea and licked the sugar off her fingers.

"About your problem," she said. "Does it have anything to do with Lucia?"

He pushed aside his plate of eggs over easy, on sliced, toasted Italian bread. "One of the guys she tossed at the Verdi, the one with the gun that went down the stairs, is Tommy Nguyen. He's an on-again, off-again member with this Asian gang headed up by this guy name of Shu Shi-Bin. You never heard of Shi-Bin, did you?"

"When you mentioned him last night, that was the first time," Andy said.

"Tommy Nguyen has a father, Li-Loh Nguyen. Mr. Nguyen came over after the war and has done really good for himself. He either owns, or has partnerships with, a lot of businesses around Westyard."

"So Tommy's father wants to sue Lucia for messing up his son?"

"He wants to thank her."

"For putting his son in the hospital?"

"Mr. Nguyen thinks that, by Lucia kicking Tommy's ass down into Mr. Delise's basement, she's shamed Tommy so much, Tommy is going to leave the gang and become the son his father always wanted."

"So what's your problem?" Andy asked.

He folded his hands. "Lucia has to go for it."

"Have you asked her?"

He curled his lip.

Andy put her elbows on the table. "Vinnie, you pick up the phone. You dial her number. She answers and you say hello."

He fretted. "How long you know Lucia?"

"Long enough to know that you shouldn't be asking me to bend her arm," Andy said. "Call her up and ask her out. Tell *her* to think of a donut."

Vinnie shifted in his chair. He looked at his hands. He picked up a donut and put it down. "The day I got my first bike, Lucia didn't want me to take her for a ride. She wanted me to let her ride it, alone."

"What's wrong with that?"

He tried to explain. "Lucia is unpredictable."

"I think she's quite predictable," Andy said. "And considerate, and loyal and capable of kicking your butt ten different ways. You've known she was right for you since you were a baby and you're scared of that, and that makes you scared of her."

He bit into a donut. "I wouldn't be so quick to say she can kick my butt. While Lucia was doing that chop-chop stuff, I went to the fight gym. They had these guys hanging around the K-O, old boxers and bouncers, most of them, with busted-up noses and ears like coffee rolls. They were mighty happy to knock the crap out of me. I put up with it because you have to lose a lot of fights before you start winning. A street fighter will beat a karate guy any day."

"What about a karate *girl?*" Andy asked. "After watching Lucia take out those guys at the restaurant, I wouldn't be so sure."

"My brother Errol went for about a year to the school Lucia went to, that Heian-Do place when Shi-Bin was teaching there. Errol used to come back from that school and beat up on me. He said that I needed to be controlled, so that gave him the right to break these two fingers on my left hand, dislocate my right shoulder and put on this double-handed front choke hold until I almost blacked out. That was his favorite thing to do, choke me half to death."

"Your father let him do that to you?"

"My father wasn't around. The only person who could tell my brother what to do was Uncle Paul, and he never said anything to stop him from beating up on me. It took a couple of years of me hanging out at the fight gym before I got my brother to lay off me. . . . Why you looking at me like that?"

She thought he was adorable, but she couldn't tell him that. "You hit him back?"

"He had me in a front choke hold, and I felt, deep down, that I wasn't going to let him do this to me anymore. I punched his face and hurt my knuckles pretty bad when I hit his jaw. But I also knocked out three teeth. A dentist got two of the teeth back in, but he swallowed one and the replacement that was made never set in right. So the side of his mouth will get painful at times. He has trouble eating anything too hot or too cold."

"So he doesn't mess with people anymore."

He became uncomfortable. "The deal with Lucia is, are you going to call her and get her to show up?"

"Why can't you just ask her out?"

"I'm not supposed to be there."

"Ask her anyway. Tell her she's been important to you all your life."

"She has, but . . ." He fretted. "If I do that, she'll start in about how I should've stood up to my father and not been a cop."

What's this? The dreamiest cop she'd ever seen doesn't want to be a cop? "You told me you became a cop because you wanted to do something decent with your life."

Vinnie saw the donut in his hand and threw it down.

Andy almost laughed, he was so cute.

Vinnie got mad. "Some things aren't funny. If I was doing decent, I would've arranged for patrol cars on Brixton Street last night."

"Vinnie, I have to tell you: you sound *exactly* like Lucia. She's always second-guessing herself."

He hunched his shoulders. "Teal Cavaletta was like . . . even if my mother wasn't dead, I could always talk to Teal. After Lucia took off with Frank for the Main Line, Teal would have me in for a pizzelle and a coffee and we would talk about things."

"About Lucia?"

"Mostly it was about me. She once showed me a Web site that said it had every American listed who had ever fought in Vietnam. It was an important lesson for me because my father's name wasn't on it. Neither was Uncle Paul's. Taught me an important lesson. You believe what people tell you, not what's on paper, or on a Web site."

"I'm sure Lucia feels the same way," Andy said righteously.

He became quiet for a while. Andy thought she could see his mind, his attention, his interest in her slip away. She told herself that it was just and proper that Vinnie think of Lucia. Just because he took her on a carefully-within-the-posted-speed-limit automotive equivalent of an orgasm and then plied her with perfectly cooked eggs and warm, sugar-glazed donuts, did not mean that she would be important to him.

But Andy *liked* being the center of his attention. She wondered how he would take it if she jumped across the table, push him down on the ground and kissed him until he had to come up for air. Could he read her body language?

But he wasn't reading her. Not at all. He had turned away and was looking at a small, drably wallpapered room located at the end of the cafe's serving counter. At the very back of the room were conspicuous, illuminated signs for the restrooms. To reach the restrooms, you would have to go past a cluster of round tables. At one of these tables, under a cloud of cigarette smoke, four thickset, middle-aged men and one woman wearing a baseball cap that said OUT A MY FACE—apparently truckers—were playing cards.

"What's wrong?" Andy asked.

"Uncle Paul used to play cards out here and bring Errol along," Vinnie said. "It's dangerous, what people will do to each other in a card game."

She wanted to tell him he was sexy when he was worried but . . . no. "I'll talk to Lucia," she said.

He looked at her with such gratitude that she felt herself melting. He reached over and put his hand on hers. He let it stay there for a while, and then he thanked her.

Then Andy asked, "Now you're going to help me with a problem. It has to do with Lucia."

He took his hand off hers.

"As long as I've known her, she's been obsessed with this girl, CeCe, and I want to help her get past it. What you can do is get me the files on CeCe's case so I can show Lucia what was done. We'll have one last cry about it, and that'll be it."

He tried to appear offhand. "You can get copies of what's in the files by asking. You write a letter to Police Headquarters, Homicide Division. There might be some kind of fee for copying."

"Vinnie," Andy said, "there are files you can get, and files you can't always get. I want those files, too. Whoever did the investigation—"

"My father did the investigation," Vinnie said defensively. "It was one of the last cases he worked on before he retired. He did it as a favor to Mr. Delise."

"You sure it wasn't a favor to you? You went out with her."

He became uncomfortable. "When we were kids, sure. But CeCe went out with a lot of guys. You're not going to write something in the newspaper about reopening the case, I hope."

"I couldn't if I wanted to and I don't want to," Andy said. "I want to help Lucia get over this."

He put the donut down. "What's in a police file doesn't always make sense if you don't know police work."

"If I have a question, I can talk to Lieutenant Nanh. And I can talk to your father."

He became anxious. "My father doesn't talk about old cases."

"I've never met a cop that didn't like to talk about his old cases," Andy said. "That's one of the things I like about them."

He sat up. "When I came into Mr. Delise's place, I figured you for the kind that didn't like cops."

"I like you, Vinnie," Andy grinned. "It's a start."

She didn't scream as he drove back to her apartment. Andy had every expectation that what began as adventure on a perfect autumn afternoon was going to end with the sun going down as two people, having made deals to each other's mutual advantage, would stay in control and not screw anything up.

But she could see it, in the way his gaze stayed on her as she got off his bike, that if she asked him to come up to her apartment, he would. She had known him for less than twenty-four hours and yet, it was what she didn't know about him that made it so tempting to push things, to go too fast in a direction that she shouldn't take. If Andy put her mouth on his and pulled him into her bed, it would be impossible not to see him again, and again and . . . then what?

Just then, an alarm going off inside her, an alarm that had never rung before, not once, not ever. It was the opposite of a warning: *You could have this guy's children.*

She removed her helmet and hoped that he would assume that it was the ride and those donuts she was supposed to be thinking of that made her face glow like a hot coal on a darkening evening.

He took off his helmet and she saw that he knew *exactly* what was on her mind, and that he liked what was on her mind, very much.

Some clouds had rolled in so the sunset was especially grand. The bright vermillion, reds and golds rippling through the sky were like fires that would be too easy for the two of them to put out.

Was she right for him? For a moment, she was shocked that she was asking that question: just because Lucia and Vinnie seemed destined for each other didn't mean that destiny would bring them together.

She wasn't in love with this guy, but she could see herself falling for him—it could happen, just like that.

"Thanks for a great afternoon," she said, her voice not quite as weak as her knees.

"Thanks for coming along." He opened his arms just a little and she wanted to jump right in.

Instead she handed him her helmet. "When do you want to . . . I mean, when is that meeting with Nguyen supposed to happen with Lucia?"

He didn't like hearing Lucia's name, but he smiled anyway. He tied her helmet to the back of the bike as he said, "Just tell her she should go and she'll do the rest." He turned his warm brown eyes on her. "You're going to call her, right?"

"In a bit," Andy said, wondering if she was really going to need a cold shower, and how cold it would have to be to do the trick.

"Keep Nguyen waiting too long and it's like you're disrespecting him. I wouldn't be asking you to get involved if—"

"If you didn't want me," Andy said, "to solve your problem."

He smirked. "A couple more afternoons like this with you, I might start thinking I don't have any problems."

"You're going to get me the file on CeCe," Andy said.

That brought him down, so she put her hand on his shoulder and he hooked his arm around her and she inhaled the odor of his leather jacket, the dry must of the leaves blowing around and a strong, salty scent that must be him as his stubble raked her cheek and his lips finally pressed themselves down on hers.

You forget how perfectly wonderful it can be to kiss, on a cool autumn day with the sun going down, especially when you're not sure if this is the right person and a kiss might give you the kind of information that an intelligent, responsible, reasonably well educated individual might use to make an intelligent, responsible, reasonably well educated *decision* as to the rightness of the individual doing the kissing. As a reporter, Andy was adept at information-gathering and she had no difficulty bringing her professional skills to the task—

Until he clamped his hands on her butt. Then she put her hands on his chest and tried—not very hard, but hard enough to let him know that she had obtained as much information as she currently required—to push him off. He held her tightly for just a second, and then he let go of her butt and, somehow, their lips were the last to part.

"I liked that," he said.

Andy did, too, but she couldn't tell him that. He should *not* have grabbed her butt. Not on the street where she lived with cars passing by.

Of course, if he *was* going to be the father of her children, none of this would matter, but as long as she wasn't sure yet, and had no intention of giving him the opportunity to demonstrate his abilities in that regard, she could come back with, "Am I going to get that file?"

"You just might," he said. He put on his helmet, hopped on the bike and roared away.

10 ring of truth

Ladderback glanced at his wristwatch. His stomach was not happy with the split pea soup he had eaten in the employee cafeteria. Was Andy going to return so he could give her an assignment?

Probably not.

He looked at his notes from his conversation with Alise Perrigore, half-sister of Paul Small and former owner of an indoor marijuana farm that, when it burned down more than thirty years ago, "made everyone living downwind so very happy, except Paul."

As a teenager, she told him, Paul Small had sold some of the family's Canadian-grown marijuana to summer kids in Wildwood, New Jersey, and to "bulk" dealers in Camden, right across the bridge from Philadelphia. Paul had even arranged for a lifeguard friend of his to get a truck, start a moving company and "import" some of the goods hidden among the possessions of affluent Canadian families who had summer homes at the New Jersey shore. The very same lifeguard was shipping Paul Small's ashes back to her.

"He wanted to have his ashes with the plants, but it's all houses now," said Mrs. Perrigore, who had sold her farm to a developer in the 1980s.

She laughed at her outlaw past. "We were children then. We were, how do you say it, making it up as we went along? You should have seen Paul with Frank at the border, telling stories to the inspectors so they wouldn't think to search the truck. He was so lucky we did not get caught."

Ladderback rose and slowly moved past the cluster of features desks (averting his eyes as he passed the newsroom's windows) to the huge map of the city on a wall next to the Metro Desk. He followed the thick line of Broad Street to Washington Avenue where, at Seventeenth Street, Sunset Zyman's old condiments factory, a mere ten stories in height, was the tallest building in the area. He let his eyes move farther south, into Westyard itself. He identified neighborhood landmarks: the firehouse, police substation, the Church of St. Mary the Redeemer and St. Eusebeo Catholic School, Sisters of Zion Hospital, the site of the Eisely Bros. Meatpacking Plant, the Ronald Avery branch of the Philadelphia Free Library. Knitting it all together was a maze of tiny streets going off in every direction.

He went back to his desk and searched the newspaper's database for every article printed in the *Philadelphia Press* and the *Philadelphia Standard* that contained the word *Westyard*. He didn't mean to read them all but, with no need for more obituaries, he soon lost himself in the fragmented, disjointed and always much-too-brief account of a neighborhood's daily travail, its back-alley heroes, street-corner philosophers, good Samaritans and inexplicable tragedies.

Then he spent another hour reading about Nashua Eagleman. A profile done five years ago in the *Press* when the Pickle Factory opened, discussed Eagleman's "distinctive strategy in partnering with non-profits and good-works organizations." After doing small developments of government-financed housing in Camden, New Jersey, Eagleman teamed with a Haddonfield church to turn a building on church property into the Rectory, a private card club that supposedly served the best coffee in South Jersey, whose membership fees supported the church's poverty outreach programs. An older *Press* article on the card club referred to the Rectory as the "Den of Sin Equity."

Mrs. Eagleman was mentioned in the *Standard*'s "Bold Facers" column. A "radiant presence," she appeared at many regional charity and arts-related social events.

Ladderback went back to his desk. He told himself he would wait one minute for Andy to return. He waited five.

He rose and went toward Howard Lange's office. Lange was on the telephone. Ladderback waited at the door. Lange noticed him but did not motion for him to come in.

"You're still here?" Lange said when he put down the phone.

"I wanted to ask you about your relationship with Captain Ferko of Not Fade Away."

"My relationship with Jack Ferko began quite awhile back," Lange said. He leaned back in his wide, high throne chair and knitted his palms behind his head. "I think it was seven years ago, maybe a little more, I got a letter from a teenaged kid telling me that his mother wanted him to be a cop but he always wanted to be a newspaper reporter and that I should print this exposé that he was sending me. It was clumsy. Spelling mistakes, too many adjectives, not enough attribution, about some old factory in Westyard where they were supposed to be enslaving Asian families. I normally throw unsolicited crap away, but when I saw the last name was Ferko, I called Jack at his home. This was before Jack had retired from the police department, so, if anybody knew what was going on in Westyard, it would be him. The older brother picked up."

"Errol," Ladderback said.

"He told me his father was off doing something with his veterans, so I asked Errol if he knew a Vincent Ferko, and he said that was his brother, but his brother wasn't living at home anymore. I asked if Errol knew anything about a slave plantation in a Westyard factory. Errol wanted to know what I was talking about. I told him that Vincent had written an exposé about this slave plantation. I read it back to Errol and Errol told me that Vincent was a big practical joker, that he had some crazy girlfriend who probably put him up to it, just to see if he could get his name in the newspaper."

"You believed him?" Ladderback asked.

"I finally got ahold of Jack and Jack confirmed it. He said that there were always some Asian illegals around Westyard and in other parts of the city, but he was pretty vigilant in assigning street patrols and as soon as any illegals were found, they were handed over to the Immigration and Naturalization Service. There was no slave plantation."

"Did you send a reporter to verify this?"

Lange sighed. "Shep, if I didn't know what the ring of truth sounded like, I never would have made it this far."

Ladderback stood silently for a while.

"Go home, Shep."

Ladderback went back to his desk. He removed several files from his cabinet, and inserted them carefully into his satchel. Then he put on his hat and coat and left.

Andy couldn't remember unlocking the apartment house's front door, going up the stairs, opening her apartment door, dropping her shoulder bag, or throwing off her shoes and jacket.

She was on her bed with her eyes closed, lolling in a post-caffeine, post-sugar, post-butt-squeezing-kiss-on-the-lips meltdown, when her phone rang.

"What's this about you feeling up Vinnie on his bike?"

"Lucia, I . . ." Andy sat up. She could never keep secrets from Lucia. "Who told you?"

"Who do you think?"

"Vinnie?"

"He calls me up, tells me I should expect a call from you, and what am I going to do? Not ask him what the call is supposed to be about? He told me he took you for a ride on his Harley and he spent the afternoon with you at that truck stop and he pumped you up on those donuts—I hope you had the wholewheat glazed, by the way, because that's my favorite—and that I should do whatever you tell me to do, and do it pretty quick. So, what went on that he left out?

When you're asked a question you don't want to answer, ask another question. "Who is this guy who wants to thank you?"

"CeCe and I used to call him Uncle Nuggy. He wants to make tea for me so I'll forgive him for his son trying to kill me. After my father went home from the hospital, there was a call from Nuggy's office on his company's voice mail."

"So you're going with your father?"

"He's with his lady friend tonight."

"What about Vinnie?"

"Vinnie's working tonight, and I wouldn't want him with me even if he could take the time off."

"Lucia, he has feelings for you."

"My best friend in the whole world gets a ride on a Harley, and now she knows Vinnie like she and him were separated at birth!"

"He said if you didn't do it, it might not be so good for him."

"He would say that."

Andy thought of Vinnie and told herself that she had tried, that, as much as she wouldn't mind Vinnie taking her for another ride on that bike, she had done what she could to remind Lucia that she belonged with him.

So she changed the subject and asked Lucia about her mother.

"She's sleeping. Doctors say, physically, she'll be okay. Mentally . . . who knows. I'm at her house now. You don't want to see what was done to it."

"I'll help you fix it up, if you need me," Andy said. "Any ideas who did it?"

"I get so mad whenever I think about it. I mean, she's not rich. There's nothing here that cost any money. She's an *accountant*. You can get mad and yell at an accountant. But you don't break in and trash their place. Not somebody like my mother. She's got stuff here, records, tax returns—she could probably shut down half the neighborhood if she decided to tell the IRS the truth."

"But what if somebody thought she was going to do that?"

"People can think what they want, but my mother would never voluntarily go to the law. Not in Westyard. She'd never get another client." Lucia asked Andy if she wanted to come with her to Uncle Nuggy's.

Andy asked her how she should dress.

"Like ladies," Lucia said.

Andy parked at the top of Brixton Street. When she turned off the engine, the street did not appear any more menacing than it had last night, but the knowledge that a woman who lived alone had been brutally attacked had changed the way she saw and felt about walking outside, alone, even if it was less than a block, to the house to meet a woman who could probably kick anybody's butt, anywhere, anytime.

Andy had been in fights. Both her parents grew up in a tough, decaying Philadelphia neighborhood. They insisted, in their own very different ways, that she should never start fights, but if she found herself in one, she had better fight back with everything you had. Once, when Andy was threatened by a rapist, she fought back and escaped harm.

But, sitting alone in a car as the cooling engine clicked and pinged to itself, Andy could not suppress the memory of Teal Cavaletta's horribly bruised face. She could not stop hearing the broken, angry remarks Teal had made in her delirium. It took a great deal of effort just to put her hand on the car door.

She heard the distant, blurry city sounds of traffic, sirens, trains moving in the night. Just before she opened the door, she reached into her shoulder bag and found her cell phone. Should she turn it on so she could hit the emergency 911 speed dial? Or should she keep it off so it wouldn't go off suddenly and draw attention to her in this dim, unfamiliar place?

She left it off. She got out, locked the door and pretended that she was invisible but her shoes made slight, grinding noises as she moved across the concrete. Soon she saw Lucia waiting on her mother's row house steps in a long, belted umber tweed coat that came down to her moss brown leather boots. With her face glowing and her dark hair glossy under a knitted woolen cap, Lucia actually looked *nice.*

"Tell me you didn't recognize me," Lucia told Andy when she heard Andy approach.

"I did recognize you," Andy said.

Lucia did a full turn. "My mother had an entire room filled with all these clothes she bought from catalogs," Lucia said, opening her arms and doing a little curtsy on the step. "She never wore them and . . . some of them fit me pretty good."

That was a matter of interpretation: to Andy, Lucia was playing a slightly more grown-up version of a little girl dressing up in her mother's clothes.

"What you have on under that bomber jacket?" Lucia asked her. "All I see is your legs."

That was all anybody saw. "It's a suit my mother bought me to wear for a job interview," Andy said.

"You get the job?"

"No." Andy changed the subject. "My car's down the block."

"We're walking," Lucia said as she came down the step.

Andy was in a pair of opaque black winter-weight panty hose, but she still felt the breeze whipping around her legs. She looked up and down the street for bad guys that might jump out of the darkness but only saw trash blowing around. She did not want to walk for any distance in a neighborhood where persons unknown broke into houses and beat up women.

But she couldn't tell Lucia that. "I don't think it's safe for you to walk on that knee. When I hurt my knees, the swelling would always be worse the second day. That was when I had to lay off."

"I did yoga stretches and applied pressure to three points above and below the knee. I'm fine."

"If you say so . . . ," Andy replied, unconvinced. "Where are we going?"

"A supermarket three blocks away." Lucia started off in that loose, flowing, effortless, straight-backed stride that Andy had always envied.

Andy caught up with her. "I used that wrist thing you showed me, to get this asshole to listen to me."

"I shouldn't've shown that to you. You learn a little thing like that, it's too easy to hurt people. You didn't hurt him, did you?"

Andy grinned.

"You keep this up," Lucia said, "and you'll end up just like me."

They stopped at the corner of Brixton and Fifteenth Street. Empty plastic bags and shredded pieces of newsprint tumbled in the wind across Fifteenth to a pocked and pitted asphalt parking lot extending to Broad Street. At the edge of the nearly empty lot, beyond the hulks of abandoned cars and a blue van whose side and rear windows had been painted over, was a strip of shops leading to the wide, high arch of a supermarket at the far end. Andy could see traces of the old Penn Fruit sign on the supermarket's facade. Below the sign was a smaller, simpler electric sign with black letters on a yellow background, and oriental characters above and below: GOOD CHOICE MARKET.

Sharing the strip was the Good Choice Drug Store, the Good Choice Travel Agency, the Good Choice Gift Shop, Good Choice Video and DVD, and the Good Choice Coin-Bakery and Cafe. A cracked glass window on the only storefront that didn't have Good Choice on it showed a barren space with a polished wooden floor, frayed canvas mats, a punching bag hanging from a corner, a pile of long and short sticks in another corner and a black-and-white photo of a frowning Asian man on the far wall.

"Was this one of those karate schools you went to?" Andy asked.

Lucia paused in front of the darkened window. "*Heian-Do* is Japanese for 'way of peace,' but this was the hardest, nastiest, most brutal martial art I've ever taken. CeCe got into Heian-Do because she got this huge crush on Sensei Ishimura's chief instructor, Shi-Bin."

That name was familiar. "And you had to do what CeCe did."

"Well, sure," Lucia said. "It seemed like it would be fun and it was, until CeCe tried to get serious with him. Then Shi-Bin punched her hard in the solar plexus. You hit somebody there, in the soft spot where the bone ends, and you can knock the wind right out of them. He didn't break anything, but he knocked her off her feet against that wall over there."

"You didn't beat the crap out of him after that?"

"This was before I knew how to beat the crap out of people. It was also my first exposure to a hard art, and the kind of people who teach hard arts. Sensei used to say you should hit your opponent as if you are honoring your opponent. And there's this tradition, in some of the schools, that whatever your *sempai*—a *sempai* is the student who out-ranks you—does is for your benefit. I just got really mad at him. I demanded that he apologize and, of course, he didn't. So I picked up one of the long sticks we'd been practicing with and 'honored' his knee. Blew his whole knee out. He went straight down and swore he would kill us both. Sensei ended the class and threw CeCe and me out."

"Was CeCe okay?"

"A bruise, but that's all. That was her last try at the martial arts. CeCe hung out around her father's restaurant for a while, and then started dating guys."

"Including Vinnie?"

"Not really. Vinnie was going to the fight gym, getting his ass kicked and trying to figure out how he was going to piss off his father by becoming the one thing that scared his father more than anything."

"A lawyer?"

"Cops don't hate lawyers when they need them. Vinnie could never be a lawyer. He doesn't have the mouth. What scared Vinnie's father was newspaper reporters. He would read the *Press* and get really mad about some reporter finding out things that embarrassed the police department. So Vinnie wanted to be what you are. More than anything."

Andy saw Vinnie in her mind and that you-could-have-kids-with-this-guy alarm went off inside her so loud that she was sure Lucia could hear it, or sense it, or figure out with that telepathy that friends have, that if Andy could make a wish right now she'd click the heels of her shoes together and, like Dorothy in *The Wizard of Oz,* magically appear in front of Vinnie and do things to him that just might make him think that there was no place like home.

Her home.

But Lucia was off again. Just past the Heian-Do school, before the glass windows of the supermarket, Lucia yanked open a windowless steel door encrusted with the remains of posters and handbills. A grimy sign above the door indicated that this was the employee entrance. Next to the sign, Andy noticed the metal housing and open eye of a video camera.

Andy followed Lucia up a flight of steps to a landing where an old man in a blue security uniform sat at a desk behind a sheet of wire-reinforced bullet-proof glass. He glanced at Lucia and then pressed a button that opened another steel door. This led to a brightly lit corridor with an old time card clock beside a shelf with a coffeemaker, hot water urn, a huge pile of tea bags, creamer packets and red plastic reed-like stirrers.

Lucia glided down a corridor where a sign pointed toward the office. She found a stairway. Andy followed Lucia down past the supermarket's ground floor, into the basement.

Andy had done a Web search on Li-Loh Nguyen before she left her apartment. She had found only two news articles about him. Both articles, one in the *Standard,* the other in the *Press,* used the same cliche—"a classic rags-to-riches story." A leader of an anticommunist rebel coalition in North Vietnam, Nguyen came to Philadelphia after the American withdrawal. He worked odd jobs for little or no pay, preferring to take his wages in trade, or, later, in partnership interests that helped him acquire numerous businesses from the mostly aging, white Irish and Italian owners who were retiring or abandoning South Philadelphia.

Nguyen refused to be interviewed for either article. The articles differed on the extent of his business empire. The *Press* article, written two years ago, confined him to South Philadelphia and Chinatown. The *Standard* article speculated that "his influence can also be felt in Asian conclaves in Upper Darby, South Jersey, and even as far away as Atlantic City." Both articles noted his fondness for John Wayne Westerns and agreed that, even if without his wealth, his six-foot-ten-inch height made him "the giant of the Asian community."

Andy had no problem identifying him in the supermarket's basement. There, among big sacks of rice piled high to the dim lights, two dozen people crowded around a battered cook pot, one of whom was so large that the others seemed no more than children around him.

His gray suit fit him like a tarp thrown over a cell phone antenna tower. His thick hair was a dusty blow-dried gray cloud. He wore a pair of heavy, tortoiseshell spectacles over a face with so many liver spots and deep creases that Andy thought of pictures she had seen of weathered stone idols that been carved centuries ago into the sides of mountain cliffs.

As Lucia bounded past the mounds of rice sacks, he opened his long arms like the wings of a great bird. Lucia hopped into those arms.

He lifted her up and put her down on a sack of rice beside him. She sat there for a few minutes as Nguyen conferred with the others, all of whom were Asian. Then she went back to Andy's side.

"This is a *hui*, a kind of secret bank," Lucia told her. "See that pot in the center? That's a *ting*, a metal cook pot. Uncle Nuggy—I mean, Nguyen Li-Loh—brought it with him from Vietnam, so his bank is the *hui ting*. It's the biggest of the secret banks in the city, at least, it was when I left."

"What makes it a secret?"

"Nothing, really. Just about everyone who is part of the Asian community knows about them. They're not registered. They don't pay taxes. What happens is, everyone you see contributes a share, sometimes several shares. Then they decide what to do with what they have."

In the faint light, Andy told Lucia, she couldn't see any money. She did see a man sitting on one of the sacks of rice scowl at Lucia.

"It's all symbolic," Lucia said. "If you looked into the pot, all you'd see is rice. If you add a share, you just drop in a handful of rice. Each handful is a share. The man with the small notebook, sitting on the sack near where I was, is the *shiao shu*, the 'small one who holds.' That's Sensei Ishimura, the one who gave me that nasty look. He keeps track of how many handfuls go into the pot so that the people who contribute shares can forget about who gave the most, though everybody knows it's Nguyen Li-Loh who puts in the most shares."

"Why did Ishimura look at you like that?"

"I told you he threw me out of his class after I blew out his best student's knee. I was supposed to come back and beg him to let me in. I did not."

"And he holds a grudge?"

"I think that's all he does, hold grudges."

"So all these people are sitting around on these sacks of rice," Andy said. "Putting in handfuls of rice, like it's money?"

"Neat, isn't it? In order to borrow, you have to be known to all the people here, or have someone with a lot of shares vouch for you. My father got a loan from the *hui ting* to buy a new truck for his moving business when he was short on cash and none of the city's banks would lend to him."

"Who vouched for him?"

"Mr. Delise. Of all the white people in Westyard, he's the one they respect the most. Nguyen Li-Loh knew him in Vietnam."

"If they respect him, how is that an Asian gang robbed his place last night?"

"I don't know," Lucia said. "I would ask him but it's a waste of time with Mr. Delise. He'll talk about music and food, but never about what he's feeling, even if you can sort of tell that he's hurting. It's like he's more Asian than the Asians."

"What about Vinnie's father? He was in Vietnam, too."

"Him, they hate. When CeCe died he was sure that the person who killed her was Asian, so he rounded up a lot of Asians and tried to get confessions out of them, but he didn't get anywhere. He also arrested a lot of Asians who were illegal immigrants. He'll tell you it was his job, but just because it's your job doesn't mean you have to do it. I heard that a lot of the people he arrested had refused to work in the sweatshops and janitorial businesses that were paying them slave wages. If you're illegal, and you get arrested for anything in this country, you get deported. They used to call him Jack Spade, because his name was Jack, and the ace of spades was the death card that the American soldiers liked to leave on the bodies of Vietnamese soldiers they killed."

"What do they think of Vinnie?"

130

"He wrote me some letters and told me he was trying to make amends for things his father did, but he didn't elaborate."

"What about your Uncle Paul?"

"I don't know what they thought of him. He would talk about them taking over the south edge, and make racist jokes. One reason I moved out with my father is that I didn't think I could deal with Uncle Paul and Errol, who was even worse. Uncle Paul never wanted me to hang around with CeCe, because she knew so many Asian people through her father. Around the time I moved out, Uncle Nug—Nguyen Li-Loh—wanted to get Uncle Paul's help in fixing up that old factory where CeCe died. But the factory's still there, so I guess nothing came of it."

They watched the people—men mostly, but some women—speak to each other around the cook pot. Nguyen Li-Loh said nothing but conversation ended when he nodded.

"Do you know what they said?" Andy asked Lucia.

"None of it. I minored in Asian Studies at Ohio State, but I never learned the languages. I really want to, one day."

The session around the cook pot ended with Ishimura, in dark blue work pants and an army surplus camouflage blouse, coming forward and putting a lid over the cook pot. Lucia and Andy followed Ishimura and Nguyen Li-Loh up the stairs to a drab, cluttered office where, against one wall, hung a movie poster of John Wayne in *The Searchers.*

On a dented metal folding chair near that poster sat a young man in a white neck brace. Most of the lower part of his stitched, darkly bruised face was hidden behind a tangle of shiny metal wires and blue compression pads.

"Cricket girl," Li-Loh said in a deep, weary voice when they entered the office. "So good see you." Lucia introduced Andy.

Li-Loh extended a hand that opened like a digger claw and encircled Andy's hand in a warm, gentle grip. He bowed slightly. "Please to meet you. What is Cosicki?"

Lucia explained to Andy, "When I first met Uncle . . ."

Ishimura sucked air.

"I mean, Li-Loh, I told him my last name meant 'cricket' in Italian and he told me his name meant 'New Prince.' So he wants to know what Cosicki means."

Andy didn't know. "It's Ukrainian. It may not have been my father's real name. He took the name of a person at the orphanage he really admired."

"Great responsibility to have name of important man," the giant said. "In Vietnam, Li-Loh was a prince who was a farmer and a leader of his people. Big question: do you take name, or name take you?"

Lucia explained. "Li-Loh calls all his businesses Good Choice because the word used for 'good' stands for something that should be favorable, but you can't be sure if it's the best because you haven't tried it yet. 'Choice' means what it does in English, a decision you can make, but it has a second, older meaning, as a place to plant where crops haven't grown before. So, to call a place Good Choice means that this may not be the best, but it seems to be the most favorable place to start something new."

Li-Loh said, "Take coats?"

Andy and Lucia removed their jackets and handed them to Li-Loh, who reverently hung them on a small rack next to a framed movie poster of John Wayne in *True Grit*.

"Please to meet, Hideyoshi Ishimura," Li-Loh said to Andy when he returned from the coatrack. "My associate."

Lucia faced Ishimura and said, with some difficulty, "Sensei."

Ishimura also bowed, not as deeply as Lucia, and said, "Sempai."

"Sensei, I . . ." Lucia blushed deeply. "I don't know what to say."

"I hear you fight good now. You will come back to dojo," Ishimura said. "I teach you not to be so little girl."

Andy saw Lucia try to repress her disgust.

"We have tea," Li-Loh said.

A petite Asian woman in a long skirt and knitted blouse cleared the closest desk and put down a lacquered tray that held a pot of water, two stoneware cannisters, a wooden whisk, a wooden spoon and five stoneware tea cups.

Li-Loh approached the table. "Please to let me."

Andy saw instantly that this was false modesty, that whatever it took to make tea, Li-Loh not only knew how to prepare tea, but he was aware that, by making tea himself, he was conveying upon Lucia a supreme gesture of respect.

The petite woman arranged chairs around the desk. Li-Loh sat first, in a chair without arm rests. Ishimura sat next, then Lucia (taking the chair as far away from Ishimura as she could) and Andy. One chair remained empty.

Li-Loh opened the cannister and, with a reverent solemnity, dropped a spoonful of green tea leaves into a cup, poured on steaming water, stirred it briskly and set the cup before Ishimura.

Ishimura studied the swirling leaves, lifted the cup to his lips, inhaled the aroma and uttered an imperious, "Oh."

Li-Loh opened another tea cannister, showing a dark tangle of tea leaves with pearl white fragments of flowers mixed in.

"Jasmine?" Andy asked.

"You choose," Li-Loh said.

Andy adored tea. She knew that serving tea was a big deal in some Asian cultures, that each part of the tea ceremony was heavily symbolic of all kinds of deep philosophical things that she couldn't understand because you drink tea because it's hot, it tastes good, it goes with every kind of food, it gives you a buzz and it's better than coffee in every way possible.

She had tried the green teas and found them lacking, empty, bland, even after all the health studies turned it into a fad drink for about five minutes. She had run through the basic orange pekoes. Earl Grey annoyed her: the bergamot oil reminded her of dishwashing detergent. The smokiness of Lapsang Soochong was fun sometimes, but mostly, it seemed contrived. The oolong blends favored in Chinese restaurants tended to taste more like the pot they were steeped in. She found some of the better Darjeeling blends pleasant, but they varied so much in quality and intensity that she didn't trust them. So, when she could ask for a tea, it was Kemmun, an astringent black blend that told you, on the first sip, to *pay attention*.

Next to a steaming cup of Kemmun, every jasmine Andy had tried was disappointing. She had heard that jasmine was the tea of teas, the Bordeaux wine of Asia, and that the absolute best jasmines came from Vietnam. Compared to Kemmun, it was flowery and so slight that, unless she let it steep too long and it became bitter, she could drink it almost without knowing it was tea.

Li-Loh sensed her indecision. "This," he said, gesturing toward the green tea mixed with brown rice and twigs, "is *bancha* for Ishimura-san. This," he extended his long fingers at the jasmine, "from Vietnam, for cricket girl."

Before Andy could say anything, Lucia announced that they would both have jasmine and, from the way Li-Loh straightened up, Andy guessed that this was the right choice.

Li-Loh put the jasmine leaves on the bottom of one cup, then poured the water over them. He gave them a brief stir and put the cup, which could have been a thimble in his huge hands, in front of Andy.

Andy picked up the cup and felt the warmth entering her fingers. She brought the cup to her nose, not because she had seen Ishimura do this and it was part of the ritual, but because if you really love tea, you appreciate how the aroma shapes your expectations of the taste. With some teas, the aroma is as good as it gets: what follows is dark water in a rusty pot. With others, the aroma sets you up for the stronger, dominant flavors of the brew.

So Andy inhaled and she smelled blossoms after a warm rain on the last spring afternoon before summer. Then she detected a fragrant, teasing sweetness. She inhaled again and she detected a third scent, a fleeting bitterness that, by itself, would have been peculiar. Jasmines aren't supposed to become bitter during their first minute or so in the cup. Here the bitterness gathered the flowery scent and its beckoning sweetness into a gorgeously complicated vision that she had never experienced.

She looked at Lucia and Lucia, who hadn't touched her cup, winked. This was one of *those* jasmines!

She took a sip and the scented sweetness was like the tentative touch of someone very young and very beautiful. The flowery essence filled

134

her, followed by a distinctly *green* taste, a playful, chlorophyl tang, like a scallion or a really good asparagus. The two flavors slowly merged into a glowing perfection, like the last ruddy gleam from the sun before it drops below the horizon.

Andy opened her eyes to see that Lucia had her eyes averted. She glanced at Li-Loh, whose attention was aimed across the room, at his son in the metal folding chair.

"Thomas," Li-Loh said. "You make."

His head couldn't hang as low as he probably wanted it to. He walked with awkward, uneven steps until he took the empty chair on the left side of his father. One of his arms was wrapped and bound against his side. He grasped the teaspoon and shoveled a dark tangle of leaves into a cup.

"Too much," Li-Loh said. "You do over."

Thomas spilled the dry leaves onto a corner of the tray. Then he put another, smaller spoonful of leaves into a cup. His hand trembled as he lifted the pot. He poured too quickly—water splashed over the side and he jerked the pot back. He approached the cup more carefully, filled it, put down the pot, stirred the leaves and put the whisk down on the tray.

"Now you give," Li-Loh said.

His hand shook even more as he touched the cup, enclosed his fingers around it, lifted it and then set it in front of Lucia.

Lucia lifted the cup, inhaled the tea and looked Thomas in the eye. "This," she said, "is very good." She tasted it and quietly said, "Thank you, Thomas."

"Now you say," Li-Loh commanded.

Thomas was crying. With his jaw shut, the words emerging from his lips sounded as if they were being dragged from the bottom of a bin of broken glass: "I am v-very sorry, Ms. Lucia."

"I am very sorry, too," Lucia said quietly.

"No need for sorry," Ishimura said. "Need for respect. Respect and humility."

Li-Loh pinched a few of the discarded leaves and was about to put them into the last cup when Lucia said, "Please." She picked up the spoon, put leaves from the jasmine cannister into the cup, poured in the water, stirred the tea and put the cup down in front of Thomas.

Thomas stared at it. He lifted the cup in his good hand but couldn't quite bring it to his face. Then he said, "Thank you, Ms. Lucia, but I . . . can't drink this way."

"You will drink," Li-Loh demanded.

Thomas began to panic. He couldn't bend his neck. He couldn't bring the cup close to his lips without tilting it over the wire brace. He couldn't open his lips wide. His hand began to tremble and tea splashed on his skin. He winced and a tear fell out of the corner of his eye.

Andy got up and, in several long, loping, utterly graceless eat-up-the-basketball-court strides, was out of the office and down the corridor to the coffee urn, where she grabbed one of the plastic straw stirrers. She returned to the table, put the stirrer in Thomas's cup and said, "It's hollow. Treat it like a straw."

Thomas gazed at Andy as if she had just performed a miracle. He poked himself twice before the top of the straw touched his lips. He sucked the tea through the straw.

Thomas couldn't move the lower part of his face. He put down the cup, turned his entire body in his chair because he could not move his neck and said to Andy, "My eyes are smiling."

An old woman with a grimy airline flight bag hanging from her shoulder found Ladderback cringing in front of the door that led out onto Filbert Street from the underground Twelfth Street Station.

She saw him shaking, his eyes shut tight, his hands clenched around his satchel. "Are you afraid of something, sir?"

"Yes," he said. "Could you help me cross the street to the bus terminal?"

"Isn't it supposed to be the other way around?"

He shrugged helplessly and she took his arm. "It's just a few cars and taxis waiting," she said to him.

He was silent until he went into the bus terminal. Then he relaxed

and gazed upon his benefactor. "You have my gratitude. Is there anything I can do for you?"

She looked him up and down. "Not be so scared." She went to a row
of seats with television sets mounted on them, popped a coin into the set
and watched the screen.

Ladderback noticed the time was four minutes to eight P.M. He went
to a pay phone, punched in his credit card number and then the number
of the Villa Verdi.

A man with an Asian accent answered. Ladderback asked if the
restaurant was open after the robbery. The man said it was. Ladderback
said he had read a review in the *Press* some years ago that mentioned
the owner sang arias from Italian operas every Friday and Saturday—

"He's about to start," the man said.

Ladderback asked him if the telephone was close enough so that the
man could just leave the handset off the hook and Ladderback could listen to the performance?

Ladderback heard the phone bounce a few times. Then he heard a
tremulous swell from the organ and a voice. . . .

At the end of twenty minutes, the departure of the bus Ladderback
was to take had been announced, and, Ladderback, who was familiar
with every aria Angelo Delise had sung, felt he knew the man.

Almost.

11 street fighter

Ishimura insisted that Lucia demonstrate what techniques she had used in Mr. Delise's kitchen, so she left the table, with Ishimura and Li-Loh, and stood in a clearing near the front door.

Andy had more of the fabulous tea, and saw that Tommy Nguyen had been giving her an eyes-bugging-out kind of stare, as if he were Moses and she was the Promised Land.

She wasn't anybody's promised land, but she found his attention a little bit flattering. She winked at him and he yanked his eyes away, a dark blush crawling out from under the bandages.

"So," Andy began. "How come you're not out there with Lucia, making yourself a punching bag again?"

The parts of Tommy that weren't wired, bound up or bandaged in place wilted. "I am not good enough."

"To be a punching bag?"

He said nothing, his face dark with shame.

"It's okay," Andy said. "Just don't try to kill her again."

He breathed with difficulty.

"So what was in the safe you guys wanted to get?"

"A piece of paper."

"Are you going to tell me what was on the piece of paper?"

He shifted uncomfortably. "It was like a share, a certificate of stock, but it was more like a contract between the *hui ting* and Paul Small. It said the *hui ting* had a share in the Pickle Factory."

"You broke Mr. Delise's fingers and you almost killed Lucia over that?"

"Shi-Bin wanted the share to prove that the *hui ting* had been defrauded."

"In cases of fraud, there are legal remedies and I'm sure your father is quite capable of using them."

"When the share was made, Angelo Delise got the only copy with the signatures because he is a member of the *hui ting*. It is his job to keep track of the debt. He had the only copy with signatures because to have more than one copy is to indicate the possibility of distrust and dishonor, and the *hui ting* is all about trust and honor."

"Until you and Shi-Bin decided you wanted to rob him."

He became proud. "We decided to use strategy, like Sensei Ishimura says: when you want something from someone, make what they think is easy much harder for them. So we would not let him go sing but he would not open the safe. He said the paper isn't there, that Paul Small took it Tuesday."

"Did you have any idea Lucia was in the dining room?"

"She made a reservation. If she was a problem, I was to deal with her because it was her mother who wrote the contract and notarized it."

"And she dealt with you," Andy said.

Tommy's eyes were welling up with tears. "I would have killed her if you hadn't pushed me down."

"That would be really honorable," Andy said sarcastically.

"Yes, it would be," Tommy said. "You don't understand that, here, it is not the individual that matters. It is the village. If the village is dishonored, a price must be paid to restore that honor."

When Tommy was a boy, he said CeCe and her father brought Paul Small to the *hui ting*. Paul Small said the men involved in the Pickle

140

Factory needed $2 million or the project would not begin. They said if the *hui ting* gave them the money, they would make low-income housing for Asian people.

"That was seven years ago and I am now a man and just now, we are hearing about Veterans Plaza, luxury condos that are bigger than big, better than new. I don't hear about low-income housing. None. We were betrayed and my father would not admit it! He wanted to negotiate, but, with the man dead, who can we negotiate with?"

"How much did this share cost?" Andy asked.

"I don't know the exact amount. I have been told it was two million dollars. Do you have any idea how hard it was for us to get that money? We are all so poor here. My father has almost nothing—everything he does is in partnerships based on honor and trust. He had tried for years to have some kind of large housing project for our people. He would go to all the politicians and they would say, yes, you need housing, but so do poor people all over the city. Paul Small told us that the problem was that most of us were not registered voters, we did not give to the campaign of Senator Tybold, but to buy a share of the Pickle Factory would turn things around. And now we know that nothing has changed. Do you have any idea of the shame? The disgrace?"

Andy started to get mad at him. "Tommy, have you seen any of the plans for this project? Has anyone? I don't think so. Right now, all you've heard are rumors. That's it. I can find out a few things in the next week that might give us a better idea. Until then, what's going to happen to all your shame and disgrace if things come out the way your father wants?"

"They won't," Tommy said. "Shi-Bin is sure of it."

"What if Shi-Bin is wrong? Tommy, you almost screwed up your entire life. If Angelo Delise and Lucia Cavaletta were any different, you'd be in jail right now, and you should know enough about America that you don't get ahead easily if you have an assault with a deadly weapon conviction on your record."

His eyes became hateful. "All my life, my father forced me to work for Mr. Delise. After school, in college, all the time. I am American-born. I am a citizen. I have a degree in business administration. My father thinks my gang is dishonorable. I must work at Mr. Delise's until I give them up."

"What if you just quit?"

His eyes went round. "The gang?"

"Everything. Do something different."

He squirmed. "My father has the respect of the Asian community. If I quit I won't get that."

"So get your own respect!" Andy said.

Tears fell from his eyes. "You sound like CeCe. She would say this to me."

"And she probably would have knocked you down if you tried to hurt Lucia," Andy added.

He glanced at Lucia, who was speaking with Tommy's father. "Did Lucia tell you about me and CeCe?"

"She said CeCe was dating you when she was killed."

"Me and CeCe were a gang. We met in her father's kitchen and we used to do everything together. When she was found, the Jack Spade said he would accuse me if I didn't say that it was an Asian gang that killed her."

"You were a teenager then, right? Sixteen years old?"

"Seventeen."

"What made them think you were a suspect?"

He began to blush. "She got killed after we . . ."

Andy saw his face go red. "Had sex?"

"We used to do it in the basement, below the kitchen, right where I fell—"

Andy held up a hand. "You don't have to tell me. There are places I used to make out that I don't want to think about."

He lowered his voice. "CeCe and me always had to be quiet because we could hear things going on, in the kitchen and in the office. While we did it, she heard someone go into the office."

"With Mr. Delise?"

"Not him. He was singing in front."

"But CeCe heard, and that made her go upstairs?"

"I told her to stay with me, but when she heard something she wasn't supposed to hear, she would tell people, just to get them mad. She went upstairs and she never came back down."

"You didn't go looking for her?"

"I waited until after her father finished singing. By then there was nobody in the office. I looked around for her, but I couldn't see her."

"Was anybody else in the kitchen?"

"The kitchen didn't have anybody in it when he was singing because, when Mr. Delise sings, the people in the kitchen have to come out into the dining room and listen. If you wanted to keep your job, you would let him see you listening."

"He didn't miss you and CeCe?"

"He . . . sort of knew. He may not have known we were going as far as we did, but he felt that, as long as she was happy, he would let us do what we wanted."

"Did anybody else know about you and CeCe?"

"Everybody knew. When CeCe was found, the police took me to the substation on Seventeenth Street and would not let me out for three hours. They wanted me to say that me and CeCe took drugs and had sex in the gatehouse by the meat factory and that I left Lucia there."

"Who wanted you to say that?"

"Jack Spade. Ferko."

"Did he come up with that story about the gatehouse?"

"He said he knew what we were doing and that I was to write it out as a statement, which I did not do."

"Didn't your father come with you?"

"My father did nothing for me. He said a son who associates with criminals is no better than a criminal. If they put me in jail he wouldn't bail me out. Jack Spade said he could put me in a jail with a psycho killer who would do to me what was done to CeCe."

"You didn't believe that."

"I was seventeen I was born and raised in a city where worse things have happened to Asians. Most of those without green cards were living two blocks from here, in the meat factory my father wanted to turn into houses. They were free people in Vietnam, Thailand and Cambodia. They came here and were turned into slaves. When one got sick, got arrested or died, do you think anyone cared? Only my father. He cared more for them than he cared about me."

"You're probably wrong about that," Andy said. "I didn't think my father cared much about me until, after he died, I found out that he really did care. Things would be much worse for you if you didn't have your father, Mr. Delise and Lucia on your side."

"Things are worse," he sniffled. "I failed. My gang failed."

"Tommy, quit the gang," Andy said. "You don't want to mess up your life just to feel cool with a bunch of assholes."

"Shi-Bin says I'm the most important person in the gang. With me in the gang, my father has to let us alone."

"With you out of the gang, you can get on with your life. You can move out of your father's house, find another job, anything."

"You don't get it," Tommy said. "My father is one of the most successful Asian businessmen in the city. But I have to wait until he decides I'm worthy. If I go anywhere else, he won't help me because he says when he came to America it was work, work, work and he doesn't think I've worked enough. I've been a busboy for more than seven years! Is that enough? Not for him. If I go somewhere else, all I'll get is the same thing: entry-level crap."

"Not always," Andy said. "I've written about people who kept trying different things and then found a great job that took them places. So get out there and start trying."

He became rigid, embarrassed, *squirmy*. "No girl's going to look at you if you fail."

Oh, so that was why he was playing gangbanger: one more example of a guy who has to turn himself into an asshole because he thinks girls like assholes.

"Tommy, girls don't mind when guys fail. We get to cheer guys up."

He didn't hear that. "With my gang, we have fun. I'd be crazy not to be with them."

Suddenly Andy remembered another film from her American Cinema Icons class. It was badly lit, badly cast, badly directed, *but* it starred Mae West, the funniest femme fatale of all time and you couldn't wait to see her on the screen, making so many worthless hunks ogle her corseted hips. Though Andy was too tall and too thin and too plain to ever even *think* of being mistaken for that winking, wiggling lampoon of feminine sexuality, she *could* use her imagination.

"Do yourself a favor, Tommy," she said, leaning close to him so her breath touched his ear. "Be a little crazy. Be unpredictable. It gives a girl something to look forward to in the morning."

His eyes bugged out. She smiled. He blushed. Andy had the feeling he would do anything for her. All she had to do was ask.

But there was nothing she wanted him to do. She could think of what she'd want Vinnie to do, and she could imagine him doing it.

She stood rapidly and headed toward Lucia so that Tommy wouldn't see the blush creeping across her face.

Andy waited until they were past the security guard and going down the stairs before asking Lucia why she didn't want to stay for dinner. "He did invite us, and he's like family to you, right?"

"Better than family," Lucia said. "But I had to turn it down, because of Sensei. Sensei wants me to teach at his place. If I stayed and had dinner, I'd be obligated to do that. I want to teach self-defense in my own place, as far away from Sensei as I can get. When it comes to being a true martial artist, he's one of the absolute best—he doesn't let anything come between him and his art. But as a teacher and a human being, forget it. He was insulting and verbally abusive to me, and to anybody else he doesn't like. I can't tolerate that. Li-Loh doesn't seem to mind. They go back to Vietnam. They came back with Mr. Delise."

Andy said, "You were right, by the way, about Mr. Delise's safe. Tommy said they were supposed to get him to open it and give this document to Shi-Bin, about having shares in the Pickle Factory."

Lucia paused for a while. "Shi-Bin is another reason I want to stay away. He's trouble. Remember that class I told you about, where he 'honored' CeCe with his punch? Before it started, Shi-Bin bragged that I'd had sex with him. What I have to offer, I want to offer to women, in my own way." She shook her head. "Funny about that safe. CeCe and I would ask Mr. Delise what was in it, and he'd say different things every time. It's never been cracked. It's built so solidly into the wall, you'd have to tear the restaurant down to pull it out."

"Did he ever open it while you were there?"

She shook her head again. "Not once."

Andy paused at the bottom of the steps before the steel door. "Well, we're all dressed up, I could use some food. Where can we go?"

"No place around here," Lucia said. "Li-Loh's got a piece of just about every place in the area. It can't get back to Li-Loh that we turned him down personally to eat at one of his places on our own. That's the kind of insult that would hurt."

"We'll go back to my car then," Andy said.

Lucia pushed open the door and then stopped. "Andy," she began, "I'm going to close this door behind me and I want you to promise to do what I tell you."

Andy waited for Lucia to move so she could go through the doorway, but Lucia blocked the way.

"I want you to stay here and don't open the door until I tell you."

Andy said, "Lucia—"

"And *don't* call the cops."

Andy looked over Lucia's head. The blue van with the painted windows was parked fifty feet away. A man in a white windbreaker leaning on a cane—no, a battered golf club—stood outside the van. As Andy pushed past Lucia, the van's headlights flashed on. Andy squinted and put her hand over her eyes. She closed the door behind her and saw the man with the cane limp toward Lucia, then stop about ten feet from her and whip his cane around in several fast, almost choreographed moves. Then he bowed to Lucia.

"Hello, Shi-Bin," Lucia said carefully.

With one hand on the cane, Shi-Bin motioned Lucia to step forward.

Lucia didn't move. Shi-Bin motioned her again. Then he looked back at the seven young men of varying heights and thickness who had stepped out of the van and were drawing closer.

"Time for a demonstration, Lucia," he said in a beautifully melodious voice, almost like a radio announcer's.

Lucia still didn't move.

Shi-Bin took a step closer. Andy saw that his nose had been broken, his upper lip had been torn and had healed improperly, and that his chin and lips were spotted with stubble. "How are we going to do a demonstration if you leave me out here alone?" Shi-Bin asked playfully.

Lucia said nothing. Andy thought she could hear the sound of metal dragging along concrete somewhere to her left. She remembered she had her cell phone in her shoulder bag and that all she had to do was reach into it—

Shi-Bin whipped the golf club around and Lucia dropped into a crouch, her left foot slightly forward of her right. Shi-Bin's men gave the kind of high-pitched giggles that suggested they were on drugs.

Shi-Bin tapped his golf club on the asphalt. "Did I scare you, Lucia?"

"Let us go," Lucia said.

Shi-Bin gaped in astonishment. "Oh, you can speak. It's nice that you can speak. Maybe you'll scream, too. Just like your mother."

Andy heard Lucia take a quick, sharp breath.

"You'll go *oh-oh* before I honor your face. Quick little scream." He glanced back at his men. "Don't want to wake up the neighborhood."

Lucia tensed as she said, "Did you hurt her, Shi-Bin?"

"Everybody around here blames Asians for their problems. They say we have nothing better to do but make trouble. Who knows?" He grinned at his men. "They could be right."

He looked at Andy. "Who's the girlfriend, Lucia? She looks like she wants to fuck me because she's tired of fucking you, okay?" He moved the golf club. "She wants something hard up those legs for a change?"

Andy told him to fuck himself.

"After we have a demonstration," Shi-Bin said. "Lucia and I must demonstrate to my guys who is the most peaceful, okay? Then," he eyed Andy, "we go for a ride and I will fuck you, and my guys will fuck you and maybe even fuck Lucia, too, if there's anything left to fuck. Okay?"

His men giggled again. Shi-Bin motioned one of them toward Andy. The man carried an aluminum broomstick. Andy moved her hand toward her shoulder bag and Shi-Bin said, "Look-ee there, guys. Think she's got a gun? Not very peaceful. Think Moe can break her before she gets it?"

Lucia said, "Andy, get back—" as Moe whipped the broomstick up over his head and brought it down in a curving arc. Andy swung her shoulder bag up to where the end of the handle should have been. The light from the headlights dazzled her eyes and she heard something make a thick, dense thud against the steel door, followed by the clang of the metal broomstick hitting the concrete.

A few feet to Andy's right, a short youth lay dazed, on his back against the bottom of the steel door. Between Andy and the youth stood Lucia, with the end of the broomstick pointed at Moe's throat. Moe tried to grab the broomstick. Lucia leaned away and brought the stick up and down, smacking it painfully across Moe's mouth. Then she spun and thrust the stick firmly between Moe's legs. Before he could pull in his legs from the pain, Lucia whipped the stick into a sharp arc that ended with the stick pointed in the opposite direction, at Shi-Bin.

"Leave us alone," Lucia said to Shi-Bin.

Andy saw Moe roll away from the door into a fetal ball, one hand on his crotch, the other over his mouth.

"You're too nervous, Lucia," Shi-Bin said, using the handle of his golf club to scratch his nose. "Moe was just giving you—"

He brought the club up in a backhanded uppercut. The metal end of the sand wedge would have shattered Lucia's chin if she hadn't stepped back. Shi-Bin lunged forward, stabbing the wedge downward at the center of Lucia's chest, but Lucia had moved to the side and brought the broomstick crashing against Shi-Bin's leg.

The stick made a loud *thwack* as it bounced off what sounded like a heavily padded brace enclosing Shi-Bin's bad knee. Shi-Bin snagged

Lucia's right ankle with the end of the sand wedge. He pulled sharply and would have swept Lucia off her feet, but Lucia just rocked back on her left shoe, raising her foot so that the wedge slid harmlessly away.

She brought that foot down, spun and aimed a kick at Shi-Bin's chest. Shi-Bin brought his sand wedge down in a fast arc that would have broken Lucia's knee, if her knee had been in the way.

But Lucia's kick had only been a feint. In the second that Shi-Bin's attention was on the kick, Lucia struck like a baseball slugger going for the kind of grand-slam home run that would put the ball out of the stadium, across the Delaware and as far away as Cherry Hill, maybe even Haddonfield.

The blow made a loud, jarring smack against Shi-Bin's left ear, knocking the white baseball cap off his head. Shi-Bin wilted slightly and Lucia followed that with a kick to his left side, pushing him down to the asphalt where Andy expected him to fall flat and lie still.

But as Shi-Bin fell, he pulled his body into a ball. Unlike Moe, who still lay with both hands on his bleeding mouth beside the door (which was now ajar), Shi-Bin rolled forward, the golf club in his hands. He bounced off the asphalt and came to his feet, using the sand wedge to stop him from wobbling.

Then Andy heard two rapid hand claps that were so loud they echoed off the shopping strip's glass windows. She saw Ishimura standing a few feet from the open door, his hands clasped.

"Stop!" he shouted. "Finish!"

Shi-Bin, the left side of his head slick with blood, turned to Ishimura, planted his golf club to steady himself and bowed.

"No more fight," Ishimura said. "No reason."

"I have a reason," Lucia said. She whipped the broom across the top of Shi-Bin's chest, knocking him backward. He broke the fall by slapping his arms on the ground. Before he could recover, Lucia brought the end of the broomstick down on Shi-Bin's nose, smashing it flat. Then she put the end of the broomstick on his left wrist, pinning it to asphalt, while bringing the pointed heel of her shoe down on the right wrist that had been clutching the sand wedge. Shi-Bin yelped and released the golf club. With one hand gripping the broomstick, Lucia kept him pinned as she grabbed the club and flung it in the air at Shi-Bin's gang, They scattered and the sand wedge banged loudly into the side of the van.

Lucia was panting as she stepped off Shi-Bin's hand. "You come anywhere near me, my mother, my friends or anybody I know," she said, "and I will make sure you never walk again."

Ishimura walked slowly toward them. Andy followed. Shi-Bin's face was a rigid mask of suppressed agony. His nose gurgled blood.

"Move back," Ishimura said to Lucia. She complied.

Andy pulled out her cell phone, and then felt Ishimura's roughly calloused hand on hers. She felt a sharp pain in her thumb as he popped the phone out of her hand and dropped it back into her shoulder bag.

"No calls," he said. He stood over Shi-Bin. "Up!"

Shi-Bin fixed his eyes on Lucia. He pulled himself painfully to one side, spat out blood that had dripped into his mouth, then pushed himself up with his hands and his good leg.

"Face each other," Ishimura commanded.

Lucia didn't move. Shi-Bin slowly turned to face Lucia.

"Lucia honor Shi-Bin," Ishimura said. "Lucia do not honor herself. Lucia break rules. To hit when match is over is not honor."

"How dare you!" Lucia said. "This was no match!"

"All confrontation a match, in one way or other," Ishimura said. He pointed to the pinhole TV camera above the steel door. "I see everything on TV. Shi-Bin challenge, you no accept. Shi-Bin student challenge, you accept. Shi-Bin defend student."

"He said he was going to gang-rape us," Andy said. "That's no challenge. That's a threat. We put people in jail for making threats like that."

Ishimura dismissed that. "He make noise. Big noise, little noise. Girls believe noise because they make so much of it."

"Lucia," Andy said, "we've just been insulted. I don't have to listen to insults from . . . little men."

She watched him turn slowly toward her, and she was ready for him with her secret weapon, the Cosicki Intimidation Beam, a stare of such utter loathing and contempt that it could reduce the most repugnant male to slime. She hit Ishimura with everything she had and saw his eyes widen slightly, then look away. "You," he said, "have much to learn."

"Ditto," Andy said.

Lucia flung the broomstick away. "C'mon, Andy. We're going."

Ishimura turned to Lucia. He said, "Sempai," and Shi-Bin almost fell over.

Lucia took a deep breath. Andy could almost hear her counting to ten. "Yes, Sensei."

"What I see," Ishimura said, "your technique is much improved. Must work more hard on balance, and to keep the back straight when attacking but, on the whole, you fight good. You come to dojo tomorrow. Teach Sunday class."

"No, Sensei," Lucia said.

Ishimura sucked air between his teeth. "I'm sorry. I am not hearing good?"

"Too much noise," Lucia said. She turned and glided away.

12 one man's trash

Andy caught up with Lucia at the edge of the parking lot.

Her best friend in the whole world wasn't gliding. Lucia took heavy steps with her shoulders hunched forward, her arms wrapped tightly around her.

"Lucia," Andy said, "that was amazing."

"That was a mistake," Lucia grumbled. "I should have ignored him."

"I would have hurt him more."

"You would," Lucia muttered. She crossed the street without looking. "If I was smarter, I would have seen through him. I would have understood why he was making noise. Now I've made things worse. Now he's going to want to get back at me." She shivered.

"What else could you have done? He wouldn't have let you ignore him. He had his gang to impress. He would have kept threatening you until you hit back."

"I didn't have to hit *back*. I wanted to kill Shi-Bin. I wanted to stick the end of my weapon in his neck and crush his larynx until he choked to death. I wanted to bash his teeth in and shove the weapon down his throat. I wanted to smash his skull."

"You did."

"I didn't. I flattened the blow against his ear and split the skin," she straightened. "The one thing I got from Sensei Ishimura was it's okay to do anything *but* kill your opponent. You want him to live because"—she imitated Ishimura's accent—" 'to live is what peace all about.' Shi-Bin's going to have an ugly ear for the rest of his life."

"His nose won't look so good either." Andy put her hand on Lucia's shoulder. "You did great. Let's call Vinnie and get Shi-Bin in jail right now."

"Vinnie would make things worse," Lucia said.

"Stop that," Andy said. "I want to hear, right now, what it is you have against Vinnie. Okay, so he threw you over for CeCe. That was stupid, but guys do that all the time, and he was a teenager then, so what did he know?"

"Vinnie knows plenty."

"And he's still around. He likes your mother. He's the most decent cop I've ever met. He looks good. He cares for you—you know that. So what's the problem? How come, every time I bring him up, you act like he's the worst person in the world?"

Lucia's makeup was running and she had her hands over her face to hide her tears.

She's been in a fight, Andy told herself, remembering the fights she had been in. When you get into a fight, it stays with you, even if you're not hurt. You can say things you don't mean.

They were in sight of Lucia's mother's house. After a few minutes, Lucia told Andy that she didn't feel like eating, that she'd rather see her mother in the hospital before visiting hours were over.

Andy offered to drive her.

"I can walk," Lucia said.

"My car is up the block," Andy said.

"You can't walk to it by yourself?" Lucia snapped irritably. "What are you afraid of?"

"With you on the same side of the street," Andy said, "I'm not afraid of anything."

Lucia put her arm in Andy's and walked her to the car. On the way to the hospital, Andy asked Lucia if she was sure she was okay, if she wasn't hungry and she wasn't going to kill anybody soon.

"No to all three," Lucia said. "I have to show my mother how I look. She'll be impressed."

Andy waited until Lucia went through the glass doors. She thought of her own mother and let the car slowly move forward.

She turned her cell phone on and saw the messages from her mother. She didn't listen to any of them.

The entrance ramp opened up onto Broad Street. At the light, Andy could do an illegal *U*-turn to head north, but she caught the glimpse of a police cruiser. She didn't want a moving violation, even if the guy writing the ticket might be Vinnie Ferko.

She turned right, back into Westyard, got lost but saw, rising above the row houses, the ten-story tower of the Pickle Factory. The building had been trimmed with decorative sconces that splashed light on the old brick. The windows glowed at night with a faintly green tint. Though it was in the next neighborhood over, the tower remained visible above Westyard's smaller row houses. Andy used the tower as a landmark as she drove the maze of narrow, switchbacking one-way streets.

Finally she made a quick right turn, stopped at a traffic light, and there it was, just across Washington Avenue, with parking valets, security guards and green uniformed doormen scurrying along a line of cars and cabs beneath a curving, dark green porte cochere that thrust out over what was still recognizable as the factory's loading dock.

And who should be at the front door, throwing a temper tantrum? The man who knew everybody, the man who could get anybody on the phone, the *Press*'s most important columnist, the man in a white dinner jacket and a blue Hawaiian shirt, ladies and gentlemen, Chilly Bains!

The light changed and she drove onto Washington Avenue, found a parking space about thirty yards from the line of cars waiting for the Pickle Factory parking valets, locked her car and took long, loping strides toward the front door.

Bains, his red stacked hair stuffed into a black cap with CHILL on the bill, spied her. "Where *were* you?" he cried breathlessly, running toward her.

"Having tea," Andy said.

"Well, *I* showed up appropriately late, down to the minute, and there's some problem about which Ferko is supposed to let me in. Howard said I was to ask Ferko and he would tell them to let me in. But these . . . *green*heads," he gestured derisively to the uniformed doormen, "won't call up until I come up with his first name. Jack, Errol or Vincent. I mean, is there a *difference?!*"

"I hope so," Andy said. She raised her cell phone, touched the speed dialer and put the phone to her ear.

"This is Cosi," Charlotte Cosicki said.

"This is Andy."

"An*dre*ah! We're . . . speaking?"

"I'm in front of the Pickle Factory. Tell the guys downstairs to let me in."

"I will! This is excellent, exquisite. Take the elevator directly to the sky lobby. Top floor. I need you to do the biggest favor. Claus would so *love* it if you would interview him for your newspaper."

"Mom, I can't." She looked at Chilly. "There was a small item about him in the gossip column."

"That was about him picking up trash—it wasn't about him, as an artist. Just pretend that you're interested in him. As a journalist, I mean. The journalists here are paying too much attention to Lyssie Eagleman and he's jealous. You *are* dressed appropriately?"

"I'm in that black cocktail dress you got me."

"The one you couldn't sit down in?"

"I learned how to sit down in it."

"Shoes?"

"Half heights. The spikers are still in the closet."

"You'll find an occasion for them. I'm never wrong about wardrobe acquisitions. For tonight, the half height heels should be just about perfect. The purse to match?"

"I have my shoulder bag."

"Not that *cloth* thing . . . You can check that before you come in. Oh, Logan is coming in tomorrow and you're to pick him up at the airport. I'll give you the details about his flight when you come up."

"How come Logan didn't call me to pick him up?"

"He wanted his mother to get him. But she fired her chauffeur again and I am not driving her around this time. Not while I have an artist to look after."

"One thing, Mom," Andy said. "I'm coming in with somebody."

"Male or female?"

Andy glanced at Bains. "What's the difference?"

"If you have to ask, I imagine there is none."

Andy closed the phone.

Chilly Bains almost pounced. "We're in?"

Andy nodded.

"Hoy, hoy!" Bains said.

She saw the doorman pick up a green and gold telephone at a rostrum just inside the entryway. The doorman looked at Andy and grinned. "Your mother said I'd know it was you, Ms. Cosicki." He noticed Bains. "You're not taking him in with you?"

Bains bowed extravagantly, kissed her hand and said, "Dahhhling!"

"He'll behave," Andy said.

They went into a narrow lobby trimmed in grayish green serpentine stone. At the center, near a set of black, straight-backed chairs that seemed too uncomfortable to sit in, a giant bonsai cucumber plant rose out of an old pickle barrel.

Bains ignored the plant. He gazed upward and said, "Oh my *God!*"

Andy looked up and didn't see God. The lobby opened into an atrium extending all the way to the building's ceiling. Fixed to the wall above the elevators, between the top floor balcony and the ground floor bank of elevators, was a towering collection of trash sheathed in clear panels.

No. Not exactly trash. She saw a few dingy, torn pages from the *Philadelphia Press* among the junk.

Bains pulled a piece of paper out of his jacket. "I got a press release about this." He opened up the paper. "What Claus Fontini does is 'create nonfigurative environments with indigenous organic substances. In this installation at the Pickle Factory, a joint project developed by Point Man/NFA, LLP, the artist collected leaves, weeds, newspapers, junk mail, organic refuse and a single cardboard jacket of singer Frank Sinatra's *Songs for Swinging Lovers,* and added these in a glass case, six inches deep, fifteen feet wide and sixty feet tall.' "

"Does it have a name?" Andy asked.

"Autumn Sinatra. It says here, this is the biggest Fontini there is. Tonight, he's supposed to add several caustic chemicals and some anaerobic bacteria cultures, and then seal up the top so its airtight—though there will be some one-way emergency air valves vented to the outside so the piece doesn't explode. Then, over a period of several years, the sculpture will 'evoke an everchanging visual interplay of natural and man-made processes on local materials.' This is so Vegas!"

He removed a sound recorder from his dinner jacket. "Thanks so much for getting me in? How about we kiss and make up?" He stood on his tip-toes, his lips puckered.

Andy blasted him so severely with Intimidation Waves that he rocked back onto his heels.

"Won't stoop to conquer, eh? No matter." He slid a card into Andy's hand. She read:

OFFICIAL CHILLY BAINS ONE-ACT COURTESY CARD

* * * * * * *

The bearer has been of service to Chilly Bains, the world's first and only KLEPTOsexual columnist of the *Philadelphia Press*. This card entitles the bearer to one act of publicity, kindness, generosity, publicity or benign neglect to be determined by Chilly Bains and the bearer at the time of the bearer's request.

Andy was about to tell him she would never, ever want anything from him when Bains said, "Read the fine print."

She did: *Non-transferrable. Expires after one year, or when Chilly Bains forgets who you are, whatever comes first. No second acts, please!*

The elevator door opened and Bains rushed in. Andy followed him but he put up his hands before she could enter the car.

"I always arrive alone!" he pleaded.

Andy stepped in beside him. "That'll make two of us."

The elevator car reminded her of those she had ridden in the hospital to visit Lucia and her mother. It had two sets of doors, one you stepped into at the bottom and another set in what would have been the back that would open up when you arrived.

"Five, four, three, two . . ." Chilly counted out the floors as the elevator ascended. "The rocket is waiting to take off!"

The car's rear doors opened onto what might have been the moon, or some version of a lunar habitat: a large, open area much wider than a hall, in quietly cruel industrial tones of gray, white, black and brushed chrome. In the center of a field of gray-and-white-striped carpet was a cluster of luminous, translucent marshmallows—chairs, evidently, because some of the men and women in gray and black, loose-fitting if not completely shapeless, tummy-and-butt-reducing ensembles were sitting on these marshmallows, holding drinks in disposable plastic cups.

Others were milling about, wandering through the open doors of the three apartments on this level, or clustered around a bar along an aluminum wall from which hung a brightly playful blue, lavender and green neon light wall sculpture, or in front a flat TV screen playing a documentary of a thin, frantic man in grimy brown coveralls gathering garbage on the city streets.

Only one person in the group wore anything with color: an arresting gold, green and vermillion Florentine wrap that began below her tanned, rounded shoulders, undulating over the sweepingly narrow contours of her waist and flaring out into a floor-length dress ending in sharply pointed shoes that made it appear that her feet were floating an inch off the ground.

There was nothing physically striking about the woman. She had attained the age, and surgical enhancements, to be "ageless," not young, not anyone's idea of a hot babe, and yet capable of drawing attention from every male in the place, especially the gay ones.

She had several men buzzing around her, smiling and nodding as she made quick, delicate gestures with her fingers. Among the men was another woman: short, rounded in a painfully tight black dress, candy red purse and matching shoes that made her feet look really, really big. Her arms were folded defensively across her chest, with one hand brandishing a small sound recorder.

Beside her slouched an impeccably groomed, broad-shouldered man in a gorgeous, gray sportcoat and a black, high-necked knit shirt. He held his face attentively. He seemed to be listening to the woman in the vermillion dress and his eyes scanned the room restlessly until they found Andy.

When you sleep with someone for a while, you not only learn how this person expresses emotions that would normally be hidden from public view, but you also recognize how this person might hide his surprise, shock and confusion.

And so, Drew Shaw, who was a vigorous if occasionally conceited lover of Andrea Cosicki when he was a mere senior editor at *Liberty Bell Magazine,* who went on to end the relationship when he began the positional jockeying and political power-playing that eventually brought him the top editor's chair, expressed surprise, shock and confusion, and then tried very hard to hide it.

Then she saw that the short woman in the tight black dress and the awful shoes who was standing close enough to him to be "with" him, was Barbara "Bombarella" Ellerbaum, *Liberty Bell Magazine*'s chronicler of the "bitchin' famous."

Now it was Andy's turn to hide her shock, disgust and the creeping blush of a former lover who, against every strategy of self-control, could imagine several scenarios in which a dour Drew Shaw might confess that in so abruptly dumping Andy he had made the worst mistake of his life, and that he was willing to put up with her being taller than he was and getting more attention than he got when they walked into a room, if she would just take him back. . . .

Of course, Drew could *begin* to redeem himself if he stepped forward and introduced Andy to the woman in vermillion.

Okay, Drew, Andy thought, now's your chance. Let's pretend that people who have slept together have little cell phones in their brains. Listen to what I'm thinking: I want you to smile and say something like, "Excuse me for interrupting, but this is my clever, insightful, earnest, interesting, talented, wonderful friend, Andy Cosicki . . ."

Drew didn't move, but Bombarella—her eyes and sound recorder still directed at the woman in vermillion—gave Drew a possessive clasp on his butt.

Worse yet, the woman Bombarella was interviewing had noticed Andy and was giving Andy a two-second friend-or-foe scan. Andy needed some kind of devastatingly witty entrance line that would simultaneously introduce her as a person worthy of the woman's attention and put Drew Shaw and Bombarella in their proper place, which was, as far as Andy was concerned, with the garbage that the artist did NOT think was worthy enough to become art.

Then she felt a breeze beside her and Chilly Bains swept by her, slipped into the ring of male admirers and said, "Lyssie, you are positively a *goddess* tonight!"

The ring of admirers closed around him and Andy was left standing there, until, just a second later, she felt a hand on her shoulder and saw the surgically enhanced face of her mother swim into view.

"An*drey*ahhhh!"

"Mom, you said the *artist* wants to meet me?" Andy fired a salvo of Intimidation Waves at Drew. "Let me at him. Now."

13 just looking

Ladderback knew from the echoing sound of the idling engine that the bus was parked in an enclosed space, most likely the bus terminal that most of the Atlantic City casinos were supposed to have.

He kept his eyes shut because he could not be sure if some areas in the terminal were open to the sky. Ladderback's agoraphobia kicked in when he found himself without a roof over his head, or when he was near a window with a view of open space.

The symptoms had begun in his youth and soon shaped his life. He now commuted to the newspaper's newsroom by walking through the subway concourses and underground shopping mall below the *Press* Building on Market Street and the subbasement of his Locust Street apartment building. In that building, safe inside his tiny studio apartment (whose windows had been covered by bookshelves), he could accept deliveries of his groceries and order other purchases over the telephone and the Internet. He could also satisfy whatever curiosity he had about the world by surfing the Internet or watching television, videotapes and DVDs. Somehow, he had to be near the outdoors to fear it. Seeing it on a screen did not bother him.

He could endure occasional travel in taxis and buses if he kept his eyes shut and forced himself to think of anything other than the anxious, panicky, nerve-shattering vulnerability in being outdoors. He could achieve a tooth-grinding sense of calm as long as the vehicle was moving. When it stopped, he dreaded the moment when he had to open his eyes and find out exactly where he was.

This time, he looked out the bus's window a short, plump, ebullient, smiling fellow filling out a gold, crimson and green fleurs-de-lis-encrusted Frontenac Casino Hotel windbreaker. The fellow stood just outside the idling bus in an enclosed terminal that offered no glimpses of the evening sky.

The bus greeter handed each arriving passenger a packet of coupons and then motioned that person toward the brightly lit entryway leading toward the casino.

Ladderback lifted his satchel, buttoned and belted his raincoat, planted his hat firmly on his head and took a position behind the woman who had helped him across the street back in Philadelphia. He followed her across the terminal into a corridor of gaudy, fleurs-de-lis-flecked carpet, throbbing pop music and murals of Paris in the style of Renoir, Utrillo and Toulouse-Lautrec.

He paused just before the first bank of slot machines and took an escalator leading upward to the restaurant level. From there, he followed signs to the Winged Victory Hotel.

Ladderback found the entrance to Winged Victory just past the Frontenac's Grand Canadian Buffet. He stepped through a curved, red and gold Romanesque archway and the casino's bright pinks and cotton-candy Renoir reds ended in a dark black walnut-paneled corridor with cracked, wing-shaped wall sconces and a mottled brown rug on a wood floor that creaked with every step. The air felt close, almost stale, as the bustling sounds of the casino faded behind him. Ladderback followed the corridor until it opened onto a mezzanine. He drew close to the balcony. Just above the balcony was a mosaic dome that was missing so many tiles that it had been "restored" by a coat of sky blue paint.

The dome framed a magnificent, twelve-foot-tall carved marble statute of a woman holding aloft an olive wreath, as a pair of eagles' wings thrust from her flowing, windswept robes.

Ladderback noted that the wreath had broken and been replaced with a coil of green plastic ivy. Pieces of the woman's stone fingers had cracked and fallen away, and there were holes in her sculpted head where a diadem might have fit.

But the statue still did what its sculptor had intended: it took your breath away with its quiet, righteous certainty. For a moment, Ladderback could imagine the veterans of the Great War coming to Atlantic City with their families. He could see them coming through the broad entrance to the lobby below and pausing, before they came to the hotel's registration, to recite the inscription: Victory Honors the Brave.

The hotel's lobby street entrance had been sealed. Where the front doors might have opened was now a blank, white wall. The marble top of the mahogany registration desk held stacks of playing cards and a cluster of battered coffee urns. The lobby's furniture was long gone. On the cracked marble floor stood several folding card tables and mismatched chairs. Some of the chairs were occupied by mostly ancient men and women hunched over arrangements of cards. One table had an especially fat youth with a single finger on the track ball of his laptop, a bowl of what appeared to be saltwater taffy on one side of the laptop, a mound of empty, crumpled taffy wrappers on the other.

Ladderback heard the faint, delicate snick and snap of playing cards in motion. From one table came the rippling of a shuffled deck. He went down a flight of marble stairs and straight to a woman playing on a laptop. He said he was looking for Osiris Jonathan Murphy. Was there a way to find him?

She pointed toward a dark-skinned man with a bushy beard who sat at a table. His eyes were aimed straight ahead while his hands moved over rows of cards.

The green felt on the table had worn and frayed in some places and the cards were covered with small, raised ridges. Before moving a card, the man brushed his fingers over those ridges.

His eyes didn't move. He wore an old pinstriped suit jacket with patches on the sleeves and faded brown corduroy pants. Against the table was a long staff ending in a pointed rubber tip.

The man arranged the cards in what resembled a Russian Orthodox cross.

The man rubbed his thumb on the face of each card he dealt. Cards that couldn't be paired were added to the cross. When the cross was complete, subsequent cards went into a smaller pile, facedown.

"It's not polite to stare at a blind man," the man said suddenly.

"I apologize," Ladderback said quickly. "I was just—"

"Looking?" The man grinned.

"I am looking for—"

"I heard you the first time. Sit with me."

Ladderback lifted a small folding chair and put it close to the table. He sat slowly, placing his satchel beside him. Then he watched the man's fingers move the cards.

"I hope you're not in a hurry because we don't hurry around here," the man said.

"They're called patience games," Ladderback replied.

"You know what's most appealing about this game?"

"That there are more ways of losing than winning," Ladderback said, "so that when one wins, one experiences an emotional uplift."

"Not for me." The man lowered his voice. "I listen to the cards."

Ladderback was not sure if he should ask for an explanation.

"Mostly I pass the time," the man added. He played a few more cards. Then he withdrew the deuce of diamonds. "Oh, that's too bad," he said as he removed the jack.

"Mr. Murphy is a friend," Ladderback said.

The man tossed in the cards and pushed them into a deck. "The less you tell me, the more I can hear from the cards." He began to deal the cards in a cross. His fingers found the king of diamonds. "This is your friend and this . . . is you." He put the king of clubs on the table near Ladderback. He shuffled the deck and arranged the cards in a cross with the king of diamonds at the center.

"My mother was born with the sight," the man continued. "She said I had it, too, but, as a young fellow, I never placed much faith in it. I was the fool that wants to believe but won't let himself because he's afraid to be caught out a fool."

Ladderback shifted uncomfortably.

"Come the war, I am in a tent, in a foreign land, camping out in hostile territory, playing a game to pass the time, when I saw myself in the cards. You hear me? Without looking for it, I saw that an important event would occur." He touched the back of his head.

"You were injured?"

"A mortar round during an armed conflict. Do you know the difference? The United States has never lost a war. An armed conflict is a game that is played out, without a clear victory or defeat. Except for myself: the impact detached one optic nerve, messed the other. I'm not completely in the dark, but close to it."

He examined the arrangement of the cards, then dealt five cards across the bottom of the cross, facedown. Moving from right to left, he turned the cards over, pausing on the last card, which was in front of Ladderback.

"Now the pattern I am feeling here suggests that there's something you want to know and it isn't what the cards say."

"This armed conflict you're describing was in Vietnam?"

"I was in Laos on an incursion, but we used Vietnam as our mailing address."

Ladderback removed from his satchel files he had printed out from last night's Web search. "During your tour of duty, did you hear anything about the Research and Studies Annex? It was known as RASA and it was responsible for covert, deniable operations against North Vietnam."

"What you're asking isn't important."

"I would be grateful for anything you can tell me," Ladderback said.

"Before I went to Vietnam, I went through basic training," he replied. "I learned what every solider had to learn, from the grunts all the way up to the officers: how to take an M16 automatic rifle apart in the dark, clean it and put it back together. I remember making a clever comment about how, if I had to fix my weapon in the dark, there was no way in hell I would fire it because I wouldn't be able to see what I was shooting at. The military being the military, the cleverness of my remark was not appreciated. Now, every day, in my apartment, I take apart, inspect, clean and reassemble an M16 automatic rifle. This particular rifle has been altered so it will never be fired. I will keep no live ammunition in my quarters. But I take apart and reassemble that rifle every day because I am proud that I can do it." He paused. "There. That is something that you needed to hear."

"I thank you for telling me this. Shall we call each other by our names?"

"My name is William Teasdale. Please don't call me Blind Willy."

"It is a genuine pleasure to meet you, Mr. Teasdale," Ladderback said after introducing himself.

"A pleasure to be met by you, Mr. Ladderback." Teasdale touched the cards, then withdrew his hand. "When I arrived, RASA was ancient history."

"But some operations were still active."

"From what I heard, RASA's mission was to create anti-Cong radio broadcasts, leaflet drops and a curious form of counterinsurgency. They would gather up Cong POWs and civilians they knew were spying for Hanoi and take them to what was purported to be an anti-Cong training camp."

"The Beach of Good Choice," Ladderback said.

"I was told that it was on an island. These inductees would be trained in guerrilla tactics and made part of a cult of some kind."

"The Staff of Life," Ladderback said. "The symbol of the movement was deliberately commonplace: a stick, a staff, a bamboo pole. They were taught to use it as a weapon."

Teasdale touched his staff. "It doesn't take much imagination to turn objects into weapons."

"From my researches on the Internet," Ladderback went on, "the RASA commander who came up with the concept for the Staff of Life counterinsurgency, got the idea from watching an American soldier from Philadelphia teaching Vietnamese children how to play stickball.

This same soldier is one of the reasons that several Vietnamese settled in Philadelphia after the war."

"Angelo Delise," Teasdale said.

"You met him?"

"He was before my time. But many Vietnamese I had the pleasure to meet had learned the game from him as children. They were teenagers when I fought beside them and they were very brave. In sharing that simple game with them, Corporal Delise did a great deal of good. There were many soldiers like Corporal Delise. The good we did in Vietnam was never recognized, never understood, never considered in the accounts of the war that followed our return."

"I have never heard the war described that way," Ladderback said.

"I am speaking of people who were strangers, coming to understand that they were not so strange. This understanding far outweighs the disgraceful acts of those who used the war to serve their own purposes."

He gathered the cards and slipped them into a worn cardboard box. Then he stood and, using his staff to guide him past the tables, went to a battered armoire placed against a wall of the old lobby. He opened the armoire, revealing great stacks of card decks, some arranged on small shelves, others locked in glass cases.

Ladderback stood near him. He remembered that the article he had read about the Patience Society mentioned an assortment of playing cards "rumored to be of great value." He asked if this was the society's collection.

"You're looking at it. We have cards from all over. Some are very old. Some of them have been touched by all kinds of people. A lot of our members are playing on computers now, but most prefer cards, because the time you spend shuffling provides a chance to think, to rest the mind, to touch and feel."

He ran his fingers along the shelves. "Our members bring cards from every place they go. I have been told there are decks here from gambling clubs in London, and from a truck stop in Pennsylvania. The ones with the holes drilled in them, we get for free. They come from the casino—it's the law, the casino has to drill a hole into every deck it discards so the cards can't be played in the casino again. But we can play them as long as they last. When they can't be played anymore, we put them here." He touched a shelf at the very bottom. "We let them rest."

He put his deck on the shelf above that. Ladderback saw that the shelf was marked MARKED.

"I will be honored, William," Ladderback said, "if you will let me help you back to wherever it is you're going."

"No need for that," Teasdale said, sliding the tip of his cane on the floor. "I know where I'm going. You're in a much more difficult situation."

Could Teasdale know about his agoraphobia? "What difficulty is that?" Ladderback asked.

Teasdale grinned. "You're still looking. Be patient. He'll find you." With that, he touched his staff, back and forth, as he made his way through a dim and dismal hallway beneath the staircase that led to the casino.

Ladderback went to the chair to grab his satchel. When he turned back, Teasdale was gone.

Claus Fontini had thinning, bleached hair, a drooping yellow mustache and coffee-stained teeth. He wore a bone-colored suit with a wilted, stomped-on cigar butt pinned to his lapel where a flower should have been. A native of Holland, he was still annoyed at the Pennsylvania Dutch restaurant that the eager members of the Arts Council had taken him to earlier that evening.

"Pennsyfahnnia *Deutch* is not Dutch," he sputtered. He sneered at Andy. "You don't like the piece."

Charlotte Cosicki raked her daughter with Cosicki Intimidation Waves. Andy removed a pad from her shoulder bag and said, "No. Actually. I'm trying to understand it."

"What's to understand?" he began. "I have spent a week walking your city at different times of the night and day, gathering objects that are unwanted, unused, discarded, unattractive, rotten and disgusting, and because I have gathered it, and put it here, it is what it was, but something more. When I put them into the case, they will become something else." He watched her write that down. Then he stuck his hand in the bag and pulled out a great glob of wet trash. "You want some? Don't say no. The art isn't just in the result. Because I have chosen this, it has a value now. You must take some home now. There is no choice. That, too, is part of the art. And it is part of the money."

"Oh, Claus," Charlotte responded on cue, "*must* you bring up money?"

He became indignant. "She wants to understand. I am to explain. She is American. America is the richest country in the world and nobody in America has enough money. But America produces more waste, per person, than any other country at any time in the history of the world. These bags of materials—let us not call it trash—were gathered for the installation, but will not be used in the installation. What is not used the gallery can price and sell." He took out a white marking pen. "I sign the bag. So. Now worth money."

He wrote ART on the bag. Then: DO NOT DISTURB/38.

Charlotte sat on one of the marshmallow chairs, crossed her long legs and leaned forward. "Not long ago, a Fortini collection in the Do Not Disturb series sold for $5,000 at auction."

"Amazing? Not amazing. It doesn't matter," Fortini said grandly. "Whatever it was, it will be something more. After it is something more, it becomes something else. Because of me. There. That is all my story." He handed her the bag. "You take."

The bag stank. Andy said, "But—"

"Okay. You don't want? I make of you a bet. I bet you that you will find something in this bag that isn't trash. In any bag. If you find it, you must pay me. Something. I don't care what. But you must pay because the selection is my art. What I chose, why I chose—what do you say in America? Life is choices? These are my choices. This bag . . ." He took out a Blackberry handheld from his jacket. "I record precisely where and when I am when I gather materials. I record what I see and hear, and what I feel, because that is part of the art."

"It is in Dutch but I translate." He read. "Tuesday night, Russell

Street. A one-direction traffic street in part of city called Westyard. It is very windy. I hear, over the wind, the sound of televisions inside the houses on the street. And on the street, in the sky, I see birds overhead. Winter gulls. I hear voices arguing. Loud voices. The sound of hitting. Is this the violence for which America is so famous. I feel fear. I am only here to take what is not wanted. Should I give assistance? I go toward the voices but I stop. A man runs into the street. He is chasing something, a white piece of paper in the wind. The paper is like a bird in the wind. It is always out of his reach. He gives up and turns back. I ask, again, should I give assistance? I look. Is anyone else giving assistance? There is no one. I see the piece of paper this man was chasing. I go to that. Do I want it? I pick it up and I hear sirens. Police. This is not a safe place. I take what I can, and go."

He put the device back in his pocket. "There. What you have is not trash. It is history."

Charlotte beamed. "She will be *delighted* to take it, won't you, dear?"

Andy was going to say she'd rather not when Charlotte put the bag in her daughter's hand and hustled her away.

"Wait here," she said.

Andy looked back at the crowd, at Lyssie Eagleman surrounded by her courtiers and a short man that her mother had identified as State Senator Henry Tybold, surrounded by his courtiers. Andy asked herself if she should ask the senator that question about development, or just let it go?

Yes. She decided she would ask Tybold about development, specifically, if he knew of an agreement made with the *ting hui* or *hui ting* or whatever it was, to build low-income housing in Westyard.

Then a male voice said, "Take out your trash?"

He was young, fidgety, long-limbed and almost tall enough to look her in the eye. He wore the standard art-crowd black, but it looked wrong on him, as if he really belonged in a button-down shirt but was trying to fake it in a black mock turtleneck.

"You might not be aware of it, but . . . I'm Errol Ferko," he said, flashing bleached teeth. "You're going to want to know me."

"I *am?*" She wanted to tell him that she knew his brother, but he wouldn't let her.

"Oh, I like that. You've got what we in Philadelphia call atty-tood. You're not from Philadelphia, I can tell. I saw you talking to that art fellow. Nobody from around here can talk to him. Most Philadelphians just don't have the sophistication. You're with the out-of-town media, I take it? Visiting Philadelphia for the first time?"

"Not really," Andy said. "I'm actually—"

"Well, you'd be surprised how easy it is to call Philadelphia home, if you're smart, if you know an opportunity when you see one and you can master the atty-tood." He put his hand on her back and nudged her toward a window that looked south over Westyard. She would have hit him with the garbage bag but he let his hand fall off as he positioned himself in front of the window and pointed toward the hospital.

For a moment, Andy forgot him and was taken up in the view. The night sky had clouded over and the moon showed feebly. Jets on their way to Philadelphia International Airport flew low overhead and the only signs of life were the flickering fires from distant oil refineries. She could see the vacant parking lot of the Good Choice Market and, about a mile to the south, the ungainly bulk of the Sisters of Zion Hospital rising like a brooding fortress, the EMERGENCY sign glowing malignantly at its base.

"Now you just follow that little alley back and, can you see that wide open space? It's an old factory but it's really a gold mine, and I'm involved in it. You can't say you heard it from me, but I can tell you, because I know you're the kind that knows an opportunity, that one of the 857 luxury dwellings I'm going to put there is going to have your name on it."

Was he for real? "You're putting them there?" Andy said skeptically.

"My father, who is over there talking with our state senator, and myself created what you're standing in. This is our work of art and, as he's approaching retirement age, it'll be just me taking the wheel of an exclusive, 100 percent secure, state-of-the-art $350 million public/private luxury residential, retail, entertainment enclave, complex that will break ground—I tell you again, you didn't hear this from me—in a matter of weeks."

"That's the meatpacking plant?" Andy asked.

He rubbed the side of his jaw. "We're calling it Veterans Plaza because we're doing it through a war veterans organization you probably haven't heard of. We can get funding earmarked for war veterans and non-profit development grants and get a whole mess of tax breaks, write-offs, write-downs, abatements, zoning adjustments—you name it, we're taking it, so we can pass the savings onto sophisticated individuals such as yourself, who are exactly the kind of people who grasp, on an instinctive level, the opportunity this kind of project affords."

Andy nodded, as if she was exactly that kind of person. "But didn't I hear that there was supposed to be a low-income element?" she said. "Didn't the developers make some kind of arrangement so that there would be housing units for Asian immigrants?"

He almost gagged. "*Low* income housing? Are you being . . . *humorous*?"

She made her skin crawl, the way he said that. "They made a deal. In exchange for buying shares in the Pickle Factory, an Asian community bank would get a low-income housing project off the ground."

He shook his head. "Hardly. There might have been a *rumor* about cutting some people a break, but . . . the person who would know is not with us anymore."

"Your Uncle Paul," Andy said.

"I don't have an uncle," he said, rubbing his jaw. "I don't believe I asked your name."

"You didn't," Andy said. She let the silence grow between them like the stench from the trash bag she held in her hand.

"Well . . . ," he said after a few seconds. "I still think you will want to take advantage, at preconstruction prices, of the opportunity that Veterans Plaza is going to be. I can assure you that the only Asian people you're going to see will be running the dry cleaning concession, and that's only if they meet our standards."

"You sure about that?" Andy said. "I don't have to ask Senator Tybold?"

He opened his arms wide, like a TV pitchman. "What I'm sure is, that for what it costs to live at the highest levels of privacy and exclusivity in this city, you're not going to find prices like these again." He gazed ahead at the darkness, rocking back on his heels, the knuckles of his long, bony fingers cracking as he nervously opened and closed his hands.

How is it that the same parents who produced the sincere, motorcycle-riding hunk whose children she could *consider* having, also came up with this phony, fidgeting, grasping slimeball?

"Uh, no thanks," she said, moving away from the window.

He followed her. "I told you, I wouldn't make this offer to just anyone. I'm quite selective about those I choose to surround myself with." He pulled out a business card and tried to push it into her hand until she stopped and opened the garbage bag.

"Drop it in here," Andy said.

His face went very cold, very fast. Then he looked down in the bag, stopped and looked again. "Excuse me. I think I see something—"

"Familiar?" Andy said. She pulled the bag out of his reach and got away from Errol Ferko as rapidly as possible. She told herself that if he followed her she would hit him with the trash and then her mother would get mad, so she'd better not hit him with the trash. Maybe she'd grab a stick and bash him on the head the way Lucia had taken care of Shi-Bin.

She was near the elevator when she turned around and saw that he wasn't following her. She heard a high, hiccuping laugh and saw Lyssie and Bombarella sharing a joke. Bombarella laughed—too loudly. Nothing could be that funny.

She found her mother. Charlotte reminded Andy about fetching Logo from the airport.

"What are friends for?" Andy said.

Charlotte rolled her eyes. "Can I at least *hope* you can get something about our artist in your newspaper?"

"Dear Mr. Action," Andy said. "Wherever I go in this city, I see garbage all over the place. How much is it worth, really?"

"Wholesale or retail?" Charlotte smiled at her.

14 double whammy

Ladderback didn't know how much time he spent wandering through aisles of noisy slot machines arranged in rows, in circles, on raised platforms, some crowned by signs that showed rapidly escalating numbers, some arranged in clusters with genuine automobiles perched above. Gaudy animated signs promising that one lucky pull put you in the driver's seat.

Ladderback had learned to drive and maintained a driver's license for identification purposes but, with agoraphobia, driving was no longer possible. He did not want to win an automobile. He found the casino appalling and went back to the Patience Society. Before he could ask a woman with a laptop if he could borrow a deck, she waved him away. He went to the armoire, and found a worn Bicycle deck. Before he could find an empty table, he saw a massive man in a red Phillies baseball cap and a shabby brown canvas hunting jacket examining a row of cards on a table.

Ladderback drew closer. He saw the broken nose, some uneven patches of skin that could be scars, a mouth that drooped at one end.

"Osiris Jonathan Murphy," Ladderback said.

"Neville Shepherd Ladderback," Murphy said without a hint of surprise, as if he had predicted the encounter.

" 'You have been in Afghanistan, I perceive,' " Ladderback said, quoting Sherlock Holmes's greeting of Dr. Watson.

" 'How on earth did you know that?' " Murphy quoted Watson's reply.

" 'Never mind,' " Ladderback recited Holmes's riposte. " 'The question now is about hemoglobin.' "

"Blood or money," Murphy said. "Didn't we once imagine, sometime before puberty, that every crime could be reduced to having the wrong kind of either?"

"Or both," Ladderback said.

Murphy looked up from the cards. "Teasdale should have warned me. You look old."

"I am old," Ladderback said.

"We should eat," Murphy said. He guided Ladderback through the casino to the Nanook of the North ice cream parlor. "We could eat a meal anywhere," Murphy said. "In this place, there's no crowd. We can get anything we want."

Ladderback scowled at the rows of banquettes set into fiberglass igloos. He averted his eyes and positioned himself away from the glass windows looking out on the Boardwalk.

Murphy ogled a waitress, a young woman in a hooded, low-cut, ludicrously fake sealskin cocktail dress and fishnet stockings with finger-sized plastic fish stuck in them. She told Murphy that it was a pleasure to see him again.

"Not as much as I get seeing you, babe," Murphy said. "Tonight I feel like a chocolate egg cream, to start. Then I want a big blob of crème brûlée on a hot Belgian waffle with a drizzle of sarsparilla sauce."

"Whipped cream?"

Murphy grinned at her. "Yeahhh." He waved a slip of paper. "This is a full food and beverage comp, Shep. You can order anything you want, anything you can think of. Doesn't have to be on the menu. Steak, lobster, stone-crab claws steamed in beer—if they can make it, you can have it."

"I will have coffee," Ladderback said. "Black."

"Food?"

"My bus will leave soon," Ladderback said.

"They have genuine Eskimo Pies here, Shep. They bring them out in foil wrappers. C'mon, Neville. Do something silly."

"You are the only person, aside from my parents, who ever called me Neville," Ladderback said. To the waitress: "Coffee is sufficient."

The waitress departed. Murphy sat back in the booth and watched Ladderback warily. They were "observing" each other. Ladderback studied Murphy's big, ugly nose. How many times had that nose been broken?

"Do you remember when you helped me with that gang of Germantown kids?"

Murphy rubbed the enlarged knuckles of his right hand. "I wanted to see if I could beat the crap out of them, and I did. I don't think you landed a single punch."

"What was important to me was that I had you on my side," Ladderback said. He saw interest flicker in Murphy's eyes.

The waitress set Ladderback's coffee before him. Murphy's egg cream arrived in a tall, frosted mug, with Ladderback's coffee.

"Delicious," Murphy said, taking a sip. "You know there's no egg in it? Of course you know. You always had that memory. Anything you saw or read, you could bring it back, right like that."

"Never as accurately as I wished," Ladderback said. "I write things down and I keep files."

"What you didn't have was the nuts. You know what I mean by nuts?"

"Poker slang for a winning hand."

"Not quite. In poker, the winning hand doesn't always win. To have the nuts, really and truly, is to be able to play the hand you're dealt, whatever hand you're dealt."

Ladderback was about to open his satchel when the waitress brought Murphy's waffle. Ladderback watched Murphy prod and poke it with his spoon. Murphy toyed with his food like a cat before pouncing.

Ladderback tasted the coffee. It wasn't quite as bitter as what he tended to get in Philadelphia. He remembered he had a file somewhere on Atlantic City's "award-winning" water supply. He asked Murphy if he had married.

"I live alone. You?"

"I also live alone," Ladderback said. "How do you earn a living?"

"I don't earn a living. Anything I want, I can get from a game."

As he watched Murphy cut his waffle into big, gooey pieces, Ladderback remembered the awkward evenings when Murphy's father, Michael, a fiercely honest plumbing contractor who never seemed to have any money, would come to the kitchen door of Ladderback's house to borrow cash from Ladderback's father. Michael Murphy would use the cash to settle his son's gambling debts, cover the doctor bills for those the son had injured in fights and, once, bail the son out of jail.

"Have you thought much about your father?" Ladderback asked.

Murphy shifted uncomfortably. "My father never respected what I could do. For him, it was all about what you did for others."

"He told my parents that he was very proud of you when you got into Drexel," Ladderback said.

"That was until I got busted for running a game," Murphy said. "At least your parents took it in stride when you told them you weren't going to college."

"They did not," Ladderback said. "They were horrified. I had to move out."

"You believed all that make-the-world-a-better-place crap."

"I still do," Ladderback said.

"You make the world better by writing obituaries?" Murphy looked at him archly.

"If I make small differences in people's lives, those differences are no less valid."

Murphy dismissed that. "Low-stakes games never interested me. When we were kids, I could make more money in one night at poker than my father made in a forty-hour workweek. I got into investigations for the same reason I got into poker. I like beating the bad guys."

"What happened to the man who wanted to be Sherlock Holmes?"

"We both wanted to be Sherlock Holmes," Murphy said. "But we had different theories about why he was so good at solving cases. You thought it was all about finding the clues, poking into places nobody else would, seeing things that others ignored. But me, I always thought Holmes was a great guesser. He was born with the nuts. He went into a case knowing pretty much who the bad guy was. What he didn't know was *how* he knew. The clues were just his way of confirming he was right."

"What about the stories in which Holmes erred?" Ladderback said.

"Exceptions to the rule," Murphy replied. "When Holmes screwed up, he did it because he didn't trust himself completely. You have to trust yourself, because you can't trust anybody else."

"He trusted Watson."

"Because he needed him. I never needed anybody."

"You worked for a commercial firm."

"Because, in government, it was only *incidental* if justice got done. That's why I got out of government and into a commercial accounting firm. But firms don't care if they're working for the devil. They just want to get paid."

"You still have contacts in law enforcement?"

"Those that don't want to lock me up, sure."

"Do you trust them?"

"No." Murphy finished the waffle and made a loud gurgling noise as he sucked the chocolate-flavored seltzer water of his egg cream through a straw. "Okay. I can't figure out, just by observing, why you came here," Murphy said.

Ladderback spent so much time thinking about his answer that Murphy put his head on the table and made loud snoring sounds.

"I want to gain a better understanding of accountants," Ladderback said.

"You're getting audited?"

Ladderback shook his head.

"I was an accountant who used to bust accountants," Murphy said. "The opportunity for creativity and invention in the field is amazing."

"I'm interested in the career of Paul Small."

Murphy grinned. "Hank Tybold's double-whammy man. You know what a whammy man is? It comes from walking-around money. Walking-around money is money from the government that a politician gives away, usually in small amounts—a couple of hundreds, a couple of thousands, maybe a hundred thousand sometimes—to arts groups, unions, charities, civic organizations, churches, schools, businesses and individuals. It serves a lot of purposes. At its lowest level, it's street money. It buys votes on election day. As you move up the food chain, it's a thank-you for voting, for making things happen or for not making things happen. You go up a little higher, it's a way of greasing wheels, a demonstration of power, of personal grandeur, of noblesse oblige. You go highest of all, the money gets washed, dried and otherwise laundered and goes right back to the politician.

"Every politician needs at least one whammy man who watches what goes where. He sits in, as a consultant, on these huge state and federal grants, funding issues and improvement projects. The Paul Small I remember was a consultant. He made sure there was no trail of evidence that connected him to Hank Tybold. Then, like a storefront accountant who tries to shave a few bucks off your tax bill, Paul Small would consult on big money projects crossing the senator's desk. He'd take a little bit out of this, a little of that, move money around and set it up so these little bits—which are not so little on these huge projects—end up functioning like walking-around money—went to the people and organizations that the Senator wanted them to go to, without it necessarily appearing that the Senator was behind it.

"It all ended up looking legal, or might as well be, and nobody really complained unless they thought they didn't get what they were expecting. That's when Paul Small would turn on the charm. He'd set up a meeting, there'd be talk back and forth, give-and-take. The senator's name was never mentioned, but Small would say, in effect, if you wanted your slice of the whammy pie, then you'd better ask not what your senator can do for you, ask what you can do for your senator."

Ladderback was quiet for a while.

Murphy filled the silence. "When I was with the Commonwealth Special Investigations Unit, there was some talk about going after Small, as a way to get to the senator. Some kid close to Small was selling bogus insurance policies out of a truck stop. We wanted to turn him to turn Small but the kid was unreliable. He claimed to have evidence that he didn't have. Something about the murder of some girl." He shrugged.

"Would that person be Errol Ferko?"

"Could've been. The name registers but it's amazing what you forget when you put your mind to it. I don't read newspapers now. I don't watch television. If people are killing each other on the other side of the world, or right around the block, I don't hear about it. I play cards. I have a happy life. You? You still doing obituaries?"

"I was considering doing Mr. Small's."

"Natural causes?"

Ladderback described the police report and how few wanted him to do the obituary.

"That's because nobody on the whammy food chain wants to admit that whammy guys exist."

"I would not have gone into such detail," Ladderback said.

"They don't know that. They're all afraid that someone is going to blow their big secret, when what really happens is, that the guy who finds out about the food chain gets on the food chain and keeps quiet after that. I've seen it happen too many times to guys that start out wanting to take down the system and end up being its strongest defenders."

"Errol Ferko wanted me to write the obituary. He said Mr. Small had raised him."

"If that's the kid that we were going to bust, what he really wanted was to talk about himself. You find that with some con men. They're hams. They do their scams just so they can get an audience." Murphy sized him up. "You don't want to write an obit about this guy. But there's something bugging you about him."

"The level of violence makes no sense," Ladderback said. "There has been very little street crime in the section of Westyard where Mr. Small was robbed. I checked the frequency of reported muggings for most of this year. There is an increase in the gentrified section, two blocks to the north. But, on the block where Mr. Small was assaulted, there have been so few as to be negligible."

"A lot of these scumbags just pass through a place. A block or two isn't going to make a difference. They see some guy with a cane and they go for him."

"Last night the woman who did Mr. Small's paperwork was assaulted, in her home. The injuries were similar, in that the assailant struck Mrs. Cavaletta with a stick or a rod until she lost consciousness."

"And you checked about break-ins, and there aren't that many?"

"She lives on the same block as a police officer. There have been no break-ins on that street. The police report has not listed stolen items. The door was not forced."

"So she might have known the creep that did it. Witnesses?"

"Neighbors say at least one man entered the house."

"But, this being Philadelphia, nobody got a good look at him." Murphy eyed Ladderback. "So how come you're asking me about this?"

"I believe I am close to discovering something rather awful. It concerns Mr. Small and his so-called war buddy, Captain Jack Ferko, the lives of possibly hundreds of illegal immigrants who were exploited terribly in that corner of Philadelphia for many years and the unsolved murder of a young girl."

"So?" Murphy said. "Write a front-page exposé."

"I am not permitted to work on investigative pieces. I have an assistant, but such work as this would have to be approved and my editor is on the food chain, as you put it."

"So why don't I just call up my law enforcement buddies and we'll break in on 'em like Eliot Ness in *The Untouchables*?"

Ladderback frowned. "My concern is serious."

"As is mine, even if I decide not to be serious about it," Murphy said. "One of the reasons I quit law enforcement was that you just don't accomplish anything. Yeah, you can disgrace the guys at the top and lock up the creeps on the bottom, but they're just replaceable parts in a machine that's going to keep chugging along because most people *are* team players; most people are willing to go along to get along."

Ladderback's frown deepened. Then he said, "Throughout my life I have maintained a belief that all situations, no matter how despairing, contain within them a sense of grace, the possibility of hope. To me, having the nuts, as you describe them, is the ability to realize that hope, especially in situations of loss."

"You want to pray to the great god Osiris?"

"Your mother gave you that name," Ladderback said. "She was an Egyptian. You became obsessed with cards when she died."

"I began to play *seriously* when she died," Murphy said.

"And your father?"

Murphy sighed. "We've lost touch." He drummed his fingers on the table. "Neville, have you ever had any experience with victims?"

Ladderback nodded.

"I don't mean people who are sad that somebody died. I mean people that get themselves into situations where the creeps can take advantage of them. These victims always have a reason. But the truth is that they want to get taken advantage of. The casinos take millions from them and, believe me, they are not fun to be around. My father was one of those. I will not let that happen to me. I don't want it to happen to you. Forget about this thing. Let it just blow past you. It's not worth the trouble."

Ladderback opened his satchel and put a copy of Michael Murphy's obituary in front of Michael Murphy's son. Ladderback then excused himself, left the restaurant and wandered about the casino for a few minutes. When he returned, Murphy had his head in his hands. "Where'd you find all these people to say these things about him?"

"It wasn't difficult," Ladderback said as he sat down. "I had tried to contact you when I learned of his death. I did not know where you were. His funeral was very well attended."

"People that owed him money, probably," Murphy said. "There were so many that never paid him, and he never went after them."

"He found other compensations," Ladderback said.

Murphy was quiet for a long time.

Ladderback looked at his watch.

"You miss your bus?" Murphy said. "There are plenty of ways to get you back."

"I have difficulty with some methods of transportation," Ladderback said.

"You have a driver's license?"

Ladderback was about to tell Murphy that he had a license but could not drive when Murphy said, "Where you living these days?"

"Philadelphia."

"No problem. You have a driver's license, I'll get you back."

Just then the waitress breezed by and asked Ladderback if he wanted anything else.

"Go ahead, Shep," Murphy said. "Blow it out. Do something silly."

Ladderback picked up the menu. His eyes fell on the Georgia Peach 'n' Pecan Soufflé. "I'd like something with"—he looked at Murphy—"the nuts."

When the soufflé arrived, Murphy put a wad of cash on the table. "This will cover what we've eaten and anything else you might want. I have to get myself into a little game. You can watch, or come looking for me at Carte Rouge Poker Salon in around forty-five minutes."

Ladderback ate about half of the soufflé and then went toward the poker salon. He saw Murphy at a table with five other men, one of whom had a cell phone shaped like a red sports car on the table.

Ladderback knew enough about poker to be uninterested in it, though he noticed that, after a few hands, the stacks of chips in front of the other men at the game began to wander over toward the man with the cell phone.

Ladderback went back to the Patience Society. Teasdale wasn't there, but several men and women had gathered around a table where a large, bearded man was chewing his nails while contemplating a laptop that showed a square layout of cards. A young woman in a maroon Frontenac Hotel Casino front-desk jacket impatiently explained to Ladder-back that the fellow with the beard was playing an Internet match of "competition Scorpion."

Scorpion was among the more difficult solitaires, she said. To play it competitively required that the player accumulate so many points over a given period of time. Points were deducted for any error that, if played differently, might not have brought a premature conclusion to the round. If the player achieved a "terminal position," that is, if he failed to win but had played all cards to the end, he got bonus points.

Ladderback couldn't see what the fuss was about: six rows with seven cards in each row. The back three cards in four of the rows were turned over—the rest were faceup. Group the cards in numerical order by suit and win when you accumulate four perfect rows, kings down, aces on top.

Then he asked why three cards were held in reserve, to be put into play at the player's request.

"Don't you know *anything* about solitaire?" the girl said. "Those cards are the *merci*. It's like, when the game is over, you play the *merci*, and it's like, your last chance, and it can be very dramatic when you play it. Some players are conservative, they play until they can't group any more cards and the game is dead, and they throw the *merci* and it's like emergency CPR: it either continues the game or the game stays dead. But a really radical player will play the *merci* unpredictably, without rea-son, like he's defying death. That's where you see a very intense game."

After watching several rounds, Ladderback grew bored and wan-dered back to the poker salon, where he noticed that the chips in front of Murphy had grown only slightly, while the stack in front of the man with the cell phone had grown quite large. Murphy motioned Ladder-back over to the table.

"Automatic or manual?" Murphy asked him.

Ladderback hesitated and Murphy said, "Automatic." The man with the sports-car cell phone punched out a number on it and muttered something quietly into it. He put his chips into an old Speed Racer lunch box and told Murphy, "Half an hour, top floor."

Murphy played a few more hands. As Ladderback was about to go, Murphy tossed in his cards, shoveled his chips back into his pocket and said to the man with the cell phone, "Pleasure doing business with you."

"As always," the man said, intent on his cards.

When they left the poker salon, Ladderback asked Murphy if he'd won.

"I bought you a car," Murphy said, lumbering slowly but deliberately toward the corridor pointing to GARAGE EXIT.

"I don't drive," Ladderback said.

"I'll drive you home after you sign the papers. I got rid of my license. I don't like pieces of plastic with numbers on them. The plastic doesn't bother me as much as the numbers. I don't want any numbers out there pretending to be me."

"You need identification to get medical care," Ladderback said.

"One day I'll tell you how I got my triple bypass," Murphy said.

"You won it from a cardiologist?" Ladderback asked.

"I had the choice of taking the bypass or his Bentley."

"Did you need the bypass?"

"What would I want with a Bentley?"

They found an elevator. Murphy punched the top floor. On the way up, Ladderback mentioned his agoraphobia. "When the elevator doors open, you will have to guide me."

"Tough it out, Neville. Ignore it."

"I can't." Ladderback closed his eyes as the elevator doors opened. Ladderback heard Murphy drum his fingers on the side of the elevator. Then he felt Murphy's hand on his arm, gently leading him outward.

The briny air almost knocked Ladderback over. He felt the panic rising in him. He heard the distant drone of an airplane and . . . seagulls crying somewhere overhead! He had to force himself to keep moving.

Then he heard Murphy chuckle. "I didn't think Oldsmobiles came in puke green."

Ladderback heard a man ask for Mr. Murphy. He felt Murphy guided toward the edge of a vehicle. Murphy put Ladderback's hands on several pieces of paper on the hood.

"Shep, you know your license number?" Murphy asked.

Ladderback recited it. He almost dropped the pen Murphy put in his hand. "I can't open my eyes," Ladderback said.

"You want me to make an X? Okay, I'll sign your name. Tell me where you live; I'll fill out the rest."

"Do we need to purchase insurance?"

"You just signed a waiver that you have a policy and will inform the holder of said policy within twenty-four hours that you're the proud owner of this vehicle, which you won't have to do because in twenty-four hours the vehicle will be right back on the lot. Think of this as a rental."

"I don't have an insurance policy," Ladderback said. "If we're stopped by the police . . ."

"We'll just hand over the keys and walk."

Ladderback heard Murphy accept copies of the forms. The key had to be wiggled into the door lock. The door opened with a rusty groan and Ladderback smelled a musty stench of oily rags and very old pizza.

The car started. Ladderback felt it pitch and swerve as Murphy went down the ramps through the parking garage.

They were on the road in minutes.

It took Ladderback a while to swallow some of his panic and thank Murphy for driving him back.

"It was getting stuffy in there," Murphy said. "Same old Saturday-night crowd. No excitement to it."

Ladderback let some silence go by. Then he asked Murphy if he belonged to any private card-playing clubs.

"I do and I don't," Murphy explained. "In the better places, where I am known, I have an open invitation to play a few games, like being a guest pro at a golf course. I don't bother with those because, when I'm known, the stakes tend to be low, and what do I need with a low stakes game? In the clubs where I am not known, it's a toss-up."

Ladderback smiled faintly. Then he asked Murphy to pull over.

"You need a potty break?" Murphy said as Ladderback felt the car sway to the right. He heard the wheels grumble as they rolled over the grooves dug into the shoulder.

"There is a file in my satchel," Ladderback said, cringing. "I would like you to open it and, if possible, take me to one of the places mentioned in the file. It should be on our way back to Philadelphia. I'm sure you're familiar with it."

"If I'm so familiar with it, why do I have to look at the file?"

Ladderback was flustered. "I always consult my files before I make a decision."

"And what *decision* are you making?"

"To . . . ask you to take me to a private club in a church."

"There's only one club in a church on a Saturday night that I'd even want to be in, but it's super-high-end, and it's made the church so rich . . . what is it . . . what is it . . . I'm getting old and my brain isn't working and I can't think of the stupid game with the numbers that all the churches have."

"I want you to take me to the Rectory," Ladderback said.

"Bingo!" Murphy merged the car back onto the highway.

15nash the slash

Murphy parked the car and Ladderback thought he heard crickets slowly, slowly chirping in the cold.

"I have to tell you the house rules," Murphy said. "Nobody asks who anybody is, though most of the regulars know each other. Nobody asks what anybody does for a living. Nobody is supposed to discuss business, but they do it all the time. Coffee and tea are free but you have to make a donation if you want decaf. You'd think, with millionaires playing in that place, they'd have free decaf, but the club is the way it is. There was a big controversy a few years ago about whether they were going to have cappuccino and espresso, because some people—we're not saying who—thought that an espresso machine would let in the goombahs until they found out that the owner of the biggest coffee distributorship in South Jersey is Jewish and he was already a member and was giving away the coffee and tea for free."

"But not the decaf," Ladderback said.

"The guy supplying the decaf is a cardiologist with a boat down in Stone Harbor and to hear him talk about his boat, he's in the poorhouse.

Anyway, you can't make your own cappuccino or espresso. Whoever is at the desk will have to make it for you and you will be expected to tip."

"I won't have coffee," Ladderback said.

"You still have to let me get into a game. Especially if the cardiologist is there. He offered to give me his boat the last time."

"And the Bentley?"

"What do I need with a boat? Now, I'm going to sign you in as my guest. I'm not going to put your name down and you don't have to give your real name if you pay cash. I always pay cash. If you want to play a game, or do anything requiring you to bet, you'll have to buy some chips and you will be charged a membership fee, which is a lot more than you can afford. But there's no charge just for playing cards. They take all credit cards, automatic teller cards or checks. If you want to play any kind of game that doesn't include cards, like backgammon, you have to pay an even higher membership fee. There's a cool-off room on the way to the bathrooms that has a TV in it that is used for sports betting only. If you don't want to play, you can sit with me and watch, or you can read. One of the members collects books, so the club has every book about bridge that Charles Goren ever wrote. Are you a bridge player?"

Ladderback said he wasn't.

"Then you should also look for *Gambling Scams* by Darwin Ortiz. There's a lot that isn't in that book, but everybody who wants to spot a cheat starts with that."

Ladderback said, "I'll need you to guide me again." He kept his eyelids shut as Murphy came around and opened the door. Ladderback felt his chest constrict as the frigid air found his face, his neck, the space of skin where his gloves ended and his coat began.

He groped for Murphy's arm. He may have held his breath until his feet touched stone steps and he heard a door open and he smelled expensive cigar smoke. He felt interior heat on his face. He opened his eyes. At a larger table in the center were five men, one of whom took a cigar out of his mouth and said, "If it isn't the Ghost of Christmas Past."

"Ho, ho, ho," Murphy said as he signed in at the small desk. He sauntered over to the table, pulled out a chair and sat in it as if he owned it.

In a corner, with his back facing the door, was the slouching mountain of Nashua Eagleman.

Ladderback told the short, gnome-like man at the desk that he came to read and went to the bookshelf. He removed David Parlett's *A History of Card Games* and sat down in a red leather chair that smelled of cherry-scented pipe tobacco.

The chair was next to Eagleman's table.

Ladderback opened the book but didn't begin to read it. He first looked at Murphy, who was muttering something about shearing sheep. One of the women playing hearts was speaking into a cell phone.

Ladderback let his gaze wander to Eagleman, whose hands were moving listlessly over seven-column solitaire, the most common version of the game, called Klondike. To his right was a small, boxy plastic machine. To his left was a Point Man Project mug.

Ladderback first looked at Eagleman's fingers: they were manicured, but two of the fingernails seemed to have been chewed on. Then he noted that one of his shirt cuffs was missing its cuff link. His camel-hair jacket was rumpled, with a stain on the lapel that could have been coffee.

Finally Ladderback observed Eagleman's face. He was unshaven. The skin was an unhealthy red. All the prominent features: chin, nose, jowls and the dark bags under eyes, seemed as if they were melting from some furious internal heat.

He may have been handsome, long ago. The vicious scar on his jawline might have given him a rakish appeal.

Ladderback closed the book and said, "Forgive me for violating custom, but I came rather far to speak with you, Mr. Eagleman."

"I came rather far not to speak to anybody," Eagleman said in an unexpectedly sharp, highly pitched voice. He dealt three cards, put down the deck, pushed the rest of the cards into a pile and fed the pile into the machine. The machine whirred loudly as it shuffled the deck, dropping it into a tray.

Ladderback watched him for a while. "I am N. S. Ladderback of the *Philadelphia Press.*"

He took the deck out of the machine, dealt the top card faceup, and six cards facedown."

"I write obituaries for the *Press* and I am hoping to get information regarding Paul Small. Would you be in mourning for him?"

Eagleman started dealing again. "I would. My wife has her thing going with the art. I got more freedom. I can be miserable when I want."

In some cultures, male mourners were not supposed to shave. They also ripped their clothes and Ladderback saw that the missing cuff link had been torn from his shirt.

Eagleman played a few cards. Then he looked at Ladderback for a long time. "You did the obit about Sunset Zyman."

Ladderback nodded.

Eagleman went back to his game. "I was just a bullshit builder of Section 8 housing in Camden before Paulie Small came here and found me. Paulie got me into Philadelphia. Paulie got me into the Pickle Factory. That put me on the map."

Ladderback opened his satchel and removed a pad. He asked if he could take notes. Eagleman said he wanted him to take notes. "You should remember the kind of man Paulie was."

"A good man?" Ladderback asked.

"Paulie was a fraud, a cheat, a no-account piece of crud," Eagleman said. "Between him and Senator Tybold, the shit they pulled, it's a miracle one or both of them isn't in jail. But he did okay for me."

"In what way?"

"He only asked me to do one shitty thing. He said it was the only shitty thing he was going to ask me to do, and if I did it, I would get into Philadelphia, in a big way. Not every developer wants to get into Philadelphia, but I wanted to. When you grow up in Camden, Philadelphia, is right there, right across the river, and you know that, if it's going to happen for you, that's where it's got to happen. Paulie promised he would bring me in right. And he made good."

"Why did he bring you in?" Ladderback asked.

Eagleman grinned. "He read an article. I think it was in your paper, maybe twenty-five years ago. I had just built this place, the Rectory. I think the article mentioned I was a Vietnam veteran, and that I always played cards every Saturday night. He came over with Jack Ferko and introduced himself. He said he and Jack were having trouble getting their veterans' benefits and would I help out. They needed me to sign affidavits that said they were there."

"But they weren't," Ladderback said.

"I can't say that. What I can say is that I never saw them while I was in Vietnam with the Army Corps of Engineers. Not on the Beach of Good Choice, where they said they'd been."

"But you signed it anyway."

"I told them to go fuck themselves. Then, a few months later, I got a form letter from the Veterans Administration thanking me for my assistance in the reinstatement of their benefits. I think what Paulie did was sign my name, but I'll never know because I didn't write the VA that I did not assist in the reinstatement. A few months later, I started to get calls, some of them from Paulie, about these little spot projects in and around Westyard, a storefront, a dance studio above a garage. I got other work for small businesses, friends of the senator. I did the Not Fade Away headquarters. The jobs got bigger and bigger until the Pickle Factory. That was the biggest of all. And, in all that time, twenty-five years or whatever it's been, Paulie didn't stiff me one nickel. Everything he said that was coming to me, came to me, like it was . . . I don't know, natural."

"Were you ever concerned that your complicity in getting those benefits for Captain Ferko and Mr. Small might expose you to criminal prosecution?"

"Never. If anybody asked me, I'd tell them what I told you: I don't know if those guys were in Vietnam when they said they were."

"You must know that government funds that were intended to aid veterans were diverted to the projects on which you worked," Ladderback said.

"I don't see it as a diversion because I'm a veteran. I hire veterans. I trust veterans."

"But you kept your doubts about your employers to yourself," Ladderback said.

"I grew up dirt-poor in Camden," Eagleman told him. "Every time there'd be some new aid program, medical clinic or welfare office open up, there was at least one individual involved who was a cheating, scheming piece of crud. But how many people would benefit from those programs. Hundreds, maybe thousands. When I was discharged, I got into Section 8 housing: government-sponsored homes for poor people. I'd get the work from a piece of crud, or by somebody who got paid by the piece of crud, but I would be able to put up housing for people who needed it? I had no doubts about Paulie and Hank Tybold. I'd seen too many like them."

"Senator Tybold didn't want me to pursue my inquiries," Ladderback said.

"What do you media people do when you find a cheating piece of crud? You set off all kinds of alarms. You do your exposés. You get people excited. They demand justice and sometimes they even get it. And while you're getting what you want, nothing's happening for the people who need things the most."

"What would you say about Mr. Small, if you were writing his obituary?" Ladderback asked him.

He paused in his game. "That I was just like him. He was a big fat slob, sort of like me, except I'm not a piece of crud. I've met enough pieces of crud in my time and I'd rather not be like them. But I can deal with them and I can appreciate the one thing that they all have in common: they fight for their ability to be pieces of crud. They work hard at it. They live high, but they put so much effort into cheating, faking, fucking the system backwards and forwards that you almost have to admire them for sticking with it as long as they do. They aren't stupid people and most of them, they aren't greedy as much as they're into keeping score. They could have ripped off more money than they'll ever spend in their lives, but they'll have to rip off even more to make sure that they get more than the piece of crud down the block."

He pushed the cards together. "What would I say about Paulie? I'd say, as pieces of crud go, he was top drawer. He was a very pleasant guy to be around, when he wanted to be pleasant. Women couldn't get enough of him. He could tell you a story and make you laugh or cry. He was a terrific cardplayer, as good as that guy Murphy over there, but, unlike Murphy, Paulie wouldn't act like a bum and dress like a bum so that stupid people would get into a game with him and think they could take advantage. Paulie was never caught for anything he did that was illegal. He was never sued. Nobody investigated him. He never ratted on anybody. To see Paulie going down a street in Westyard was like watching an old boxer come into the gym where he trained for his first fight. He was like that, like a street fighter, but I don't think he ever got into a fight because he was too good at talking his way out."

If he was so good at talking his way out of trouble, Ladderback asked himself, how is it that he was murdered with his own cane?

"Mr. Small did not marry," Ladderback said. "Was there any tragedy in his life?"

Eagleman shuffled his cards and began to deal another game. "Paulie went to funerals like the rest of us. If you're asking if things pissed him off, I've seen him pissed off. If you mean, did he ever want something to happen that didn't happen; on the political level, you get that all the time. On a personal level, I think it had to do with kids. Paulie knew he didn't have it in him to be a family man, but he had Jack Ferko's son hanging around with him and Paulie was always disappointed in him."

"This would be Errol?"

"Tall kid, nervous all the time. Errol wanted to be just like Paulie but nobody could be like Paulie. Paulie brought Errol to the golf course and Paulie would always make par while Errol would hit into the rough all the time. I can't tell you how many times I'd see Paulie lose it in front of Errol. Paulie would yell at him for being stupid and Errol would stand there, opening and closing his hands. Or Errol would take a sand wedge and go out into the rough and beat up the trees."

Ladderback removed the SMALL, P file from his satchel and reviewed his notes. "I've heard two accounts of whose idea it was to develop the

Pickle Factory. The senator claims credit, while Jack Ferko said it was Paulie's project."

"It was Paulie's, no question. The senator had got his hands on the state and federal money and he needed something to spend it on. He was thinking of putting Section 8 housing on the site of a meatpacking plant behind the hospital, but Paulie didn't want that in his neighborhood. He said empty nesters were the way to go. Empty nesters raise the tax base, contribute to the economy, give to political campaigns and vote. Give them a luxury building with views and you'll have a monument to good government. The meatpacking plant was three stories. We'd need to put up a new tower to get the views, but if we bought Zyman's building, we had ten stories and could also get historic redevelopment credits. Which we did."

They paused as groans from another table announced a win by Murphy.

"Didn't the project come up two million short?"

"It did *not*. It was as on budget as you could get, and this would be the only reason I would ask you not to write Paulie's obituary, or, if you did, leave this out, because people wouldn't understand."

Ladderback put down his pen and put away the pad.

"Not even Paulie told me about this, but I figured it out, based on what I heard. What happened was, Errol Ferko fucked up, big time. It was over some insurance policy scam that Errol was selling, and it went under. One of the investors got some of the others together and they said they were going to sue if they didn't get their money back. A lawsuit like that would get all kinds of law on Errol's back, and this wasn't the worst of the scams he had pulled, so Errol needed about two million in cash, fast. Paulie said the project was under budget, found the money and got Errol off the hook, nobody said anything more about it."

"Did Errol repay this loan?"

"I don't know if it was a loan. Maybe Paulie was feeling guilty for getting so mad at Errol all these years. As I said. I never heard anything of it, and I don't think you'll find anybody else who will say anything about it, especially now, with the funding for Veterans Plaza finally opening up. Nobody wants any boats rocked, least of all me."

He thought about it. "Maybe you should leave that pad here."

Ladderback sat up. "I am not sure if I will succeed in writing an obituary about Mr. Small. It is more likely that I won't publish anything about him. What is it about an obituary of one man, one of hundreds involved in this project, that could possibly effect its funding?"

"Background checks," Eagleman said. "The level of funding on this project is higher than we've ever received. Ever since the New Jersey Casino Control Act, when anyone doing business with a gaming company had to attest to good character standards, contractors receiving funding at these levels from federal and state sources can be asked to submit statements affirming their good character. It's become standard operating procedure to submit these statements in advance of the approval process. The statements are usually not investigated, but the principals must also sign a waiver authorizing an investigation if the agency granting the funds so desires. You put what Paulie did in print, the investigators might get ideas. This doesn't scare me—I've kept my nose reasonably clean in this business. But it may frighten others."

"Might one of those others be Jack Ferko?"

"That's not mine to say. Jack wanted to retire before we made the initial applications for Veterans Plaza but Paulie insisted that he stay on. Errol has wanted to become a principal but both Paulie and Jack would rather have him on the sidelines."

"How could Errol possibly be a threat?"

"Because Paulie raised him and taught him all his tricks. With Paulie gone, the all-important cheating piece-of-crud position holding the public/private partnership together is now vacant. Just because Errol is a fuckup doesn't mean he can't use what Paulie's taught him to make a huge mess of things if he doesn't get his way. Errol does not keep cool. You can't play cards with the man."

"Why is that?"

"When Paulie played cards, he'd beat you in the long run but he did it so smoothly that you wouldn't mind. With Errol, there's no long run. He needs to win every hand. A skillful player can use that need against him and clean him out. Some of those federal investigators are just as skillful as your friend Murphy. Errol doesn't stand a chance against them."

He pushed the cards together one last time. "Which is why I, a professional practicing optimist, can't shake the feeling that Veterans Plaza isn't going to happen, at least, not in the way Paulie wanted it to happen. It's like I'm hearing Paulie's ghost whispering to me that Errol's going to fuck things up, if he hasn't already."

You don't have to write obituaries to learn that you shouldn't probe too closely the workings of the human heart. Irrational emotional agony can be explained as a troublesome neurochemical interaction, a dysfunctional pattern of behavior, the acting out of childhood hopes and fears. But explanations only trivialize the situation: they do not reduce the pain or help the sufferer come to terms with his grief.

Ladderback asked Eagleman to give him the cards.

Ladderback dealt out the seven-column board of Klondike that Eagleman had been playing, with a difference. He took three cards from the deck and put them in a pile facedown.

"Play the game as before."

Eagleman stared at the game for a minute. "But I can't win without those cards."

"Play until the game stops."

Eagleman did so, finishing with nearly half the cards faceup, in one of the four finishing piles. "Okay. I have a new way to lose."

"Not yet," Ladderback said. He pointed to the three facedown cards. "These cards constitute the *merci,* which, in my understanding, is best translated as 'grace.' Grace is always uncertain until it makes itself known. It does not always fulfill our expectations. It may not help us win a game. It may not make a difference we can recognize. But when we think of grace as a given, a *fact,* an ingredient in any human conflict rather than an accident or an element of luck, we arrive at an inescapable conclusion."

"What's that?"

"That no situation is without hope."

Eagleman stared at the game. He touched the cards with his fingers and snapped them back as if he had received an electric shock. Then he turned them over.

"Yes," he said. "Yes, yes, yes!"

"So now you're best friends with Nash the Slash," Murphy said, when he parked the car on Locust Street some distance from Ladderback's Philadelphia apartment building.

"I'm accustomed to speaking with the aggrieved," Ladderback said, his eyes shut tight. "He sincerely misses Mr. Small."

"Because he plays fair and every man that plays fair will wish he knew a cheat who can play dirty when the game isn't going his way."

Ladderback ignored his cyncism. "I'll be pleased if you can guide me to the lobby door," he said finally.

Murphy yawned, and it was like those long nights they had when they were kids before they discovered girls, when Murphy came over to Ladderback's house and did Ladderback's math homework while Ladderback slowly typed Murphy's English homework until a great, gasping yawn from Murphy signaled a decision: would Murphy stay and sleep on the floor of Ladderback's room, or would he manage the long walk home?

Ladderback heard the car door open. He almost panicked as Murphy led him to the building's front door, but he managed to open it.

They took the elevator up. Ladderback unlocked his apartment door and experienced that rare emotion that comes when you bring another person into a familiar space, and that person makes everything unfamiliar.

Upon turning on the single light in the small vestibule that opened into the studio's one room, Ladderback saw the mountain of newspapers, magazines, books, videotapes and DVDs piled up on the couch, three cocktail glasses whose contents had evaporated, a coffee cup and a half-eaten English muffin on a chipped plate on the end table with all his remote controls on it, his crimson velvet smoking jacket in a heap beside his chocolate-colored recliner, and the open bathroom door, showing a frayed and faded towel hanging askew from the shower curtain rod.

Murphy wrinkled his nose. "It smells like a crypt in here," Murphy said. "You got a window you can open?"

"I have a ventilation fan over the kitchen stove. There is another fan in the bathroom," Ladderback said. "You are welcome to sleep here tonight."

Murphy didn't take off his coat. He went into the bathroom, shut the door and turned on the fan.

Ladderback put his satchel on the floor by his recliner. He took off his coat and hung it on a hangar in a small closet by the vestibule. He put his hat on the shelf above.

He went to the couch and saw that he might be able to put most of the magazines and newspapers on the small dinette table. As he removed the newspapers from the couch he saw a dark stain on the earth-toned plaid fabric. He remembered how he had been ill with a cold and had sneezed while holding a cup of . . . what? What had he been drinking? It could have been coffee or a rum concoction. He had gone through a period of experimentation with different rums, and one of them had been a nearly undrinkable, 180 proof Grenadian blend called "Jack Iron" that had been sent to him from a state liquor store that specialized in peculiar rums. It had been the color of lubricating oil and so powerful that, no matter what he mixed it in, he tended to spill it. Maybe that had caused this stain or . . . maybe not.

It was late and Ladderback's memory became especially unreliable late at night. Ladderback wanted to turn on some awful cable TV program or catch a rerun of a terrible movie (careful to set the timers that would turn off the lights and shut down the TV set after an hour or so), fix himself a concoction with sweet vermouth (he was currently going through a vermouth experimentation period) and let the drink and the presence—or absence—on the high-definition TV screen lull him into a mindless release, so that he would sit in the recliner and have one of those dreams where he was watching television with his eyes closed and what he was watching was the dream itself, and that, by being aware that he was dreaming, create from the shreds and fragments of recent experience a wholly new and secretly delightful series of fantasies that would leave him groggy and awake at the unlit beginning of a new day.

But first Ladderback had to use the bathroom. He *really* had to use the bathroom and the door was shut, the fan was on and, over the whine of the fan, Murphy was singing marginally obscene Frank Zappa songs about poodles, pygmy ponies and a "dental floss bush."

Ladderback believed that the careful contemplation of movies, television and other elements of popular culture yielded insights about everyday life that were as important as those derived from great art, but he was not in a contemplative mood. Murphy didn't sing the songs all the way through: he lingered on vocal fragments, repeating them out of context, lingering over the more ludicrous constructions (what *is* a "modified dog"?). Murphy might be in the right place and the right time, but Ladderback had to wait, and wait, and wait.

Ladderback frequently didn't change for bed: he sat in his recliner and sometimes fell asleep in whatever he was wearing.

But he had a guest now, so he dug through the clothes that he had accumulated and never got rid of and found a pair of ridiculous red and black plaid pajamas. He put them on and found that he got the pants on backward. He took off the pants and saw an oversized white sweatshirt and matching sweatpants shoved into the back of a drawer. The ensemble came free after he ordered too many clothes from a catalog company. He put the pants and shirt on. He looked like a melting snowman.

Murphy was singing a song about a disco boy who was always going to the toilet to comb his hair when Ladderback decided he had had enough. He turned around and raised his hand to bang on the bathroom door, but the door was open.

Murphy stepped out in a maroon Frontenac Casino Hotel Royale Slot Club T-shirt. Across one arm he had draped his jacket, his flannel shirt and his trousers. His face was scrubbed a bright pink. "All yours," he said.

Ladderback pulled the door shut and backed into Murphy's grimy shoes. He saw that Murphy had washed a threadbare pair of gray socks and hung them from the shower-curtain rod in such a way that framed Ladderback's face in the medicine cabinet mirror.

When Ladderback emerged he saw Murphy stretched out on the carpet in front of the couch, his clothing folded into a makeshift pillow, his naked feet and legs sticking out from under his jacket, his eyes closed, a gentle sigh emerging from his mouth.

He was asleep.

Ladderback stepped over him. He was alarmed at how loudly the recliner squeaked and groaned as he settled into it. He reached for his TV remote control, and then he remembered he had a guest. Where were his headphones? He had them somewhere . . . on top of the shelf beside the smaller file cabinet. To get to the headphones, he'd have to leave the recliner and that would make the same horrible noises.

He picked up the remote control that turned off the lights. He looked at Murphy and tried to fix the man's location in his mind so that if he got up at night he wouldn't step on him.

He turned off the lights and asked himself what would happen if Murphy woke up and needed to find the bathroom? He didn't have a night-light. He could leave the bathroom light on, but to turn the bathroom light on, he'd have to leave the recliner, and that would make noise. . . .

The sighing sound from Murphy's mouth developed a ragged edge and turned into a gurgling snore.

He waited for Murphy's snoring to quiet down, but it got louder and louder. It just got louder until Murphy said, "Uhh, yes," made a swallowing noise, and yawned and the sighing sounds began again, getting louder and louder. . . .

Murphy's snoring reminded Ladderback of an article in his file on sleep apnea. Ladderback wasn't sure if the file was here, in the small cabinet near his computer, or in the larger cabinet at the *Press*. If it was at the *Press,* it might be part of the larger file on sleep—which included sleeping disorders, sleeping sickness and sleepwalking.

Ladderback put on headphones and found the remote control. Even with the speakers enclosing his ears he could hear Murphy snore and then mutter, again, "Uhhh, yes."

He made sure the sound would flow only through his headphones and turned on the television. He surfed the channels and, this time, watched most of that 1974 Sonny Chiba movie called *The Street Fighter.*

Watching the movie made the Westyard situation clear in his mind. He wasn't completely sure about some of the details, but he could guess. And the guesses aroused a sobering emotion, and a sense of purpose. It all had to do with the unsolved murder of Angelo Delise's daughter. That murder would have to be solved.

How?

Ladderback closed his eyes and imagined he had three cards, face-down, in front of him. He would play the first card tomorrow.

Sleep came easily after that.

16 hoops

On a dreary, drizzling Sunday morning, Andy woke slowly with a mouth that had soured from the pint of chocolate-peanut butter ice cream she had gobbled in a fit of righteous sorrow last night. She pulled the twisted mess of sheets, blankets and quilts around her.

She felt awful and there was only one cure.

She was still in the sweats she had put on after she had tossed the outfit she'd worn last night into a corner. She couldn't remember what corner of her apartment the pile was in, and she didn't care if she never found it, but the apartment didn't have that many corners and it would probably turn up somewhere.

She found the socks, put on the basketball shoes, stuffed her keys into a zippered pocket in a hooded fleece windbreaker and picked up one of the basketballs crowding out the shoes at the bottom of her closet.

The wet cold hit her in the face. She defiantly smacked the basketball hard on the sidewalk outside the apartment house. She started with small steps, bouncing the ball as she cut through the Philadelphia morning odors of automobile exhaust, bus fumes and roasting beans from the coffee bar on the corner. She lengthened her stride as church bells and a recorded voice from a mosque summoned the faithful. Soon she was over the wet, cracked leaf-strewn concrete, dribbling the ball as she crossed the street and raced the few blocks to the back of the graffiti-encrusted public school where a row of basketball courts awaited.

She didn't see the dismal clutter of soggy leaves, windblown trash and glass shards on the asphalt. She didn't feel the spray of rain on her forehead, on her hair soaking through to her scalp. She didn't care about the teenage boy and his towering, bulked-up enforcer, both in rain-drenched hooded storm parkas. She didn't hear the boy say, "Look at a bitch."

She smashed the ball down on the asphalt, let it rise and drop into her hands and saw only one thing: the bent, naked hoop of metal extending from the backboard. Then she moved under the hoop, let the ball rise on the jump until it brushed the backboard and fell just outside the hoop.

She didn't hear the drug dealer giggle.

She caught the ball as it came down, let it touch the asphalt then shot it up like a missile, pushing the ball up and nudging it toward the hoop.

The ball hit the hoop and bounced off. She had to run two steps to catch it. She spun around and launched it back toward the hoop in a high arc that did not seem as if it would go anywhere near the hoop—until it went in, singing through with such miraculous grace that Andy felt a sudden, sharp, focused rush of joy.

Then she was racing after the ball, her shoes skidding on the slick asphalt. She slapped the ball down, sent it back again. It hit the backboard and dropped straight down, away from the hoop.

She got the ball again and felt the warmth filling her arms and legs. She dribbled the ball in a crescent, stopped, pivoted left, ran in at high speed and tossed the ball gently upward.

This time she ignored the joy as the ball went in. She was with it as it came down, slapping it faster so that it bounced into her hand as the soles of her sneakers touched the asphalt.

It took a few more successful shots, and far more misses, before she felt her body loosen. A warmth that started somewhere under her sweat jacket spread to her arms and fingertips, and down her legs to the end of her toes.

And then she just disappeared. She forgot who she was. She became part of the dance-like process in which the ball moved through the space between the asphalt and the backboard. She was aware of a slight qualitative difference when the ball went through the hoop, but what mattered most was just to stay with it, keep with it until the ball began to escape her grip and she found herself chasing it into the corners of the court.

The chase returned awareness to her. She picked up the ball and stood, the muscles in her arms, legs and lower back burning, the rain-soaked sweat suit hanging heavily off her shoulders and bagging at her ankles.

She felt good. Finally.

Ladderback was on the Internet when Murphy woke. He wanted to go out for breakfast to spend some of the cash he had taken out of the Rectory last night. "It's Sunday. Let's eat until we can't move."

"I can order breakfast delivered," Ladderback said. "Or we can go"—he steeled his face—"for a drive, assuming your vehicle has not been towed."

"It's your vehicle," Murphy said. He yawned and scratched his belly. "I thought you can't go outside."

"I can, with difficulty. I need you to be my eyes," Ladderback said. "You will drive and tell me what you see."

"What if I don't see anything?"

Ladderback pondered why Murphy would say anything that stupid.

"Hey, Neville, I'm being silly, okay?"

Ladderback gave him a long look. "Okay," he said.

They took the elevator down to the lobby and Ladderback, his eyes clamped as tight as the deck hatches of a boat sailing into a storm, tensed when he felt the faint patter of rain against his face.

"This is Irish weather," Murphy said as he led Ladderback to the car.

"I'm not—"

"Fake it," Murphy said. "Pretend you come from a long line of brawling, brutal, scheming, raging, loudmouthed sons-a-bitches who don't give a shit about the weather and have better booze, better poetry, better music and better sex than the English."

"Holmes was English," Ladderback said.

"Don't be so sure. He played the violin."

The car was where Murphy left it. Ladderback asked if any parking tickets had been inserted between the wiper blades and the windshield.

"None."

Ladderback straightened and inhaled the bitter fumes of a passing bus. "This might be an omen."

"It's nice to feel lucky, eh?"

"Not lucky. Ignored. The car was ignored by those who would have ticketed and possibly towed it. Important, vital and interesting facts of a situation are most often ignored."

"So you're taking me on a tour of Ignored Philadelphia?"

A gust of wind licked against his face and Ladderback clutched the handle of the car. "I am asking for your help."

Murphy unlocked the door and helped him in. Then he started the car.

Ladderback said, "We are on Locust Street across from Rittenhouse Square facing east, correct?"

"Looks like it."

"Drive east and make a right turn on Broad Street. Take Broad Street all the way until you see the Sisters of Zion Hospital on your right. Make the first right turn after that."

"You got a map in your head?" Murphy asked as he whipped the car out of the space.

Ladderback clutched the door handle tightly. "I examined a map while you were sleeping. On occasions when I must take taxis, I memorize the direction in which I wish to go."

"You don't trust the driver?"

"No," Ladderback said.

When they stopped at a traffic light. Ladderback asked Murphy for the cross street. At Washington Avenue, Ladderback asked him if he could see the Pickle Factory on his right.

"It's about two blocks up, but that's not what you see. There's this building on the corner, wrapped in black plastic . . ."

"A wooden plank should be across the entrance," Ladderback said. The light changed and they moved on. "Describe the storefronts on the right."

"A store that only sells black clothes, a kitchen gadget place with copper pots in the window, an art gallery, no, *two* art galleries."

"Continue south. What do you see in the following block?"

"Shabby. Reminds me of parts of the Atlantic City inlet before the Casino Redevelopment Authority nuked it. Rundown houses with low-end retail. Cell-phone and junk electronics. A place that does nails. What looks like it might have been a decent restaurant that's now a Chinese takeout, a cheap clothing place, a corner bar, a pizza joint that's one Board-of-Health violation from closing."

"Tell me when the signs on the stores change languages."

"Right about . . . now. The signs are in block letters, but they're phonetic spellings of something oriental, with translations below."

"Do you see anything with Good Choice in the name?"

"In what looks like an old Woolworth's: Good Choice Everything Store."

"The Vietnamese signs began before the hospital, correct?"

"At least a block before."

"And the stores with the Vietnamese signs are in better condition than the previous block."

"It's not just Vietnamese. I see that yin-yang Korean flag on one. All Asia Travel could be anything. They're newer, brighter, lots of neon."

"The Asian community has expanded considerably northward," Ladderback said. "We're at the hospital now, correct? Turn west at the next light. The parking lot of the Good Choice Market will be just beyond that, on your left. Tell me about the condition of the housing just past the market."

"Classic Philly row houses. But mixed. Some are run-down. Some look okay." He stopped short. "I'm at a red light with all these streets going all kinds of places."

"Anything in the windows of the houses?"

"Let me see . . . over there, it looks like a town watch sign, but it's in Vietnamese. I see a statue of the Virgin Mary."

"This is a transitional neighborhood. Are any houses boarded up?"

"I can see two."

"The boards are tightly secure, correct? You don't see any evidence that the houses have been entered or taken over by squatters? There is no graffiti or vandalism?"

"None. A house gets abandoned, it's trashed. Here, you'd almost want to move in if they didn't have plywood on the windows."

"What shops are on the corners?"

"A dry cleaner and a hole-in-the-wall photography studio."

"For pictures from the *Viet Kieu*—what Vietnamese people call their overseas relatives—to those in the home country. Go straight."

"No can do. The street directly in front of me is do-not-enter, one-way, heading toward me. There's a no-right-turn on the street to my right. I can make two different left turns."

Ladderback guided Murphy through a series of turns until they were heading north. "Do you see a restaurant ahead of you called the Villa Verdi?"

"I see this green stucco thing . . ."

"Before you reach that restaurant, to your right will be an alley extending down to the hospital. Turn east down the alley and describe the housing."

"On the left, it's the sides of row houses."

"There should be very few windows. The building on the right was a slaughterhouse, meat processing and packing plant. The odors were not pleasant. Tell me what is on our right."

"A fence."

"Chain-link?"

"I guess, but not secure. You can see parts where it's fallen off the posts. A factory is just inside. It's three stories, brick, with some pipes coming out. There's a gate coming up."

"Stop the car. The gate is not secure, correct?"

"One of the doors is gone. The other has fallen off one of its hinges."

"This was the meatpacking plant's employee entrance. Directly inside is a gatehouse where a guard would have sat. What's the condition of the gate house?"

"Pretty awful. It's mostly concrete block. There may have been windows, but no more. The wooden door is rotted and open. There's some garbage around. Looks like a shooting gallery, you know, where dopers go to give themselves a fix."

"Look inside and tell me if you see any evidence of illicit drug use."

"I don't do dope dens. What would I be looking for?"

"Just tell me what you see, especially on the inside walls."

Murphy left the car idling. He opened the door, got out and didn't close the door. The sudden rush of cold air threw Ladderback into a panic. He became momentarily irrational: feelings of abandonment, vulnerability and helplessness overwhelmed him. He had to force himself to breathe, in and out, in and out. He blunted the fear slightly, but it did not subside until Murphy returned and closed the door.

"You okay?" Murphy asked.

"No," Ladderback said. "What was on the walls?"

"Graffiti. Hearts with arrows. JT loves DJ. On the floor were cans and bottles of beer and . . ."

Ladderback kept his eyes closed. "Prophylactics and other evidence that would indicate this is a lovers' lane. Did you see any Asian graffiti?"

"The walls were messed up really bad. But nothing was written on them that was recognizably Asian."

"And you saw no broken syringes? Plastic needle guards? Loose strips of cloth, rope or rubber tubing?"

"I didn't dig under the trash, but there was nothing in view."

"We have a lovers' lane, then, an area normally considered taboo that, when used by adolescents taking their first important steps into the adult world, becomes symbolic of subversion, defiance, risk and refuge."

"So?"

Ladderback settled back into his seat. "Let's consider what Holmes really was for us: a hero whose ability to solve problems and dispense justice became a way of organizing our youthful expectations as we entered the adult world."

"Neville, they were a bunch of stories written before we were born. Holmes was a drug addict, a social failure, a total prig. We read those stories when we were kids. We're about as far away from being kids as we can get."

"Not as far as you might wish. I suspect that at the heart of this situation is a failure, by adults, to understand the distance between childhood and adolescence."

"Difference?"

"Distance. We tend to see ourselves removed from our childhood by time, experience, sexuality, the grim knowledge of our personal limitations. And yet, the adult turns back into a child when he is threatened, when he fights and when he plays."

"Some of the sheep I beat at poker cry like babies when they lose."

"Or they might jump for joy when they win. But what of those who can't give up an element of their childhood, or their adolescence? What happens when they can't let moments of pain and pleasure slip safely into memory?"

"They become . . . I don't know . . . difficult to live with," Murphy said.

Ladderback agreed. "How close is the time to 11 A.M.?"

"You forgot your watch?"

"I can't open my eyes to look at it."

"Eight minutes."

"Let's imagine that we have never really left our childhood. At this point, the game we are playing has ended: the most important elements are in place, we have realized why someone was murdered here seven years ago and why her single death changed the entire community in

214

ways her murderer, and those who kept him from the law could not predict."

"You didn't tell me anything about a person dying."

"In the same way that a solitaire that is not won seems inconclusive, so has our game ended here."

"So we give it up and go for a big feed."

"I want you to take me somewhere else."

"For food, I hope."

"You can get food after you leave me there," Ladderback said. "It's time to invoke the *merci*. I want to play my first card."

17 rice

Andy didn't remember the walk back to her apartment. She didn't remember opening the door. She was in the shower when she finally remembered who she was and that she felt really, really good.

She came out, wrapped an old beach towel around her and saw on her cell phone that Lucia had called.

She dialed her back.

"I might be crazy but I'm still your friend," Lucia said. "I need to borrow your car." She wanted to go to at least a dozen stores in and around the city to buy things for her mother's house.

Shopping. Who was the comedian who said God invented shopping so women could get men off their minds? Andy told her that in the afternoon she had to go to the airport to pick up this guy who Lucia might remember, the one who had invited them to a Halloween party in a huge mansion in the tiny Main Line township of St. Anne's.

"Was he the one that bragged to me about driving a motorcycle into the swimming pool?"

"That was him," Andy said.

Lucia said she would rather go with her to meet him, if Andy didn't mind. Andy didn't mind.

She showered, changed, found her car, unlocked it and stepped back from the stench when she opened the door. Fortini's trash bag had stayed in the backseat of her car overnight. She pulled it out and looked for a place to leave it.

She saw other bits of debris, man-made and otherwise, blowing about the street. With trash pickup a few days away, she couldn't just leave the bag on the curb where the squirrels would tear it open. She went back to her apartment house, to the rows of cans lined up around the back. The cans were full. She left the bag on top of the nearest can and went back to her car.

She went into Gina's Gas and Service Station on Biltmore Avenue and bought the only air freshener available, a blister-packed, four-inch-tall ivory plastic set of praying hands with a "dry stick base" that would adhere to an automobile dashboard. She took the plastic off and the odor of frankincense and myrrh was so overpowering that she drove to Westyard with the windows down. Just before she got to Lucia's house, she put the air freshener back into the blister pack and shut it away in the car's glove compartment.

They visited two "urban resource" stores near the Pickle Factory, and then the Home Depot and the Wal-Mart off Columbus Boulevard, and they lingered over a lunch of gazpacho soup and tabouli salads at the Izmir Cafe. Lucia said nothing about Vinnie or CeCe and Andy said nothing about having met Errol Ferko last night and just like that, they were back in the days before they went off to college, when they would go to Main Line pizzerias and sandwich shops and coffee bars and spend hours having conversations that never quite went anywhere but left them both feeling good, restored and at peace with the notion that it was possible for two people who felt so much at odds with the world to sit and talk and just get along.

Andy asked her, "You figure out when your first women's self-defense class is going to meet?"

"I can reserve Wednesday nights at 7:30 at the Tiburno Academy of

Dance. CeCe and I used to take ballet there and my mother still does Mr. Tiburno's taxes. If I can get some flyers printed up and distributed, I'll start this week. Although I don't think I'm going to get much of a turnout. Wednesday's the day before Halloween. I don't know if any women are going to want to attend a self-defense class on Mischief Night."

"Leave that to me," Andy said. "Deal?"

Lucia shrugged. "Deal."

As soon as Ladderback was through the door, he smelled the sour odor of human steam.

Just inside the doorway was a railing made of grimy white polyvinylchloride plumbers pipe that set off the scuffed, wooden floor on which Ladderback stood from a broad stretch of canvas matting. On his left was a row of pegs from which hung jackets and khaki duffle bags, some of them with the vertical staff and Heian-Do logo. On his right was a small metal desk with a laminated top that might have once been inside a schoolroom. On top of that desk was a single telephone and a box holding green file cards.

Just past the desk was a line of chairs facing the mat. Ladderback sat in one of the chairs, put his hands in his lap, glanced at his watch and faced the mat.

The Heian-Do Web site had said that this class was scheduled to begin at 10 A.M. If so, it had been going for at least an hour and a half. Most among the twenty or so young and middle-aged men appeared so weary that they were barely capable of standing. They stood barefoot in loose cotton trousers and T-shirts in various shades of khaki, olive drab or dingy white. Around their waists were knotted colored belts, some with stripes on the ends. They paired off, some on the mat, some on the hardwood floors past the mat, and came at each other with their bare hands or with sticks of varying length. The object seemed to be for one person to parry the attack, remove whatever weapons the attacker held and then force the attacker to the floor, or throw him on the mat.

These antics were supervised by a young Asian man with a faded, frayed black belt tied around his waist. At the end of the belt were three stripes of yellow electrical tape. He moved among the students, showing them different ways of practicing their violent play.

On a small three-legged stool, under a black-and-white picture of an Asian man that hung on a wall at the very back of the room, sat a slight man, in faded military fatigue pants and an oversized Good Choice Food Market T-shirt. He could have been Ladderback's age, or older. He wore no belt and didn't seem to be looking at anything specific.

Ladderback watched him for a while until he felt his gaze returned with an unsettling hostility, even if the man across the room wasn't looking directly at him. The man pointed at Ladderback and the supervisor with the worn black belt crossed over the mat and asked him if he wanted to know more about what was going on.

Ladderback glanced at the supervisor's sweat-streaked face. "I do have some questions," he said. "I can wait until you're finished."

"You wish to learn about Heian-Do?"

"I am seeking information about individuals who have learned it," Ladderback said.

The supervisor took in Ladderback's raincoat, hat and white button-down shirt. "Some of our students are senior citizens who want improved health and a greater feeling of confidence."

"I write for the *Philadelphia Press*," Ladderback said.

"I'll tell Sensei," the supervisor said. He crossed the mat, bowed to the man in the chair and whispered in his ear.

The man—Ishimura, Ladderback concluded, from his resemblance to the photograph of Hideyoshi Ishimura on the Heian-Do Web site—stood and clapped his hands twice.

Everything stopped. "Be sit," Ishimura said. They gathered their weapons and sat on their knees in a line on the mat against the left wall. The supervisor sat facing them, with his back against the right wall.

"Before end of class," Ishimura began, stepping onto the mat, "we talk about punch. Punch everybody think they know about punch, but not everybody know."

He assumed the center of the mat, his attention on the students, though his body was aimed toward Ladderback. He held up his right hand. "Most people think a punch is a fist." He made a fist with his right hand. "You make a fist and you hit, bang-bang, you dead!"

It wasn't funny, but the supervisor laughed and the students followed. He turned and glanced at the supervisor, who bowed and jumped to his feet.

"Punch must be more. Have spirit and intent." He turned toward Ladderback, Ladderback saw the students also turn toward him.

He said, "Come," to the supervisor. The supervisor bowed again and stepped forward.

"Punch can begin match"—he left fly his fist, stopping it an inch from the center of the supervisor's chest—"or end match."

His fist shot smoothly into the front of the supervisor's T-shirt and the supervisor crumpled forward and fell backward, openmouthed, banging the back of his head on the mat.

"Intent make difference," Ishimura went on, oblivious to the gasping sounds coming from the stricken man. "With intent, America win war against Japan. Without intent, America lose in Vietnam. To defeat opponent, defeat opponent's intent. How to defeat intent with intent?"

One of the students waved a hand. Ishimura's eyes popped with irritation. "With stronger intent?" the student piped.

"No such thing!" Ishimura barked. "In Heian-Do, no such thing as big, small; strong or weak. In Heian-Do, only one thing matter: truth. In Heian-Do, all fight lead to end of fight. In Heian-Do, all intent lead to truth. Truth lead to peace."

He opened his right hand and the supervisor scrambled for a long, battered bamboo stick in a corner against the wall. Ishimura closed his hand around the stick.

The stick was taller than Ishimura. He raised it, waved it over his head and then whipped it in front of him into a two-handed grip, the point aimed at Ladderback.

"Truth make peace. With truth . . ." He smacked the stick on the mat, making a loud cracking sound. "Fight over before begun."

Then he bowed to Ladderback. "You, newspaper. Come."

The students looked at Ladderback expectantly. Ladderback looked blankly at Ishimura.

"You afraid, newspaper?"

Ladderback sighed. "No."

"You afraid of nothing?"

Ladderback was afraid of only one thing: being outside, unprotected, with no roof over his head. Nothing else aroused such overwhelming feelings of dread. This fear had no physical existence. It was meaningless, insubstantial, nothing.

Ladderback answered Ishimura's question, "Yes."

"Come, newspaper," Ishimura said.

Ladderback did not move. The supervisor called out in a choked voice, "If you're going to step on the mat, you'll have to take off your shoes."

"Okay to keep feet with shoes!" Ishimura overruled him.

"What is intent of newspaper? To make bad lies about Vietnam people so Vietnam people give up war against Communist? To make bad lies about Japanese people in America to put them in concentration camp? To say Asian people too many. Too smart. Too quiet. Work too hard, make better cars and take job from American? What is truth? Truth is, American make own problem, blame rest of world for problem, make people suffer who are not American. Right, newspaper?"

Ladderback said nothing. Ishimura's analysis revealed a shameful ignorance of world history. But informing grandstanding media critics that their criticism was based on what they did *not* know only increased their antagonism. "I'm sorry," Ladderback said.

"What you sorry about, newspaper?"

He was sorry that he could not correct Ishimura's ignorance, but to say that would only make the situation worse.

The supervisor scurried over to Ladderback's side and whispered loud enough so everyone could hear, "when Sensei asks a question, you must answer, challenge or leave our school."

Ladderback remained silent. He studied Ishimura's lively eyes.

Ishimura smiled. "You challenge, newspaper?"

Play his game and you'll lose. Refuse to play his game and you may not get the information you want.

"You may challenge me," Ladderback said.

The students fled from the mat.

Ishimura put the tip of the stick over Ladderback's heart. "What weapon you want?"

"The truth," Ladderback said.

"Stick is truth," Ishimura said, bringing the stick up until it hovered under Ladderback's chin. "My intent must be to defeat."

"By your own words, any intent to defeat the truth is to defeat yourself."

Ishimura whipped the stick up and held it just over Ladderback's head. "What truth you want, newspaper?"

"The truth about a conflict that has harmed this part of the city for several years."

"Many conflict here, newspaper. Too many to solve for one old man."

Ladderback almost smiled. They were both old men. In trying to mock Ladderback, Ishimura had let him hear the sound of his soul.

"Solving a problem can make the world seem new," Ladderback said. "Old men can feel young when they solve a problem together."

Ishimura saw his students getting restless. He raised the stick.

"Let's solve your problem with Caprice Delise," Ladderback said.

Ishimura handed the stick to his supervisor, clapped his hands twice, and said, "Class finish."

Then he bowed to Ladderback and said, "Come."

Lucia didn't want Andy to write her into the "Mr. Action" column, but Andy insisted. "Mr. Action is going to get asked a question: how can a single woman walk down the street without being afraid? And Mr. Action will say something like what you told me last night: that everybody has the right to walk down the street without being afraid, and then I'll mention you, a self-defense teacher, I'll throw in a quote or two from you, with a *fomi* at the bottom and your phone number."

"A *fomi*?"

"That's what we call For-More-Information in the newsroom. If you were giving a demonstration, or a lecture, or putting on a show, I'd end it with a *fyugo*. That's If-You-Go. I'm sure you have special names for things in self-defense."

Lucia dabbed her mouth and thought about it. "When two people are sparring and they hit each other at the same time, with the same punch or kick, in Japanese, that's called *I-uchi*."

"Sounds like *ouch* to me."

"It's that, too," Lucia grinned.

Andy suddenly noticed that it would take too much time to backtrack to Westyard and drop Lucia off before getting Logo at the airport. Would she mind coming along for the ride?

Lucia didn't mind. "All assholes look alike."

As Ishimura led Ladderback down steps into a basement changing area. This opened into a short tunnel that opened into a dry, dusty stockroom beneath the supermarket next door. Huge sacks of rice were stacked high against the walls. A small paper screen marked off a section of the basement between two great columns of rice sacks. Behind the screen was a tatami mat, a small chest of drawers, a writing table, a desk lamp and two small cushions. Against a dim concrete black wall was stacked an assortment of long and short sticks, staffs, lengths of bamboo and broomsticks.

"Please to sit," Ishimura gestured to a cushion. He opened the chest of drawers, wrapped himself in a plain, worn cutaway robe and sat on the other cushion. "Many rice. From all over," Ishimura said. "To know people from China, Japan, Korea, Vietnam, is to know rice. It is most basic thing. To be with rice of home is to be home, almost."

Ladderback glanced back into the basement and saw, small packages of clothing and bundles of other belongings rolled up among the rice sacks. Stretched out on the sacks near the massive boiler were groups of young men, sleeping in their clothes. "You live here?" Ladderback asked.

"Many live here. Men, that side. Women, behind boiler. When I come to this country with Li-Loh-san, we sleep on rice. I get used to it." He grinned. "Li-Loh-san say wife don't like sleep on rice. He have a bed now. House of own. I stay with rice."

Ladderback heard a groan. Ishimura rose. "For a moment, you will excuse." Ishimura stepped beyond the screen and ducked down a short corridor among the sacks of rice. Ladderback glanced down the corridor, knowing it was rude of him to do so, but hoping that he was unobserved. He saw Ishimura bending over the supine form of a man whose nose was encased in a blob of white plaster. His knee was bundled in a makeshift splint. Beside him was what appeared to be a golf club.

He saw Ishimura wipe the man's face with a cloth and examine a bandage over the man's ear. He then examined a line of acupuncture needles on the man's face.

When Ishimura returned, he said, "I am also doctor here. Some can't afford doctor. Some afraid—what if asked question, what if no green card? Some want traditional medicine. Too many tradition, but only one doctor."

"Were you taught field medicine in Vietnam?"

"I was teacher, in Vietnam. A great honor to teach Heian-Do people to American soldier, police and Vietnam people." He saw Ladderback's eyes go to the bamboo staffs. "Heian-Do is a way of life. Heian-Do about using everything for peace. American commanding officer like stick, we teach with stick."

"When you were in Vietnam, did you know Angelo Delise?"

Ishimura nodded vigorously. "Oh yes. American soldier with stickball. His girl, Caprice, everyone call CeCe. She was my student, his daughter. Tragedy for all when she die."

"Did you approve of the way the investigation into her death was handled?"

Another inhalation across his teeth. "What is to approve? In Heian-Do, first thing to tell student: if something attack at you, you get out of the way. We get out of way. Police make blame on us. Heian-Do, we teach blame is nothing. Ignore blame. Ignore police. Keep peace by self."

"Did Angelo Delise approve of the investigation?"

"He stop it. He say bad for community. You know Angelo san?"

"We haven't met," Ladderback said.

"Sad for him, because him, big heart. In Vietnam, always playing with children."

"And what about Jack Ferko and Paul Small?"

Ishimura froze again, and took a longer pause, before the effusive smile. "They not . . . play. I come here. I start my school. The boy, Errol Ferko. Jack say, make man of you. I say, he already man. Heian-Do make him better man. I teach him a little. Not enough."

Ladderback heard the emphasis in that last comment. "What was not enough?"

Ishimura sensed that he might have given something away. He covered with, "All student leave before learn enough."

Ladderback changed the subject. "I saw a fascinating motion picture called *The Street Fighter*," Ladderback said.

Ishimura almost laughed. "Oh yes, Sonny Chiba very good. Rip out bad guy throat. Different from Jackie Chan."

"The plot was similar to films about the American dream, but, instead of the hero beginning poor and ending rich, the hero's mastery of violence and dedication to personal honor helped him rise to a much higher level of society."

"Yes, yes," Ishimura nodded. "But it was, like you say, only movie? In America, no rise for Asians, unless stop being Asian, become American. But, Asian become American, what is he? Build railroad. Run laundry. Make restaurant. Fix computer. Work in factory. Just one more American with funny face. No rise."

"Caprice Delise was found near a meatpacking plant that was used to house immigrant Asian families."

"Very sad," Ishimura agreed. "Still, many sad memory. No place to leave. Police on street, arrest. Call INS. INS deport back. Never seen again. So we get them out of the way. We. Heian-Do students. We make peacekeepers. They protect families from police."

So Ishimura's students kept illegals out of sight. "Could some of these immigrants learn Heian-Do with you?"

"Some, yes. Help keep order. Help keep peace. No other choice."

Ladderback remembered that the Nazis turned concentration camp inmates into trusties who collaborated eagerly with their guards at the expense of their fellow inmates. The Americans did the same thing when they "interned" Japanese-Americans during World War II.

"Were your peacekeepers questioned when Caprice Delise's body was found?"

Ishimura's face grew dark. "Many questioned. Police go crazy. Jack Spade—Jack Ferko, go crazy of all. We say, no way can keep peace all time. One girl. Anything can happen. Peacekeepers not responsible. Jack Ferko not see truth."

"And that truth was?"

"We—Asian community—want to build new house at factory. We need government help—permits, approvals, money. We ask Angelo Delise. We ask senator. We ask Paul Small. They say they will help us build new house, and then, they decide not to build new house. CeCe says unfair, she will tell newspaper. She says with son of Jack Ferko, she will tell newspaper."

"With Errol?"

"Not with Errol. Vincent. Then they come to the *hui ting,* to our community bank, and they ask us to buy a $2 million share in Pickle Factory, which we buy, because Angelo Delise says it will be okay, that there will be a new house for us when the Pickle Factory is finished. Now, there is to be Veterans Plaza, all for the rich, and we have no new house."

"Where is this share?"

"Angelo Delise has the paper in his safe."

"Whose signatures were on the share?"

"Li-Loh-san. Mine. Paul Small. Ferko."

"Which Ferko?"

"Errol. The son."

"Not the father?"

"The father is not welcome here."

"The money given was in cash?"

Ishimura nodded. "The bags were quite large. We use bags you put garbage in. We should have thrown it away."

"The project hasn't been officially announced," Ladderback said. "Changes can be made in the course of construction."

"How?" Ishimura said. "You can do what Li-Loh-san cannot?"

"We must find who killed Caprice Delise," Ladderback said.

Ishimura rose. "You talk, newspaper. You talk to top student. You talk to him."

Ishimura led him past the screen to the little corridor where the injured man with the knee splint lay breathing through a plastered nose.

"This man newspaper," Ishimura said brusquely. "Sempai Shu Shi-Bin."

Ladderback introduced himself and was appalled at the rage that radiated from the man's eyes.

"He says he want to know the truth," Ishimura said. "Tell him about CeCe girl."

Shi-Bin glared at Ladderback. "She was a girl who wanted to fuck me. Her bitch friend hit me during practice."

"Shi-Bin teaching class," Ishimura said. "Lucia girl break Shi-Bin knee with stick."

"And then CeCe got fucked and killed," Shi-Bin said. He tried to sound tough, but his plastered nose made him sound like a duck.

"As the best student, were you also one of the peacekeepers?" Ladderback asked.

"I make Shi-Bin boss," Ishimura said.

"Did you live in the meatpacking plant?"

"Yeah. Sure. It was shithole but we lived there. Sensei said the people need a boss and the best student can be the boss and I was the best. When we had a problem, when we had runaways, when we had snitches that tried to tell the city inspectors about where they were being kept, I was the one that went to the cops."

"You assisted in the punishment and deportation of your own people?" Ladderback said, trying to control his contempt.

"All the cops wanted was Asian bodies," Shi-Bin said. "We gave them bodies."

"Was there any specific police officer you went to?"

"Yeah," Shi-Bin snarled. "We went to the cop we could trust. Right, Sensei? We went to your big war buddy, Jack Spade."

Ladderback looked at Ishimura. "Someone you knew from Vietnam?"

"Someone," Ishimura sucked air.

"But I wasn't boss of the peacekeepers all the time. I had a job, okay? Then, the stupid girl dies and they close it down. Everybody have to leave. Sensei let me stay here with him. My mother went to Baltimore. Father to New York. I don't know where they are. I never see my brother or sisters again."

"What was your job?"

"I worked the night shift. I was chief vegetable sorter at the Zyman Condiments."

"I was told Mr. Zyman let his employees watch the sunset when they were at his factory," Ladderback said.

Shi-Bin glanced at Ishimura.

"Tell him," Ishimura said.

"He let us up there. He even put telescopes on the roof so we could look at the city, the kind you put the coins in, but he fixed them so they didn't need coins. We'd use them to try to find naked women behind windows. Zyman thought he was being such a nice man."

"My newspaper ran two small items about Caprice Delise's death," Ladderback said, "which, I believe, occurred in the summer, in the early evening. The time she died was estimated to be somewhere between seven and nine P.M. At that time, the sun would have been setting. Is there any possibility you could have been on the roof of the factory at that time?"

Again Shi-Bin looked at Ishimura. "Tell him!" Ishimura said. "Tell him about the car."

Shi-Bin recited it as if he had said this before. "I was on the roof. I saw a car come down the alley."

"Can you tell me anything about the vehicle?"

"It had four wheels and it was dark, okay? Cars don't come down that alley because some of the kids where I lived would throw stones at cars. But this looked like it was going to the hospital. It was going fast. Then it stopped at the place where we went in and out."

"The gatehouse," Ladderback said.

"I saw somebody get out of the car, carrying her, okay? I saw him carry a black trash bag into there. There was a foot sticking out of the bag, okay? I saw him come out of the gate house and look around. I saw him open the trunk of his car and get out a golf club. I saw him go into the gatehouse and come out a little bit later with the trash bag in one hand and the golf club in the other. He threw the trash bag in the alley. I saw him put the golf club in the trunk, close the trunk, get back into the car and leave."

"Were you looking in one of the telescopes? Could you recognize this man?"

"I could."

"Did you tell this to the police?" Ladderback asked.

"They never asked me because I was working, okay? I had an alibi, okay? I saw everything but I didn't go near them because you don't go near anybody who can make trouble for you. You just don't. So they went after my peacekeepers. They rounded them up. They even got Li-Loh's kid, Tommy, who was banging the girl. He banged her before that guy killed her and Tommy was so scared, because Tommy knew it all. He saw it all. But all the cops wanted was to blame it on an Asian gang. Say it was some Asian gang that killed the girl, and we wouldn't get deported. But he couldn't deport us. There was this other cop, an American-born Vietnamese named Nanh, and she made him back off. There was no Asian gang. It was just us, the peacekeepers. We got together after that. We say, 'Police want a gang, we'll make a gang.' So, from then on, we're a gang, okay?"

"Will you tell me who killed her?" Ladderback asked.

"No," Shi-Bin said. "It would not be peaceful for me. It would not be peaceful for Sensei. It would not be peaceful for his students."

Ladderback looked at Ishimura. "The killer was one of your students?"

"I teach all students not to kill," Ishimura said. "Some students don't learn enough."

Ladderback saw a golf club leaning against a wall. "And that?" Ladderback asked.

"That's my stick, okay?" Shi-Bin said. "I need one to get around."

Andy drove her car up to the top floor of the bleached-gray concrete parking garage that surrounded the swooping curves and jagged edges of Philadelphia International Airport. She liked parking on the very top level, even when the weather was dreary and dismal. She liked the view. She liked watching jet planes leap effortlessly into the sky.

Andy would have waited for Logo at the customs exit, but Lucia recognized one of the airport security guards from her Heian-Do martial arts classes and he let them into the area where arriving VIPs were met and received.

Standing against a wall, Andy and Lucia could see over the customs inspection lines to the baggage carousels. A monitor in the VIP area indicated that Logo's plane had just landed and so she turned her attention to the distant gate through which the haggard passengers where taking their first awkward steps after a long flight.

When in public, Logo liked to affect a rolling, heavy-legged gait that he adopted in imitation of the hulking swagger of steroid-enhanced sports stars. But he lacked the height and muscle mass of his thick-necked idols and, because he was so frequently inebriated from numerous substances he abused, his macho swagger was closer to a traipse. When you added a scruffy, untrimmed beard and a wardrobe of ill-matched thrift-shop castoffs that he wore to annoy his mother, there was no way the unimaginably wealthy slacker heir to the nation's oldest bank could be mistaken for anything other than a homeless derelict.

Andy had warned Lucia that even if Logo wasn't sneaking in packets of marijuana or other banned substances, he might do something stupid, like make a joke at customs about flunking out of terrorist school. If that happened, and Logo was arrested, detained or had the crap kicked out of him by the security guards, Andy would call to a lawyer, or two, or three, and she and Lucia would have to wait until the lawyer arrived to save Logo from the embarrassment of being himself.

Having said that, she only glanced at the clean-shaven man in the warm, lustrous forest-green suit and knit sweater the pale golden color of a tropical sunset. The man was very good-looking, and men who were good-looking were usually only that.

Andy gave him another glance, just because the rest of the people coming off the plane weren't good-looking and, well, if you see somebody who is kind of *scenic,* you can at least admire the view.

The guy walked erect, his back straight, his dark, vaguely curly shoulder-length hair behind him in a kind of retro-European way. He had a pencil mustache riding over his lip. Why did he have a pencil mustache? It was a smudge that Andy wanted to wipe away, and it annoyed her in a way that was too familiar.

She saw it was Logo and she got *really* annoyed. He saw her and he was grinning because he just *knew* she was mad at that mustache, and he looked so damned marvelous, pleasant, breezily at ease with himself, unaware of the unescorted women around him who were brushing back their hair, striking poses, sizing him up and counting the money that they were sure he was worth.

For the first time ever, Logo looked like he was worth more than mere money. He had no carry-on bag. He strode through the immigration checkpoint as if he owned the place but understood that the officials had to do their jobs and who was he to interfere?

He slipped his passport into his jacket pocket, strode up to Andy and, before she could react, he put his arm around her, pressed himself against her bomber jacket and kissed her on her cheek. Logo never kissed Andy anywhere, because he typically smelled so bad that Andy wouldn't let him get close enough.

This time she was too shocked to move.

"Andy," he sighed when he stepped back and gazed at her. "I can't think of anyone I'd rather see."

Then his eyes went to Lucia. "Except, perhaps, you?"

Andy introduced them. Logo took Lucia's hand in his, looked her in the eye and said, "Charmed."

Another one who was charmed. What was it with guys who said they were charmed?

Andy waited for Lucia to whip her hand away or do one of those fancy moves that would bring intense pain to Logo and his idiotic mustache.

But Lucia let him keep her hand while a bright flush spread over her face.

"I hope you don't have much baggage," Andy said flatly.

"None," Logo sighed, as if tearing his eyes away from Lucia was very difficult. "I got rid of everything I had in Europe. I decided to come in with the clothes on my back and nothing else."

"It's cold out," Andy said. "That jacket you're wearing doesn't look warm."

"It isn't," Logo agreed. "Would you like to buy me a jacket?"

Andy glared at him. "Since when have I bought you *anything?*"

"We're not going to steal a jacket, are we?" He stepped easily toward the exit. He became blithe: "Life becomes so interesting when we discard the superfluous, don't you think?"

"Logo, it's wet and cold outside," Andy said as she followed him. "You need a jacket this time of year."

"Or you can use your inner breath to create warmth," Lucia said, gliding beside him.

"Yes!" Logo exclaimed, as if it was such a fabulous idea. "The yogis call it"—he fluttered his fingers—*"prana!"*

"In the martial arts, it's called *chi,*" Lucia said. "It's the life force that holds everything together."

Logo paused. Lucia paused with him.

Andy saw them looking at each other. Lucia flashed an embarrassed smile. Logo grinned, as if to ask, what's so embarrassing?

Lucia pushed her hair away from her face. Logo moved closer to her.

They looked at each other again. They liked what they saw enough to look another time. And another.

I am not seeing this, Andy said to herself.

18 *rivincita!*

Murphy took Ladderback for *pho* when after he walked him back to the car. "You know what *pho* is?"

Ladderback forced himself to think of food, of a roundup on "Philly Ethnic Treats" that the *Press*'s food critic had done some time back. "It's a soup made with a clear meat or fish stock, served with bean sprouts, mint, hot peppers, lemon grass, rice noodles and various cooked meats," Ladderback said. "It has been called the chicken soup of Vietnam."

"Have you had it?"

"I have not."

"There's a place that makes it in Atlantic City. It cures what ails you."

Ladderback felt the car shake and swerve. Murphy led him into the Good Choice Pho restaurant, a brightly lit, high-ceilinged building redolent of salty steam. Long tables filled the dining area, where mostly Asian families lingered over bowls big enough to be soup tureens. A top-40 radio station played breathy American pop tunes.

Murphy was right—the rich soup was perfect for a cold, dreary afternoon, but Ladderback had to force it into his mouth.

"You look like you've seen the Hound of the Baskervilles, Neville."

"Forgive me if this summons difficult memories," Ladderback began. "I must ask you, how did you feel when your mother died?"

Murphy closed his eyes for a while. When he opened them he said, "She died of an aneurysm when I was twelve. I found her on the kitchen floor. You were the first person I called. You're the one with the memory. You tell me how I felt."

Ladderback said nothing.

Murphy dumped a plate of hot peppers into his soup. "There was never one feeling. Abandonment, anger, fear, betrayal, rejection, helplessness, a conviction that it was my fault when it obviously wasn't—all that came and went. My father just prayed all the time and I couldn't accept that. I couldn't see a god killing off a thoroughly loving and gentle person like my mother. I suppose the dominant feeling was that life was unfair, unjust and unreasonable and that nothing mattered. I started getting into fights because I just didn't care about myself anymore."

"You did care," Ladderback said. "You were testing how much you cared."

"I might have been. As much as I tried to be completely dead to the world, I would get hunches, intuitions that there might be things worth caring about, that there might be a possibility of . . ."

"Grace?"

"The cards were another way of testing that, especially the solitaires."

"And another way of fighting," Ladderback said. "What might have happened, when your mother died, to make you feel differently?"

"To stop me from becoming a forensic investigator so I could go around beating up the bad guys?"

"To stop you from putting yourself in situations where you could be harming others, and yourself."

Murphy sipped his soup for a while. "What kept me going then was this need to hurt myself, and others, so I couldn't hurt anymore." He regarded Ladderback. "You're thinking of someone in the same situation?"

"A few individuals," Ladderback said. "The phenomenon of loss, or rather, a life without grace, seems primary to them."

Ladderback tasted the soup and the salty broth began to warm him. He took another and his despair began to fade. By the third sip, he glanced about the dining room and began to savor the experience of being in an unfamiliar place. The aroma of the soup calmed him. The sight of other people eating, talking, enjoying themselves with simple pleasures, helped raise his spirits.

What was it that Teasdale had told him about Vietnam? About goodness being shared, about strangers finding they were not so strange?

Ladderback was warm and glowing when he finished the bowl. He thanked Murphy for taking him to the restaurant.

Murphy shrugged it off. "I was just driving around, waiting for you to come out, and I saw this place. It was close."

"And thank you for being at my side," Ladderback said.

Again Murphy shrugged. "What else would I be doing? Taking money from losers?" He stirred the bowl. "Any other places on your itinerary?"

"Not today. This morning, while you were sleeping, I contacted Mrs. Cavaletta's attending physician," Ladderback said. "He informed me that she would be in better condition to answer any questions tomorrow, after she is released from the hospital."

"I'm thinking of heading on back to Atlantic City," Murphy said. "Don't worry about the car. I can get rid of it just as easily as I got it."

Ladderback smiled. "You've found quite a life for yourself."

Now it was Murphy's turn to frown. "You know what I miss now? I miss those times when we were kids, when I was pretty good at cards, but still rough enough to do stupid things, to make mistakes, to feel that tightness in your throat when you're too deep in the game and you're going to have serious problems if you lose."

Ladderback regarded him for a while. "Are you saying that, having had the nuts, you prefer to be without them?"

"I guess I'm saying that"—he looked at Ladderback—"it's been too long. We should do this again. No silly adventures this time. Just us. Doing nothing."

"How can I contact you?"

"Call Teasdale, William T. His number is listed. He can always find me."

"I will."

"And Neville? Thanks for what you wrote about my father. It was just words on paper, but they changed everything."

Ladderback was happy for the rest of the day.

Logo asked if Andy didn't mind if he sat in the backseat with Lucia and he and Lucia continued talking about energy and spirituality and the cosmic flow of the universe.

Andy couldn't get over the fact that Logo actually buckled his seat belt. He never did that. And he never talked about energy, spirituality and the cosmic flow of the universe.

Lucia ate it all up. She started touching him, as if to make a point, and he touched her back. Yes, they agreed, there were unseen forces connecting people, even if they didn't know they were connected and you had to attune yourself to a higher reality so you could live fully in the moment.

Andy never gave much credence to Lucia when she got cosmic and spacy. She dropped Lucia off at the hospital. From the front seat of the car, Logo watched Lucia go through the glass doors. He stayed quiet as Andy drove back to Fifteenth Street and down to Broad.

"You want to go to your apartment?" Andy asked finally.

"It's gone," he replied emotionally. "Before I left, I didn't pay the rent."

"So that leaves your house," Andy said, as she turned down Washington Street toward Columbus Boulevard and the northbound entrance to Interstate 95.

"What would happen if we circled around and I bought flowers and made a surprise visit?"

"You want to visit Lucia's mom?"

Logo rubbed his mustache. "I want to show I care."

Andy was incredulous. "Logo, as long as I've known you—"

"I've only cared for myself, so now . . ." He put a warm hand on Andy's wrist. "I want to help."

Andy pulled her wrist away. "Help *what?*"

"I want to make everything better."

She stopped at the light. "Logo, what the hell are you talking about? My father gets killed, you go off to Europe and now you're back and you have that *mustache.*"

"You don't like it? I wasn't sure how much of my beard I should retain. Look, I see a drugstore on the corner. Pull over, give me some money and I'll get a razor and shave it off."

She pulled over. "I don't want you to shave. I want you to tell me what happened!"

He folded his arms. "I decided to clean up."

Andy drove forward. "Just like that?"

"No . . . but, while I was in Europe, it got me thinking. About the bank. Nobody likes a bank, except, for maybe five minutes, when we agree to lend money. Then they hate us, or they try to cheat us, or they tell themselves that we really don't want their money back. The Swiss always had the most incredible banks. So I hooked up with some of their people who know our people, and I spent about a month studying how they keep track of assets, manage accounts, handle fraud. Especially fraud. For three weeks I learned the basics for the most common dirty tricks, and they're not quite different from parlor magic. And that's when I started thinking about my relationship with you."

Andy became nervous.

"I started to feel really bad about you. Then I started feeling bad about everything else—you know, my mother, money, the bank."

"You didn't tell me any of this when you would call me."

"Because I know you really like me, love me, probably."

She almost wrecked the car. "Logo, I know you, okay? I've grown up with you. You've been rude, disgusting and thoroughly inconsiderate with me as long as I can remember."

He patted her on the thigh. "That's all right. I accept that. We can never fully understand our feelings while we're feeling them. And yet, it is possible for feelings to change so rapidly, so suddenly, that we get to a point where we can see the future and . . . it changes everything. Well, not everything. My mother is a problem. And the bank has incredible difficulties right now. It's positively gushing money. And . . ." He glanced at the backseat. "I really like your friend."

She became tense. "What do you mean by that?"

"I'm not sure. I just . . . you know, like her. Really."

Andy hit the accelerator and the car screeched ahead. "There are things you don't know about her."

"And there are plenty of things she doesn't know about me."

"I'm taking you home," Andy said.

"Turn around and lend me twenty dollars," he said. "Better make it forty. I can't walk in with any old bunch of flowers."

Why was she looking for a way to turn back toward the hospital? Why was she trying to remember if she had $40 in her purse? "Logo, you don't know what you're getting into."

"I like her and she likes me. We'll get around to the other stuff sooner or later."

She loaned him the money. She took him to a place to buy the flowers. She dropped him off at the hospital and she felt totally, completely utterly alone. She picked up her cell phone and dialed.

Of course Andy could drop in! The kitchen was almost completely finished, but there wasn't much in it, just things he kept for the staff, his experiments, his almost-but-not-quite-there-yets and other things he wasn't quite sure about because, "because you are never, ever sure about a menu until two months after your opening and then you have to change it all because some things just don't work, no matter what and, after two months, everyone in the city has done an awful job of copying the menu and the critics have published their stupid reviews in which they act like they know all about the food but they wouldn't know dog food if we served it. Wait a minute. What about a high-end restaurant for people and pets? We could call it, Les Chiens de Rotissoire, Le Gran Pooch, Les Chats Meow! What do you think?"

She didn't tell him she needed an emotional lift, she needed a friend, she needed somebody to be with, a little bit.

And Matthew Plank was just perfect for that.

"I love it," Andy said into her cell phone, looking for a place to park among the vans and trucks clustered around the tarp-shrouded building on Broad Street with the plank in front of it.

"We could do mousse of mouse," he replied, "petit Fauves, Fettucine al Fido, Bone Appetite! Andy, you always inspire me! Well, not always. This place *was* my idea. But you were there when I got the idea. You were with me. You were part of the creative flash! You know where it is? If you can't find parking on the street, there's the lot I had to buy for parking just behind the place. It's your first right going west from Broad on Hockawingo. God, what a name! How will I *live* with an address that sounds like Native American for spit?"

His voice began to fade. She found a parking space. A young, weary woman in a stained white chef's jacket and houndstooth pants waited for her at the back of the building. She raised the tarp for Andy, exposing a wide set of double doors in the cooly luminous sheen of metal-flake "Ferrari red" paint that would be the restaurant's exterior color. She led Andy along a grimy, concrete block corridor that smelled of machine oil, drying paint and hardening spackle. They went through an employee locker room, past an enormous storeroom and a walk-in refrigerator the size of a bank vault into a dazzlingly bright kitchen trimmed in milky almond and olive green.

In the center of the kitchen stood a small, frightfully thin man who could have stepped out of a jungle, or a forest. He held a short, crudely carved wooden club in one hand. The other hand pressed a cell phone to his ear. He wore a short black cap with a tiny bib over brown, wavy hair that cascaded to a dark gray shirt of coarse weave and similarly roughly stitched woolen trousers that ended in knee-high leather boots.

Matthew Plank turned, saw Andy, said, "The guest of honor has arrived!" and ended his phone conversation.

Then he tapped the club on the stone tile kitchen floor and displayed his clothes. "This is the traditional getup of a *massere*, a dream-hunter, a souvenir of my trip to Corsica." He twirled the club. "The *masseri* are an elite group in Corsica, shamans who mediated with the underworld, got into fights with evil spirits and, according to legend, killed by first going to sleep and dreaming a spirit to death, then going out, summoning their prey, which could be human or animal, and killing them with their bare hands, or with a club, like this."

Andy saw that a table for two had been set in the center of the kitchen. He pulled back an elaborately carved bentwood chair for her. She took her place. Plank put down the club and zoomed about the kitchen.

"The world does *not* need another cute, cozy, shabby-cool Center City Italian BYOB!" Plank said, putting a dish of olive oil on the table. He went to a wood-burning oven and removed a round, dark brown loaf big enough to be a tire on a small car. He put it on a cutting board, put the cutting board on a wheeled tray and brought it to the side of the table.

Plank said, "The original concept was for a restaurant called Vendetta! Food as revenge, eating to get even. Who does revenge better than the Corsicans, where the vendetta was born? I read Merimee's *Colomba,* a creaky old story in which the cure for so much senseless blood feuding is—religion! Merimee was French and, to a Frenchman, the only cuisine possible is his own. Merimee probably didn't go near the local cuisine, which, in the nineteenth century, consisted almost entirely of goat, lamb, wild boar, water, cheese, dreadful wine, crudely pressed olive oil, fish and bread. But not just ordinary bread. A bread of dreams! A bread that you eat to experience a unity with nature, a bread of cosmic consciousness, a bread that summons dark forces from the earth!"

He ripped off a chunk of the loaf. "Corsica is too mountainous for wheat, so the *masseri* made their bread with coarsely ground chestnut flour—the very same chestnuts we roast on an open fire while Jack Frost is nipping at our nose. You can still get it in places. I had to be taught to make it like this. This is *pane di legna,* the bread of wood, made like the *mazzeri* make it. You don't cut this bread with a knife. You use your hands. You tear yourself a piece and taste."

She eyed the bread suspiciously. It was a dark, grayish brown and retained a smokey odor from the oven. She touched the mottled, crusty surface. The crust yielded to her touch. Her fingers sank into the warm, spongy heat. She pulled a piece away. It was a lighter color than the crust, but scary in an earthy, primitive way.

"Come on, Andy, it won't kill you," Plank urged. "This bread is lower in calories, lower in fat and lower in carbs, high in fiber and absolutely spectacular in taste. This is a supreme example of rustic peasant food that is better than civilization and its discontents can dish out."

She brought it to her nose and inhaled a deeper, darker earthiness, almost like a roasted mushroom.

"Taste, taste. You can dip it in the olive oil, if you must. It's Corsican oil, a first pressing, but first, taste."

The roasted, chewy, faintly sweet flavor of the bread filled her mouth. It was like dropping slowly into a soft, warm, cozy bed piled high with your favorite old blankets. She took another taste and the warmth claimed her. She wanted to forget what was bothering her and just curl up somewhere, with or without someone, and let everything go.

"It . . . takes over," Andy said.

"Indeed."

The bread began to dry her throat, so she dipped a chunk in the olive oil. It was *too* good.

"Merimee was wrong in assuming that religion—which, as we all know, has caused more misery, heartache and bloodshed than anything else in history—would end a vendetta. He would have had to live in the American century, when food is culture, cure and redemption. Food unites us. Food redeems us. Food sustains us and inspires us to . . ."

Andy stopped chewing. "Mmmuft?"

Plank hopped up from his chair, vaulted over a divider isolating the kitchen from the unlit dining room and came back with several bottles from the bar.

"I could have done an entire restaurant based on that bread, but it wouldn't be enough for this market. Not at my prices. I had to get something closer to where people live, something that speaks to their deepest obsessions. So I looked around this neighborhood. Who's moving in? Boomers, coming back to the city to blow their money on a lifestyle they never had while they were raising kids. Whatever they want, they want it better than they've had before. They want food that symbolizes dignity, sophistication, panache and triumph, and that they can eat on a diet!"

Andy became desperately thirsty. She tapped on the milkshake glass. The bread had absorbed so much moisture from Andy's throat that she couldn't talk. She lifted the glass, pointed to it.

"Be patient!" Plank commanded. "There is an *art* to the building up of suspense!"

He resumed his rhetorical stance. "While I was in Ajaccio, I heard two Italians arguing over a card game. The one who lost threw his cards down and shouted, *'Rivincita!' Rivincita* is a demand for a 'rematch,' an opportunity to do again what wasn't done properly the first time. Imagine: a restaurant for people who feel that whatever modest success they have attained is not enough. They want status they never had, glory they never attained, diet food so extraordinary, spectacular and unique that they wonder why they ever bothered to get fat in the first place. They want an American life with a second act!"

Andy pointed insistently at the shake glass.

Plank opened a fuse box and threw some switches. A cluster of theater spots splashed light on the dining room walls. Illuminated columns of bottles, stacked with their tops facing forward, rose to the steel ceiling beams. "I got the idea for them while staring at these magnificently vertical rock formations in the red cliffs near Piana. You know about bottle lockers? Where you overpay for a single bottle of vodka and make a big deal of not finishing it so it can be locked away in your own tiny personal shrine and all these people who don't know you can be so

244

impressed that you have your own piece of turf in a public restaurant? That is *so* weak. Why go to a restaurant where they overcharge you to cellar a single bottle when you can come here and cellar from five—for the Baby Back—to as many as twenty-five bottles, for the Max Rack— in a locked, temperature controlled, vertical stack with a glass front so that people won't know exactly what you have, but they will see, real fast, how *much* you have? Instead of conspicuous consumption reduced to a single, overpriced branded bottle, the affluent empty nester—who has had a lifetime to accumulate a range of peculiar, ironic, or merely awful favorites—can flaunt his favorites with the equivalent of his parents' living-room china closets, in which he can stack anything from Chateau Petrus to Mad Dog 20/20. And get this—I sold all the racks to my backers a month ago. They resold the racks several times, with the restaurant getting a percentage on each transaction. Andy, this is the first restaurant I've done that's made a profit before it's opened!"

He snatched the glass from the table. "And what's a bouncing *boite de boisson* without a gimmick drink? What did I serve you last time? Drabyak Siberian Pepper Vodka?"

She could only nod, rapidly.

He opened the bottle, added it to the goblet, then added whiskey and dry vermouth and then "not one, not two, but three dashes of bitters."

He added other liquids to the glass. From a drawer he removed a long spoon with Rivinceta! embossed on the handle. He swished the concoction briefly in a way that reminded Andy of the way Li-Loh had stirred tea. "We must consider the theatrical element," he said. Then he vaulted again over the divider and returned with a red metal bucket reminiscent of the water buckets used to douse weary boxers. He plucked from the bucket what appeared to be a black bean. He dropped a bean into the glass and, instead of floating, the bean sank in the swirling liquids in a descending spiral.

He put the glass in front of Andy. "I call this a Bitter Pill."

Andy swallowed the bread that was in her mouth. "What did you put in there?"

He folded his arms. "You'll have to drink it and find out."

Andy took a sip and almost recoiled from the conflicting tastes of spicy vodka that wasn't quite cold enough, burning whiskey, thoroughly inappropriate sweet vermouth and an astringent taint that made the whole thing taste rude, brackish, *bitter.*

She almost pushed the drink away until she noticed, underlying so many conflicting tastes, a subtle, smokey sweetness. She took another sip and Plank said, "Ah ha!"

The sweetness was stronger. She noticed a curl of what appeared to be liquid smoke emanating from the bean at the bottom of the glass.

"It's an unusual variety of anise sour made by this old candy maker I found in Bonifacio. It's so dense it refuses to float. It goes right down to the bottom where it dissolves slowly enough to impart a faint, licorice sweetness that, by the time you get to the bottom of the drink, unites all the flavors until it tastes better than anything you could think possible." He grinned at her. "Don't you love it?"

Andy was about to tell him that she did when the woman who had let Andy in rushed up to him and whispered in his ear.

He paled. "The sewage backed up—where!?" He rushed off, came back, rinsed his hands, and insisted that he would cook for her, but as a different, less appetizing aroma invaded the kitchen, Andy told him it was okay, they could do this some other time. He wrapped a large piece of the bread in a dark red Rivinceta carry-out bag while she drank the rest of the Bitter Pill. He made her promise that she would attend the opening on Halloween—"No one's allowed to come as they are—they have to come as what they're definitely *not!*"

She was in her car when the alcohol in the drink hit her. She didn't know how long she sat in her car and cried. She had needed a friend and the people she thought were her friends were either falling in love with each other or trying to find a plumber on a Sunday night. She told herself she had no right to feel sorry for herself and that made her cry more.

She started the car and headed up Washington Avenue, across the Grays Ferry Bridge and then up Baltimore Avenue to Forty-second Street.

Cars lined the streets. She had forgotten that, on Sunday nights, the

246

Penn students came back from wherever they went on the weekends and parking got tight. Then she saw the light bar on a police car flashing behind her.

What had she done? Did she run a stop sign? Her first thought was her breath. What had Plank put in that drink? She covered her mouth with her hand and smelled the sweet fumes of top-shelf alcohol.

She heard a voice on the loudspeaker telling her to turn onto Forty-second Street and pull into the space marked off by the cones.

Cones?

She saw an empty space right in front of her apartment house with TEMPORARY NO PARKING signs hanging on two traffic cones. She slipped the Focus between them and saw the police cruiser pull up beside her.

In the red, white and blue glare from the light bar, she saw that the guy in the driver's seat was Vinnie Ferko. He waved. Andy waved back. He took something from the car, got out, came around to her side. She rolled down the window and he handed her a large brown envelope.

He peered at her. "Andy, you look terrible—I mean, you look good, you're very good looking but, you look upset. I didn't mean to bother you. This was too big to leave on the doorstep where anybody could take it. Lucia said you'd dropped her off at the hospital and I figured I'd save you the space and—"

"Vinnie," she said as she held the envelope, "what is this?"

"CeCe's file. It wasn't back at the district headquarters. I had to get it from my father's place. He lives in the Pickle Factory. You been there?"

She began to cry.

"Andy, I'm sorry. This is what you wanted, right?"

Just like that, she was in his arms. She didn't remember getting out of her car. He was a little bit surprised when she put her mouth on his, and then his arms were around her and they locked together, hard and tight. Andy closed her eyes and her lips, slightly numb from the alcohol, slipped deliciously over his. Lights went off somewhere inside her skull. A car horn hooted behind them and, before they broke apart, Andy said, "Vinnie, it's you I want."

For a moment, he just stared at her as if he was the happiest man in the world. Then he said he had to put his car somewhere. He got in, zoomed up the street, turned hard and hit the brakes and left the car in front of a fire hydrant.

He ran back to her, but to Andy, he was moving so slowly, until he was in her arms and they locked again, tighter than before.

It took them a long time to get into her apartment because Andy had to keep kissing him to make sure he was really there. And he had to kiss her right back, a little bolder each time. When Andy didn't get the apartment door open fast enough, he turned her around and pushed her against the door. She was going up the stairs when he grabbed her left ankle and came up her leg, hand over hand, not stopping until his hands were under her skirt. She dropped the file. Her shoulder bag slipped off, the notebook computer inside making a thunk as it hit the stairs, and she pushed his jacket off, started unbuttoning his shirt and stopped at this black wall of fabric around his chest.

She started laughing.

"It's a Kevlar vest," Vinnie said hesitantly. "It can stop some kinds of bullets and knives."

"It looks like a sports bra," Andy giggled.

"So what do you got on?" He said and slipped another hand under her bomber jacket, through the suit jacket, to the blouse, opening one button, two buttons, diving under the elastic of her brassiere and finding the nipple that was waiting for him, sticking up shamelessly like one of those stupid traffic cones that had saved the parking space.

She sent her hands down past his back, then into between his shirt and his belt. She had to find out if Vinnie wore boxers or briefs. She hit elastic but kept going until she grabbed warm skin.

"Your hands are cold," Vinnie said, on top of her, the hardness of his lust bearing down on her. He disentangled himself from her. "I'll go out and get you a pair of cop gloves," Vinnie said. "They're made of a special fabric that resists knife slashes."

She looked at him. "Not now."

He yanked her panty hose down. "Later."

248

19 what are friends for?

The lunch hour was approaching when Andy strode into the newsroom as if she owned the place.

Her face glowed. Her eyes were bright. A long, russet-and-gold woolen dress swirled beneath her bomber jacket. She doffed her shoulder bag, draped the jacket over the back of her chair and slid languidly into her seat.

"And how are you this morning?" she asked Ladderback.

Ladderback took his hands away from his keyboard. Andy *never* asked him how he was.

"I am well, thank you," he said. "And how are you?"

"How *am* I?" She extended her legs under her desk, stretched her arms, arched her back and yawned. "Let me count the ways. . . ."

Ladderback went back to his word processor.

Then she asked, "You know what happens when people get killed?"

He stopped writing. "I don't understand your question."

"Your folks. They did autopsies, right?"

"My parents were medical examiners. In the course of determining a cause of death they performed autopsies."

"And they wrote reports?"

"Their findings were dictated and transcribed," Ladderback said.

"Have a look." She reached into her shoulder bag and pulled out a Homicide Case file marked PROPERTY OF THE PHILADELPHIA POLICE: DO NOT REMOVE. She extracted from the file a yellow Cause of Death form.

Ladderback asked her how she got this.

She stretched again. "It was gotten for me."

"For your friend?"

"If you asked me yesterday morning, I'd say, definitely," Andy said. "If you asked me before I called her this morning, I'd say most likely. But I called her to tell her I got this file, and I found out she spent the night with this guy I've known all my life, which was okay, because she's known *this* guy all *her* life, but she doesn't really respect him. He got the file for me and . . ." she rolled her eyes. "The guy I slept with . . . I mean, well, this place where they live, Westyard? Things can get kind of thick down there."

"They certainly can," Ladderback said.

Ladderback told her he would give the file a thorough reading when he went to lunch. He added that she was welcome to join him, even if the subject wasn't easily discussed over food.

Andy told him she'd love to but . . . she had other plans. She looked at the newsroom wall clock. Only forty-seven minutes until Vinnie, who had court time that morning, would come by in a police patrol car, take her to a secluded spot and, in broad daylight . . .

She gazed at the stack of mail in front of her. She started with the pile closest to her. She went through five letters. When she saw the sixth, she laughed and called Logo.

He answered with a yawn.

"So, how was she?" Andy asked.

"How was . . . how could you ask me that?"

"I just did."

"Andy, I'm offended."

"*You're* offended by *me?*" Andy smirked. "That's a first."

"We didn't just fuck. We talked."

Andy and Vinnie didn't talk. Not for the first hour, at least. "About me?"

"More about your relationship to us."

"Let me tell you something about Lucia. You know how I'm calling you to . . . compare notes? This morning, right after I called her to tell her I got this file? Did she go somewhere and take her cell phone? And who do you think she called this morning?"

"I don't care. She's at the hospital with her mother. She's bringing her back today."

"She called me."

"Then why ask me how she was?"

Because I like annoying *you,* for a change, Andy would have told him. Instead, she changed the subject. "Lucia doesn't have a car. How is she bringing her mother home."

"I'm letting her use the stretch limo I rented last night."

"You said you had no money!"

"I carry my credit card and pin numbers in my brain. How else am I going to dine out with her?"

Andy was immediately jealous. Vinnie didn't go anywhere with her last night. They were too busy, so very, very busy, that, after he left, it took her three tries to program his personal cell phone number into her speed-dialing cue.

She asked Logo where he took Lucia. "Loup Garou. My bank holds some of the notes on Matt Plank's restaurants, so they let me in without a reservation."

"I can get in without one, too."

"You're lying."

She hadn't told him about her friendship with Plank because . . . he hadn't asked her. "I had one of their cheesesteaks."

"You definitely lie. The menu's all Voodoo Hungarian."

"It's Caribbean Transylvanian fusion, but you can get a cheesesteak if you ask for it."

"You can?" Logo was genuinely surprised. "How much they charge?"

"I got it free."

"Now I know you're lying. Plank runs a tight ship. He doesn't give anything away."

Andy glanced at the red bag and the lump of bread in her shoulder bag. "I like the way you said 'my' bank. You used to call it 'the' bank or 'our' bank or 'the goddam fucking bank.' "

"It *is* my bank. Or it will be when my mother gives it to me."

"You're going to have to show her you can work for it."

"People of my class do not *work,* Andy."

Ahh, that was some of the Logo old, Logo the Loathsome, Logo the Jerk who annoyed her because he liked to annoy her. Logo annoyed other women, but Andy liked to feel he gave her special treatment. Had he begun to annoy Lucia? Andy doubted that. Lucia wouldn't take any crap from him, no matter how much money he spent on her.

"You're going to have to call your mother eventually, Logo," Andy said "She's still your mother, even if she thinks you're utterly worthless."

"My mother has *never* referred to me in those terms!" he said, as if she'd just slapped him.

"You're right. She's said much worse." She *loved* annoying him. She felt like she was a little girl trying to get her father's attention. She changed the subject. "When you *dined out,* did Lucia pick at her food?"

"It was more like surgery. She took everything apart put it in little piles and she wanted a Diet Coke, no caffeine, and it had to be a Coke. Matt Plank serves his own cola there, but she had to have Coke. You didn't have a Coke when you had your cheesesteak, I hope."

"I had 120-proof Drabyak Siberian Pepper Vodka, chilled to minus five centigrade, poured straight."

"That's the thing about you," Logo admitted. "You always know what you want."

Did Andy hear correctly? Had Logo almost complimented her? He should sleep with her best friend more often. "So . . . how do you like her mother's place?"

"It's absolutely hideous, especially with all these tacky, cellophane-wrapped flower-and-food baskets coming in. I guess her mother was somebody important."

"She's an accountant," Andy said.

"Lucia told me. But, really, the place is a shock. I can't tell you how many times I've gone past those quaint little working class row houses and never *once* wanted to look in them. Now I know why. I woke up in the middle of the night because my body still thinks it's in Europe and I looked around. I think I figured out the break-in. There's this huge room full of files on the third floor, I know Lucia tried to straighten the rest of the house up a little, but she hadn't gotten to the third floor. I think whoever got to her mother had wanted the files. The S-files were all over the floor."

"Has Lucia's mom said anything about who hurt her?"

"Nothing comprehensible. She's drugged up. She goes in for more tests later this week. Right now, whenever she sees me she calls me Errol and tells me to get out of her house. You don't know who this guy is, do you? Do I look like him?"

"Exactly like him," Andy lied.

He broke the connection.

Oh, I am *too* mean, Andy said to herself. Then Andy remembered that Lucia was holding her first women's self-defense course on Mischief Night at . . . where was it?

Andy did a Web search for "dance Westyard" and found it: Tiburno Academy of Dance at Fifteenth and Panati Street.

She pulled up the template for her column and wrote, in boldface,

Dear Mr. Action:

Recently a woman who lives nearby was attacked and seriously injured by an unknown assailant. Would she have been able to prevent this if she had taken a self-defense course?

Worried, M. P., Kings Grant

Would Matt Plank know she had used his initials? Probably not. When he was developing a restaurant he was too busy to read newspapers.

Now Mr. Action had to answer the question. Andy could call Lucia and ask her, but Lucia was probably with her mother right now so . . .

> Dear M. P.:
>
> No self-defense course can guarantee your safety. But a self-defense course can give you ways to cope with threatening situations, as well as show you a few tricks that can let potential assailants know that you won't be pushed around. Lucia Cavaletta, who will teach self-defense every Wednesday evening at Tiburno Academy of Dance in Westyard beginning this week, says that "a woman has the right to walk down a street and be treated with dignity and respect. A self-defense course won't turn you into a street fighter, but could make the difference between being a survivor, or a victim."

Andy would get Lucia on the phone and get some quotes from her about how to find a reliable self-defense course, how much they cost, what special clothing or equipment you might need, and what health or medical problems might arise.

Or she could find that information on the Internet. But Lucia would get a plug and maybe that would get her some good students.

She looked at the wall clock: Vinnie was coming in eight minutes!

Before she signed off, she asked herself if she should use Lucia's cell-phone number for the *fomi*. With Lucia's mother coming home today, Lucia needed to keep her cell-phone line open, just in case she was out of the house and her mother needed her. She didn't want to use Teal's number. Teal might not be in any condition to answer the phone.

She put Logo's cell-phone number in the *fomi*.

What are friends for?

Ladderback watched Andy rush out of the newsroom.

Then he dialed a number with the police department. He was told to call a cell phone. The woman who answered said, "Sex Crimes, Lieutenant Nanh."

Ladderback identified himself. He said he was aware that it was unusual to be asking about an old case that occurred some time ago, but he would be grateful if she could tell him what she remembered regarding the death of Caprice Delise. "You were among the officers investigating that case."

Her voice became guarded. "I was, yes."

"I must ask you a difficult question, but before I do, I want to assure you that your answers are not for publication."

"Then why are you talking to me?"

"I have a copy of the Cause of Death report in front of me. I also have some knowledge of terms and procedures. What I was hoping to obtain from you is not in the report."

"I see so many cases," she said. "I cannot remember much about that one."

A wariness in her tone suggested to Ladderback that she remembered a great deal from this case. "Whatever you can tell me about this one will be helpful," he replied.

She began, "A girl, I believe she was sixteen years old, was found dead."

"Physical trauma about the head and torso," Ladderback read from the report. "Cause of death is asphyxiation. Bruising about the neck indicates pressure from assailant's hands. The report goes on to indicate sexual assault. What I find peculiar is the lividity—the way the blood collects in a body shortly after death."

"I know what lividity is."

"It seems likely, from the lividity pattern on her back and on her arms and legs, that her sexual relations, as well as the murder, occurred elsewhere and that she was carried to the site."

"That was my opinion also."

"What I wanted to ask you, Lieutenant Nanh, if it is possible that the body was left in the Eisley Bros. Meatpacking Plant gatehouse intentionally."

"Do you mean for some other purpose than merely hiding it, or getting rid of it? I can't say. The gatehouse is a bad place to hide a body in the summer. The windows were broken and it was open to the air, so the odor would have eventually informed us where the body was if we were not summoned."

"I also have a copy of the incident report that says you were summoned by an anonymous caller. Could you determine anything about the caller from the tone of voice?"

"The caller was male. He used a pay telephone in the lobby of the Sisters of Zion Hospital. I have no way of knowing if the caller was Asian. If you are thinking that one of my people in the factory might have called, that isn't possible. There were no working telephones in the factory. No one there could afford a cell phone."

"You had relatives living inside the plant?"

"Some. They risked their lives to come to this country. They wanted to be citizens but they were not permitted. They were exploited. They were used as prostitutes. They were worked until they were sick and when they were sick they couldn't go to the hospital. Many of them died. Their bodies were dumped in abandoned houses, empty lots, everywhere but near the factory. I made sure these bodies were reported but nobody from your newspaper called me about them. Then this girl dies, and I was called from your newspaper."

On his word-processor screen, Ladderback pulled up the only articles about the Caprice Delise murder in the *Press*. The first was a single paragraph in the "Police Story" column mentioning that a teenaged female homicide victim had been found in Westyard, and that police were withholding her name until the family was notified. The second, appearing a day later in the same column, identified Caprice Delise by name and mentioned that the medical examiner had determined she had been sexually assaulted. A "source" mentioned that police believed she had been the victim of Asian gang violence.

Items in the "Police Story" column could have been written by any of a half dozen reporters covering police matters all over the city. Contributors to the column did not get a byline.

"Do you remember who called you?"

"He said he was the top man."

"Howard Lange?"

"It could be him."

"Did he say why he called you?"

"He said he had been contacted by a Caprice Delise previously and he wanted to know if this was the same one. I said I had told her to call the *Press*. She came to me and said a boy she was friendly with wanted to be a journalist and the two of them thought they had a big story about Asians living in the factory and what should they do?"

"Why did she contact you?"

"I am American-born Vietnamese. I was raised in Upper Darby, but my parents would go often to Westyard, to the market there, because it is the best place for rice. When I became the first Vietnamese woman in the police department, I became known in the Vietnamese community. Caprice was Caucasian, but she was dating a Vietnamese boy, a different boy than the one who wanted to be a journalist. This boy she was dating said she should contact me. She said she and this boy wanted to do a big exposé, so, should they call TV or a newspaper?"

"Why did you recommend a newspaper?"

"I read the *Press*. I don't watch much TV. At crime scenes, the TV newspeople come with their lights and cameras and they make a lot of fuss. The newspaper people are easier to get along with. I told her to call the *Press*."

"Did she tell you what happened after she called the *Press*?"

"She said the boy who wanted to be a journalist was afraid he would get in trouble. Caprice wasn't afraid, so she kept calling until she got to the top man and told him about it. The top man said she should send him something in writing and he would get back to her."

"Did he?"

"I don't know. I did not see her again until she was dead."

"And Howard Lange called you after that?"

"Just the one call. He also asked me about Asian gangs. He said he had heard from his sources that the factory was used by the Asian gangs and that I was put on the case because I was Asian. I told him it was true that the police department will assign people to a case who share a similar background with those involved in a case, but I believed I was assigned to the case because it was a sex crime and I was competent at working with those cases. I told him that a few of the younger people in the factory were in the gangs, but most of them were just suffering terribly and that it was shameful that no one was willing to help them. He said he knew all about squatters. He said there were squatters all over the city and that nobody wanted to hear about them. What people want to hear about was the police catching a killer. He wanted me to tell him as soon as we found out because he wanted the *Press* to be the first with the story. He said he had friends in the police department who would look out for me."

"Did you ever speak to him again?"

"I did not want to."

"Captain John Ferko investigated the crime. Did you think his efforts were competent?"

She wanted to say more, but she merely replied, "Yes."

"Were all the suspects Captain Ferko questioned Asian?"

"All the suspects I was aware of were Asian."

"I have something else that I must ask you, Lieutenant. I will understand if you do not want to answer."

"I know what you want to ask. You want to ask me if Captain Ferko directed the investigation at the Asian community so he wouldn't have to investigate the white community."

Ladderback waited. And waited. And waited.

"You must write more obituaries about Asian people. Many, many more. We have given up so much to build our future here."

"I am sorry, Lieutenant Nanh," Ladderback said.

"I am sorry, also. And I will not speak further about this."

Ladderback finished two obituaries, one of a retired schoolteacher who started a morning walking club before she was overwhelmed by Alzheimer's, another of a mortician who died in an automobile accident while driving to find a nightclub where he was scheduled to perform as a comedian, when Andy blew in, her dress swaying as if carried by an autumn breeze.

"Don't stare at me," she said to him when she had taken off her jacket and signed on to her word processor.

"Are you aware of the time?" Ladderback asked her.

"No," she said. "Why should I be?"

"It is 3:37 P.M.," Ladderback said firmly. "We accomplish more when we are here."

"Before I left I wrote a new lead for tomorrow's column. I have the equivalent of three columns of secondary material carrying over from last week. Since when do you set my hours?"

"One of your duties is to assist me. That requires you to be present."

"So I took a long lunch."

Ladderback opened his mouth.

"And don't ask me what I ate."

He closed his mouth. And opened it again. "Would you like—"

"An assignment? I would *love* an assignment," Andy said sarcastically. "I can't *wait* for you to mess up my day by sending me out to talk to some obscure wacko and then come back and listen to you tell me I didn't ask the right questions."

Ladderback watched her for a while. "You're different today."

"I'm *what*?"

"Your attitude. When you have been antagonistic in the past, it has been in response to rude, abusive and impertinent treatment from members of the newsroom staff, who are, by and large, rude, abusive and impertinent. Since you have had your position here, I have done my utmost to treat you with respect and courtesy."

"You want an award for that?" Andy asked. "You want me to congratulate you for being one of the few people in this place who isn't an asshole?"

"I want to give you an assignment," Ladderback said.

"But, as long as I'm *different* today, why don't we do things differently? I'll give *myself* an assignment. I'll write about . . . truck stops! Did you know that the most critical item on a truck-stop menu is eggs-any-style? Truckers, and others who happen to go to truck stops because they serve breakfast twenty-four hours a day, are very particular about their eggs."

He said nothing.

"Okay. This one I *know* Lange will go for. I can see big play on the front page, a truly *fat* lead: the police commissioner has recently issued a confidential memo to police supervisors ranking sergeant and above reminding them of harsh penalties for officers who are found to have *done it* in their patrol cars."

Did his nostrils flare, just a tiny bit?

Andy pulled two lumpy black gloves out of her shoulder bag. "These are not just gloves you're looking at. These are FIRBA hand protection garments. Do you know what a FIRBA is? Flexible Impact-Resistant Body Armor. What they used to call a bulletproof vest, which was never really bulletproof. Now you can get FIRBA ware for your entire body, including your hands, at your local police or personal security supply shop. Watch this."

She put one of the gloves on her left hand, picked up a ballpoint pen with her right, and rammed the pen into her palm. "Monofilament weave. You can't even stick a needle in it."

Ladderback's eyes went to the glove. "How is the fabric stitched together?"

Andy peered at the glove on her hand. "I didn't ask but . . . I can find out!"

"The source of these gloves is no doubt the same as the source of this," Ladderback opened the Homicide case file that Andy had given him. "I will not ask what you have offered in exchange."

She stared at him. "Have you been spying on me?"

Ladderback said, "I don't spy. As Sherlock Holmes would say, 'I observe. I deduce.'"

"Isn't he the one that fell off a cliff?"

"A waterfall. Holmes had to be willing to sacrifice his life to end the criminal career of Professor Moriarty. They went over the Reichenbach Falls together but Holmes did not die. He could not die."

Ladderback opened a white envelope stamped with the words "images taken" with a time and date written in pen. Inside were 8-by-10-inch black-and-white crime-scene photographs. He took one out and put it back. "How is the victim's last name pronounced? Is the patronymic spoken in the Latin variant?"

"What?"

"If it is pronounced in the Philadelphia fashion, Duh-*lease,* then Caprice Duh-*lease* becomes a trite rhyme. But if we use the Latin variant, Day Lee *say,* we have a name of uncommon beauty."

"I've heard him called Mr. Dee Lease."

"I've already called the restaurant. Though it is closed on Monday, you can interview him in the apartment above the restaurant. Your assignment is to profile him as a neighborhood hero who has not missed a single weekend performance since he returned from the Vietnam war." He took a piece of notebook paper from his satchel. "I've compiled a list of some of the arias he sings. 'Nessun Dorma' from *Turandot*; 'Questa O Quella' from *Rigoletto,* and, of course, 'Vesti la Giubba' from *Pagliacci.* Greet him tonight as Mr. Del Lee Say and ask him why he sings."

"But I don't understand opera."

"Most people don't, which is why they fail to appreciate it. All you have to do is listen. If you wish, I can accompany you. We can have dinner at an excellent restaurant within driving distance of the Villa Verdi that serves an exquisite Vietnamese soup called *pho.*"

Did she see a yearning in his eyes? Not like what she saw in Vinnie's, nothing like that. It was more like he didn't want to be alone.

But she was meeting Vinnie later tonight, before he came on shift. She could barely wait. "I'm sorry," she said. "I already made plans for dinner."

He paused. Then he said, "In the course of doing your interview, ask him about some of the well-known people who have dined at his restaurant. He will mention several. Then ask if you can look through his reservation books. A traditional restauranteur would keep them all. Ask to see several books, but make sure you go to the book that records this date."

He pointed to the date written on the envelope of crime-scene photos.

"That's the day she was killed," Andy said.

"According to the autopsy, her last meal was most likely prepared in that restaurant's kitchen. It was a Friday evening. Mr. Delise would have sung that night. She was killed while he was performing."

"How can you be so sure?"

"According to a statement by Mr. Delise included here, when his daughter was in the restaurant, he let her go where she wished, but he was always aware of where she was. It is likely that she had sexual relations while Mr. Delise was singing. The time of death can be calculated as happening no later than the moment the police were called to the scene, which is eight thirty-one P.M. Mr. Delise sings for exactly twenty minutes. It would take no more than fifteen minutes to transport the corpse to a car, move the body to the gatehouse, mutilate the corpse, and drive to the Sisters of Zion emergency room, where an unidentified male called the police."

He replaced the documents and envelopes inside the Homicide case file. "Make sure you write down the name and telephone number of every individual who made a reservation that night."

"One of those will be the killer?"

"Or may know the killer. Ask Mr. Delise if he let some people dine without reservations. Try to get as many names as you can."

Andy rolled her chair away and sat quietly for a while. Then she looked at the wall clock.

"You figured all this out while I was . . . at lunch?"

"I have figured out nothing!" he said, then went back to his word processor.

20 need to know

She thought, when she kept her Ford Focus just behind his Crown Victoria patrol car, that he would take her to a quiet, safe, lonely place, like the one where they went at lunchtime. Vinnie had met her at the front of the Press Building in a patrol car, then he went south on Tenth Street to Orley's Emperor of the Steak. They grabbed steak sandwiches and drinks from the take-out window and he continued going south, then east on Oregon Avenue, until he turned on a dirt road lined with tall brown stalks of marsh grass. The road ended on a lump of muddy soil strewn with odd bits of trash. Seagulls swooped and dived overhead. The grass was so high that the only sign that they were anywhere near civilization were the great, gray piers and soaring arch of the Walt Whitman Bridge heading east into the cool blue, mostly cloudless sky over New Jersey.

After they had made love in the car and eaten their sandwiches, she asked him how he had found the place. He told her she didn't want to know. She told him that whenever anybody told her that, it was like waving a red flag in front of a bull. He waved his underwear at her (blue and green plaid boxers) and they made love again, but, when it was nearly 3 P.M. and she figured she'd better show her face at the newspaper, he mentioned to her that he had been part of a squad that had been called to this spot because some bodies had turned up there.

"What kind of bodies?" she'd asked, expecting him to say, again, that she didn't want to know.

"Dead ones," he said simply, "sometimes without much clothes on. No identification. The animals get to them and they look pretty bad."

He had utterly ruined the mood, until she asked him what would have happened if, when he had taken her there, they had found a body or two.

Vinnie put his arm around her and, giving her that sincere look that she loved said, "I would've asked them to leave."

It wasn't funny but she gave him a smile. He smiled back. She kissed his cheek and then licked his ear and the good mood was back.

She needed him again to lift her mood, now that a moonless night had fallen. She followed his patrol car's red taillights onto an old shipping pier thrusting out into the Delaware, waiting for him to stop so she could join him in the patrol car and maybe do what they had done again, or just talk, because she needed to talk.

She had been late for her interview with Mr. Delise because she couldn't find the entrance to his apartment. She had finally located it behind a large truck that was parked in the alley behind the restaurant. The truck had ONWARD AND UPWARD painted on its side.

The door to the apartment was open. She took creaky wooden stairs two at a time until she had to duck. The ceiling of the dark little apartment was so low she had to look out for lighting fixtures hanging down. Furniture tilted and leaned in odd directions on the sloping hardwood floor.

Mr. Delise sat in a rocking chair beside a table with a reading lamp and a large shortwave radio. His splinted hand rested on a plum-colored blanket that covered his knees. He got up when he saw her, asked her if she wanted tea or coffee, and showed her a plate of pastries, including a stack of pizzelles. She opened a small folding chair that had been leaning against a wall and apologized for being late. She was five minutes into the interview when she realized she had forgotten to greet him with the fancy pronunciation.

He told her that he was amazed that anyone would want to write him up, talk to him as a singer, "not just some bum who feeds people." But she was a little late. He had decided to deed the restaurant over to Not Fade Away. Jack Ferko had a place for him in a senior adult community out in the suburbs where he could sing every night if he wanted.

"So I guess you wasted a trip," he said.

It was a stupid question, but Andy had to ask if he was leaving because of the robbery.

"They want what's in the safe, they can have it," he said bitterly. "My father put that safe in, right after he opened this place. He put it in the wall, so, if you take out the safe, the whole wall comes down. He knew the combination but he liked to keep secrets. He never told me. He never told my mother. And then he died. He was a mean man when he died. Angry. Not happy. He didn't leave the combination in the will. When he died, they said I should drill the safe. The week we buried him I was going to drill it, but then I went out and did my singing and, when I was done I figured, whatever is in the safe can stay in the safe. I don't need it.

"But everybody knew I had the safe. Even after I put in the pay phones, the big shots, the celebrities, the people who had to run off and make a call and they couldn't just use the pay phones, they'd come back to the office and they'd see the safe, and they wouldn't believe me when I said I never opened it. Paulie Small—did Lucia tell you about that louse? He thought I kept things in the safe. He used to write me letters when I was in Vietnam, tell me all kinds of stories about what he was doing in Canada. Never signed the letters, but I knew it was him. I wrote him back a few times, him and Jack Ferko. They thought I had his letters in my safe. I told them I threw those letters out. They never believed me."

"If you couldn't open the safe, what did you do with your valuables?"

"I don't have any. When my wife left me, she took her jewelry. I have my medals from the war. You want them? You can have them. What's here to steal? Pots and pans? My wristwatch? A recipe for meatballs? The cash money the restaurant makes goes into a paper bag that I used to give to Tommy Nguyen to walk down to the Hampton Bank. I had no problems with Tommy all these years until him and his stupid punk gang tried to rob me. His father told me it's all a mistake, that he's a good kid now, but I don't know . . ."

"What about the deed to your restaurant?"

"That's in a safe-deposit box at the bank. Anything else I stuck in a bag in the office behind the reservation books."

"Did that include the share in the Pickle Factory?"

She saw him die then, just a little. "Lucia tell you about that? Yeah, I had that until Paulie asked for it. What was it, last Tuesday. He comes in, has a big meal like always, with Lucia's mother, and he says he needs it and I told him, what are you going to do, tear it up? I tell him, if you're going to tear it up, then let me tear it up, and then let me sell my place and get out. Because if you go back on your word, I can't face my neighbors no more. I can't stay here.

"He said, no, no, he wasn't going to tear it up. He said the plans for Veterans Plaza didn't have the low-income housing, but he came up with a way he could put it in and that just might work, but he'd need the share to show the senator that it wasn't just an idea, that there was a legal obligation to provide the housing. I couldn't believe it. Paulie always hated Asians. He would always go on about how they were taking over. Now he's saying to me, 'They're good people, too.' I ask myself, was it something in the food? What turns a man around like that? What brings the light into his life? Then he gets killed, poor Teal Cavaletta, she gets beaten half to death and Vinnie Ferko asks me if I have any idea why Asians want to rob my place."

He died a little, again. "The people who used to come out for a fine Italian meal, they're dead, they moved out, they go someplace else. I don't blame them. Time for something new."

"Lucia doesn't think so," Andy said. "Lucia told me your place was the best. She said I had to hear you sing, even if . . ."

"What an angel she is, that Lucia." He looked at his damaged fingers. "To me, what happened to CeCe, my wife, Vietnam, Paulie . . . it's like that safe. When I think about what's in it, I wait until I can go out and sing, and when I'm finished singing, I don't need to open it."

But you have to open it, Andy thought. How can I get you to open it?

Then he gave her a look that told her, without words, that he *knew,* that he had always known who murdered his daughter, and that the interview was over.

"We're done now," he added. "You go."

"Mr. Delise, you can't keep this to yourself."

"What's to keep?" he said bitterly. "You try getting out of bed in the morning when everything you love and work for and live for is taken away from you. You go and fight a war, for what? So this one can be in charge, instead of that one? Because one side is good and the other side not so good? I saw nice people, good people, wonderful, kind, loving people, lose so much. The lucky ones were killed, because they didn't have to lose no more."

"Mr. Delise, I just have a few more questions—"

He didn't hear her. "My beautiful, wonderful daughter lived while, two blocks away, who knows how many were dying. I gave them as much food as I could. I tried to help where I could. She helped, too. I would try to get doctors to go to them and help. We both knew who was keeping those people in that hell, so that the department stores and the sweatshops would have workers who would take a dollar an hour and not complain. We both knew who was turning his back on these people, because they didn't have enough money or enough votes. I asked myself, every day, when was the light going to shine into his life?"

He held himself against the wall. "The light came because of my CeCe. They needed money at the Pickle Factory. She brought them in. Nguyen Li-Loh did not trust them because he had asked them many times before—and had offered to provide seed money—for housing projects and they had ignored him. But I said, this time, we would trust them. We would have a share, and an agreement. And I made the agreement say that the loan would be repaid in the form of seed money for

low-income housing. Ishimura put his chop on the paper, and it was notarized by Lucia's mother.

"And when my daughter was killed, when I thought about opening
my mouth and shouting down who took her life, I knew that I would not
be believed. What is the word of a father against these bastards, who
tried to make it seem as if she was killed by people she loved? But
CeCe, God bless her, didn't die for no reason. The hospital sealed the
factory and Paulie Small told me that, because I kept quiet, the process
of acquiring the land, getting the permits, drawing up initial plans for
the housing could begin."

He turned to the wall. "Do you know what it's like to wake up in the
middle of the night and hear your daughter's voice, in your ear, in your
heart, telling you that it's okay, that things will come out all right, when
all you want to do is to kill the bastards, drag them down and destroy
them so they'll never harm anyone again?"

He wiped his eyes with his sleeve.

"You can go," he said finally.

Andy didn't budge. "Tell me who it was."

He shook his head.

"I'm not going until you tell me."

He turned on the shortwave radio and found a station. Something that
could have been music came out of a tiny speaker.

"Mr. Delise, please! You have to do this!"

The droning turned into words in Italian. He was singing and it
sounded horrible to her. Her *amusa* made most music sound like noise,
but this was worse. This was pain, agony, suffering so intense, so ugly,
so empty of hope, that she had to leave.

She went downstairs into the alley. She saw that the door leading to
the kitchen was open. Inside, just past the glassed-in office, she saw
Frank Cavaletta, in his ONWARD AND UPWARD jacket, a clipboard in his
hand. He was running down a checklist of items to be packed up.

"Angie said you were coming by to write him up. How did it go?"

Andy couldn't say anything.

"I move all kinds of people," Frank went on, as if he were talking about the weather. "When they've lived in the same place all their lives, getting used to the idea that they have to leave can be very tough for them." He made a check mark on his clipboard. "Hey, I heard you introduced Lucia to this rich guy and she actually likes him. Think it'll last?"

Andy brushed past him and Tommy Nguyen moving through the kitchen wearing distressed blue jeans and a soiled white windbreaker with PEACEKEEPER printed on the back in red. His jaw was still wired and the bruises on his face had darkened to the dark plum color of the blanket that had been on Mr. Delise's knees.

"Tommy," she called to him. "Help me with this."

She went into the office, where a piece of plywood had been fitted over the shattered glass that the bullet had gone through.

Andy saw the safe, a dark, brooding bulk. The shelves around it were empty.

"Where are the reservation books?" she asked him.

"Packed up," he said through his wired jaw.

"Get them out," she demanded. "I need to see the one for the year when they killed CeCe."

He didn't move. "They're packed up," he repeated.

"Tommy, if you help me get the book, I might be able to figure out who killed her."

"Why?" he said.

Was he stupid? Was there something she hadn't explained properly?

She turned and saw that he was no longer looking at her like an infatuated adolescent. "It wasn't me," he said.

She stepped out of the office. His eyes followed her. She slowly went down into the basement, turned around and looked back up the stairs. If the wooden board hadn't covered the shattered glass section, she could have seen into the office.

She went back up the stairs and into the office. Tommy's eyes were not smiling.

"He had made arrangements to meet her while her father was singing. He was mad at her for going to a newspaper about the people in the meatpacking plant."

"Who was mad at her, Tommy?"

"He came into the kitchen. He said he needed to use the office phone. He wanted her to open the safe and give him the paper, the share from the *hui ting.*"

"But she didn't know how to open the safe," Andy said.

"That's not why he killed her," Tommy said, his eyes on hers.

And so, Andy learned that CeCe Delise was not killed because she was an adolescent girl who liked getting attention from males. She could flirt, she could tease, she could scamper around, she could trip people up, play practical jokes and find other ways to annoy them.

CeCe was not killed because she came up the stairs and told this man that it was wrong the way people were suffering in the city and that housing should be built for them, not rich people from out of town.

When she said that, Tommy told Andy, the man grabbed her, pulled her down, got his hands around her throat and, while Mr. Delise sang outside, demanded that CeCe open the safe.

CeCe was not killed because she didn't know the combination.

CeCe was not killed because she failed to fight back. "There's this move in Tai Chi called a warding blow," Tommy said. "You see the old men and women doing it in the mornings." He made a soft, fluttering, backhanded movement. "CeCe and Lucia took tai chi. That's where I first met them. They didn't last long. I didn't either. If you were going to learn to fight in Westyard, and you were white, you went to the fight gym, K-O on the Corner. If you were going to learn to fight in Westyard, and you were Asian, you went to Mr. Ishimura. Mr. Ishimura thought tai chi was sissy stuff. He taught us what to do if we got a warding blow, and this guy did the very thing."

CeCe was not killed because she tried to break this man's grip on her throat by hitting him in the face with a warding blow.

CeCe was killed because the man who had his hands around her neck wanted to kill her. What was horrible about it, Tommy said, was how long it took for her to die. When the skin on her face went dark and she stopped struggling, he kept his hands on her neck and shook her, as if he wanted to wring the last bit of life out of her. Then he dropped her, stepped back and touched his face. Only then did he show he had felt any pain.

The man in the suit had looked at his watch. He left CeCe in the office for a few seconds. He came back with an oversized black plastic garbage bag used to line the kitchen trash cans, pulled it over CeCe and carried her out. Only when Tommy heard the back door slam shut did he emerge from the basement.

Andy's need to know had carried her this far, but it didn't carry her far enough. You can get people to talk to you, and they'll tell you what you want to hear, but you can turn them off if you ask the wrong question.

"Tell me who killed her."

Tommy became afraid. "You have to tell me!" Andy said, pursuing him. She reached for him. He scurried away and ran out the back exit.

She wanted to chase him but she had to leave the place. What she had heard was too terrible to bear. She suddenly needed to be with someone who might touch her, kiss her and tell her she didn't have to think about these things.

And yet, when she stopped her car, slipped into Vinnie's patrol car and saw through the windshield a fabulous, northward view of a grand and glittering city rising into a starless, moonless night sky, she had to ask him one thing as he put his arms around her.

"Vinnie, you arrest a lot of people, right?"

"Not enough. For every one that we get, there's at least ten I wouldn't mind putting away. . . ."

She remembered what Vinnie had told her about Errol liking to choke him after Errol had come back from his Heian-Do lessons, and how, only after Vinnie had knocked three teeth out of his brother's mouth, causing Errol intermittent bouts of pain, did Errol lay off.

"Do you think, if it ever happened, you would be able to arrest your own flesh and blood?"

He let go of her. "I don't know, Andy. I just don't know."

They sat quietly for a while. Then he kissed her face.

Andy kept reminding herself that there could be lots of guys who wore suits and strangled girls. She asked Vinnie about wanting to be a reporter. He told her he had felt that way when he was a kid, but just because you feel one way when you're a kid doesn't mean you have to follow those feelings.

Andy told him she felt that way when she was a girl and she stuck with those feelings.

He said that's why he loved her.

Finally, he told her he would wake up early (for him, a guy who works nights, early was anything before 4 P.M.), come by the paper on his motorcycle and take her to lunch. He wanted her to meet some people.

She didn't ask who, because she wanted to believe that Vinnie could save it. Or explain it. Or show her that it wasn't possible that the brother he described to her, the sadistic creep who had choked him as a child, had murdered CeCe, dumped her in the gatehouse and beaten her corpse so it would look like one of the stick-wielding creeps in Shi-Bin's gang had killed her.

Please, Vinnie, Andy said to herself as she went back to her car. Please be the cop we all want: be the guy who rushes in when all seems lost and saves the day.

21 the wrong question

On Tuesday morning, Ladderback was enduring what journalists experience most often: frustration, confusion, obfuscation and a great mass of unreturned phone calls.

Ladderback had lived long enough to be accustomed to this. One of the benefits of writing obituaries about so-called "ordinary" people was that those who have rarely, if ever, been anywhere near the spotlight of celebrity tend to respond to journalistic inquiries courteously, openly and honestly. They have little, if anything, to hide. And they return phone calls.

But the day had begun with Ladderback leaving a message for Teal Cavaletta on her voice mail. He considered a conversation with Teal a second card to play.

While waiting to play it, he looked at the morning's death notices and selected three possibilities from the list. He needed more information about them and left messages with the funeral directors involved. All three funeral directors said they would get back to him.

Then Andy's phone started to ring.

Ladderback dialed the number of Not Fade Away and asked for

Captain Ferko. He was told by a voice he recognized as belonging to one of the cronies Ferko had dined with when Ladderback first met him, that the "commander was not in headquarters." Was there a message?

There was indeed. Ladderback had questions about the commander's tour of duty in Vietnam.

"He's booked up for lunch and dinner tonight, and lunch tomorrow. We'll be at Jimmy D's tomorrow night. You can ask the commander then. We're organizing Mischief Night patrols and the commander wants us to get a good feed on."

Couldn't Ladderback just talk to the commander on the telephone?

"The commander left orders: if it's anything involving members of the media, it's done over a meal and the commander always picks up the check."

"I don't need a meal, I need to speak to him," Ladderback said testily. "This doesn't involve the media."

"We'll see you at Jimmy D's tomorrow night, then."

Ladderback went on the Internet and found the Atlantic City telephone number for Teasdale, William T. He got voice mail and left a message.

Andy's phone kept ringing.

Then Ladderback called the telephone number on the card that State Senator Henry Tybold had given him. He was told the senator was in Harrisburg and that most media requests were handled by Senator Tybold's press secretary, with whom Ladderback could leave his telephone number. Ladderback said he wanted to know if Senator Tybold could confirm that a $2 million share in the Pickle Factory had been sold to an Asian community bank. Ladderback was put on hold and then disconnected.

Andy's phone was ringing, ringing, ringing.

Ladderback then called the Harrisburg office of State Senator Henry Tybold but did not identify himself as a reporter for the *Philadelphia Press* because, he decided, his reasons for calling did not strictly concern the newspaper. Senator Tybold had asked him to call him, so he was returning the call. Ladderback was informed that the senator was in

Philadelphia and was not expected in Harrisburg until tomorrow. Ladderback repeated his reasons for calling and was given Senator Tybold's assistant, who first asked Ladderback if he lived within the Senator's district. Ladderback replied that he did not understand how the location of his residence and, by implication, his ability to vote for the senator, had any bearing on his reason for speaking with the senator, which was based on a relationship initiated by the senator to benefit the senator. The assistant said that she had just a few more routine questions that needed to be asked to "qualify and prioritize" Ladderback's request because, though Ladderback was very important to the senator in the same way all were important—

"All *was* important," Ladderback said. " 'All' takes the intransitive singular."

The senator's assistant put Ladderback on hold. He was disconnected.

As soon as Andy arrived, her phone stopped ringing.

Andy was in a lousy, lousy mood. She hadn't wanted to come to work. She was wearing an old pair of blue jeans and a black blouse and if anybody messed with her she'd just blow out of the newsroom and never come back.

But no one messed with her.

She didn't say anything to Ladderback because she didn't want to tell him that she had screwed up, that she had gotten as close as she could possibly get, and then . . .

Ladderback glanced at her and he observed or he deduced or he just read her mind that he should leave her alone.

She signed on her word processor. She didn't bother to open any mail. She asked Mr. Action a question:

Dear Mr. Action,

　　In my place of business, I have an old safe with a combination lock that I no longer know how to open. What can I do with it?

　　　　　　　　　　Secure but unsure, C.F.

There, Andy said to herself. Claus Fortini got his initials into the *Philadelphia Press.*

So how was she going to answer this? She did a search for locksmiths. She called a locksmith with a cute name. He answered. She introduced herself. She asked. He answered. She thanked him, hung up and started to write:

Dear CF,

According to Weldon Tarrow, a locksmith at Redmonton's Lock, Stock & Tarrow, there are a surprising number of old safes of various kinds and sizes in the Philadelphia region, some of them dating back to the 19th century. Because so many of the early lockboxes were custom made by master locksmiths, the wheels, mechanisms and handles of some older safes are prized by collectors, who have paid up to $100,000 for a fully functioning wall or free-standing lockbox.

As you might expect, Tarrow recommends you call a locksmith. "A competent professional can visit your home or place of business and, within a few minutes, assess what needs to be done."

The one thing you should never do, Tarrow says, "is try to jar, strike, bang or force the mechanism. Even if you know the combination, and the mechanism has stuck or jammed, a screwdriver, crowbar or a drill will, at least, mar the finish, which can reduce the safe's value on the collector's market." At worst, Tarrow adds, you might destroy components of the mechanism that "can be surprisingly fragile, especially after dust and corrosion have done their work. And forget about what you saw in movies—dynamite is more likely to blow *you* up than the safe."

Though safes are not made to be disassembled easily, there's hope, in the form of the Internet. Lock and safe collecting enthusiasts have put several

Her phone rang and she picked it up. "Why the hell did you put my cell-phone number in your shitty little rag for that self-defense course?"

Logo yelled into her ear. "I can't use the thing, it's ringing so much. I can't get any work done."

"Work?" she said. "I thought work was something your class didn't do."

"Well, I can, if I want to. I used Teal's computer to access the bank and I got into our transactions log to see if your cop boyfriend has an account with us. Next time you see him, ask him about his brother."

"I'd rather not."

"I've already put our forensics onto Errol. They're going to talk to him really quick and either shut him down or force him to take his business to another bank."

"What's he doing that's so bad?"

"Errol Ferko's little one-man financial services company is using our bank to make it seem like he's doing more business than he is. He's taking payments that are supposed to go to insurance companies, mutual funds and brokerages and ramming them through six different accounts, and billing his clients, and the businesses he's supposed to serve, for each transaction. Each time he does a transaction, he generates a fee which he bills to both the client and the business."

"I did an item on insurance salesmen," Andy said. "They're not allowed to double bill."

"This is more than double. He's paying himself twelve times over. But the businesses he represents are so marginal that they don't care as long as some money comes in. And his clients, as far as I know, haven't checked up on him, though one of our forensic team remembers a case some time ago when a group of clients requested transaction records from us covering about two million dollars. I don't know what came of that, but I'm going to find out."

"Because you're jealous?"

"What I am is diligent. If my bank is used in a scam that we could have found out about, and we failed to find out about it, we can be fined rather severely and named as a party in a suit. Small-time dipshits like Errol Ferko don't have deep pockets—he can go bankrupt and nobody's going to cry. But my bank has deep pockets, and I don't want them emptied for any reason."

"So how come it took you so long to find this out?"

"Fraud is like parlor magic. You don't see the trick unless you know where to look, and you don't look unless you have a reason to look. The brother—the one you're fucking—is okay, by the way."

"I'm so grateful to hear," Andy said. "You're actually making yourself useful."

"I kind of like it. I mean, I could be fucking off, but doing something like this . . . kind of fun. I may get bored with this but . . . if I stick with it, who knows? My mother might not think I'm so worthless."

"Have you called her yet?" Andy asked.

He hung up.

Andy put her phone down. "Errol Ferko," she repeated sourly.

"Indeed," Ladderback said. He called up a Web site that rated local investment companies and found Incentive Investments at the bottom. "Last year was not good for Mr. Ferko," Ladderback said. "His one-man company suffered from stock market reversals, insurance claims, commission reductions and real estate projects were not approved. He needed cash infusions. How did he get them?"

He peered closer at the screen. "I am curious to know exactly what Mr. Ferko does for a living."

Andy noticed it was close to noon. "I think I'm about to find out," she said.

They had a fight, in public, right in front of the *Press* Tower.

Vinnie hopped off his bike, pulled off his helmet and said, "I want to know who this Brickle piece-a-shit Lucia's seeing is!"

Andy folded her arms. "He's rich, he's good-looking, he's cleaned up his act and it was love at first sight."

"I did a search on him," Vinnie said. "He's got a sheet a mile long." He pointed his finger down, making jabbing motions as he talked. "He's been arrested for drugs, drunk-and-disorderly and just about every other petty crime there is and he never got convicted for a damned thing and there's the name of this guy Ben Cosicki all over his file and I want to know what he had to do with this kid."

"My father had a sideline business of getting people out of trouble."

"Just the rich ones?"

"My father never talked about it," Andy said.

"So how come this piece-a-shit is asking all these questions to Teal about me?"

"Vinnie, you can ask him. He's sleeping with Lucia."

"But you know him. You put that thing in the paper about her and you used his fucking number!"

"I wanted to piss him off," Andy said.

People who were closest to them kept walking, but a few stood back to watch the show.

"What about me?" he yelled. "Why didn't you want to piss me off? I'm not worth it?"

"You're worth it, Vinnie. It's your family I'm not sure about."

"You're talking about my family? How dare you talk about my family when your father paid off cops to keep this piece-a-shit out of jail, and your mother sells garbage!"

"How do you know if he paid off cops?" She wanted to kick him. "Were you standing there? Did you take some money?"

"I talked to the piece-a-shit. *He* said your father paid off cops."

Was everybody talking behind everybody's back? "You know nothing about my father and you know nothing about art!" she yelled at him.

"And you don't know people!" he said.

Andy didn't get that.

"I mean family," Vinnie said. "The people who are family. My family."

"Then tell me, right here," Andy said. "Tell me to my face that your brother had nothing to do with CeCe's death."

"Why would he have anything to do with her death?"

"Was he at the Villa Verdi the night she died?"

"He could've been. I had moved out of my father's house then. I was living on the couch in Teal Cavaletta's living room. My brother was hanging out with Uncle Paul. I'd see him when Uncle Paul would visit Teal. But we didn't talk. Not then. We talk now. It took a while."

"You talk to him this morning?"

"As a matter of fact, I did. He says he got a call from his bank, the same one that this Brickle piece-a-shit works for."

"He doesn't work for it, Vinnie. He *owns* it. And he thinks your brother is screwing around with other people's money and he doesn't want his bank involved."

"You put him up to that, right?"

"I did not."

"So who's telling you that he killed CeCe? Tommy Nguyen? What the fuck does he know? He was going with CeCe at the time. Who knows what they could've done. Who knows why she would get herself in that gatehouse."

"Did you see the pictures, Vinnie?" Andy said. "The pictures of her, in the file you gave me, that were taken where she died? I saw the pictures. Who could've done that to her, Vinnie? Shi-Bin?"

"Not Shi-Bin," Vinnie said. "He was working at the time. At Zyman Condiments. He had plenty of witnesses putting him at that factory. When we did finally talk about it, my brother thought whoever killed her might've wanted to make it look like Shi-Bin did it."

"And how would he know about Shi-Bin?"

"He's known Shi-Bin since he trained with Ishimura. My brother gave him one of his clubs, a sand wedge, to use as a cane."

"I saw Shi-Bin try to kill Lucia. He threatened me with rape. How you feel about your brother being friendly with a piece of shit like him?"

"There's a lot about my father I don't like, there's a lot about my brother I can't stand," Vinnie said. "But they're my family and, compared to the rest of the piece-a-shits in this world, I'm sticking by them."

She could have told him to say "piece*s*-of-shit," but she wanted to put her arms around him instead. In his voice she heard that terrific sincerity, the desire to be good, to be right, to help people and to stick up for those who needed him. She calmed down and remembered why she was so attracted to him. And she remembered something else.

"Mr. Delise knows who killed her, Vinnie. He wouldn't tell me, but maybe he'll tell you. He needs to tell somebody. His world is coming down around him. He shouldn't suffer that much, Vinnie. Nobody should."

"Whatever Mr. Delise knows, he never said to me. From what I was told, he was out singing. The next anybody hears about CeCe was the phone call about a dead girl in the gatehouse. Sure, I've heard talk about having sex with her. I've heard what he's had to say. What kind of kid is it who hides in the fucking basement when his girlfriend is in trouble? Not somebody I'd want to believe. Why Mr. Delise trusts him, I'll never know."

He came close to her. "Now Andy, come with me on the bike. Errol's meeting us for lunch. My grandfather's getting some tests done with his doctors, so he's in town. It might be just me and Errol. Or you might get my grandfather and even my father, too. You can ask us anything you want. You can settle whatever's bothering you. And then you and I can get back to the way things were Sunday night."

Andy wanted to hug him and he looked like he needed a hug. Some of the people standing around were expecting it. They had their hands up, waiting to applaud when Andy and Vinnie kissed and made up.

But one last thing was bothering her. "Where were you, when CeCe died?"

He was confused and he was adorable when he was confused. "Oh, I get it." He held his right hand in the air. "Your Honor, I cannot tell a lie. I was with Lucia."

Andy was close enough to smell him and she really, really liked how he smelled. She gazed into his gorgeous brown eyes, put her FIRBA-wrapped hand on his leather jacket and let her voice become as melodramatic as his. "And what were you doing, Sergeant Ferko, with Lucia Cavaletta, on the night of the murder?"

It was the wrong question, but it was silly enough so that anyone other than Vinnie Ferko could have laughed it off and said something silly, like, they were getting punchdrunk.

But Vinnie didn't laugh it off. He broke eye contact and faltered. "I was . . . her mother was away with Uncle Paul so . . . we were, you know, doing it."

She asked Wrong Question Number Two: "I thought you broke up with her?"

He became sheepish. "We would get back together sometimes."

Two wrong answers should have alerted Andy to the fact that in all human situations, especially those regarding love and affection, some questions you shouldn't ask.

But Andy had that need to know. So she asked Wrong Question Number Three: "Then why aren't you with her right now?"

Of course, that question would not have been so wrong if Vinnie gave the one right answer possible, that he wanted to be with Andy, more than anything, or anyone.

If Vinnie had said that, Andy wouldn't have cared if Errol was all the things you don't want in a brother. Or even a brother-in-law. Because she was standing on a cold but bright day at the end of October with the first man who had ever tripped the alarm on her biological clock.

She wanted this guy's kids. Not right away. Maybe not for a year or two. But soon enough. If he said the right answer, she would follow lunch with a suggestion that they take the afternoon off so he could show her the Westyard apartment he lived in and they could make an even bigger mess of his bed than they made of hers on Sunday night.

But he didn't say that. He didn't say a thing. He hesitated. He became uncertain. He looked at the sidewalk. He looked around.

"So *be* with her!" Andy yelled. She turned and went through the front door of the *Press* Tower and, instead of waiting for the elevator, where there would be people who might recognize her if she started to cry, she took the stairs all the way up to the eleventh floor. She was in her chair looking at the "Mr. Action" column about safes when she remembered that a newsroom filled with men and women who are paid adequate but in no way decent money to be nosy, prying, gossipy and downright obnoxious was the worst place to be miserable.

"Come with me," Ladderback said.

She followed him downstairs to the screaming yellow and orange employee cafeteria. He sat her down at a table in a windowless corner, with her back to the door. He put a pile of paper napkins in front of her. Then he went to the cafeteria chef and asked if he could cook to order. The chef asked what did Ladderback have in mind?

He returned a few minutes later carrying a tray with two huge steaming bowls of beef broth. He came back carrying another tray with a bottle of hot sauce, dish of lemon wedges, a plate of cooked spaghetti without tomato sauce, a dish of chopped scallions, a dish of canned bean sprouts, a bowl of meatballs without tomato sauce and a chopped, skinless chicken breast.

"This is an approximation of what is called *pho,*" Ladderback said. "You put whatever you want into the broth and eat it like a soup."

He sat down and added some of the items, stirring them briskly with his spoon. The only words he spoke during the rest of the meal were, "It worked for me."

It worked for her, eventually.

22 mischief night

Some believe that there is no god for journalists, that the media is an invention of the devil and that journalists are the minions of the Evil One, whether they know it or not.

But, if the squabbling, bickering and gossipy inhabitants of the *Press*'s newsroom had a god to pray to, you could almost believe that their prayers had been answered.

The no-news weeks ended.

First, the Philadelphia Eagles beat the Miami Dolphins.

Then, at 4:30 A.M., agents of the Federal Bureau of Investigation served search warrants on the residents and offices of three members of the mayor's staff. Inspired by the mayor's "You gotta pay to play" speech, this was just the beginning, an FBI spokesman announced, of Operation Playbill.

With their contract expiring in less than twenty-four hours, the city's sanitation engineers staged a "sick out" in anticipation of a strike. Trash collection was suspended in most portions of the city.

After closing down all of Rittenhouse Square so that filming could begin in "undisclosed locations" of former *Philadelphia Standard* columnist Mindy Haggismanner's latest chick-lit best seller, *Not That Fat,* the film's female star "happened to let slip" to Chilly Bains that she was pregnant with the director's child.

Rival gangs in North Philadelphia engaged in gunplay on a street in front of the Arthur Bourgeau Public School during recess, killing two students, ages nine and eleven.

And, finally, *The Wanderer,* a travel magazine based in New York City, published its December list of America's Worst Holiday Destinations and Philadelphia finished in first place for cumbersome transportation, unsightliness and unfriendliness.

Andy finished her column and revised her interview with Angelo Delise. She recast the story as another in the "local-business-calls-it-quits" genre. When she thought she needed more information, she called and was surprised to hear him apologize to her when she identified herself. "I'm sorry because I act so rude," he said. "Just because you ask me something, doesn't mean I have to throw you out."

He told her he read her article and had summoned Weldon Tarrow of Lock, Stock & Tarrow to open his safe. "He's got to research the serial number and the mechanism, but he says, if he can't turn up the combination, he can go in through the outside in, so we can at least find out what's inside. Why leave it for the next guy?"

Andy suddenly felt good. Better than good. She had written something, passed on information and a reader had benefited.

Mr. Delise then invited her to come for dinner some night with Lucia.

She reminded him that he had closed his restaurant. "Well, maybe I'll reopen. Things are packed up, but they're still here. I may decide to stay. I don't know. My father used to have a silver tray that I couldn't find after he died. We'll see what's in the safe. Maybe I can sell it or something."

Wow. Is this the power of the press, or the power of people to change their minds? A little of both, she hoped.

Logo called to tell her that he'd found an apartment in Center City and that he probably wouldn't make it for Lucia's debut self-defense class. From the tone of his voice, she guessed that his fling with Lucia might have been no more than that.

Andy didn't point out to him that Lucia's Wednesday class was for women. "I'll have to find some other way to kick your butt," Andy said. To her delight, he found that offensive.

She went home and changed into long sweatpants and a sweatshirt. She then returned to Westyard and found the Tiburno Academy of Dance above a two-door garage at Fifteenth and Panati Street, right across a five-point intersection from the police substation.

At 7:15 P.M., bright light streamed out of the three windows above the garage doors. Andy looked up and caught a glimpse of a mirror and a ballet barre. The door to the Tiburno Academy of Dance was on the left side of the building, sunk about five feet into an alley. Lucia had taped a poster to the door: SELF-DEFENSE FOR WOMEN. "Because Fear Sucks . . ."

Andy opened the door and felt a comforting blast of heated air.

She went up the long, single staircase to a landing that opened onto a gleaming wooden floor. At the center of the floor was Lucia, barefoot, in faded blue sweatpants and a white, oversized, long-sleeved Ohio State T-shirt, facing the mirrors along the far wall. Andy was about to say hello when she saw Lucia bow, then slowly move her hands in front of her face, then describe a wide, downward circle that returned her hands to her waist.

Again, Andy was about to say hello when Lucia suddenly whirled into motion. She waved her hands in fast, fan-like movements, snapped out high kicks with her legs, spun around, seemed to drop on the floor and roll back up and delivered a flying double kick as she shrieked, "Eeeeyahh!" Then she dropped, turned slowly and, with open arms, described that same circle with her hands arcing upward.

Andy waited until Lucia noticed her. Then she asked if she had to take her shoes off. "Only if you're more comfortable with them off," Lucia said. "There are some lockers in the back room by the office, if you want to change, but you can just dump your stuff in the corner there."

Andy put her shoulder bag in the corner and threw her bomber jacket on top of it. "Why did you shriek?"

"It's called a *ki-yai*. It's a sound that helps you tighten your body, summon up your energy, shock your opponent."

"Is that what you're going to teach tonight?"

"What I teach depends on who shows up. Thanks for being here."

"Ditto," Andy asked about Lucia's mother, who was recovering well, Lucia said, because she had already begun to accuse the nurse of being out to get her.

They said nothing about boyfriends, past or present.

Andy put her shoulder bag in a corner of the room and changed into the same worn pair of sneakers with which she did layups. Soon, three women arrived: a mother and daughter, and a teenage girl with tattoos over her arms.

"Okay," Lucia said, summoning them together. "This is for women, women only. I'm not saying that you can't do this with guys. If you know guys who want to work with us, I'll set up a mixed class. But right now, this is for us."

She paused, took a breath. "First thing I want to say is that, we have a right to walk down a street, work our jobs, raise our children and go about our lives without fear of violence, abuse or harassment of any kind. What we're going to learn and practice here is only one way to achieve that. But it's most important because it starts with us. What we believe about ourselves means a great deal. It's where our power begins and ends. Right now, we're going to believe that we can be strong and live without fear, and that, in every situation that confronts us, we have choices. One of the most important choices we can make is to fight back."

Andy saw that the girl with the tattoos was looking at the door. She didn't like something about Lucia, or the class, or the dance studio and she wanted a way out. The mother's eyes were on her daughter, and the daughter, in low-slung look-at-my-navel red pants and a plum-colored skintight blouse, stood in front of her mother, annoyed at the attention she was getting, but also needing it.

Nobody was paying any attention to Lucia.

"So let's feel, right now," Lucia went on, aware of the discomfort in the room but talking over it, "that we're strong, that we will not let anyone, or anything scare us."

A brief stretch of silence was filled by the building's heater grumbling to life. The girl with the tattoos giggled and said, "I gotta go."

"The bathroom is over there," Lucia said.

The girl giggled again. "I didn't mean . . ." She stayed put.

"I guess a lot of us didn't feel it," Lucia continued. "We were distracted. Or we thought it was kind of dumb—how can a belief stop a rape? Andy, show us."

Andy wanted to collapse and hide. "What do you—"

"My friend Andy, here, can look at somebody in such a way that they get the message that bothering her is exactly what they don't want to do."

Andy blushed. "But, Lucia, that's—"

"What? Just a look, right? An attitude that you project. We will have this attitude in us, and it starts with a choice, deep inside, that we do NOT want this person in our space. Andy, you've used that, right? You've projected that attitude, and it's worked."

"It's worked, but—"

"Not always?" Lucia completed her thought. "That's because every confrontation is different, and you can never be a hundred percent sure how things are going to turn out. But this has worked often enough, right? So you learn self-defense by starting with what you know, what you can depend on, what has worked for you most of the time, and you go from there."

"What I know is," the mother began, "I've always been small and short, so me giving out a look is not the same as somebody like her giving out a look. Some guys, they get a look from me that I don't want to be bothered, and they start to bother me. What am I supposed to do then?"

"The first rule is to avoid conflict, any way you can," Lucia replied. "You can run."

"Most of the time I'm on the street, I'm in heels," the woman said. "I'm not going to run in heels, and if I just pick up my pace a little, they come on even faster. It's like, to them, me just being there, in certain places and at certain times of the day or night, is enough of an excuse."

"The kind of individual you're describing is in need of an education," Lucia replied. She asked Andy to come forward. "Now pretend Andy is the biggest, strongest, nastiest jerk there is. He still has weak points. We all know this one." Lucia kicked and the woman flinched even though Lucia stopped her foot an inch in front of Andy's groin.

"You can do this in just about any shoe but a sandal or open-toe," Lucia said. "The problem for us, is, depending on the guy, his balls can be a tough target. He might be wearing a jacket that could cover them up. He might be in thick trousers. So one of the things we'll practice is kicking *through*."

She moved away from Andy and demonstrated. "Imagine the target of your kick is a little farther back into him, and kick *into* the crotch so the force of the kick goes into him. If you're in an open-toed shoe, the contact point is your instep, and not the toe. Puts some force into the kick. It's the force, not whether or not you hit his balls, that can let him know that you're not going to be an easy victim."

The mother shook her head. "But I can't remember the last time I kicked anybody. And, when you're in heels, you can't balance right."

Andy expected Lucia to tell her not to wear high heels. But Lucia said, "No matter what you're wearing, there are plenty of other things you can do, far more than you thought. You can go for the solar plexus. It's that soft spot right below the breastbone, just about at the point where your bra strap crosses." She touched the area on her sweatshirt that happened to be on the I of OHIO STATE.

"Everybody, put your fingers on it. Just at the place where the bone ends—if you connect there hard enough with a punch, or even two fingers of your hand—you can knock the wind out of a guy. Knock the wind out of him, and he goes down. Sometimes, that's all it takes to end the fight."

"And then what?" the teenaged girl asked.

"You go about your business," Lucia said as the front door slammed loudly.

They heard two pairs of shoes step slowly, deliberately, *aggressively* up the steps. Andy turned around to see two young men enter, one holding what appeared to be large, metal paint cans; the other, a baseball bat.

"We deliver a message from Shi-Bin," the one with the baseball bat said.

Lucia took a breath. "This is a women's class," she said. "Classes for men can be scheduled later."

One of the guys hurled one of the paint cans at her. Lucia stepped aside as the lid flew open, spilling a noxious liquid on the floor. The can hit the floor and rolled toward the mirrored wall.

"Everybody out," Lucia said. "There's an exit in the back, through the locker room. Get your stuff on the way out."

The teenager and the mother and daughter didn't wait for Lucia's command. They rushed through the door to the locker room. The floor began to wrinkle and buckle as the fluid attacked the resins on the wood.

"Andy!"

Andy spun and felt the wind as the second can zoomed past her face and shattered the mirror on the opposite wall. She found the guy with the baseball bat grinning at her.

"Get out of here, Andy," Lucia said.

"No way," Andy said. She sent the guy with the bat her biggest, nastiest, get-out-of-my-space blast of Intimidation Waves.

And they didn't work.

Ladderback was at his table at Jimmy D's when Jack Ferko came in with his cronies.

"Captain Ferko," Ladderback said, standing.

Ferko was drunk. "I see you have company tonight."

"Joining me from Atlantic City," Ladderback said, "is Mr. Murphy and Mr. Teasdale."

Murphy looked up from his cards. "Howdy, guys."

"When I was at the Beach of Good Choice, I never had time for games," Ferko said. He turned to his cronies. "Not on Mischief Night. I supervised armed patrols, because the Cong liked to attack us then."

Teasdale paused. He and Murphy using the Original Trenton Crackers on the table as gambling chips. "You carried a gun?"

"I had my rifle out, cocked and ready."

Teasdale nodded. "You had it cocked . . . ," he repeated.

"We had to be ready for anything, because those Cong, they used every excuse, every chance they got, to sneak up on us," Ferko said. "They were a tough bunch, but we were tougher."

Teasdale said, "I'll raise you four," and pushed four OTCs into the pot.

"Captain Ferko, I was hoping that you could join me for a moment," Ladderback said. "I'm curious about something."

Ferko looked at his cronies. "I don't know if I have much time. I have to make the rounds tonight. I'm organizing street patrols to keep the peace."

Murphy threw down his cards. "Lost again," he grumbled. "This just isn't fair. I *know* I'm supposed to get lucky tonight."

Ladderback tried to affect a poker face. He had told Murphy that if Captain Ferko came in with his cronies, he could try to get them into a game while Ladderback spoke with Captain Ferko, but Murphy shouldn't be too obvious about it. Murphy had replied, "There's no such thing as being too obvious when you're fleecing sheep."

One of the cronies regarded the deck. "What kind of luck, sir, did you have in mind?"

"The horoscope I read in the *newspaper*"—Murphy eyed Ladderback—"said this would be my lucky day. And so far, it's been right on the money. Before we decided to come up here, I went into the casino and, you know how it is, guys," he took out a wallet stuffed with cash, "when it rains, it pours."

"I guess we do." The crony gazed at his buddies meaningfully.

Whitey Goohan rolled up. "Anybody playing for real money in my establishment kicks the house a ten percent rake of the pot. That's twice what the casinos take, because my place is twice as better."

"You're taking how much out of the pot?" Murphy replied, astonished. "I never noticed what the casinos were taking. I was winning too much."

"And what game," the crony said slowly, "were you winning too much at?"

Murphy shrugged. "I don't know. Three cards facedown. Two faceup. Or was it two facedown and three faceup? Whatever it was, they called it poker."

The crony stood over him. "You can try your luck with us while the commander has his conversation."

Murphy thrust back his chair and stood. "I don't know, guys. I'm a street fightin' man. I'm tough to beat."

"We'll see about that," the crony said.

The guy who had thrown the cans was wearing oversized yellow polyester warm-up pants with red stripes down the sides and a white PEACE-KEEPER windbreaker open over a black T-shirt.

He smiled at Andy. "Get me, bitch!" he implored.

Andy took a step toward him but Lucia slipped in front. The guy with the bat went for her. She threw up her hands, touched the arm and shoulder of the guy with the bat, pivoted and sent the guy and the bat slamming into the wet, warping floor.

The guy howled as his face hit the caustic liquid, but he bounced up and came right back at Lucia as the guy in the windbreaker charged. Andy tried to kick him but he reached down with his arm, scooped up her leg and dumped her onto the floor.

Andy fell hard on her side. She saw that the guy who had dumped her was wearing scuffed, black street boots. She saw one of the boots float upward and position itself over her right hand, but before she could think that this guy was about to stomp on her hand, she saw the guy's other boot lift off the floor as Lucia drove her foot into his stomach, shoving him back and away.

It took another second—and the sound of another mirror shattering—for Andy to figure out that being on the floor might not be a good idea. By the time she wobbled to her feet, she saw that Lucia had thrown the guy with the bat again, right into the mirrors.

Andy found her shoulder bag, got out the cell phone and hit the emergency speed dial. She heard a crash behind her, and the seconds that it took for the cell phone to connect into the network and place the call went by so slowly . . .

Vinnie Ferko said, "Hey, Andy, how you doin'?"

She had meant to dial 911. "I'm at the dance school and these guys are trying to hurt Lucia."

"Hold on, I'm coming," Vinnie said as the guy in the windbreaker knocked the phone out of Andy's hand. He grabbed her sweatshirt and, without thinking, Andy smacked him across the face.

He laughed and smacked her right back.

Captain Ferko took Murphy's empty chair. He pulled the chair in and the chair leg hit something that made a *clunk*. He looked below the table. "Something in that duffle bag I should know about?"

"Give it a look-see," Teasdale said.

Captain Ferko reached down and pulled up the scuffed, faded black duffle bag. Ladderback cleared a space on the table. Ferko opened the bag and found several objects of varying sizes, each wrapped in oil-stained cloths.

"You may unwrap them," Teasdale said, putting a ten of clubs on top of a jack of spades.

Captain Ferko removed a few cloths. "Looks like parts to some kind of a gun," he said.

"Is it familiar to you?" Teasdale asked.

"It's a gun. I mean, if it looks like a duck and quacks like a duck . . ."

"What *kind* of duck?" Teasdale pressed.

"How should I know?" Captain Ferko said. "It's in pieces."

"I have been told you served in Vietnam, sir," Teasdale continued.

"You were told correct," Captain Ferko replied, unwrapping the rest of the parts.

"And you cannot recognize the parts of an M16 automatic rifle?"

"Whoa." Captain Ferko sat back. "What did you bring that in here for?"

"Mr. Teasdale had one in his possession," Ladderback said. "It's been disassembled in respect for the law. It's illegal to carry an assembled automatic weapon across state lines. Mr. Teasdale thought you might like to see it."

"This is the baby that would've won us the war, if the government had let us win," Captain Ferko said. "It looks well cared for." He studied Teasdale. "You're a military man, Mr. Teasdale?"

"Former military man," Teasdale said. "I am now considered disabled."

"You haven't let it get to you," Captain Ferko said, putting more parts on the table. "Once a soldier, always a soldier." He turned to Ladderback. "You said that there was something you wanted to discuss with me regarding my tour of duty."

Ladderback waited for a few seconds. "Tell me about your son, Captain Ferko. The older one. Are you concerned about him?"

"I'm always concerned about my boys," Captain Ferko said.

"Is Errol in some difficulty?"

"Something with his bank. Nothing he can't handle."

"Will this affect Veterans Plaza?" Ladderback asked.

"I don't see how it will. We've got the money. Everything's set. Nash Eagleman and I will announce the groundbreaking in a couple of weeks. Pity that Paulie isn't here to share it with us, but it's just as well. Errol said he wanted to change the plans before he died. That would have pushed us back some."

"Mr. Small was in communication with your son before he was robbed?" Ladderback asked.

"When Paulie'd get ideas that required some legwork, he'd ask Errol to run things down for him. Errol might have been the last person to talk to him. On the phone, that is."

"You said you and Mr. Small served together in Vietnam," Ladderback said.

"We fought side by side in Vietnam."

"Where?" Teasdale asked, dealing a solitaire.

"Army," Ferko said. "Army Intelligence. I don't know what Shep here has told you about me. . . ."

"He has said very little about you, Captain Ferko, other than that you are a retired police officer. He asked me, as a veteran of the Vietnam war, if I could determine if you were, in fact, a fellow veteran."

"You're looking at the genuine article," Ferko said. "I mean, not *looking* but—"

"That's quite all right, Captain. I have the gift of sight."

Captain Ferko became wary. "Are you blind or not?"

"Both and neither," Teasdale said.

"Well, whatever you are, you must know that matters concerning Army Intelligence, especially counterintelligence, are still classified."

"They are not," Teasdale said. "All records pertaining to American military operations in Vietnam have been declassified."

"Because the records about deniable activities were shredded long before that," Captain Ferko began. "And don't forget that fire in the records warehouse in St. Louis that wiped out any trace of half the guys I served with."

He eyed Teasdale, as if he had been challenged. "Before I was shipped back, stateside, I was told, by my C.O., that I would get this kind of treatment coming home, that my military service would be doubted, my pride, my bravery, my *good word* would be disputed by folks from all walks of life, even my very own comrades in arms. And I accepted that, as part of the honor of serving my country."

"Several Web sites list every American man and woman who served in Vietnam," Teasdale said. "These Web sites were created by veterans, for veterans, and were compiled and cross-checked. The military keeps *several* sets of personnel records in different locations."

"And what's a blind man," Ferko raised his voice, "telling me about what's on a Web page?"

One of his cronies called out, "You need assistance, Commander?"

"Nothing I can't handle," Ferko said, his forehead slick with sweat. "*Mister* Teasdale, are you impugning my honor?"

Teasdale put down the cards and reached forward to touch pieces of the rifle. Then he withdrew his hand. "I am not impugning you, or your honor, sir. I am concerned that you failed to recognize your weapon."

"This is not my weapon. Army Intelligence was issued .45-caliber sidearms that I kept holstered throughout my tour."

"What, then, did you have cocked during your patrols?" Teasdale replied.

Captain Ferko picked up the rifle barrel and set it down. "If you weren't disabled, Mr. Teasdale, I'd ask you to step outside." Captain Ferko turned to Ladderback. "Where'd you dig this fellow up? I'm not the enemy, Mr. Teasdale. I'm the guy that's on your side, fighting for you, and for every veteran."

"Then why don't you just surrender?" Teasdale said, his finger on the jack of spades.

Andy didn't feel pain from the blow as much as surprise. This guy had no right to hit her. No right at all. He hit her again and her surprise turned to rage. She punched at his face and her fist landed in his left eye. She hit his right eye with her other fist. Then she brought her knee up into his groin and . . . it worked! He went down.

Andy stepped over him and saw Lucia standing near the mirror, glaring at the guy with the bat who no longer had the bat. He slowly rose to his feet and then started screaming as he rushed at her with his hands out. Lucia just stood there for what seemed to Andy to be far too long. Then she stepped back and, as the guy reached for her, she moved quickly to the side. He twisted to grab her but she shot out with her hands, one, at his face, the other at his side under his arm, pushing him faster so he hit, face first, into the mirror.

"Andy, I can handle these assholes. Get away from here!" Lucia yelled, her attention on the guy Andy had just dumped, who had picked up the bat and was smashing the mirrors.

Andy suddenly had a crazy idea that you get when you're in a fight, things are moving too fast and your mind can't handle it. Your attention becomes diffused, unfocused as your brain goes down a list of familiar objects, reference points, thoughts, feelings—anything but what's happening in front of you.

Andy became fixated on her shoulder bag. Inside it were the things that connected her to her world, things that represented security, safety, identity; things like her cell phone (which had been knocked against a far wall near the bathrooms) and her notebook computer.

She thought if she could get her hands on her shoulder bag, she could use it as weapon. She was halfway to the bag when she felt a stabbing pain in her back, below her shoulder blades, that made her legs momentarily go dead.

She'd been hit hard in the lower back. She fell forward, landing awkwardly on her arms and almost on one of the empty paint cans. She saw a guy in the Furs T-shirt standing over her, waving his fists.

And she heard, coming up the steps, the sound of a man with a cane. No. Not a cane.

Andy's fingers found the paint can. She didn't feel the liquid burn her skin. In her mind, the can became a basketball and she got into a squat. Where was the basket?

She jumped up, leading with the can, her legs shooting her toward the ceiling. The guy moved back, his eyes following Andy but not moving away fast enough as she brought the can down in a spectacular slam dunk—into his face.

Andy heard the wet crunch of a nose breaking. The guy grunted in surprise, then roared in pain. Andy ran again for her shoulder bag. She had her hands on it when she felt wind again, as the can sailed past her face.

She turned and saw the guy coming at her, fists flailing, his flattened nose gushing blood across a mouth set in a fearsome grimace. She froze. She was suddenly terrified. This guy could really hurt her, maybe even kill her. What the hell was she going to do?

Then she heard Lucia yell. The guy heard it, too, and he turned around in time to see the ball of Lucia's bare foot go into his side right below the floating ribs where Andy's high school anatomy books said his kidney was. He folded in half, as if he were no longer flesh and blood, just stained and bloody clothing descending in a heap.

Ladderback spoke up. "Mrs. Alise Perrigore, Mr. Small's half-sister, returned my telephone call."

Captain Ferko's mouth twitched into a grin. "She tell you about that time Paul and I came up to visit and found out she was growing pot in the barn?"

"She told me you and Paul lived for four and a half years with her in Canada because you were afraid you would be drafted. As it happened, your numbers didn't come up."

"And you believed a woman who supported herself in a criminal enterprise?"

"She said that you assisted her in her criminal enterprise quite handily. She also said that you corresponded with a friend in Vietnam, and that you sent letters to this friend to mail from Vietnam so that your father, who had been in the Korean War, would believe that his son was following in his footsteps in Vietnam. Was that friend Angelo Delise?"

"If he told you any of this, he's no friend of mine."

"She said you incorporated in your letters what Angelo Delise told you about his service on the Beach of Good Choice. Mr. Delise also wrote to you about returning GIs who were having difficulty getting their benefits from the Veterans Administration. After a fire in her barn destroyed her crop, Mr. Small decided that, instead of waiting interminably in Canada, you and he would return to Philadelphia as if you had been honorably discharged and claim your benefits. It was an election year and your father introduced you to Senator Tybold, who agreed to write letters on your behalf if you recruited veterans who would vote for him."

Captain Ferko's face darkened. "My involvement with veterans was based on my respect for what a man goes through when he serves his country," he said. "It had nothing to do with politics."

Teasdale shuffled his cards. "Down at the Atlantic City Soldiers Home, we call folks like you wish-a-beens. They skipped the country, they went to college, one of 'em tried to get himself 4-F'd by cutting off one of his toes. Then, when the war was over, these fellows would come around and listen to us talk about what we'd been through. They figured out they'd missed out on something, and they did miss out. You could tell from the way they hung on us, they wished they'd been through it. They wished they'd been there."

"I am not disputing that you assisted veterans," Ladderback said. "Not Fade Away has done a great deal of good, for the city in general and veterans in particular. But Mr. Small also used your organization to launder kickbacks from city businesses that used illegal Asian immigrant labor, as well as cash contributions to Senator Tybold's campaign."

Ferko went rigid. "I want to know who told you this, because I don't take false accusations lightly. What you have just told me defames my good name and character, as a police officer and commander-in-chief of my organization. If it's printed, I'll sue."

"I have no intention of publishing," Ladderback said. "But you must be aware that if this information was to be published in some way, and you did sue, the process of legal discovery would bring to light the fact that no records exist whatsover of your alleged military service. There is also the matter that, while you were in the police department, you assisted in the detention and eventual deportation of Asian residents of this city."

"They were living here illegally! They were taking jobs from law-abiding citizens," Captain Ferko said, hands beginning to tremble. "I want to know the name of the bastard who made that slander."

"Mrs. Prentiss, a lawyer who, as Noah Zyman's daughter, spoke with some of the immigrants Mr. Zyman employed."

"You can't sit there and tell me you'd believe some story from a lawyer!"

"You might want to find one," Teasdale said. "Fast."

*　*　*

Lucia turned to the guy with the baseball bat. "It's over," she said to him. "Stop it, now."

He grinned and shook his head. "Shi-Bin said not to stop until . . ." He smashed the last mirror.

Lucia made an ugly sound and slowly moved toward him across the ruined floor.

He moved in front of one of the windows. With one eye on her, he shoved the bat through the glass. The glass shattered and dropped down onto the street.

Lucia picked up a can.

The guy held the bat as if he had just stepped up to the plate, and Lucia was about to pitch him a fastball.

Andy found her shoulder bag, and then her cell phone. This time, she was going to dial 911. She flipped open the cell phone and saw the man Lucia had knocked down was slowly getting up.

Maybe he was dazed from being knocked around. Maybe he had a woman smack him with her purse once or twice and he didn't think that the soft, woven cloth bag that Andy had would hurt him. He didn't raise an arm to protect himself. He just stood there, daring Andy to knock him down before he could get his good hand on her throat.

So Andy whipped up the bag, and the hard edge of the notebook computer inside that woven cloth, caught him on the side of his head, right above his ear, and he went down like the kind of tree that falls in the forest that *everybody* hears.

Andy watched him fall. Then she looked for Lucia and the guy with the bat, and, though they were across the room, she thought she could see a moment of fear cross the guy's face, as if he was thinking, as she had, a few seconds ago, that he just might get hurt, *bad*. What the hell was he going to do?

Lucia didn't give him a chance to find out. She hooked her right foot around his left, pulling it out from under him. As he fell, she brought her knee up, hitting him, not in his groin, as Andy had hoped, but under his jaw.

He didn't get up.

Andy flipped open the cell phone. "Lucia, we have to call the cops."

Lucia came over to the man beside Andy. She stomped on his hand.

Then they heard a voice: "No cops!"

Before Andy remembered she'd heard a third set of footsteps coming up with a cane or something like a cane, before Lucia could turn and see Shi-Bin leering at her. Shi-Bin brought the sand wedge down on Lucia's right shoulder. She cried out as she fell, and Shi-Bin brought the golf club down on her again and again until Andy saw what was happening and the anger and fear came out of her in a scream so loud that Shi-Bin stopped, settled his feet, whipped the sand wedge around his head with one arm and stopped it one inch from Andy's face.

"You're next," he said.

She tried to hit him with her shoulder bag but he just took a step back. She came at him again and he grinned this time, stepping back so the bag just missed him. She took a third swipe at him and he brought the wedge down, hooked her ankle and pulled.

She fell on one of the gang kids, who groaned painfully, and felt, in the wooden floor, the vibration of someone else coming up the stairs, someone coming hard, heavy and fast, boom, boom, *boom!*

Jack Ferko went red. He put his hand over his mouth, as if he had to stop the contents of his stomach from coming up. He glanced nervously around the room, and finally took his hand away.

Teasdale moved the king of diamonds near the jack of spades.

"As a police officer," Ladderback said, "you must have known that when you cover up a crime, no matter how awful, when you obstruct justice, when you hide truths that must be brought to light, you open yourself to exploitation not only by your enemies, but more often, by the very people you want to protect."

Ferko shook his head. "You can't prove one word of this."

A chorus of rude, angry epithets arose from the other table. "How the fuck did you pull that off?" one of Ferko's cronies said to Murphy.

"Pull what off?" Murphy said innocently. "Hey guys, I thought I told you," as he pulled a pile of cash toward himself, "this is my lucky day."

The one who had been so confident, became even more confident. "We're cutting you no more slack. No one's saying you're cheating. It's just the way you played that hand, like you kind of teased us along."

Murphy held up his hands. "Okay, guys, I'll level with you. I'm a shark. I'm a street fighting man. I eat sheep like you for breakfast, lunch and dinner."

They laughed. "In your dreams."

Ferko pushed himself to his feet. "Company, attention!" he shouted. "We're moving out."

Ladderback leaned close to Teasdale and said, "Let's play our last card."

Ferko's cronies complained, but they threw in their cards, divided the cash and were passing by Ladderback's table when Ladderback said, "Before you go, may I ask you to come to our table please? I want to ask your commander to do an old soldier a favor."

"C'mon men," Ferko said. "He don't need any favors from us."

One of the cronies came close enough to see what was on the table. "Damn!" he said. "That's an AR15!"

"M16," another said.

"It was known under both designations," Teasdale said.

One of Ferko's cronies was already assembling the rifle. "Remember how, back in Basic, we had to do DCR all the time? Disassemble, Clean, Reassemble?"

"Sergeant Teasdale was blinded when his platoon came under fire during an incursion into Laos," Ladderback said. "He acquired these parts after his discharge and I invited him to bring them here tonight on the possibility that Captain Ferko would assemble them."

Ferko shook his head. "C'mon, men. We have patrols to run. We've stayed here too long as it is."

"Aw, Commander," the crony replied. "It shouldn't take more

than . . . how many seconds? They used to time us." He put the part down on the table. "All yours, Commander."

Ferko didn't touch it. "It's been years," Ferko said. "You forget these things."

"Impossible," the crony said. "When we were in basic training, they had us doing DCR at night, during the day, when we just woke up, when we were dead tired after a march. Got to the point where I could do it in my sleep."

"You do it, then," Ferko said.

"I wouldn't take the honor from you, Commander." He examined the barrel. "I hate to tell you, Sergeant Teasdale, but the barrel's been plugged and your firing pin's been altered. You'll never be able to fire this."

"It is enough to hold it in my hands," Teasdale said. He turned his empty eyes toward Ferko. "Would you do it for me, sir?"

Ferko put a shaking hand on the barrel, another on the stock and tried to jam them together.

The crony became confused. "Commander, it doesn't go that way. The manual says—"

"Don't you think I know what I'm doing?" Ferko said, trembling. He dropped the barrel on the table. Then he dropped the stock.

"Commander. . . ."

"I don't recall giving you permission to speak," Ferko yelled. He picked up the oily firing pin and held it so tightly in his fingers that it slipped out, bounced on the table and fell to the floor.

"It's okay," the crony said, diving below the table. "I'll get it, Commander."

Ferko announced that he had to go the men's room. He set off toward the back of the dining room and went down the steps to the kitchen.

The crony asked, "They have other bathrooms down there?"

They waited for a few minutes. The crony who had started assembling the rifle wondered if he could put it together, and then take it apart so Ferko could have the honor when he returned.

Ladderback excused himself and went down the stairs.

Shi-Bin limped toward Lucia, whose breath was coming out in small, broken gasps. He raised the stick and slammed it down on her, spraying her blood on his white windbreaker.

"Lucia!" Vinnie Ferko bellowed as he shoved Shi-Bin to the floor in a flying tackle. Shi-Bin rolled away from him and, using the wedge, lightly pushed himself upright.

Vinnie, in his police leather jacket, police blues and polished shoes, did not reach for his holstered pistol. He did not reach for his mace, his nightstick or his gun.

He just went for Shi-Bin, who stepped back toward the windows while bringing the sand wedge down on Vinnie's left collarbone. Did it break the bone or did Vinnie's FIRBA vest save him? Or was it the effort of a man who was avenging the woman he loved that kept him going as his arm took a hit and shook with pain?

Shi-Bin took a larger step back toward the windows as Vinnie lunged for him, taking a blow from the sand wedge on his leg. Vinnie almost fell, but his fall turned into a stumble and he pushed himself forward. Shi-Bin felt the cold of outside air coming through the broken window and he struck back viciously, hitting Vinnie rapidly across his face, on his arms, on his legs as Vinnie opened his mouth, gave out one final roar and wrapped himself around Shi-Bin, pushing them both out and through the window, where they landed with a brutal thud on the sidewalk below.

Andy found her cell phone and dialed 911.

Ladderback found an ashen-faced Captain Ferko hanging up the potwasher telephone. "The senator will fix this. The senator will make it right."

He put a hand on the wall. He took a step away from Ladderback. "Why did you destroy me in front of my men?"

"I didn't destroy you," Ladderback said.

"I can't go up there now. I can't face my men."

"You can," Ladderback said.

"Paul wanted the benefits because he wanted the money. I did it because of my father. I didn't want him knowing I was a draft dodger. It would've broken his heart, just as it's going to break the hearts of those men, and all the rest, when you tell them I—"

Ladderback said, "You can choose what you inform them."

"What if I just don't? What if I just take my men and go and we can keep our little secret?"

"Then you are only prolonging the moment when another confrontation will arise and, perhaps then, you won't be able to keep the secret. Mr. Teasdale told me of a group of military personnel who have made a second career of exposing fraudulent veterans."

"I had one of 'em give a speech at one of our monthly meetings. He said it's a federal offense. He said there's some long, hard time awaiting."

"Perhaps you can join the group that is exposing the frauds."

"What, like those hackers that get caught breaking into the government's computer and turn around and get hired by the government to stop their buddies?"

"I'm only pointing out to you that there are other possibilities. No situation is without hope."

Captain Ferko became wary. "What's that supposed to mean?"

Ladderback played his last card. "While I do not approve of dissimulation, I am aware of your accomplishments as a civic leader and I respect them. Mr. Teasdale and I will agree not to mention what has occurred here, if you are willing to make significant changes in the plans for Veterans Plaza."

"What do you mean by significant?"

"I have been informed by Nashua Eagleman that the current plans for Veterans Plaza do not include a provision for low-income housing desired by the Asian community. I have also learned that an obligation, initiated to benefit your son Errol, was undertaken with the Asian community to construct this housing on the meatpacking plant site."

"Errol said . . ." He closed his eyes. "Errol said that he made Paulie give him the agreement and that he got rid of it. He said he checked

306

Teal's place because notaries keep records of what they notarize and he said he couldn't find any."

"Mrs. Cavaletta let him search her premises?"

"Errol's a family friend. There's nothing stopping him from ringing her doorbell and coming in for a friendly chat."

"When did he do this checking?"

"He didn't tell me."

"What did he tell you?"

"That Paulie got it into his head to put in the Asian housing. Errol didn't want it because . . . well, he's been selling the units at preconstruction prices. You tell some of the people he's sold units to that their neighbors are going to be poor people, and they'll back out on the deal. Too many backing out and the whole project can go down the tubes."

"Some might back out, as you say," Ladderback went on. "But what of the ones who don't? Wouldn't you rather have, as your neighbors, those who see similarities instead of differences, those who find diversity stimulating, interesting and rewarding, for its own sake?"

"Nash Eagleman won't go for it."

"We know enough about Mr. Eagleman's origins and career to know that he will."

"The senator definitely won't go for it."

"What the residents of Veterans Plaza can't contribute to him in political donations, they will contribute with loyalty. Their votes are just as good as anyone's."

"You don't understand the politics of high-end real estate," Ferko maintained. "It's not for people like us."

"Why *not?*" Ladderback said.

Captain Ferko eyed the doors that led to the underground concourse. "You stay here for a while, okay?"

He went up the stairs to the dining room.

"Freeze and *drop* it!" a female voice behind her yelled.

Andy saw a female police officer with her pistol out, aimed at her.

She was so surprised to see a gun on her that she dropped the cell phone.

"The bag. Drop it. Slow."

Just then Lucia said, "Vinnie. Was that my Vinnie?"

The policewoman looked at Lucia and the two gang kids and said to Andy, "What the fuck did you do?"

"Nothing!" Andy shrieked, and fell apart.

23 beginner's luck

Andy stayed in the emergency room of the Sisters of Zion long after the X-rays of her face revealed no fractures. She was told not to drive a car for at least eight hours, not to have any alcoholic beverages for twenty-four hours, to call a doctor immediately if she suffered any loss of feeling in her extremities, any loss of mobility, feelings of vertigo or blurring of her vision. She was also advised to sit up for the next eighteen hours, just in case the blows caused internal bleeding in her skull.

When Frank Cavaletta arrived, Andy told him that Lucia and Vinnie were in the Intensive Care Unit. She showed him where they could look at them through the glass. They were unconscious. The chances of them surviving were not great, but good enough.

"Who did this?" Frank wanted to know.

"Two of the guys are here. They'll be okay. Shi-Bin is at the morgue."

"Lucia's attitude, this was bound to happen sooner or later," Frank said. "I should never have let her take those martial arts classes."

Andy cried again. Or rather, she resumed the crying she'd been doing since she fell apart when the cops came. She told him this wasn't his fault, it wasn't Lucia's fault. "It's mine," Andy said. "I put it in the paper that Lucia would be there."

"Blame the media, eh?" Frank said. "I don't think so. I'm tired of all this fault business. Let's just hope we can all get through this. Food? It's on me."

The sun was high when Frank dropped her off at her car. She wasn't supposed to drive, but she had to do something to persuade herself that she was still capable of functioning.

She found a place to park that was near enough to the space that Vinnie had once saved for her. It was another reason to cry, but she couldn't cry anymore.

In her mailbox was a small, dark piece of chestnut, a *plank,* with Rivinceta! burned into it. Printed on the bottom was "come as you're *not.*"

Easy, she thought as she fell asleep, flat on her back on her bed.

It was dusk when she woke up and called in sick. Bardo Nackels said, "Sick of whom?"

The remainder of the masseri bread had hardened into a dark lump. She sawed off a piece with a serrated knife and couldn't eat it.

She called a place that delivered. The guy who came to her door with the cheesesteak and the Diet Coke was wearing a rubber Richard Nixon mask. He saw the yellowish purple bruises on her face and said, "What happened to you?"

What could she tell him? "It's my disguise," she said. "I'm going as a battered shrimp."

He looked up at her. "Shrimp? I get it."

Her gums had swollen a little bit so it was hard to chew. The carbonation in the Diet Coke was annoying. How long had it been since she was annoyed? She thought of Logo. Should she ask him to go to the restaurant opening tonight?

Should she go at all?

She called Logo's cell phone and got a message: "If you are inquiring about a self-defense course, please call . . ."

Did he know what happened to Lucia? Did someone tell him?

She showered, got out and dabbed her face. It was *hideous*. She didn't have a costume. What could she wear to this thing, assuming she would go?

Come as you're *not*. She tried to think of some of the things she *wasn't*. She looked in her closet. Her eyes found that ridiculous black cocktail dress her mother had bought. She saw the four-inch spiked inlaid heels. What could her mother have been *thinking?* This kind of outfit would be worn by a young Lyssie Eagleman. *Not* a woman six feet, one inch tall who wanted to be appreciated for something other than being tall.

Exactly!

It was dusk and raining lightly when she left her apartment. Garbage danced around the stone pathway to the street. She looked at the side of the apartment house and saw the black plastic bag holding her Fortini "Do Not Disturb" collection had been torn apart by squirrels. The wind lifted the smaller pieces and she remembered Fortini's description of the man chasing the white paper.

Could one of the "objects" dancing before her be the one that this mysterious person had chased through the streets of Westyard? She stepped closer, tottering on her heels, but the odor stopped her.

She noticed a white, folded piece of paper that had blurry blue and red spots—ink that had become a pale wash in the rain. The red ink reminded her of chops—the ivory stamps that oriental illustrators, calligraphers and printmakers dipped in and used to sign their works.

She took another step and, again, the odor forced her to pause. What was it Fortini said about his art? That first it becomes something more, and then it becomes something else?

She turned around and let the piece of paper stay where it was.

*   *   *

She went first to the hospital. Even if Vinnie and Lucia were still in intensive care, she could practice walking on her heels in the hospital corridors, and then drive from there to the restaurant and give her car to the parking valets. Maybe she would run into Logo.

She wore a long coat so people wouldn't stare at her legs. She didn't get a second glance from the hospital staff in gorilla masks, Frankenstein heads, vampire teeth and pig noses.

Standing at the glass in front of the Intensive Care Unit was a tall, lanky man in a dark suit who absently touched the left side of his jaw. He heard the sound Andy's heels made on the floor and turned.

Errol Ferko was more haggard than when she first saw him. His eyes were unsteady. Was he unsettled by what had happened to his brother? Or were Logo's forensic accountants getting to him?

"Vinnie said the girl he was going with was . . . up there." He curled his mouth in what was supposed to be a smile, but wasn't quite. "He said you had these questions about me."

"I don't want to get into it now," she began. She wanted to run away from him. She told herself she was not going to run. She'd come to look at Lucia and Vinnie and she would do that and then she would leave.

She came closer to the glass.

"Vinnie wanted to be a cop," he said. "These things happen to cops. I was going to be a firefighter but I quit that because . . . who wants to get burned?"

Andy tried to ignore the hardness in his tone. "It's nice for him that you're here for him."

"Last night my father was with someone from your newspaper. A man named Ladderback." He gave her a creepy smile. "What can you tell me about him?"

A voice inside Andy said, *Run. Get out of here. Now!*

But Andy didn't want to run because, if she did, he would know she was running way from him and she didn't want to give him that satisfaction.

"He sits next to me in the newsroom," Andy said. "He's old. He's nice, when he isn't grumpy. He's quiet. He's considerate. He knows a lot more than you'd think, about a lot more than you'd think." She shrugged. "He writes obituaries."

"My father has changed the plans for Veterans Plaza. He's putting a low-income wing into the first phase, and that is just not what I want to happen. Did that Ladderback have anything to do with this?"

Andy smiled to herself. "You'll have to ask him that."

"I was told that my father met with him because he had questions about me. Why would he have questions about me?"

Andy looked him in the eye. "Because I have questions about you."

He touched his jaw. "I suppose I should answer them then."

"This isn't the time," Andy said.

He shook his head. "No, I think it is. I think this is the right time. You're in the business where you think you have the right to know about me and my business and I don't have any problem with that."

"It's more than your business," Andy said. "It's about . . . forget it." Andy saw Vinnie's bundled, bandaged form and would have cried if Errol hadn't been watching her. "Your brother is a good man. You shouldn't have been so hard on him."

"I was hard on him *because* he's my brother," Errol said. He brought up his hands, as if he were at a business meeting. "I would have explained that to you if you'd come to lunch the other day. I don't know if it would have made any difference but, really, if it's something that concerns me, that I would be the best person to comment upon, why shouldn't I be the person you come to?"

What had he just said? Andy couldn't quite figure it out.

He put his hands in his pockets. "If you ask me, I think you owe me a chance to settle the score."

"What score?"

He took his hands out of his pockets. "What I mean is, there are doubts in your mind—I'm not sure what about—but, given what's happened to these people that we are both connected to, that we both love, in our own ways, I think you owe it to me to just lay it out."

"Lay what out?"

"Whatever it is you want to know."

"About you and Lucia and CeCe?"

"About anything," Errol said. "There are a lot of things I might help you with, with your column or whatever."

"Okay," Andy said. "On the day CeCe died—"

He held up his hands. "Whoa, there. This isn't the time. I mean, this *is* the time, or it *could* be the time, but it is definitely not the place. My apartment is in the Pickle Factory. I also have my office there. If it's a question of facts or figures, I'll be able to get it out for you and lay it out on the table."

"I have plans for tonight," Andy said.

"Don't we all. I'm just saying, if you want to get it over with, now's the time." He started toward the exit. "We'll sit there, we'll talk, I don't know, fifteen minutes, whatever."

Andy followed him. Why was she following him? For Vinnie, she told herself. Out of respect for Vinnie. "Just don't try to sell me anything."

He grinned. "If I knew who you were then, I would *never* have wasted my time."

When Errol locked the door of his apartment behind him, Andy knew that she should never have come with him.

He turned and grinned. "Well," he said, his fingers rubbing the right side of his mouth. "I've got you now."

He was on her quickly, his hands around her neck. He brought her face toward his and put his lips on hers, then he tightened his hands on her neck, crushing her throat. This was the choke hold that Vinnie had told her about.

She no longer cared if he killed CeCe. She wanted him to get his hands off her.

She hit him a few times against his chest and he just crushed her tighter. She tried to work her fingers around his wrists and pull his hands away, but his grip was solid. She flailed about, her long arms tangled with his and, as she gagged, she started to panic. She brought her hands in again, as if she were answering a phone, and her left elbow came up and hit his jaw.

Hard.

She must have hit where Vinnie had knocked out his teeth, because he grunted and let go. He grabbed his face and kicked her leg. She stepped back and stumbled over a chair.

He shook his head, opened the hall closet and extracted a set of golf clubs, including a sand wedge with dark, bloody brown crusts caked along the shaft.

As part of an intro psychology course Andy had taken called "Sociopaths and Society," she'd read that beneath the raging fury that drove him to hurt and kill was a small, traumatized, needy child who wanted a parental figure to stop him. Did he want to kill Andy because he was angry at his mother for dying and abandoning him?

Or did he just like having power over her, like he had over his brother, until Vinnie hit him back? Could he have killed CeCe for the same reason? Did he try to get Teal to tell him where she had hidden whatever he wanted? Or was this some sick message he was sending to Lucia.

She watched him raise the club and she said, feeling stupid but needing to say it, "You don't have to do this. You can just go."

He said, "Nahh."

"Shi-Bin's dead. You can't blame this on him."

"I wouldn't worry if I were you."

He brought the cane down slow enough for her to step back so that the tip of the cane came down on the gray carpet with a soft thunk. She saw the grin: he was playing with her. He liked her being afraid of him.

She told herself that she wasn't afraid, that she wanted to slip past him, unlock the door and get the hell out. No, she admitted to herself, she was afraid of getting hurt. She didn't want to be hurt.

She stepped back into the living room, with its cold, cruel, chrome, leather and smoked glass furnishings that he probably thought were so masculine. He came closer, bringing the club up, pausing to savor his power, and then bringing it down in an arc that would bring the tip close to her head.

Did he want her to move her head? Or did he think he would rip open her skin? She ducked and felt the air against her cheek as the cane rushed past and shattered the edge of a coffee table.

The crash of breaking glass scared her. She turned away and found a window in front of her. The view looked south, into Westyard. The alley and the gatehouse were easily visible. How could he live here with that view reminding him of what he had done?

Or did he like the view? Did he see his placement of CeCe's body as a good thing? A clever thing? Another con job well done?

She turned to him and saw he had positioned the tip of the sand wedge a few inches from her right eye. From where he stood, he could just lean forward and shove it into her eye. He probably wouldn't do that, because she could step back and avoid it.

She stepped back, tripped on a chair and came down on the leather-and-chrome armrest. She felt a quick, sharp pain in her ribs as she rolled off the chair onto the carpet, and the shards of the shattered coffee table.

He touched the sand wedge to her face.

The touch made her cringe, and he seemed to like that. Errol raised the cane into the air (for a moment, she thought of the pun-raising Cane, get it?) and smashed it down beside her head.

She cringed against the chair. "Errol, please stop!"

He smashed the club again and she moved away, behind the chair, against the wall below the window. He smashed the club a third time, on her right arm.

He didn't break it but the pain was astonishing. It made her shriek and he liked that, too.

She saw what she would have to do. It was like basketball. She was going to feint, as if she was going to do one thing, and do something else.

He raised the club up and she became weirdly calm, the way she was when she was doing layups and she was so tired she no longer cared how tired she was. She pulled her legs in, folding the right on top as she twisted and exposed to him the right arm that he had just struck, as if she was agreeing that he had become powerful over her, so powerful that she would just have to give herself utterly to him.

He brought the club down. He put his body into the blow and she heard the bone in her arm break. The pain came—more horrible than she had ever felt—but with it came an anger, a focused fury that narrowed all sensation to one thought: no matter what happened to her, she was going to hit him back.

She pulled her body in to protect herself. It was instinct, and sometimes yielding to instinct is the right thing to do. Because, in trying to protect her right side, she brought up her left leg, and when she saw him standing over her, raising the club one last time for the blow that would come down on her skull, she was filled with such defiance that she kicked out at him.

Andy did not execute the perfect toe-point kick that Lucia would tell her later takes years to get exactly right. And she did not do the rising instep kick that the kickboxers like. No, this time she put all her strength, all her effort into a heel kick, the dumbest kick of all, the kick that does nothing unless you happen to be wearing a shoe with a heel on it, the narrower, the better.

Andy was wearing the narrowest, spikiest heel she owned and, possibly because she had listened to Lucia tell her that hitting someone in the solar plexus might knock the wind out of the attacker and stop the fight, or because anyone who is learning a new skill gets a small bit of beginner's luck, or because Andy had an overwhelming need not to let this man take her life, the kick went exactly where it had to go.

And because her mother had bought the shoes in a Main Line shop whose owner cared about selling quality goods, the heel did not break, as narrow, spikey heels can and will do when they are made to do what they were not intended to do.

The heel hit Errol on the edge of his breastbone, stopping him dead, knocking the wind out of him. He folded forward and the heel slid down into, and through, the skin on his chest, burying itself deep into his solar plexus, where it hit some combination of nerves that informed Errol in

317

the deepest, most basic way possible, that he had finally encountered a situation with a woman that he could not control.

His arms twitched as if he had been hit with an electric shock. He dropped the club. It fell on the floor somewhere near Andy. For an instant his body was suspended on the heel of Andy's shoe. Then Andy's leg bent on his weight, bringing him close enough so that she saw the surprise in his eyes, the arrogant disbelief: this is not happening to me.

She couldn't hold him up. He twisted to the left and a gout of blood shot from the hole in his chest as her heel came out.

He gripped his chest and the blood began to gush. He shuddered and tried to breathe. "Am I going to . . . ," he gasped, ". . . am I going to die?"

"You just might," Andy said. With her good arm, she reached into her shoulder bag, brought her cell phone to her ear and called the cops.

24 better than new

It's amazing the things you can learn to do one-handed, like answering the phone.

Andy was in the newsroom when the call came. "I got a question for Mr. Action."

"Vinnie!" Andy shouted so loud that Ladderback stopped typing. "How you doing?"

"I heard you got your arm broken."

"Only one," Andy said.

Silence fell between them. What was it that he wanted to tell her?

"I'm sorry about Errol," he admitted.

"Me, too." Andy told him that his brother was going to live.

"You're pressing charges, I hope."

"I am," Andy said.

"Good."

"Tell me what the doctors are saying."

"Eight to ten months from now, I'll be just fine. Until then, I have a few minor skull fractures, my hand is messed up, I have a broken arm, a broken leg, a broken ankle and a broken pelvis, a half dozen cracked ribs, but the *good* news is that my vest probably saved my life. So you wear those gloves, you hear?"

"I hear," Andy said. "So what's your question for Mr. Action?"

He told her.

She closed her eyes. Then she said, "A reader asked about how you buy stones and it's pretty complicated, but, basically, the distributors fix the prices by controlling the supply, and the jewelers factor them up, way up from what even they think is fair. It's almost impossible for the average person to recognize a decent stone from a flawed one and the rating system is really designed to make it as easy as possible to sell the stone, so it all boils down to the relationship between the salesman and the buyer."

"Can you do it?"

"Sure. How are you going to decide which one it should be?"

"You can take a picture if you want me to choose one, but I think you know what will do it. I'll give you a credit card number."

"Vinnie, are you *sure?*"

"I'll never be sure, Andy. I just want to."

They spoke for a few minutes more, then she slowly dug out of her shoulder bag a card and went to Chilly Bains's desk.

He was on the phone but when he saw her, he put his hand over the mouthpiece.

She handed him the Official Chilly Bains One-Act Courtesy Card.

"What's this about?"

"A happy ending," Andy said.

She called Logo and asked who the bank used when evaluating gemstones. "We have experts we can call, but . . ."

He asked her who the stone was for. She told him.

"In that case, it's going to be me."

"What do you know about gems?"

"I learned a little bit in Europe. She's a decent person," Logo said. "I got to know her really well, well enough for me to want to help, even if I have to do it with you."

"Logo, this is the first time you've ever wanted to do something with me that doesn't involve annoying your mother."

"Strange, isn't it?"

Andy checked it out with the doctors. They *could* move Vinnie to the solarium on the hospital's roof. Lucia's injuries were actually more complicated than Vinnie's, but, given the situation, they would move her, too.

Andy made more calls. The hospital asked if they could photograph the event for their newsletter. She asked Vinnie. He didn't mind.

Two days later Andy, her arm in a dark blue sling that actually matched the warm, navy and russet tweed suit she had bought for the occasion, rode the big elevator up to the top floor of the Sisters of Zion Hospital. Vinnie was beside her on a gurney, most of him enclosed in gauze, padding, wires and soft casts. He released Andy's hand when the elevator doors opened.

The nurse wheeled him forward into the solarium, a dusty room with faded, mismatched furniture and grainy glass windows that offered a fabulously bright view of the refineries. Airplanes hovering over Philadelphia International Airport in the pale sky that hinted of the winter about to come.

Joining them in the solarium were two representatives from the hospital's public relations office, the six doctors, a photographer, Jack Ferko and a slower Joseph Ferko, who wore a black armband and moved slowly forward on his walker until he came close to Vinnie. His mouth trembled as he said, "I'm proud of you, son."

"I haven't done nothing yet," Vinnie said as they wheeled the gurney around to face the corridor.

They heard the elevator doors open and Andy put the box in the only hand Vinnie had that worked.

Teal Cavaletta's voice arrived before she and Frank did. "If I missed this because of you—"

"You didn't, okay?" Frank Cavaletta said. "Not everything's my fault."

Another elevator door opened and Angelo Delise emerged, pushing a cart crowded with dark, filled unlabeled bottles of wine. He went to the nearest doctor. "This is homemade. All of it. I make it myself, from the finest imported juices, so you're going to let them have it, you understand?"

The doctor agreed that, as far as he knew, the patients could have a taste.

Finally came Nguyen Li-Loh, Tommy and a diminutive woman that Andy guessed was his mother. Tommy held a tray upon which was a small bag of rice, a beautiful lacquered box of tea and two teacups. He still couldn't open his mouth wide. "This is for—"

"Thanks, Tommy," Vinnie said. "I'd shake your hand but . . . they don't want me shaking any more than I already am." He glanced around. "Okay. Let's bring her up."

The hospital PR rep picked up a house phone, and the solarium was so quiet you could hear the wind whipping across the glass.

A nurse pushed in the gurney on which Lucia lay in a mess of bandages, casts and wires. Flanking the gurney was another nurse, making sure the intravenous drip was hanging just right, and a doctor, and Logan Marius Brickle in a dashing dark suit and obnoxiously bright blue and pink paisley tie.

"Vinnie," Lucia said as soon as she saw him. She saw the other people in the room. She started to cry when she saw her mother.

Another elevator door opened and Chilly Bains rushed toward them, his stacked hair tilted over as he fumbled with his disc recorder. "Don't do *anything* yet. Not a single *thing!*"

Andy glared at the hospital's public relations director, who shrugged helplessly.

"I heard you were okay, Vinnie," Lucia sobbed. "I wanted to thank you but . . ."

"You don't need to thank me," Vinnie began, tears filling his eyes.

A camera clicked. "Mom, could you wipe my face?" Lucia said. "I can't reach it."

Teal Cavaletta's heels went pock, pock, pock as she strutted toward her daughter, pulled an embroidered handkerchief out of her purse like a magician about to make a rabbit disappear and gently dabbed her daughter's eyes.

Andy took some tissues out of her shoulder bag but Vinnie said, "I can take it."

He took a breath. "Lucia, I'm going to marry you. I mean, I *want* to marry you. If it's okay."

Lucia started to choke up. "Oh my God, Vinnie."

"I got . . . something for you here." He tried to open the box.

Andy opened it for him.

He said, "Could we get moved a little closer?"

The nurses complied, but Vinnie couldn't quite turn his head to see Lucia's hand.

"Just a second!" Mr. Delise said. "I got the thing." With his good hand he came up with a polished silver serving tray. He angled the tray so Vinnie could see his hand, and Lucia's, reflected in the tray.

Andy held her breath as Vinnie's fingers awkwardly extracted the ring from the box. She hoped there weren't any superstitious customs about bad things happening if the guy dropped the ring.

Then she felt Logo at her side. He touched her good hand and she held it, tightly.

The nurses adjusted the gurneys. The camera clicked again.

Vinnie paused. "Lucia, you're not saying nothing."

She replied so softly Andy almost couldn't hear her. "It's okay, Vinnie."

"Hoy, hoy!" Chilly Bains exclaimed.

"It's okay for me to try to put this on you? You sure about it? This is all a new thing for me."

"Oh, Vinnie," Lucia sobbed as he gently nudged the ring onto her finger. "It's better than new."

And it was.